JADE DRAGON MOUNTAIN

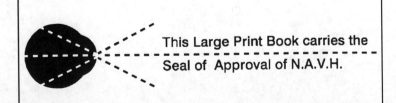

JADE DRAGON MOUNTAIN

ELSA HART

THORNDIKE PRESS
A part of Gale, Cengage Learning

GALE
CENGAGE Learning

Farmington Hills, Mich • San Francisco • New York • Waterville, Maine
Meriden, Conn • Mason, Ohio • Chicago

GALE
CENGAGE Learning·

LIBRARY OF CONGRESS CATALOGING-IN-PUBLICATION DATA

Names: Hart, Elsa.
Title: Jade Dragon Mountain / Elsa Hart.
Description: Large print edition. | Waterville, Maine : Thorndike Press Large
   Print, 2016. | © 2015 | Series: Thorndike Press large print historical fiction
Identifiers: LCCN 2015041052 | ISBN 9781410486707 (hardback) | ISBN
   1410486702 (hardcover)
Subjects: LCSH: Jesuits—Crimes against—Fiction. | Librarians—Fiction. |
   China—History—Qing dynasty, 1644-1912—Fiction. | Large type books. |
   BISAC: FICTION / Historical. | GSAFD: Mystery fiction.
Classification: LCC PS3608.A78455 J33 2016 | DDC 813/.6—dc23
LC record available at http://lccn.loc.gov/2015041052

Published in 2016 by arrangement with St. Martin's Press, LLC

Printed in Mexico
1 2 3 4 5 6 7 20 19 18 17 16

To my mother

AUTHOR'S NOTE

Yunnan Province is located in the far southwest of China. To the Chinese elite of the early eighteenth century, Yunnan was an uncivilized, dangerous frontier. It was also one of the major producers of a commodity fundamental to Chinese culture: tea. From the mountain jungles in the south of the province, the dried leaves traveled north on mule caravans along a path known as the Tea Horse Road. The city of Lijiang, which I refer to by its older name, Dayan, was a hub on this trade route. The ethnic group native to the region is called the Nakhi.

In Imperial China, the Emperor was considered a divine being, chosen by the heavens to rule the world. Because the heavens selected only just rulers, no action taken by the Emperor could be unjust.

PROLOGUE

April, 1780.

. . . You must understand, before I continue, that seventy years ago we in the West did not know very much about China. There were no crates of opium stamped for delivery to its shores. Our alchemists could not replicate its porcelain. The promise of silk and tea and spices made our merchants sick with desire, but China had no interest in the paltry, scrabbling kingdoms of Europe.

The Emperor, called the Kangxi, tolerated only one kind of foreigner: the Jesuit. They were his advisors, his astronomers, and his amusement. The others, be they merchants or adventurers, were turned away. And the Company, the poor Company, whined at the door like a hungry dog, a frustrated brute who smelled meat but could not reach it. Now the situation is very different. The Company would be better likened to a wolf. Be wary, nephew, of the creature you have taken as your employer.

Memory, I have always thought, is like deepening waters, and every day the sunken objects on the sea floor are a farther and more frightening journey away. I know that they are there, but I do not look at them. The ripples on the surface distract me, and call my attention to the flotsam and jetsam that are within reach. Now, as I imagine your ship being readied to sail, a light shines into the depths. It illuminates an evening, one of Galland's last. As usual, he and I were hunched and freezing over our books in his wretched apartment at the Golden Circle.

The university had not paid him in three years. He spent the coins he gleaned on ink for his projects — a dictionary of the Orient, an encyclopedia of Arabic, and his tales of the thousand and one nights that so delighted the nobility of Versailles. I was his student, urging him to sit closer to the fire, for I could see his face becoming gray and his hands turning to bones bound by translucent skin.

A knock announced a visitor. How I stared at the figure outside, cloaked against the cold night. He seemed to have stepped from the pages of one of my master's tales. He was tall, with black eyes and a beard oiled to a point. His clothes were simple, but in his self-assurance I detected a suggestion of regal vanity. Galland greeted him as an old friend, and rushed to prepare tea. I knew that he had only one portion remaining, and no money for more. But Galland kept the tin hidden from our guest's view, and put the last of the dry leaves into the old teapot. Our guest said nothing, but I think he must have known, for through some trickery I found on the following morning that the tin was full of tea so valuable it is reserved for emperors and kings.

The man said that he had come to tell a story, and that it would not be like the other tales. It was a story, the man said, that would take the whole night to relate. Galland brought a fresh pile of paper from the drawer. In the hours that followed, I did not hear the scratching of the quill, or the sounds from the street. I did not feel the itch of wool, or the damp, or see the open texts I was meant to be studying. The storyteller replaced my world with his own.

Time passed very quickly after that night, and Galland died before he had completed the dictionary, the encyclopedia, or the tales. My memory of the story sank into the dark. But Galland left all of his notes to me, and several months ago I found among them the jottings he made on that evening. My circumstances being better than his were at my age, I have had the leisure to compile his work into a kind of order. I include the results of my efforts with this letter to you.

I must burden you with a few details of history. You are about to embark on your own adventure, and your mind is on what is ahead. But you must never neglect the past. It pulls at our decisions like a magnet, and can block our progress as if it were in front of us, not behind.

So it was for the Kangxi Emperor, who began his rule encumbered by the past. He was only the second emperor of his line. His people, the Manchu, were horsemen from the north who invaded China and toppled the native Ming. The Manchu founded their own dynasty, and took the name Qing. Anxious to be accepted by their new subjects, they adopted traditions of the conquered. They studied the intellectual and aesthetic interests of the Chinese elite, and imitated the Ming style. But the horsemen of the eight Manchu banners enforced their rule to the very borders of China. Ming revolts were crushed without mercy, and native rulers were replaced with Qing magistrates.

The Jesuits had first come to China during the late Ming years. They had brought with them the principles of Western science, and a willingness to teach what they knew. Not averse to degrees of assimilation, they had devoted themselves to the study of the Chinese language and customs, and had earned a place at court.

The Kangxi elevated the Jesuits to still higher rank. This was, you understand, a result of their usefulness. He was unmoved by the Christian faith. But as long as the Jesuits behaved as his subjects, their knowledge — mathematics, engineering, cartography — was assumed into his own aura of divinity.

Years passed, and the Jesuits began to lose influence in Rome. In 1704, the Pope sent a Dominican envoy to China to persuade the Kangxi to replace the Jesuits with Dominicans. Although the Kangxi defended his favorites, his patience had begun to wane. He was annoyed by the squabbling between foreigners. He dispatched a message to the Pope suggesting that if he truly wished to reform the Jesuits, the Emperor could perform the service by cutting off their heads.

That is what I know of the world in which this story took place. I do not know if any of its characters really lived, but they walk with me now in the twilight garden of my home, and sit with me in my little study. I wonder if any of the Chinese books in my humble collection were read by the librarian in this tale. Of the incredible device brought to the Emperor of China by the English East India Company, I have found no record.

— EXCERPT FROM A LETTER
WRITTEN BY THE BOOKSELLER
PAUL-HENRI D'AUBIGNE
TO HIS NEPHEW ARMAND BADEAU, CARE
OF THE CAPTAIN OF THE *RESOLUTION,*
TO SAIL THE FOLLOWING WEEK TO CANTON

6 Days

CHAPTER 1

It was a cold morning in early spring when Li Du came to the top of a small hill and saw below him the city of Dayan. The sun had not yet touched the valley, and the only perceptible movement was in the pale smoke that blurred the rigid curves of the tile and wood rooftops.

Beyond the city to the north, a mountain emerged slowly into the dawn. Its base was blue and featureless, a shape without dimension against the brightening sky. But on the distant summit, the snow and ice glowed golden pink in anticipation of sunrise.

Li Du could see the pass that would take him over the mountain and down to the river valley on the other side. But between him and that ridge lay Dayan, unavoidable. With a small sigh that puffed into the cold air, he rose, rinsed his bowl in a stream that ran by the hilltop temple where he had stopped to drink tea, put out the little fire he had made, and began the descent into the valley.

It took him a little over an hour to arrive at the houses on the edge of town. By that time the sun had risen and the road was crowded with travelers, farmers, and horse caravans. The farther into the city he went, the more packed the narrow streets became. Soon he was moving at a shuffle, surrounded by people and cows and horses, all bumping and jostling and making noise. The ground was littered with dung, peels, chewed and trampled sticks of sugarcane, gristly chicken bones, and discarded rice disintegrating in puddles of water. He tried at once not to step on porcelain cups, not to hit his head on copper kettles strung on ropes, and not to trip over the dogs that scampered or slept or wandered in search of bones.

Li Du was a man of middle age. He wore old clothes that were neatly patched, and a velvet hat that had lost its shape and faded from black to graying blue. A rough woven bag was slung across his back, and he carried a book, his pointer finger inserted between two pages to mark his place.

Vendors misread his small, polite smile, and called to him to look at what they were selling. He stopped each time he was addressed, and with raised eyebrows and creased brow, gave dutiful attention to the items for sale. But when the merchants saw that he did not intend to buy anything, they turned their attention to other customers, and Li Du continued on his way.

He did not hear any Chinese amid the clamor, only a confusion of different languages and dialects, most of them unfamiliar. *An empire so large,* he thought, *that the people at its borders speak a different language from those in the capital is like a person who cannot feel his own fingers.* Li Du took off his hat and scratched his head, wishing for a moment that he had remembered to neaten his hair. It was bristly as a brush on top where it should have been shaved, and he imagined that the soldiers in pale gray standing at a corner gave him reproving looks. *Lose your forelock or lose your head,* the saying went. He replaced his cap and decided to wait a little longer before asking for directions.

He came to the street of tea and regarded the dusty, humble leaves with some solidarity. A month earlier he had traveled through the hot jungles where they had been picked. He remembered, as perhaps they did, the lush mountains on which they had grown, where heavy flowers stirred like slow fish in the mist. These leaves had been dried, knotted in cloth, and enclosed in bamboo sheathes, ready to be strapped to saddles and taken north by trade caravans.

As they traveled, they would retain the taste of their home, of the flowers, of the smoke and metal heat of the fires that had shriveled them. But they would also absorb the scents of the caravan: horse sweat, the musk of meadow herbs, and the frosty loam of the northern forests. The great connoisseurs of tea could take a sip and follow in their mind the entire journey of the leaves, a mapped trajectory of taste and fragrance.

On another street, bridles with polished bells dangled from hooks, and smooth wooden saddles were stacked in rickety piles. Sandalwood, jasmine, and a drift of rose belied the frost that still chilled the ground and the air. The road became hazy with the smoke of lit incense. Beyond that, the decadent perfumes were overcome by a salty, metallic odor, and when he turned the corner, Li Du found himself among the fish sellers.

Here, everyone was stepping carefully to avoid the inflated guts that spilled like bubbles over the edges of buckets, surrounded by slippery puddles of water and blood. As he passed a shallow trough teeming with carp, one of the fish threw itself from the water and landed on the ground. It began to beat its body wildly in the dust. Li Du tucked his book securely under one arm, bent down, scooped up the fish, and dropped it back in the water.

"What are you, some kind of monk?" the seller asked. "Why did you do that?"

Facing the gruff merchant, Li Du's confidence in his private reasoning wavered. Before he could say anything, the man shrugged. "Well," he said, "at first I thought you were stealing my fish. That is all."

Never adjust your hat in a plum orchard, thought Li Du, and then said, "I was wondering, could you tell me where to find the magistrate's residence?"

"Just up that way." The man gestured. His hand was reddened and chapped with cold, and crusted with torn and gleaming fish scales. "Big place with a wall around it. Easy to find once you're out of the market."

"I had not expected such a crowd," said Li Du. "Is it market day?"

The merchant grunted. "Never crowds like this on a regular market day. Been this way for a week now, and thousands more on the way. Don't you know? It's the —"

The man's words were lost in the clamor of haggling voices around them, and Li Du shook his head, confused. The merchant opened his mouth to repeat what he had said, but at that moment he was distracted by a customer. He waved again vaguely in the direction he had indicated before, his attention now on making a sale. Li Du nodded his thanks and left.

Away from the market, the streets became quieter. He passed several teahouses, several brothels disguised as teahouses, and a wine shop crowded with large stoneware vessels. It occurred to him that a hot cup of wine would go some way toward making his errand worthwhile.

A colorful sign pasted to the wall of a house brought him to an abrupt stop. The words that had caught his attention were painted in blazing red: *The Emperor to Arrive.* After he was sure he had not misread, he looked at the top of the paper. It said: *Spring Festival Events and Performances.*

Li Du's eyes moved restlessly from one bright announcement to another: *At noon on the field of the dragon, the great singer Madame Wu.* Below that: *Performances of the Popular Plays:* The Departure of the Soul, A Visit to the Garden, *and* The Dream. And written in gold paint: *The Emperor Commands an Eclipse of the Sun.*

This explained the crowds, the chaos of the market, and the fishmonger's words. The Emperor of China was coming. Li Du again removed his hat, rubbed his head thoughtfully, and put his hat back on. It seemed that he had chosen an unlucky time to come to Dayan.

CHAPTER 2

Outside the imposing gates of the magistrate's residence, a small commotion was taking place. A foreign merchant stood beside three carts stacked high with wooden crates packed in straw. Several of the crates had been taken down and were open on the ground. Five soldiers — Manchu bannermen in robes of blue satin embroidered with white dragons and yellow flames — were examining the contents of the boxes, while the foreigner berated a sixth.

The merchant, a bald man with a ruddy face and rich clothing, slapped a roll of documents against the soldier's chest and said in crisp, competent Chinese, "I am an ambassador. My cargo is not subject to inspection, and if you continue to open these crates I will hold you personally responsible for any damage to their contents. Order your men away, and take me to the magistrate at once."

The soldier avoided the man's gaze, but his posture did not change. "All merchant caravans are subject to inspection. There are no exceptions."

"But this is unacceptable. I am not to be treated this way. The magistrate will hear of it. The Emperor himself will hear of it. Yes, I have an audience with the Emperor. Do you understand your error? Do you know how much trouble you could bring upon yourself if you continue to treat me like some common trader?"

The soldier stood, baffled and uncomfortable, and the atmosphere was suffused with painful embarrassment. The foreigner's undignified behavior was humiliating to everyone there, but until he said or did something to give the guards a script that they could recognize, they were at a loss for what to do. No one had noticed Li Du, who stood some distance from the gate, and he waited to see what would happen.

The situation was saved by the arrival of a young man with an official bearing, who took the papers from the red-faced foreigner's hand, unrolled them, and scanned their contents. "Sir Nicholas Gray," he said, pronouncing the name carefully. He switched to Chinese. "The magistrate is expecting you, and will be delighted that you have arrived. You will, of course, stay in the guest quarters here at the mansion, and we have arranged for your cargo to be kept in the magistrate's own personal treasure room. Please accept my apologies — the city has never before hosted so many important dignitaries, and we are unused to foreign visitors. The soldiers should have known who you were. Please come with me."

"I must insist that this cargo does not leave my sight until I am assured of its security."

"Of course. We will have the boxes carried in with us now."

The young official gave instructions to one of the soldiers, who hurried through the gate and returned with a group of servants. They mingled awkwardly until the official told them to take the boxes from the carts and carry them inside.

The foreigner helped lift each box, which made the servants nervous. When one of them fumbled and almost dropped a crate, the merchant turned on him. "The contents are fragile," he said. He addressed the young official. "Instruct them not to set anything down too roughly. I cannot do it all myself."

"But you have traveled over very rough roads to get to Dayan. Surely the crates are packed securely?"

The man nodded grimly. "And I would not like to see the finest crystal in all of Europe shattered now by a clumsy servant."

Li Du watched the group pass through the massive doors, painted bright red, into the mansion. Once they were gone, he hesitated a moment before he approached the guards. They were armed with polished bows and quivers of matching green silk embroidered with golden vines, and muttering among themselves.

"Excuse me. I am here to beg audience with Magistrate Tulishen," said Li Du to their leader, who had recovered his poise now that the irate foreigner was gone.

"Do you have letters of introduction?"

Li Du presented his documents from where they were tucked in the book he carried. The paper was old, crumpled, and thin from being rained on and dried out many times over the years. The soldier took the papers, went into the mansion, and returned some minutes later with a servant, who escorted Li Du inside.

As he passed into the cold shade of the entrance, Li Du could sense the weight of the wall above and around him. The curved ceiling was painted with clouds outlined in bright blue and green, in imitation of the sky. The intended effect was one of grandness and space, but Li Du was only aware of the bulk of plaster and stone. The painted clouds were still and flat, and he was relieved to step out from under them.

The mansion was not a single house, but a complex enclosed by the thick stone wall. The grandest pavilions were set one behind the other along the central axis, while the smaller buildings, gardens, and courtyards were arranged along the edges, separated by paths and covered walkways. The far end of the mansion was set against a wooded hill dotted with picturesque pagodas and crowned with a grove of cypress trees.

In a quiet reception hall not far from the main gate, Li Du drank tea and waited for a summons. By the time a servant came for him, he had replenished his cup seven times, until the exhausted leaves barely tinted the water. He rose, feeling the stiffness in his back and knees from the long wait in the cold stone room, and followed the servant to a scented chamber decorated with large paintings and bookshelves crowded with jade sculptures and antique porcelain.

Magistrate Tulishen was seated in a carved mahogany chair behind an ornate desk. He wore a silk robe, brightly embroidered and trimmed at collar, shoulders, cuffs, and hem with squirrel fur. Above and below his eyes were the swollen crescents of fatigue, and Li Du saw written on his face the stratagems and schemes of a successful bureaucratic career. He acknowledged Li Du's kowtow with a short nod, and for one hopeful moment Li Du thought that perhaps the magistrate would not mention their connection, would simply put a seal on the letters of permission and send him on his way.

Tulishen said, with an effort at warmth, "Cousin, how long it has been since we saw each other. One day, one thousand autumns. I do not know if I would have recognized you. Have you been unwell?"

"No — but I have been traveling, and am perhaps a little tired."

Tulishen waved his hand slightly, as if to accept an apology that Li Du had not actually made. "Since your departure from the capital," he said, "my mother has joined the ancestors. She is with your mother now, sisters together in the afterlife. You may pay your respects in the temple here, if you wish."

"I thank you, and offer my deepest condolences."

Tulishen made another small, dismissive gesture. "The mourning period is over," he

29

said. "The old generations give way to the new. My son scored in the top rank on the provincial examinations."

"That is a great achievement."

"He is in Beijing now preparing for the national tests. If circumstances had been different, perhaps you would have been one of his tutors. Instead, you and I find ourselves in the borderlands, far from home. Though we have come here by very different paths."

One by advancement, the other by exile, thought Li Du. But he said nothing. Tulishen made a show of unfolding Li Du's worn and wrinkled travel documents, and scanned them while Li Du waited in silence.

Tulishen's name, Li Du remembered, was Li Erfeng when he had received his first assignment to a small eastern city of little significance. Li Du had been just a boy then. He had listened to the stories of his elder cousin's success, and shared his family's pride in the news of Li Erfeng's promotions. Li Du had imagined a handsome, talkative adventurer, like the heroes in the novels. He had been disappointed when the man who returned from the east had proved to be cold, uninteresting, and knowledgeable only on the subject of the wealthy nobles with whom he had dined and drunk wine.

Li Erfeng had continued to rise through the ranks, in connection with the implementation of certain tribute collection strategies. He was praised for his sound and effective legal mind, and eventually he received honorary Manchu status. This reward was given only to the most trusted Chinese nobles. Li Erfeng had chosen for himself the Manchu name Tulishen as proof of his commitment. Though it was difficult to see amid the jewels that crowded his hand, he wore the simple archer's ring in deference to the Manchu past as archers of the steppe.

Li Du wondered how his cousin felt about his current position: magistrate in the farthest corner of the empire. To the south of Dayan were the tea jungles, feared because of the fever their insects carried, and to the north was the Tibetan plateau, feared because of the bandits who roamed it. The magistrate of a town like Dayan had an opportunity to demonstrate his skills and to rise in the bureaucracy, but also ran the risk of ending his career in obscurity deep in the mountains, surrounded by peasants barely aware of Qing rule.

He waited for Tulishen to address him again, conscious of the ritual that had

31

brought him to Dayan. He understood the humiliation of his position, the required deference, and, above all, the imperative that he not cause trouble, scandal, or any embarrassment whatsoever to the local officials. He had only to act out his role, and he could be on his way.

Tulishen kept his eyes on the papers in front of him as he spoke. "You were a librarian of the Forbidden City. Almost five years ago you were sentenced to exile from the capital for your friendship with traitors. Had it been determined that you knew of their treachery, you would have joined them in the lingering death." Tulishen waited for a response. When none came, he looked up at Li Du. "Our family was spared that, at least," he said.

There was mutual understanding in the short silence that followed. Li Du was well aware that his family's concern from the moment he was arrested had been for their reputation, not for his life. This had not surprised him. He had never been ignorant of his family's priorities, and, in the end, the knowledge had eased his departure.

"I have come," said Li Du quietly, "to fulfill the condition of my sentence, to register my presence upon arrival in a new prefecture."

"Then let us observe the formalities," said Tulishen. "Where were you before you came to Dayan?"

"I have been in the south, in the tea forests."

"You are alone? You do not travel with a guide or translator?"

"No. I prefer to travel this way whenever it is possible. I carry a small collection of published travel journals with me. I rely on their geographical descriptions of the area."

"And you have not caught the fever?"

"I read that chrysanthemum smoke is toxic to the insects who carry the disease. I burned it when I could, and avoided the lakes."

"Not many will go so far south. Even in Dayan there have been cases of the fever. But the weather is cool now and travelers are safe." He paused delicately, then continued. "Do you plan to stay long in Dayan?"

"I have no plans to stay at all. I will leave as soon as it is convenient, and go north, toward Gyalthang."

The tension around Tulishen's mouth eased slightly. "Why to Gyalthang?"

"Simply because I am more content when I am traveling. It is not my habit to remain long in any city. I am going to Gyalthang because I have not been there before."

"Gyalthang is crowded with Kham Tibetans. They are violent people. Their men are bandits, and their women have no grace. The local people here in Dayan have been fighting them for generations. The bickering of the uneducated. Of course, the situation is improving. We are civilizing this part of China, slowly. But if the savages and their bad food do not deter you, I will give you the permissions you need to go there." He paused, and Li Du waited for the expected dismissal.

It did not come. Tulishen leaned back slightly in his chair, and looked at his cousin with some curiosity. "I admit, Li Du, that when I saw your papers and realized who you were, I thought that you were here to take advantage of your connection to me. I assumed you meant to beg the Emperor for leniency, an end to your exile. But it appears that is not your object."

Li Du was stung. He wanted to say that if he had known the Emperor was coming to Dayan, he would have avoided the province completely. He wanted to say that he had made a life for himself, a solitary one, but one with which he was, in his own way, entirely satisfied. He had no wish ever to see the Emperor of China again.

He said merely, "I did not know he was

34

coming to Dayan. Not until I saw the announcements in the city today."

"In that case, you are possibly the only visitor to Dayan who has *not* come to see the Emperor."

"I imagine word of his travel has spread through the area. But I have been very much on my own."

"Have you spoken to no one at all?"

"Not for some time."

"Ah," said Tulishen, looking pleased with himself, as if he had solved a puzzle. "You have become a scholar recluse, have you? You write poetry and commune with the trees like the old poets."

Li Du gave a little smile. "Honestly, Cousin, I considered it. But in spite of the romantic potential of my situation, I have no skill in composition." It was true. Li Du had the advantage of knowing most of the poems ever composed in Chinese, but he found that this left little room for originality on the subject of clouds, mountains, or bamboo groves.

Tulishen did not return the smile. "You were always modest. You did well enough on your exams to earn a position in the royal library." There was an edge to Tulishen's voice, and Li Du remembered that Tulishen himself had never passed the national examinations. He could not imagine his cousin envied him now.

"As you can see," said Tulishen, "I am very busy. Dayan is to be the southernmost point in the Emperor's tour. When the festival is over, he will turn north, and begin the journey back to the capital."

Li Du, sensing that some expression of interest was required, asked, "How long has he been away from it?"

"Almost a full year. And all for this. All to come here, now, to my city. The festival is to be so grand that he has even invited foreigners to cross the southwest borders and attend."

"Does this mean that the Emperor has relaxed his policy on foreigners in China?"

Tulishen shook his head. "It is a limited invitation. It will expire when the festival is over. But when we are so close to the border, why should they not come? The arrogant foreigners will witness the Emperor's command of the heavens, and know his superiority over their own kings. The Son of the True Dragon has bestowed on my city the great honor of hosting this demonstration. Nothing like it has ever been seen in this distant corner of the empire."

"His command of the heavens?" Li Du remembered the schedule he had seen on the wall. "You mean the eclipse."

"An unmatched honor, to host the event," Tulishen repeated. Li Du saw fear in his cousin's expression, and understood it. Tulishen had always been ambitious, but even he was intimidated by what was being asked of him now.

The Emperor of China had the power, according to ancient tradition, to predict astronomical phenomena. Displays of this power confirmed the Emperor's divine legitimacy, and were taken very seriously. The more accurate the prediction, the more effective the demonstration. Members of the intellectual elite, of which Li Du and Tulishen numbered, were aware that for many years it had been the Jesuits at court who had provided the Emperor with a yearly calendar of astronomical events. Their calculations had proven reliable and accurate to the minute. Naturally, public acknowledgment of their role was forbidden, as it would tarnish the pageantry of the Emperor's predictions.

And what better way to assert control over a notoriously unstable province than to impress its people with a spectacular festival and an eclipse of the sun? It had fallen to Tulishen to organize the unprecedented event in an area known throughout China only for its disease and barbarism. He would be blamed if the Emperor was disappointed.

"Thousands will gather in a field east of the city," Tulishen went on, with forced enthusiasm. "And the Emperor will appear before them as a deity, on a towering golden pavilion. The foreigners, and the uncivilized people of this province, will know our Emperor's power. They will not forget."

"I saw one of the foreigners at your gate earlier today, a merchant."

Tulishen shifted his shoulders uncomfortably. "He is the most recent arrival. The first one came three days ago, an old man as bleached as a dead tree on the plains. One of the religious men in black robes, but he did not come from Beijing. He says he lives in India. That is not all he says. The man does not stop talking. Obviously he does not know *the more words spoken, the more mistakes made.* And that is not the extent of his foolishness. He journeyed here with Khampa traders. I am surprised they did not rob and murder him and his friend."

"His friend?"

"A performer who has come for the festival. A storyteller from Arabia." Tulishen brightened a little. "The storyteller is amusing and speaks good Chinese. I have hired him to perform here tonight."

For a moment Tulishen was lost in thought. Then he recalled himself and continued. "There is another one in black robes, but he arrived alone. A young man, unimpressive. He speaks Chinese like an imbecile. And he has a weak stomach — he has not left his room at the inn since he arrived. I sent my doctor to bring him herbs, and now the strange man wants to know everything about the plants the doctor used. He has a fascination for plants, he says. Did you encounter these religious men in Beijing?"

"The Jesuits?" Li Du said. "I was tutored by one."

Tulishen's expression wavered. This was an unwelcome reminder of Li Du's academic superiority, but Tulishen had not become magistrate by ignoring opportunities to use the knowledge of others. "Did you learn to speak their language?"

"Most of the ones I met in Beijing spoke good Chinese. But yes, I learned their Latin."

"Tell me about them."

"What is it you want to know?"

Tulishen was irritated. "I never wasted my time with foreigners in the capital. I am not interested in distant places that do not affect us. But now they are here and I am responsible for them. Tell me something useful."

Li Du considered. He had not thought of the Jesuits in years. "To me," he said, "the Jesuits always seemed more scholars than holy men. They spend their time studying our language and reading our books, instead of reviewing their own. As I recall, that is how they fell out of favor with their leaders even as they earned the Emperor's respect. I doubt these visitors wish to cause any offense or inconvenience. They simply want to know more of the world."

"But they have caused inconvenience already," snapped Tulishen. "They conduct themselves awkwardly. And the old one speaks unwisely on subjects that are forbidden. You do not understand the burden that has been placed upon me. I have no time for such disturbances."

"I am sure that all will go as planned," said Li Du, vaguely. He was thinking of the map to the mountain pass, and beginning to make a list of the modest supplies he would purchase in the market on his way out. Perhaps a little bottle of wine to warm over the fire, and some preserved ham, and a small bag of bean paste pastries. . . .

Tulishen observed Li Du's distraction.

"You have always acted above society."

Li Du blinked. "I am banished from my own home," he said. "I am an exile, invisible to society."

"And yet, for a man who has wandered in the mountains for three years, you speak of court matters with some elegance."

Li Du could see that Tulishen was struggling with an idea that was unpalatable to him, and with a sense of dread Li Du guessed what it might be. "I require a favor of you," said Tulishen. "I want you to remain in Dayan for a few days."

Li Du spoke carefully. "I am grateful, Cousin, for your hospitality. But I am here merely to provide a record of my presence, as required. I should not be in the city when the Emperor comes. I was exiled at his order."

Tulishen waved his hand dismissively. "Of course you were. But you were exiled from Beijing, and we are far from that city. I have need of you here. I want you to talk to the foreigners. Question them, politely, tactfully, and tell me what you learn. I don't want any surprises when the Emperor is here. If this talkative old Jesuit makes a nuisance of himself I am the one who will bear shame. You will leave before the Emperor arrives."

"But I —"

41

"Any further protest will offend me, Cousin."

They both knew the request for what it actually was: an order.

"Then it is decided," said Tulishen, satisfied. "You will stay in the guesthouse, and you will meet the Jesuit in my library this afternoon."

"You have a library?"

"In remote areas like these," said Tulishen, "it is important to keep reminders of more refined places. It sets an example for the locals. My father and grandfather were renowned collectors, as I am sure you know. I had the entire library moved here from my residence in the capital. Its design has been praised in the highest circles of society, but is, sadly, underappreciated here."

"I will enjoy seeing it," said Li Du, honestly, though aware that his cousin's interest was in acquiring books, not reading them. "And who was the merchant at the gate? Am I to speak to him also?"

Tulishen frowned. "He has brought tribute from a powerful foreign company. They want access to our eastern seaports, but it is unlikely that they will get what they want. The Emperor has refused them for years — he will not be persuaded to change his mind by a few boxes of trinkets. But the man is to be treated with deference until the Emperor makes a decision."

"Your soldiers were inspecting the crates he carried."

Tulishen nodded. "We must be very thorough. This region is wild. The Ming loyalists still lurk at the borders. And Tibet cannot be trusted." Tulishen put his hand to his forehead as if it pained him.

A young official had just entered the room, and Li Du recognized the man who had so adeptly managed the situation at the gate. He had the clean, unremarkable presence of a young scholar. Under his arm he carried a bundle of dirty, crumpled papers. He bowed respectfully and, after a brief, curious glance at Li Du, directed his gaze forward and waited to be addressed.

"This is my secretary, Jia Huan," said Tulishen. "He arrived from Beijing a month ago and already has taken great initiative in the matters of this province. With my guidance he may become a magistrate himself one day. What is it?"

"The merchant from the English East India Company is concerned that the treasure room is not secure enough. He says that he does not trust Mu Gao to guard it, and Mu Gao has gone away to drink with his friend the clerk."

Tulishen rose from his chair with a sigh of exasperation. "Mu Gao," he said to Li Du, "takes care of my library. He is barely literate, but his family used to be powerful in this province. That is the only reason he has a place here. If you meet him, advise him on the proper care of books. His skills are only adequate."

He turned to Jia Huan. "I will reassure the merchant that the treasure room is as secure as the mansion itself. There are guards at the gate and at every corner of the wall. He will have to be satisfied until the Emperor's own soldiers arrive. What is that you are carrying?" Tulishen indicated the papers.

"I found more graffiti on the walls in the market. I have peeled it away so that it can be copied and filed, according to the Emperor's new mandate."

"You did well," said Tulishen, directing a nervous look at the offending papers. "Of course, these foul slanders against the Emperor are unavoidable with so many people crowding the city. The Emperor must understand that. But someone will see the culprits and report them soon. It is inevitable."

He returned his attention to Li Du. "I will attend to these other matters. You will be

44

shown to your room, and you will meet the Lady Chen. She is first consort, and responsible for the household."

"Your wives arc not here with you?"

"Of course not. They are in Beijing. Lady Chen is of a local family, though one of high rank, naturally. She is very capable in this rough setting."

Li Du perceived no lack of opulence or comfort in the mansion, however rural its surroundings, but he said nothing.

"Tonight there will be a banquet," continued Tulishen. "You will attend." He paused and added, "It is not necessary to tell the foreigners that you are an exile. It is better that they consider you an authority. If they do not respect you, perhaps they will not talk to you. You will be introduced as a scholar traveler."

A maid in crisp red-and-white robes led Li Du through the mansion along shadowed paths. A series of flat bridges took them over three deep pools, from which rose last year's lotus flowers, brown and dry, swaying drunkenly on their long stems. Ponderous carp, golden, white, and red, swam under the bridges and through forests of water greens. Occasionally their wet backs slid above the water, and submerged again.

It was in a small courtyard at the edge of the third pool that Li Du met the Lady Chen. She was sitting on a stone bench, her back to them and an easel before her. A filigree ornament was set in her coiled hair — five silver phoenixes surrounding a golden sun. Her shoulders were covered by a heavy fur cloak, and cold sunshine lit her pale, raised hand. The only movement came from the tremble of dangling silver in her hair, and the sweep of her brush as it imparted a slope of gray mountain onto the white paper.

She turned to them, wearing on her beautiful face an expression of calm authority. It was an unusual face, with angular cheekbones and a profile that did not presage the appearance of her features from the front. Her skin was startlingly pale, a quality that the noblewomen of the capital tried hard to achieve with the application of thick creams and powders.

"I am mistress of this house," she said, rising to her feet. Li Du noticed as she approached that, though she imitated the tiny steps of a Beijing lady, there was concealed strength in her stride, revealing that her feet had never been bound. She reached him and bowed her head in polite deference. "You are very welcome here."

46

"I am —" He paused, unsure what she knew.

"You are the magistrate's cousin. I was just informed." She smiled. "I am relieved that you have come to help us. You will counsel me on how to host our strange guests? Their etiquette is very . . ." She searched for a tactful word. "Surprising."

"I remember a dinner in the capital," said Li Du, with an answering smile, "at which a Jesuit explained that in his country they never eat rice with their meals."

Lady Chen's delicate eyebrows went up. "How extraordinary," she said. "You must tell me more of what you know. I would not embarrass the magistrate by showing poor hospitality to his guests. But you are tired, and I am keeping you from your refreshment." She turned to the maid, who was escorting Li Du to the guesthouse. "Bring him tea and something to eat before he meets the other guests."

Honored consort, thought Li Du, as he and the maid left the courtyard. A woman whose lineage denied her the security of marriage to the magistrate. But here, far from the Beijing residence where the magistrate's wives held sway, Lady Chen had power. His interview with Tulishen had ended only minutes before he met her, but she had known already who he was and that he would be staying at the mansion.

The guesthouse was nestled against the hill at the far end of the complex. Li Du and the maid entered through a keyhole-shaped door in a low white wall. It led into a square, enclosed courtyard with black and gray pebbles embedded in the ground, depicting the animals of the zodiac. In the corners stood potted boxwoods and azaleas that had been trained into elegant, sculptural shapes. Immediately to the right of the door, against the wall and far from any foliage, there was a small, lit brazier, over which a blackened kettle was suspended from a metal frame with a hook.

The other three sides of the courtyard were defined by the three guestrooms, each of which opened onto a marble porch that ran unbroken in front of them. The sloping tile roof, supported by thick painted beams, extended over the porch. Each row of tiles ended in a round clay medallion stamped like a coin. The doors and windows were made of pale wood carved with elaborate floral and animal motifs, so that the light shining through would cast shadows like pictures on the walls of the rooms.

Li Du's room was the center of the three, directly across the courtyard from the door in the wall. The maid, after bowing and gesturing him inside, bowed again, and left him there. The walls were jade green and painted with golden peacocks. Against one wall was an ornate compartment bed enclosed in a green curtain. Against the other was a dark cherrywood desk, on which stood a small cabinet, its doors open to reveal writing tools arranged on shelves. Four brushes dangled from a brush stand. Also on the desk was a tea set arranged on a slatted tray. It consisted of two teapots, a set of small cups, and a set of large cups for drinking tea more casually, with the leaves loose in the water.

A soft knock on the door announced the return of the maid, carrying a tray laden with fresh dumplings and an assortment of savory sauces in colorful porcelain bowls. He inhaled the dark, salty fragrances with grateful pleasure. Another servant had brought tea, and offered him the choice of green, chrysanthemum, or red. He chose the green, and she prepared it. Before she left, she explained that the brazier and kettle in the courtyard were for the convenience of guests. The water in the kettle was boiled, replenished often, and kept hot over the coals. He thanked them, and breathed a sigh of relief when they were gone.

It was cold now that the sun was behind a cloud, but the food and drink revived him, as did the silence. He unhooked one of the brushes from its stand and touched it to the clean surface of the desk, idly testing the give of the bristles.

The last time he had stayed in such luxurious quarters had been in the earliest days of his exile, when he had gravitated automatically toward the inns that most resembled what he was used to, silk and polished sandalwood. As the months passed and he had spent his silver, these establishments had begun to lose their appeal. Their common rooms made him feel like an unaccounted-for shadow on the wall, ignored or acknowledged with unease. Occasionally he had run into the scholar recluses, and had listened to them bemoan the intellectual decline of China and complain about the uncivilized provinces. These meetings always left him dispirited. For years now he had avoided populated areas.

And now?

It's only for a few days, he told himself as he returned the brush to its hook.

Li Du thought of the coming eclipse. He refused to be one among the thousands of people willing to take part in the performance. He would not watch the Emperor pretend to command the heavens. No — he would find a good vantage point on the mountain, as high as the wind and snow would allow him to climb, and he would watch the eclipse alone. Taking comfort in this certainty, Li Du left his room to meet the travelers who had come to Dayan more willingly than he.

CHAPTER 3

The stairs leading to the open doors of the library were guarded by four creatures of white marble: a lion, a dragon, a phoenix, and a tortoise. Li Du passed through the doors and into a large room furnished with bookcases that radiated from a central point like spokes on a wheel. He started down the nearest aisle. Its shelves were full of books bound in identical black silk and arranged in matching boxes like stern ranks of soldiers.

He looked around him and, seeing no one, pulled a volume from its place and opened it to a crisp white page covered in words as familiar to him as the tree in the courtyard of his childhood home. *Outlaws of the Marsh.* He closed it and reached eagerly for another, for a moment lost in memory. *Genzhai's Jottings, Judge Bao and the Steward's Suicide* — books of romance, adventure, mystery.

"Hello! Hello, sir!"

Li Du hastily returned the volume he held to its place on the shelf, and turned to see a smiling figure in black approaching him from the other end of the aisle. He was an elderly foreigner with a long white beard that flowed in a thick wave against his robe. He was very tall, though his thin shoulders were curved slightly inward with age.

"You must be the librarian from Beijing," he said, speaking with the energy of a much younger man. "It is a *great* pleasure to meet you. A great pleasure. Forty years since I last saw the library in Beijing, but I remember it still. I had the honor of studying a text in the hand of Du Fu himself. Such words. Such sadness. A poet of unrivaled skill, and reliably forlorn in his choice of subject. You *are* the librarian?"

His Chinese was perfect, and Li Du, startled and disoriented, struggled for an appropriate response. "Yes," he said finally.

The Jesuit studied him, blue eyes twinkling with merriment. "I would be surprised too," he said, "were I a scholar recluse just emerged from isolation. I assume that you are a recluse, for what other purpose could have drawn you from so great a library as that of the Forbidden City itself? But the task of the scholar recluse is also commendable. And now here you are, used to those silent oaks and lonely cottages, and the first person you meet is a doddering old foreigner who cannot pause for breath. I do sympathize. But where the Emperor of China goes, the Jesuits follow, do we not? When I heard of the Emperor's invitation — not, of course, that it was a personal invitation to me — but when I heard of the festival to be held in Dayan! Well, it was not so far to travel from Agra. And it has been too long since I saw these mountains. But I am prattling. I am afraid it is a habit of mine. What of this library? Is it not impressive?"

The Jesuit had delivered this speech with all the nods and gestures of a person engaged in conversation, but without at any point pausing for a response. Anticipating interruption, Li Du said tentatively, "I — I have not seen anything beyond this aisle. But it appears to be a fine collection."

"Ah, then you have not yet taken my meaning. I refer to the arrangement of the shelves. A compelling formula, and one that you, as a fellow scholar, will surely appreciate. Come, come, I will show you." His tone was one of such genuine warmth that they might have been old friends meeting after a long separation, and his gesture for Li Du to accompany him was as eager as a child's.

Li Du followed the Jesuit down the aisle, which narrowed as they approached the center of the room until the bookcases on either side of Li Du almost touched his shoulders. They emerged at the edge of a large round table, white marble veined with black and circumscribed by a frame of gold filigree. This was the center from which the bookshelves emanated.

"Now," said the Jesuit, "I will be patient while you examine the design." And he waited with obvious delight and anticipation for Li Du to pronounce judgment.

Li Du inhaled with pleasure the scent of paper and dry cedar wood. Then he scanned the shelves. He counted twenty-eight bookcases in total, with books arranged by color into four sections. Across the marble table were seven cases of books bound all in deep red. To their left, the books were silken blue, and to the right, the pale color of pearl.

Carved into the wood at the end of each bookcase, facing the central table, were two symbols, one above the other. The upper carving was the abstract likeness of an animal: a lion, a dragon, a phoenix or a tortoise. Below each animal was a word.

"The twenty-eight constellations," he said, picturing the four stone guardians outside.

The Jesuit clapped his hands together. "I knew that a librarian would know," he said. "Are they not elegantly linked to the four subject matters? The histories associated with the red phoenix who rules the southern skies, the classics with the white tiger of the west, and the philosophies with the azure dragon of the east. And of course the tortoise, here, where the literary works gleam black like obsidian. You know that we do not share your four celestial beasts, or the twenty-eight constellations they rule. This one, for example" — he indicated a carving on a shelf that stood for the constellation *emptiness* — "how can emptiness be a constellation? It is very intriguing to me. But I imagine you wonder why I am so taken with this heavenly library?"

"I am curious," Li Du admitted.

"It is, you see, a personal interest of mine. I am a student of astronomy. And," he added, modestly, "a teacher of it, in my time. I am at present composing a manual on the construction of astrolabes. You must have seen the armillary sphere that sits atop the Observatory in the capital?"

Li Du pictured the dark silhouetted iron dragons, their serpentine forms holding aloft a sphere composed of tilted rings. He nodded.

The Jesuit was nodding back at him with some pride. "That instrument — I designed and calibrated it. Of course, I was only a novice at the time, but I assure you, it was entirely of my design. So you understand my excitement at seeing a library here in this rural place arranged according to ideas that have long held great fascination for me. Your cousin must be a fine scholar."

He asked the question innocently enough, but something in Li Du's face made the Jesuit's eyes flash with mischief. "I see," he said, with a chuckle.

"As an astronomer," said Li Du, "you must be in great anticipation of the coming eclipse."

"Indeed I am, though I am not alone in that. I have heard that there will be thousands here to witness it. Decadence beyond imagining . . . but that is only to be expected. When I was in Beijing the Emperor was making his own study of astronomy. Has he continued?"

"I believe the Emperor's attention was called from it by his many other pursuits. He appointed a Bureau of Astronomy."

"That is a disappointment. He was very promising. He might have learned to make his predictions himself, without the aid of astronomers. That would have reduced the need for pretense. And who is to say that the wise use of mathematics is not in itself divine?"

Beginning to understand Tulishen's concerns, Li Du replied cautiously, "The Emperor has great respect for Jesuit scholars, but it is not permitted to speak of their work in a manner that impugns the Emperor's divine —"

"Great respect, yes," said the Jesuit, not hearing, or ignoring, Li Du's gentle warning, "for our clocks and our maps, not our faith. I must confess that this does not sadden me as it should. Our efforts have brought us here, have they not? To this empire. I am thankful that I was allowed to see it, when so many others who wish to have been turned away . . ."

"But come," he continued. "I will introduce you to my friend."

They had gone only two steps when the Jesuit stopped, distracted by a book on the shelf next to him. He picked it up and opened it. "The *Ming History,*" he said, holding the vermilion-bound volume close to his face and peering at the text. "I recall that the authors who first attempted this were all executed. Unfortunate men, commissioned by their conquerors to write the history of the defeated dynasty. A deadly exercise in tact. This appears to be the later edition. Hm. Well, come and drink some tea."

Li Du's anxiety on the old Jesuit's behalf was approaching alarm. But the Jesuit appeared unconscious of any misstep, and replaced the book with a sigh and a wistful smile.

At the far wall of the library were two doors. The one on the right was closed, and brilliantly painted with gold and silver dragons holding pearls in their jaws. The Jesuit, following the direction of Li Du's glance, said, "I've heard it called the 'hall of hidden treasures.' The people of your country have a wonderful habit of giving tantalizing names to all your rooms and gardens."

As he spoke, he ushered Li Du through the open door on the left into a room filled with light. It was an enclosed veranda with windows that looked down a steep incline to the south. The sun had come out and the room's stone floor radiated warmth. The space was empty but for a jumble of wooden racks in one corner, and a low table and chairs in the center.

At the table sat a man with broad shoulders, an angular face darkened by sun, and a short black beard oiled to a point. Li Du guessed that he was slightly younger than Li Du himself, but it was difficult to say for sure. He wore a belted tunic, voluminous trousers, and high leather boots rubbed smooth by stirrups and saddles. He nodded in greeting, but as he opened his mouth to speak, the Jesuit began again.

"Hamza, this is the librarian Li Du, cousin to the magistrate. I knew it at once — there is no mistaking the face of a librarian in a library. I am afraid I startled him, but we will reassure him with tea." He turned to Li Du. "I have a passion for the tea of this province. This red tea especially. In my opinion, there is no tea that compares to red tea. It has the ability to stimulate the mind without the irritation of coffee. I could drink it all day. It drives out the superfluous humors. I also drink it every evening. It lends clarity to my dreams. But let me pour it for you. Let us not call a maid. I do not like to be fussed over." He motioned Li Du toward one of the chairs.

"Sit here. This is the room for sunning books, but I am told the season is not right for that, so now it is a room for drinking tea and sunning old scholars. Please have a seat. I wonder if we have met before? No, you must have been just a small child when I was in Beijing. You cannot be older than forty-five. And now I realize I have forgotten to introduce myself. My name is Pieter van Dalen. I am called Brother Pieter."

The man seated at the table said, in competent but less fluent Chinese, "And my name is Hamza. I am a traveling storyteller by vocation."

"And by avocation," added Pieter, and went on, conversationally, "in keeping with the traditions of his tribe. I refer to his profession, for he is of the brotherhood of Homer and Taliesin — in keeping with tradition, he is a wanderer on this earth."

Pieter displayed none of the cynicism, none of the bored defeat that Li Du associated with scholars. The joyful spontaneity of his speech warmed the room almost as much as the sunshine.

Pieter turned to Hamza. "But I do not know whether you choose to travel or are doomed to it. Perhaps the fairies have placed you under a geas, my friend. I wonder if we can help you placate them."

Hamza raised his eyebrows. "You Christians think that all the magical spirits of the forests are demons hunting your souls. We are more sensible. Our djinn may be good or evil, as may men. I knew a woman who one day was fishing on the shores of the Caspian Sea. When she drew in her nets she saw a strange bottle shining blue amid the struggling silver fish —"

"Enough!" Pieter interrupted, smiling and shaking his head. "We are becoming acquainted with our new friend. Do not confuse him with false tales before we have told him any true ones." He addressed Li Du. "You must be cautious when you speak to this man. He is a performer and, like all quality performers, he can inhabit different personalities as it suits him. Never assume you are talking to one, when you might be talking to another."

Hamza acknowledged this with a slight bow.

In the last five minutes Li Du had heard more conversation than he had in the past three years, and he struggled for something to say. "The magistrate told me that you met in India," was all he managed.

"On the road from India," said Pieter. "Hamza had already found the caravan of Khampa traders, and I was fortunate to join them also. Very hospitable people, those merchants from Kham. Hamza tells me that he is of a Mughal family, but has been in Aleppo, or was it Istanbul? He is employed by a Frenchman to collect the stories called *The Arabian Nights.* Blasphemous, and, needless to say, extremely popular with the nobility in France."

Hamza nodded. "He is willing to part with his silver to get them. But I do not know why people want to buy the tales bound up in books. A storyteller leads an audience through the underworld. It is unwise to navigate these places without a guide."

"Ah," said Pieter, delighted, "but perhaps the librarian, the guardian of silent tomes, disagrees. Shall we debate?"

Hamza smiled and stood up. "Another time, perhaps. I have an assignation with a language tutor."

"May we assume," said Pieter, "that this tutor is a pretty young woman?"

"I have made but little study of your religion," said Hamza, "and yet I believe that question is outside the scope of your knowledge."

"You are correct in that," said Pieter, pleasantly, "though I did live some years in the world before I took the cowl. And what of you, my good librarian?" He turned to Li Du. "Are you married?"

Li Du hesitated. "I was," he said.

Pieter closed his eyes and bowed his head. After a moment he looked up, and Li Du read genuine grief in his expression. "I am very sorry," Pieter said. "That is a terrible loss, a most terrible loss."

The misunderstanding was inevitable, and Li Du debated whether there was any appropriate way to correct it. He was not a widower. He and his wife had married according to the arrangement made by their respective families, and had maintained a cordial, if never warm, relationship. They had not been blessed with children. Upon Li Du's sentence of exile, his wife had been released from the marriage under the principle of destined divorce, which held that the immoral action of a husband could dissolve a union, if that was the wish of the wife's father. Li Du's wife had gone back to her home, relieved that the situation had not turned out any worse for her. The last Li Du had heard, her father had begun negotiations for her to marry a man of wealth and good standing in her own city.

But before Li Du had decided whether to speak, Pieter, in an apparent effort to spare Li Du painful memories, returned the conversation to its previous topic. "But what need have you for a language tutor?" he asked Hamza. "Your Chinese is almost as good as mine, may the Lord pardon my boast."

"That is true," replied Hamza, with straightforward immodesty. "But the magistrate has hired me to entertain his guests with a story tonight. If I am to do well, I must know by what names the demons of this country are called. The universal villains, heroes, and clowns have no power if no one recognizes them."

"Go, then, to your research," said Pieter, cheerfully.

After Hamza had gone, Pieter shook his head in puzzlement. "A strange fellow," he said. Then he turned an attentive face to Li Du. "Hamza is fortunate. He carries his stories with him. For you it is more difficult. We have among our Christian saints one Jerome. Like you, he was a librarian and a wanderer. When he wandered, he longed for his books, and when he was with his books, he longed to travel. Is it so for you?"

Li Du, unsure how to respond, said after a moment, "I do miss the library." He spoke quietly, his gaze directed at a dark stain on the surface of the low table. *Spilled tea leaves,* he thought idly.

Pieter sighed. "It is appropriate for a library to be like the heavens. One should be able to consult books as easily as one enjoys the night sky. I am a great admirer of words, you know."

"Of — of words?"

Pieter took this as an opening to a conversation. He leaned forward. "Our departed

65

brother, Athanasius Kircher, was one of the wisest Jesuit scholars, if at times a little eccentric. He wanted to assign every unique word a written symbol, and to teach those symbols to every person in the world. Consider the implications. Spoken languages could remain as varied as they ever have been, but everyone would be able to communicate with each other. And it was your written characters that inspired him! When a person from Japan says *takara* and a person from China says *bao,* they may resolve their confusion by writing what is in their mind. Both will write 寶." He traced the character quickly with his finger on the table. "And there is no reason why a man from England, or Holland, couldn't do the same, and simply pronounce the word *treasure* or *schat.* There are some flaws in the theory, but what an idea, no?"

Pieter spoke with the eager curiosity of a student only just beginning to glimpse the possibilities of an endless universe. He was soon distracted by a new idea, and the minutes passed quickly as Li Du listened and the old Jesuit talked.

Li Du was aware, as Pieter spoke, of movement in the library. He heard the silken rustle of robes, the click of a cane on tile floor, and the thump and scrape of heavy objects in the adjacent room. He had the impression of shadows moving past the door, and, obeying an instinct he could not explain, he said suddenly to Pieter, "You should be careful of what you say in this place."

"Ah," said Pieter. "You think I am unwise? But I am an old man, too old to worry about words that powerful people do not want spoken. In my final years I have no wish to waste time and thought on what I should not say."

Li Du persisted. "The *Ming History,* and the Emperor's use of Jesuit science . . ."

Pieter made as if to wave Li Du's words away, then stopped. "Perhaps," he said. "Perhaps you are right. I know well that the Kangxi fears this province that he does not know. I know also that the last of the Ming rebels still hide and plot in nearby forests. With several brothers of my house among them, I fear. I know that one of the East India Companies has sent a representative with tribute. These are dangerous times. The Companies are not to be trusted. They are more powerful than the Emperor knows. They are ruthless. No one here wants an old Jesuit like me talking about what is happening behind the stage."

"Behind the stage?"

Pieter smiled. "Ah, Li Du, I am old and foolish. It is time for the younger ones, who understand this world better, to manage things. Have you met the young Jesuit? Apparently he is a botanist. Perhaps when he is better he will wish to consult Boym's *Flora Sinensis*. I have a copy with me."

Li Du shook his head. "I have not met him. The magistrate told me that he is unwell, and confined to his room at the inn."

"That is so. I spoke with him only briefly, before he was taken by a fit of nausea and forced to end our conversation. I pity his suffering. And yet, it is a strange thing. He called himself Walpole, Brother Martin Walpole. . . . But it is nothing. A coincidence. I should rest in these hours before the evening begins. You see that even I become tired when I talk too much."

CHAPTER 4

"In the palace of the capital of China, there ruled a Sultan."

"There are no sultans in China!" This declaration came from a salt merchant with plump cheeks. As he spoke he flung up his arm, spilling wine onto the scarlet silk sleeve of his robe.

The audience cheered and laughed. Servants scurried among them, refilling wine cups and replacing picked-over dishes with fresh ones. The lantern light gleamed on peeled lychees and caught on droplets of steam rising from rice cakes stuffed with pine nuts and minced yak tongue. At the edges of the courtyard, prostitutes with red lips tilted their shoulders in dainty postures, and watched without seeming to the expressions of the noblemen and the soldiers. Warmed by wine, furs, and glowing brazier fires, the magistrate's guests were relaxing after a sumptuous meal.

Hamza was the sole figure on the covered outdoor stage. In front of him, tiered rows of potted camellias burst with pink and red petals. The roof above him was supported by lacquered blue columns. From the courtyard tables where the audience sat, it was just possible to glimpse the back wall of the stage, across which mosaic dragons, whiskered and serpentine, stretched from floor to ceiling. They grinned and spread their claws, appearing in the flickering light to float in weightless revelry behind the seated figure of the storyteller.

He was dressed in gold and crimson, and a turquoise coat embroidered with flowers. A dark jewel suspended from a blue cap glinted on his forehead. His black beard was sculpted and sleek, and his eyes were in deep shadow. The only indication that he was cold was the faint cloud of his breath as he spoke into the chilly night.

"Allow me to clarify," he said. "I am not speaking of *this* China. *This* China is in the thrice tenth world. The story I am going to tell now takes place in the thrice seventh world, where there exists another China. I once met a blind fortune-teller who knew the way to that land. She told me of the peach trees that blossom in the morning and bear fruit the same evening. She also told me that in that place, the rivers are made of tiny jewels that tumble over each other until they chip away to nothing and fill the air with rainbow mists. The mountains in that world are lodestones that draw nails from the hulls of sinking ships and wear them like bristling armor."

Li Du glanced over his shoulder at Tulishen, curious. No storyteller in the capital would ever tell a tale of another China, certainly not at a formal function in the home of a magistrate. To suggest that there were other versions of the empire was to invite unhealthy memories of past rulers and dangerous speculation about the figure. An alternate China, more beautiful even than this one? The idea would not be tolerated.

But Tulishen was not attuned to that kind of threat. He sat on a platform heaped with silk cushions and the skins of bears and tigers, surveying the audience with puffed-up pride. His guests were enjoying themselves, and would compliment his hospitality. The Emperor would notice his popularity among the elite and his success in fostering powerful relationships. A magistrate's effectiveness was determined by the list of people who owed him favors, and Tulishen's list was growing by the day with the approach of the festival. Lady Chen sat beside him.

As for the guests, they were drunk and charmed by Hamza's impudence. Each small irreverence they accepted increased their appetite for another, and with delighted giggles or exaggerated gasps of shock they encouraged him. It was as if they were darting their fingers over a scorpion, holding their hands in danger a little longer each time before snatching them away in excitement. The Emperor was six days away, but in the courtyard, inhaling the smoke of exotic incense and drinking cups of warming wine, they had forgotten all but their present surroundings. The bright moon was a slice in the black sky overhead, and the morning seemed far away.

Li Du was not so completely distracted, and his mind drifted to the conversation at the banquet that had preceded Hamza's performance. After a welcome rest in his room, he had followed the sound of the gongs to the grand hall, and had been introduced to Brother Martin. The young Jesuit had emerged from his sickroom at the magistrate's insistence, and had greeted Li Du in halting Chinese with a look of ashamed apology. Like Pieter, he wore black robes. His black hat was perched on top of unruly, golden red hair. His face was very gaunt, his hollow cheeks softened by a short beard. He had large, ocean green eyes framed by almost invisible lashes. When Li Du had addressed him in Latin, his expression had transformed from embarrassment to haggard relief.

They had just sat down in their appointed places when Pieter arrived and apologized for his lateness. "I have been occupied," he said breathlessly to Li Du, "most agreeably since you and I parted in the library." He turned to Brother Martin. "Ah, good. I am pleased to see you are better. Let me serve you plain rice. It will settle your insides." Brother Martin had been looking with trepidation at a skinned bear paw arranged over a whole fish in a pool of red oil, and he accepted the rice gratefully.

"Occupied," Pieter continued, "by an item of such wonder I never anticipated its invention. And yet, now that I have seen it, I cannot think why it has not been thought of before. We have our clockwork and our star charts. But I am getting ahead of myself. It is called a tellurion."

Li Du did not recognize the word. "I apologize," he said, "but I have not heard —"

"But that is just it," Pieter interrupted.

73

"No one has. It is a new invention. I found it in the Company's tribute. Ah, but it puts all the other heavy baubles to shame."

He was so excited that his hands shook as he served rice to Li Du, impatiently waving away the maid who tried to serve it for him. "It is a model of the heavens that moves by clockwork," he continued, "just as the planets move. An astronomer can use it to tell how the planets and stars will align tomorrow, months, or even years from the present moment. Difficult to understand — I was unable to master it in such a short time — but extraordinary. I do not like the Company, but I must admit that this is a worthy gift." He sighed, and looked expectantly from Li Du to Brother Martin.

"But how did you come to see it?" asked Li Du, remembering the merchant's refusal to allow inspection of his cargo at the gate.

"Ah," said Pieter, with a twinkle in his eyes. "It required subtlety. But after I overheard a discussion of the inventory and the mention of clockwork suns, how could I restrain my curiosity?"

"This Sultan had a trusted old vizier, whose two sons, Shamsaldin and Nuraldin, were inseparable as children, youths, and young men. And when their father died, they decided to share the post of vizier between them. Sitting together one night, the brothers drank wine and planned their future. Together, they said, they would find a pair of sisters, marry them, and, if it were the will of Allah, get them with child on the same night. They then agreed that, if it were the will of Allah that one union should produce a daughter and the other a son, these two children should in their own time marry.

"But as the two brothers discussed the details of their plan, they began to argue. Shamsaldin, the older brother, said that if it were the will of Allah for him to have the daughter and Nuraldin the son, then surely Nuraldin's son should offer a gift of at least three pleasure gardens to Shamsaldin in exchange for the daughter's hand in marriage. Nuraldin was shocked. 'Surely,' he said, 'it is through our son that our memory will be preserved. Why should he have to give you anything when all you have is a daughter?' Shamsaldin grew very angry and declared that he would never marry his daughter to his brother's son, not for her weight in gold. And Nuraldin replied that he would not marry his son to his brother's daughter even to save himself from death."

Li Du glanced at Brother Martin, who was sitting in the audience on a low stone stool. He looked uncomfortable, his long legs stretched out in front of him, and he seemed aware of the curious looks he was receiving from the other guests. With his shoulders hunched as if to repel the attention, he studied the shell of a lychee that he was picking apart nervously between his pale fingers. Without Chinese, he could not understand the performance.

Sir Nicholas Gray, the merchant, sat at a low table designed for a chess game — the lines of the playing board were etched into the stone. He was almost outside the reach of the light, in a corner close to the stage. Like Tulishen, he was focused more on the audience than on the storyteller, and at the moment his gaze was resting on the women of pleasure arranged nearby. He had a silver coin, which he moved deftly across his knuckles and from one hand to the other. It seemed to skip across his fingers, melt into the stone of the table, and reappear soundlessly in his hand.

Li Du was distracted from the flashing disk by a brief, whispered exchange between Tulishen and Lady Chen. She rose with a rustle of silk, walked to the edge of the lantern-lit courtyard, and disappeared down a path enclosed by dense rhododendron trees.

A moment later, Jia Huan entered the

courtyard through the same gate. Careful not to interrupt the story, he spoke quietly to Tulishen, who grunted softly in affirmation of his secretary's questions. Li Du had seen Jia Huan throughout the evening issuing instructions to servants and performing various errands for the magistrate. If the young man was tired, he did not show it. His step was light and purposeful as he departed the garden once more.

"The brothers were still fuming the next day, when the Sultan announced that Shamsaldin would be married to the Sultan's beautiful daughter (for he had only one daughter, and the brothers could not share her as they did the office of vizier). 'You see,' said Shamsaldin to his brother, 'I am the favorite. You have always been the less important brother.' Nuraldin, feeling that there was nothing for him in the capital, and that travel was the only way to find new friends to replace those who had deserted him, quit the city forever.

"Nuraldin traveled far, across the whole kingdom, through Kashgar and Tashkent and Samarqand and Shiraz, and had many adventures along the way. Finally, he stopped in Bassorah. There he met an old man, an astronomer and adviser to the magistrate of that place. The astronomer was so impressed by Nuraldin's fine bearing and handsome speech that he immediately liked him, and invited him to his house.

"Now, the astronomer had a young daughter who was no less impressed than her father with the newcomer. The next day, the astronomer told the magistrate that Nuraldin was his brother's son, and that he had promised this brother, now dead, that he would marry their children. So Nuraldin married the astronomer's daughter and before very long, they had a son, whom they named Hassan."

Lady Chen returned with two servants in tow, each carrying large clay jars with bright wax paper seals.

"I know those jars," whispered a drunk man close to Li Du. "That's the finest wine in the entire province she's carrying. The Lady Chen's family wine is famous. Plums . . . tasting of poetry. Nothing like it in all the province, did I mention?"

The jars were opened, and Lady Chen herself moved through the crowd, pouring it into cups. Her dark blue robes skimmed the ground like spreading ink.

Li Du accepted a cup of the wine, and sipped. The clear liquid was infused with the tannic pull of plum skins and softened by the full, sweet taste of the fruit. A hint of flowery honey turned the sip into a reminder of sunshine on mountain limestone. Warmth

78

spread through Li Du's chest. It was a remarkable wine.

A gust of wind blew through the courtyard, extinguishing several of the lanterns. The servants began to relight them, but Tulishen gestured for them to stop. It was late, and the darkening courtyard would help draw the entertainment to a close.

"But even as Bassorah brought fortune to Nuraldin, back in the capital of China Shamsaldin grieved his brother's disappearance and wished they had never quarreled. And yet, despite his grief and regret, he fell deeply in love with his betrothed, the Sultan's daughter. They married, and had a daughter, so lovely that they called her Beauty."

Brother Pieter was listening intently to the story. When his turn came to be offered wine he waved his hand in polite refusal. Lady Chen offered again and, almost impatiently, Pieter accepted. He had not been drinking wine, and had no cup, so she summoned a maid to bring a fresh one. This done, she filled it.

Li Du saw Pieter sip the wine, but as he reached down to set the cup on the table before him, his hand trembled so violently that some of the wine splashed onto the hem of Lady Chen's dress. There was a quick exchange between them, Pieter apologizing, Lady Chen insisting that it was nothing. Lady Chen refilled the cup, but Pieter simply stared at it, and did not drink. Tulishen, who had noticed the upset, was frowning. Lady Chen, her mouth set in a tense line, handed the wine jar to a servant, and returned to her place at the magistrate's side.

"Perhaps you, wise audience, know what I am about to tell you. Yes, Hassan and Beauty were indeed born on the exact same day, though the estranged brothers did not know it, and Hassan and Beauty knew nothing of the plan their fathers had conceived so many years before.

"Now, in Bassorah, the old astronomer died and Nuraldin descended into melancholy. He missed his brother deeply, and became so despondent that even his wife's famous spiced pomegranates could not cheer him. Finally he told his poor wife that he would retire to a monastery and live as a recluse. Before he left, he gave his son, Hassan, a sealed letter and said, 'Here is written the story of my life and the truth about who you are. I give it to you now with a command not to open it until I am dead.' And with that he departed."

Pieter got up and made his way slowly to the magistrate. His expression was agitated, and when he reached Tulishen he bowed and said quietly, "I am afraid I must excuse myself. I am very tired." Hamza paused in the story and Pieter, noticing that Hamza had stopped, raised his voice and said, "Continue, friend! Do not let the tale be broken by an old man who has had too much wine. Bring Hassan and Beauty to their appointed fates." He made an effort to smile, bowed again to Tulishen, and left the garden.

Li Du felt the heat of the wine in his own cheeks. He took another sip from the cup that had been refilled for him. As he did so, he noticed that the table where Nicholas Gray had been sitting was empty and the merchant nowhere in sight. He felt a sudden chill, and looked around him at the dark edges of the well-lit and crowded courtyard.

Hamza straightened his shoulders, raised his hands in welcome to pull his audience back in, and continued:

"Hassan grew to be a kind and gentle young man, and the handsomest in Bassorah. However, he always felt some lack in his life, and was restless. One day he wandered through the fields outside the city, and when the sun set he fell fast asleep in a graveyard. As it happened, this graveyard was haunted, and that night a *jinniyah* — a distant cousin of your fox spirits — came to the cemetery.

"The *jinniyah* saw Hassan asleep and marveled at his handsome features. Presently she was joined by an *ifrit* — another spirit — who said, 'I saw one even more beautiful earlier this evening, asleep far away in another city.' The two spirits argued for a while over which human was more lovely, and finally decided that they must see them side by side in order to judge. So they took the sleeping Hassan and carried him over many cities and forests and deserts until they reached the young woman's bedchamber. They set Hassan next to the sleeping woman and sighed in admiration, for the two were indeed perfectly matched in beauty.

"At that moment Hassan and the young woman woke. It was too dark for them to see each other, but she reached out her hand and felt his soft skin and the hard muscles beneath it. And being a young and vivacious woman, she found pleasure in what she felt and pulled him to her. And he, not knowing where he was or how he came there, knew only that he was with a woman whose hair smelled of jasmine and whose bottom was as round and plump as a —"

There was a chorus of gleeful protestations that drowned out whatever word

Hamza had chosen to complete the sentence.

"Well, after a time, the two young lovers fell into a deep sleep. When dawn began to glow on the horizon the *jinniyah* and the *ifrit* realized that they had to take Hassan away before the young woman's father discovered him. For her father was the vizier, and violently protective of his daughter."

"It's Beauty!" came several voices at once from the audience. "I knew it was Beauty."

"Quiet!"

"Yes, this lovely young woman was none other than Beauty, and the vizier was Shamsaldin. His guilt and misery at the treatment of his brother made him a stern father, and he guarded Beauty so carefully that she was rarely allowed to leave her little room in the palace."

Brother Martin was asleep with his face on his folded arms, but the cries of the audience jolted him awake. He looked around him, for a moment baffled.

"So the *jinniyah* and the *ifrit* took Hassan from Beauty's room, and rather than transporting him back to Bassorah, they left him just outside the castle walls. You see, this is how these spirits behave. You cannot rely on them to do what is convenient for mortals. So quickly had they taken Hassan, that they never noticed his father's letter, which he had slipped under the bed as he fell asleep.

"Outside the castle, Hassan awoke, not knowing what city he was in and why he was there. He told everyone he met that he had spent the night in a palace with a princess. They laughed at him and called him a fool. But a kind chef took pity on him, and hired him to work as an assistant in his kitchen. Hassan, who had lost his sense of who he was or where he was from, devoted himself to his work and henceforth was often to be seen covered in flour.

"Meanwhile, at the palace, Shamsaldin had discovered Hassan's sealed letter under Beauty's bed. He demanded that Beauty tell him who had been in her room. Her story enraged him, but when he opened the letter and read it he began to weep, for it was written by his brother. Determined to find him, Shamsaldin asked the Sultan's permission to journey to Bassorah. The Sultan, intrigued, granted permission and declared that he would come too, for he was of a mind to see more of his kingdom.

"While preparations were made, the Sultan, wandering the market as he sometimes liked to do, ate a dish of pomegranates served by a local chef. They were, he declared, the most deliciously spicy pomegranates he had ever tasted."

Lady Chen left the courtyard again, just as Nicholas Gray reemerged from the darkness. He returned to his place at the chess table, pulled a square of cloth from a fold of his clothing, and dabbed it across his forehead and neck, which shone with perspiration despite the chill of the night. He glanced back at the dark gardens from which he had come.

"And so the vizier, the Sultan, and Beauty came eventually to Bassorah. While Shamsaldin and his daughter looked for Nuraldin and Hassan, the Sultan stopped with his guards to eat some pomegranates in the shop of an old woman. He remarked to her, 'These are very fine pomegranates, but I have had better in my own city.' The woman replied, 'Surely that is not possible. My pomegranates are the best in the kingdom. The only person who could possibly make them better than I can is my own son, and I do not know where he is.' She went on to tell of her sad life, how her husband had left her for a monastery, and how her son had disappeared one night not three months ago.

"Upon hearing her story, the Sultan deduced that she was none other than the wife of Nuraldin, and that the man who had served

85

him pomegranates outside the palace was none other than Hassan. He told the woman, 'Go to your husband at the monastery and tell him that the Sultan of China has summoned him, for even though he left my palace many years ago, he is still my subject.' The woman agreed — she could do nothing else.

"Then the Sultan went to Shamsaldin and Beauty and told them that he had heard sad news — Nuraldin had died several years ago, and his son had disappeared. Shamsaldin and his daughter wept, and despaired of ever finding Hassan.

"The group returned to the capital city, and as they entered the gate the Sultan seemed to remember something and, turning to Shamsaldin, said, 'I know that you are weary from the journey, but just before we left I was served the most disgusting pomegranate seeds, and I have been determined to have the chef's assistant who prepared them arrested. Go see to it.' So Shamsaldin arrested Hassan and had him put in prison, not knowing that the young man was his own nephew.

"That night, as Hassan slept in his cell, the Sultan revealed to Shamsaldin that his prisoner was in fact Hassan, whom they had journeyed so far to find. 'But,' said the Sultan, 'we must be sure. Summon your daughter.' The Sultan and the vizier instructed Beauty to put Hassan's letter under her bed, and go to sleep. When all was quiet, the Sultan's guard carried the sleeping Hassan to Beauty's room. In the morning, as the dawn light shone through the gold silk curtains and on the green silk pillows, Hassan awoke. He looked at the beautiful woman next to him, and she opened her eyes and looked at him. He looked confused, then reached beneath the bed to look for the letter he had put there and thought lost. 'Ah ha!' cried the Sultan, stepping out from behind a curtain with Shamsaldin. 'You are Hassan, lost nephew of my vizier!' And Shamsaldin embraced Hassan and wept. 'If only my brother could be here,' he said. 'Ah,' said the Sultan, 'that reminds me. A man from Bassorah has requested an audience here today. Let us see who it is.' And the great golden doors of the audience chamber opened —"

At that moment Lady Chen returned. She whispered something to Tulishen, who gave a start of surprise and stood up. He raised a hand to stop the performance. "I am afraid," he said, in a strained voice, "that an urgent matter compels me to end this delightful evening. I thank you all for the honor of your company in my home. Tonight's dinner is the first of many fine entertainments to come."

87

The guests began to murmur and crane their necks, searching the courtyard for a clue to what could have happened.

"Please do not worry yourselves," continued Tulishen, "or allow this domestic upset to diminish your good spirits. I am sure that the storyteller is eager to continue his performance in the common room at the inn. The braziers there are warm, and the wine plentiful." This statement made, he exited the courtyard.

Murmurs rose to a clamor as galvanized servants ushered guests from the mansion to the sound of the evening chimes. Through the shifting jumble of people, Li Du glimpsed Lady Chen. Someone was with her, a small man with white hair. They hurried away in the same direction as Tulishen and disappeared into the shadows of the gardens.

As soon as he could free himself from the crowd, Li Du followed the same path, walking quickly from one pool of lantern light to the next. He passed the library, dark and silent in its cage of cypress trees, and the temple, blurred by smoke from the incense sticks that protruded like spikes from iron cauldrons outside the doors. There was no one in sight.

He came to the pond and hesitated, listening. At first he heard only the hollow splash of fish breaking the surface of the water. The lanterns at the edge of the pond scattered chaotic glints across the ripples. Then he caught the sharp sound of a voice raised in rebuke or a command. It had come from the other side of the pond, from the direction of the guesthouse. He thought he glimpsed a slight figure, a woman, hurrying away from the guesthouse, but he could not be sure. It might have been merely a trick of the lantern light on the swaying willow branches.

Li Du traversed the crooked angles of the footbridge and came to the far bank. His heart beat faster as he approached the low white wall. He passed through the keyhole door. As he entered the courtyard, a breeze moved through it, sending a cloud of glowing ashes up from the brazier and causing the lanterns to sway on their hooks. Through the smoke and shifting shadows, Li Du saw Lady Chen and Tulishen standing silently on the veranda outside the room next to his own.

Tulishen turned a stiff, expressionless face to Li Du. "Cousin," he said, "a grave misfortune. He suffered a fit. The doctor is here, but there was nothing to be done."

At that moment a figure stepped from the

room. It was the same person who had left the stage with Lady Chen. *That must be the doctor,* Li Du thought. He looked at the three faces before him, searching for emotion and finding none. Lady Chen stood as if frozen.

"Who?" He asked the question, knowing the answer.

It was Tulishen who confirmed it.

"The foreign priest is dead."

CHAPTER 5

The body of Pieter van Dalen lay face down, the head turned to one side. Light from two candles that stood on the desk against the wall shone on the pale face and hands that seemed to emerge from a puddle of black robes. Li Du had not realized that the man had been so frail. His eyes moved from the body to the chair beside it, drawn away from the desk and askew. Pieter must have been sitting at the desk when he was taken ill. *A scholar at his desk,* thought Li Du, *alive, full of thoughts, ready to set brush to paper.* Now, though all the words in the world remained, this man's mind would never again assign them order.

Li Du did not know how long he had been standing at the door, staring into the room, when Tulishen's voice pulled him from his reverie. "A natural life-span cannot be measured," Tulishen said. "This could have happened at any time."

"That it true," said Lady Chen, her voice low and calm. "Doctor Yang," she said, "will you repeat what you told us?"

The doctor, a short man with a wisp of white beard and a face grooved like a walnut shell, cleared his throat. "The man's breathing stopped," he said. "It was very sudden."

"Of course," Tulishen said, "the foreigners are unused to this landscape. The mountain air is thin. I have heard of it causing illness and death to those who are not accustomed to it."

"It would be wise," said Doctor Yang, "to conduct rituals of protection for this house. A sudden death upsets the spirits."

Tulishen frowned. "I see no cause for overt displays. I will take appropriate action. You may go, doctor."

Doctor Yang bowed and departed. Tulishen turned to Lady Chen. "You will inform the servants that no gossip on this matter will be tolerated. There will be no talk of ghosts or inauspicious portents. I trust you to enforce this with strict discipline."

Sensing that his presence was all but forgotten, Li Du stepped inside the room. The back wall was lined with display shelves partitioned, like a labyrinth, into irregular shapes, and cluttered with objects: bulbous vases, black lacquered sculptures, and bouquets of feathers, oily and iridescent. The candle flames stretched high from untrimmed wicks, causing the shadows of the objects to jump across the walls and bed curtains. In the far left corner was the empty bed, a grand piece of furniture with high posts supporting a tester, from which geometric latticework spread across the heavy curtains.

Li Du's gaze moved to the desk and the mundane objects arranged on its surface: slim porcelain vases of varying height, a wooden brush holder from which hung four brushes suspended over a tray to catch ink, jade paperweights, an ink stone, a cabinet with tiny drawers inlaid with pearl, a pot of fragrant oil, and the familiar shape of the tea set, almost identical to the one in Li Du's room. Arranged on a slatted tray were a jar of tea leaves, a teapot, four tiny cups with translucent edges as thin as flower petals, and four large, cylindrical cups, all decorated with the same glaze of red flowers on a blue background.

Li Du looked again. There *should* have been four large cups. There were in fact only three. *That is not so strange,* he thought. *The fourth cup must have been broken, or lost, and never replaced.* But old habits born in his library made him conscious of objects not in their proper place, and he glanced around the room in search of the cup. It wasn't there.

He returned his attention to the tea set, and noticed something else. There was a very faint blur of steam rising from the spout of the teapot. He touched the rounded porcelain and found it hot. He bent closer and sniffed — it was just hot water. Pieter must have filled it from the kettle over the brazier.

Hearing footsteps and voices outside, Li Du turned around to see a group of male servants entering the courtyard, carrying a dark, lacquered casket. They were led by the young secretary, Jia Huan. The other Jesuit, Brother Martin, was with them. Li Du observed the trepidation in the faces of the servants, though they were trying to keep their eyes lowered and their expressions fixed.

Jia Huan alone succeeded in presenting an appearance of complete composure. He bowed to Tulishen. "I have done as you asked," he said. "There is a place prepared in the temple. And here is the other priest."

Tulishen nodded. "Do it quickly. The man's ancestors are searching for him. They will find him more easily in a holy place, with fragrant incense to guide them."

Li Du watched silently while the servants, under Tulishen's direction, moved the body into the casket, sealed it inside, and carried it away.

When they had gone, Tulishen turned to Brother Martin. "I wish to speak to you on matters of ritual," he said.

Brother Martin stared at the magistrate with apparent incomprehension, his eyes wide and bewildered. He opened his mouth to speak, closed it again, and shook his head.

Tulishen frowned. "Li Du, will you translate for this man?"

"Of course." Li Du turned to Brother Martin. "The magistrate wishes to know the proper rituals," he said gently in Latin, "to show Brother Pieter respect in the tradition of his own faith. The magistrate hopes that you will counsel him in this matter."

Rather than calming Brother Martin, Li Du's words seemed to increase his confusion. "I — I would like to help, of course, but I only just met Brother Pieter. I do not know what his wishes were for — that is, in case of . . ." He trailed off, and Li Du translated.

"His wishes?" Tulishen was impatient. "This man misunderstands, or you have not translated well. Explain to him that there are bad omens associated with the death of a guest. For the safety of my house I will do what can be done to avoid those ill fates. I want to know what formalities to observe. I can bring Buddhist monks to say prayers for his easy journey to the next world, or Taoist monks, should their beliefs agree better with the foreign faith."

Brother Martin listened to Li Du, his continued agitation evident in his clutched hands. He said, "I — I am not of sufficient rank or education — that is, I do not have the authority to perform a service for the dead. It would be —" Brother Martin stopped, as if searching for an appropriate phrase. "It would not be correct."

Again Li Du relayed Brother Martin's words. Tulishen, becoming exasperated, said, "Is he to be buried or burned to ashes? Should mourners be hired to scatter money for the afterlife on his grave? And if he is to be buried, how long should his coffin remain in the temple before the burial? I only need to know the most basic requirements. The Emperor will want assurances that our actions were proper, you understand."

Brother Martin's eventual response was tense and quiet. "Our tradition is . . . is burial, not cremation."

"Very well," said Tulishen. "We will summon Buddhist and Taoist priests. They will burn offerings to appease his ancestors and those of this house where he died. We will bury him quickly, if there is no need to keep him aboveground for any time. You may —"

"Wait," Li Du said. He was surprised to hear his own voice, but he went on. "You should not perform those rituals. The Christians consider them blasphemous."

Tulishen raised his eyebrows. "Are you a convert?"

"I am not a Christian. But I have read the book of instructions on how to become a Christian without disrespecting the ancestors. Father Ricci wrote that Christians cannot invite monks from other religions to their funerals, and cannot burn paper money for use in the afterlife. I do not know what Brother Pieter would have wanted, but Father Ricci is considered an authority."

Brother Martin raised his pale eyebrows at the sound of Ricci's name. He broke in hastily. "You speak of Father Ricci? Of course, of course Father Ricci's instructions are clear. But I have observed that many brothers of my order are so accustomed to Chinese rituals that they consider them acceptable. I thought Brother Pieter might wish to be buried according to local custom." His voice shook slightly.

Li Du translated, and Tulishen gave him the barest nod. "Then he will be buried at first light. I will have it done quietly. There is no need to draw the attention of those who would stare and gossip. He will have a small tomb with the Mu kings on Lion Hill there." He indicated the dark silhouette of the hill rising at the back of the mansion. "In this part of the empire I can think of no greater sign of respect. We will not invite local priests."

Brother Martin turned to go, but Tulishen stopped him. "It would be appropriate," he said, "for you to keep vigil here tonight, to cleanse the room. It is a dangerous time, dangerous for the man's soul, and for this household. If you will stay and recite the prayers of your faith, it would reassure me."

Li Du watched Brother Martin search for a way to refuse the request. He failed, and with a wan face and stiff movements, moved to the doorway of Pieter's room. He stepped inside. "I do not have my prayer book with me," he said. "I will read from Brother Pieter's Bible, if it is here."

The book was on the desk. Brother Martin sat down and opened it.

"I will have fresh candles brought," said Jia Huan.

Tulishen nodded his approval. "Jia Huan," he said, "go and prepare ink and seals for official correspondence. I will meet you in my offices. Li Du, I would speak with you." Li Du followed Tulishen down the stairs into the courtyard. Together they exited onto the path. Li Du looked back toward the welcoming solitude of his own room, but followed his cousin into the uneasy darkness of the gardens.

Now that orders had been issued and Li Du was his only audience, Tulishen allowed some of his personal distress to show, and paced nervously while he spoke. "You realize," he said, "that this puts everything at risk. All of my plans. Why did the man have to die here? And dealing with that one" — he gestured toward the guesthouse where Brother Martin kept vigil — "how can these people expect to have any influence on the Emperor when they are so clumsy? How have they built their own kingdoms when they are all such buffoons?"

"I do not think that Brother Martin is a stupid man, but I agree with you that he seems a strange choice for his church to send as representative."

"He is wasting everyone's time."

"Perhaps he will appear to better advantage when he has recovered from the shock of what has happened. And remember that he has been ill."

"He should have concealed his illness in order to save face. But that is a separate matter. I will tell you what I want from you. In the morning, I want you and Jia Huan to search the dead man's belongings. You can itemize the books and documents — I want an inventory of everything that he has."

"But why? What need is there for such an invasion of his privacy?"

"Has your exile made you so naive? Any of these foreigners could be spies, and even if they are not, they have in their possession letters or books that could enlighten the Emperor on some relevant or interesting matter."

"Do you have doubts about the manner of his death? He died so suddenly, and I —"

"The man's breathing failed, and he died." Tulishen spoke in a sharp whisper. "It could not have been prevented, and he was, we could all see, an old man. The travel was too much for him."

"Yes, but perhaps there should be some inquiry at least. You are the magistrate."

"What do you know of the duties of magistrates? It is upsetting enough that a guest has died in my house. Now you would make it worse with unfounded speculation. You have no idea what damage could be done to my house, to my reputation, should this disturbance have some ill effect on the Emperor's festival. Consider what the people who came here tonight are saying to each other now. Consider how much effort I will have to put into reassuring them that there is no cause for concern. And already I am overwhelmed with preparations, introductions, negotiations, and worries of every kind."

He stopped, breathing hard.

Li Du spoke carefully. "If, as you said, it is certain that Brother Pieter died naturally, then there can be no scandal to trouble you."

"You have been away from society too long, Cousin, if you believe that. There can always be scandal. Rumors require nothing to feed them other than people who talk. Rumors must be controlled. That is the priority now."

There was a short silence. *Yes,* thought Li Du, *I understand your priorities.* He said quietly, "I ask your permission to leave tomorrow, after I have concluded the inventory."

Tulishen gave a curt nod. "I have no objection. Jia Huan will find you in the morning. When you have finished, your papers will be returned to you, and you may depart."

Li Du returned to his room by a meandering route. He passed the library, where a small light now glowed from one window. Even as he watched, it went out. A solitary figure descended the stairs and left in the direction of the servants' houses.

A night bell sounded the time, three hours past midnight. Its ring recalled to Li Du an old memory of a morning twenty years ago. It was the day Li Du sat for the final round of the national examinations. He remembered the shivering crowds of students waiting in the darkness before sunrise for the examination hall to open. He could almost feel the ink stone he had gripped, so cold he had to switch it from hand to hand to relieve his fingers from the marble's freezing weight.

In the exam room, the sleet had dripped through the ceiling tiles as he wrote, and he shielded his paper from the drops, knowing that an examiner in an unkind mood might fail a student rather than spend time deciphering a smudged character. Li Du's eyes became so tired that his eyelids swelled and stung, and he relied on the proctors calling out topics because he could no longer read the questions in the book.

And then, emerging from the hall of examinations still clutching his blanket around his shoulders, going over in his mind what he had written, miserably regretting answers, he heard the mourning bells sound from the Drum Tower. The tower itself was hidden in the mist, and the hollow, echoing strikes seemed to come from the very clouds that hung low over the Forbidden City. They went on, solemnly, and he lost count of their number. Someone important had died. Who could it have been? A concubine, perhaps, or a wife of the Emperor's father?

Word spread quickly that it was the Emperor's Jesuit friend, Father Verbiest, who had died that morning, and that he was to receive the greatest funeral honors that had ever been bestowed on a foreigner in China. The Emperor himself would write his eulogy, and had withdrawn from the public world to meditate on how best to express his grief. In the days that followed, it was rumored that the Emperor ventured out alone at night to the astronomical observatory where Father Verbiest had taught him to read the stars. They said that he stayed there, among the sextants and armillary spheres, mourning the loss of his confidant.

That was a time when Jesuits were more secure in their place among the Kangxi's advisors.

Li Du's own education had taken place at the height of Jesuit influence in the Forbidden City. As a boy, he, and the other children of nobles, were tutored by a succession of the foreigners. Most of them were as old and white-bearded as Brother Pieter. A few were younger, and Li Du had always found them the more disconcerting. Their faces showed the sombre intensity of men devoted to a cause. The expressions of their elders were kinder, their eyes more understanding of the world and of the compromises that had to be made within it.

The Jesuits were most often to be seen in the library of the Forbidden City, poring over scrolls and calibrating bronze and iron instruments, lighting candles to continue their work long after the evening shadows had silenced the palace. As Li Du grew older and spent more and more time in the library, he had found ample opportunity to converse with the Jesuits, practicing his Latin and assisting them in their translations. Some were adept at Chinese, others not. Some devoted themselves to bringing converts to their religion. Others put all their energy into their intellectual pursuits.

Some had concubines, some had wives, and some adhered to their vows of celibacy. Some were outspoken, others reticent. They were as strange in their individual proclivities as they were in the oddities they had in common.

Li Du had reached the guesthouse again. The hanging lanterns had been extinguished. The door to Pieter's room was open, and Brother Martin was silhouetted at the desk, hunched over his open book, supporting his head in his hands.

"He hath put down the mighty from their seat, and hath exalted the humble. He hath filled the hungry with good things; and the rich he hath sent empty away . . ."

Li Du climbed the four steps up to the porch and went into his own room. He lit a candle. Then he picked up his teapot and the thick cloth folded beside it, and retraced his steps across the courtyard to the brazier. As he passed between the eerie, hulking figures of the sculpted plants, his shoulders tensed. He had the feeling that he was being watched.

When he reached the brazier, he set down his candle and teapot, and used the cloth to lift the hot kettle from its hook. He poured the simmering water into the teapot carefully, and replaced the kettle. By the time he had finished, the courtyard was silent. Brother Martin must have fallen asleep.

He turned around, teapot in one hand, candle in the other, and caught his breath. In front of him, blocking his way, was a figure. He raised his candle in order to illuminate the face, but in his surprise he moved his arm too quickly. The flame went out.

"Who is there?" he asked the darkness.

"I have startled you," came the voice. "I can give you a flint, but it would be easier simply to use the brazier."

Li Du recognized the accented speech. He set the wick of the candle against a glowing coal, then turned and raised it again, this time slowly. Its light caught the pendants and rings adorning the velvet robes of Sir Nicholas Gray.

Even in the soft glow of the candle, Gray's face showed the effects of hard travel. The skin was irritated and peeling where the sun and wind had chapped it. The deep-set eyes were further sunken by the bruised shadows around them.

"I thought you knew I was here," said Gray.

"I did not." Li Du tried to steady his breath.

Gray looked at the silhouette of Brother

Martin across the courtyard. The young man's head now rested on his folded arms. "What has he been doing there?"

"The magistrate asked him to pray for Brother Pieter's soul."

"He chose an unusual prayer."

"What do you mean?"

"Only that he was reading the Canticle of Mary."

"What is that?"

"I'm not much of a religious man, but that prayer is not usually said in the middle of the night. The young brother must be tired. He is not a seasoned traveler. And the shock — well, we were all shocked."

Gray remained standing in front of Li Du. The full teapot was heavy, and Li Du struggled to hold it steady. He looked over Gray's shoulder, hoping that Gray would step aside, but Gray made no move to do so.

"An interesting man," said Gray. "I have not had many dealings with the Jesuits, myself. They have their ways of approaching China, and we have ours."

" 'We'?"

"The Company. The English East India Company, my employer."

Li Du searched for a response. "Brother Pieter was impressed by the astronomical piece in your tribute. He said that it was a magnificent gift for the Emperor."

It was difficult to read the man's face in the strange light of the flame, but it seemed to Li Du that Gray's expression tightened. Li Du recalled Pieter's unrepentant confession that he had gone into the treasure room without permission.

But if Gray was upset, he controlled it quickly. "It is a marvelous invention," he said. "I have some experience with construction, but that device is far beyond my understanding. It was calibrated by our astronomers and watchmakers in Calcutta. Jesuits, jewelers — the Company consulted every expert. I brought it here undamaged, which was no small feat, through the forests of the headhunters on barely passable trails. The box itself required the skills of fourteen carpenters to make."

"Why —"

"To protect it from damage. The tellurion is splendid, of course, but there are many pieces in the tribute more wondrous still. Brother Pieter was an astronomer — I assume you knew that already — so I am not surprised that he liked that particular treasure. What matters, though, is that the tribute pleases the Emperor."

"I understand that your company hopes

to enter into a trade agreement with China."

"Just so. You see, I believe it is the businessmen, not the men of the church, who should be the ambassadors to China from Europe. We are the ones who will bring China into the world. The Jesuits have had their time. They are a passing fancy, like those clocks with which they bought their way into the Emperor's court. But the Chinese can only learn so much from them. This empire is not like the colonies. China is in possession of wealth and knowledge beyond what England can comprehend."

Li Du heard the rising excitement in Gray's voice. He shuddered inwardly, chilled by Gray's animation in the aftermath of Brother Pieter's death. "I have studied so much about China," Gray continued, apparently oblivious to Li Du's discomfort, "but this is the first time I have set foot inside its borders. I've been waiting, along with others — merchants, explorers, scientists. We are all waiting, studying your language from the Chinese traders prepared to teach it, ready for the moment the empire finally decides that it is time for us all to share in a new prosperity."

"These political considerations are outside my understanding," said Li Du, whose arm was beginning to ache from the weight of the teapot. Still Gray did not move.

"Because you are an exile?" asked Gray, looking intently for Li Du's response. When Li Du made none, Gray shrugged. "I saw you as you waited by the gates of the mansion yesterday. A man of my experience knows not to ignore strangers who watch from the shadows. I asked the magistrate who you were, and now that I know, I have need of your advice. The opinion of an exile is valuable to me."

"On what matter?"

"Will the Emperor agree to trade with the Company?"

"I cannot be of any use to you. I do not know the answer to your question."

"But you must know something. You know the political games of your empire. You know what is effective, and I must assume from your exile, if you pardon my straightforward speech, that you know something of endeavors that are doomed to fail."

Li Du's reply was firm. "It is the Emperor, and the Emperor alone, who will decide whether your ships will be allowed to come to China. His is the only opinion that should concern you."

Ignoring the finality in Li Du's tone, Gray said, "In my own room there is a small vase, very beautiful. I asked the maid its value, and she said it was nothing of any great worth. And yet its glaze is made from gold suspended in glass, a material of color and quality I have never seen before, one that our alchemists cannot yet duplicate. If you could see what I see, the possibilities . . ." He let the sentence hang.

"The Jesuits," said Li Du, "came to China to learn and to teach. The Emperor respects these motives. I would not expect him to share the empire's wealth with Western merchants unless he sees good reason to do it."

"You are naive if you think the Jesuits do not have their own more subtle agendas. But I do not disagree with you entirely. Desperation is always a weak position. And there are certainly those who are desperate. Before I left Europe I heard that Prince Frederick of Saxony has imprisoned an alchemist in a tower, and vows not to let him out until he has discovered a way to re-create Chinese porcelain."

"And?"

"My point is that it will be through diplomacy, not stealth and medieval methods, that any person in this world who has some sense may become wealthy. We don't want to possess China. There is wealth enough for China to benefit just as much as we will.

111

Those who can control the wealth will be powerful. The Emperor could become even more powerful than he is now. He must think beyond China. Think of the whole world." Gray gesticulated eagerly. His open hand caught the light, exposing a dark slash across his palm.

"But you have hurt yourself," said Li Du, pointing to the wound.

This stopped Gray. The gleam left his eyes, and he dropped the injured hand to his side. "It is nothing," he said. "I cut it when I was moving the crates into the hall in the library. It is not serious."

Li Du took advantage of Gray's momentary distraction. "It has been a long evening," he said. "I will go now."

To his relief, Gray moved aside, allowing Li Du, finally, to pass him. But he had only taken several steps when instinct compelled him to ask a question. He stopped and, half turning, said, "Where did you go during the story?"

"What?"

"I saw that your place was empty. I thought you might have gone to speak to Pieter. You left around the time he did."

"Why do you ask that?" Gray snapped. "Why does it matter?"

"I was only curious. I did not mean to offend you."

As before, Gray controlled his temper quickly. His eyes met Li Du's, and after a moment's deliberation, he smiled. "I had an assignation with one of the young women provided for the occasion. But I have always considered such matters my own private business."

"Of course," said Li Du, politely. Gray's smile, almost a leer, chilled him.

Li Du went into his room and closed the wooden doors. They scraped heavily against the frame, and the iron handles clanged. Nicholas Gray's words remained in his mind. *What matters is that the tribute pleases the Emperor.* He meant, of course, that this was what mattered to the Company. Li Du frowned and stretched his tired legs. A man had died that night. If anything mattered, it was nothing to do with jewels or clockwork or the Emperor's opinion of these cold things.

5 Days

CHAPTER 6

Li Du awoke from a troubled sleep to the sound of his door closing. There was no one in the room, but the trail of steam rising from the teapot on the desk told him that a servant must have slipped in quietly and filled it while he slept. It was a conventional courtesy, but this morning it made him uneasy. The wisps of steam spread and hung in the air like wraiths.

He sat up, gathered his robe tightly around his shoulders, and shuffled to the desk. The air held the blue cast of early morning, but he could see through his latticed window a slash of golden light across the far side of the courtyard. He shivered, feeling that he occupied, in this dim and silent room, a remnant of the night that would soon be burned away. He prepared and drank his tea, then began, with practiced assurance, to pack his belongings.

When he was ready, he emerged from his

room onto the shaded veranda. He could feel the cold marble through the soles of his shoes. The door to Pieter's room was open, the sun now shining directly into it. On the opposite side of the courtyard, still in deep shadow, the door to Nicholas Gray's room was tightly shut. As Li Du crossed out of the shade into the sun, he looked up and was momentarily blinded by the white brilliance that poured over the roof. He turned away from it, and stepped into the room that had, until recently, been occupied by Pieter van Dalen.

There was no one there. The body had been taken away. In the corner there was a small pile of saddlebags, and on the desk a worn stack of books. Li Du picked up the top volume and opened it to its title page, on which dark-inked cherubs held aloft a map of China, its northern boundary defined by the sketched crenellations of the Wall. The area around the capital was a dense fabric of cities and rivers, meticulously labeled. The southwest provinces, in contrast, were a blank expanse. There was no mark for Dayan — only the tentative tracing of the Golden Sand River. A province, Li Du was reminded, still largely uncharted by the empires of the West, or by the Chinese empire that claimed to govern it.

He turned to the next page, where the author, Athanasius Kircher, explained in passionate language the need for Christianity in the pagan empires. *The devil's wrath fills the world with hatred and lies, and is not satiated, even with the destruction of men . . .*

A soft step on the veranda announced the arrival of Jia Huan. He looked tired, but spoke crisply. "The magistrate," he said, "wishes to be prepared for any question put to him by the Emperor. If you can translate the titles of the foreign books, I will make a list. After that, we are to inventory his possessions. The magistrate is grateful for your help in this matter." As he spoke he walked to the desk, took a seat, and began deftly to prepare paper and ink. "You are ready?" he asked.

"Yes," Li Du said, his eyes still on the open book. "This is the *China Illustrata.*"

"I have not heard of it," said Jia Huan.

"To my knowledge it has not been translated into Chinese. It was written by a Jesuit who took it upon himself to compile into a single tome the notes and observations of all the Jesuit brothers who had traveled to this empire."

"Were their observations accurate?" asked

Jia Huan.

"Their observations, yes. His interpretations of those observations, perhaps not always so. But I believe he was a man of great intelligence."

Jia Huan's reserved expression became momentarily skeptical. Li Du raised his eyebrows, curious to know what the other man was thinking. Jia Huan, noticing, said quickly, "I apologize. It is not my place to criticize the foreigners when the Emperor shows them favor."

Li Du found the glimpse of real feeling in the secretary a welcome relief from strained formality. Hoping to draw more honest conversation from Jia Huan, he said, "You do not believe that the Jesuits merit their reputation as superior scholars?"

"It is not my place," Jia Huan repeated, "but I believe that our own scholars have the advantage of understanding older, more fundamental philosophies. There is nothing new that can be brought to China. Everything that exists, exists here, and has existed since long before the other kingdoms of the world began."

It was gracefully delivered, but Li Du recognized the words. This was a rote statement, learned and repeated by all the young scholars in the capital. Li Du sighed. "Well," he said, returning his attention to the book, "it seems that Brother Pieter wished to improve upon the work of his predecessors. In the same way that our scholar recluses like to correct the errors in old travel journals, so he has endeavored to correct their mistakes."

He had turned to the section devoted to Agra, the margins of which had been annotated in a small, neat hand. Li Du skimmed the notes. "These are suggested alterations to the original text," he said. "Here he corrected the recipe for the antidote to the venom of the hooded snake that the Portuguese call the *cobra de capelos.*"

Jia Huan responded with a nod of polite disinterest. "And the title of the next book?" he asked.

Li Du lingered for another moment over the page. Then he closed the *China Illustrata,* set it down, and picked up the next volume. One by one, he read the titles to Jia Huan: *A Chinese Dictionary, Geography on a Universal Map, Flora Sinensis, Reply to the Mirror Polisher* — a Persian text devoted to legal disputes, Li Du explained — and *The Sphere of the Earth.*

Among the unbound documents were letters of invitation, appropriately sealed, and several maps showing the route from Agra to Yunnan. In addition, there was a stack of papers tied with twine. Li Du untied the string and glanced through the pages. They were filled with astronomical illustrations: concentric circles, rings in twelve partitions, quadrants and axes labeled with the words *orizon* and *arcticus.* On one page was a detailed diagram of an astrolabe labeled in Arabic script.

"What is that?" asked Jia Huan.

"It is a draft of the manuscript that Brother Pieter was writing on the subject of astrolabes," said Li Du, quietly. "But I cannot tell you very much more than that — I have not studied astronomy. Do you know the discipline?"

Jia Huan glanced at the manuscript and shook his head. "I was assigned minor secretarial duties at the Bureau of Astronomy. But these drawings mean little to me."

"What was your concentration in school?"

"Calligraphy. My father was a master of the art. My ancestors have been scholars and advisors to the emperor since the Tang. It is my wish to honor them."

"And do you hope to become a magistrate yourself?"

Jia Huan averted his eyes, but not before Li Du saw the flash of ambition in them. "I want only to prove myself a good servant to the empire," said Jia Huan.

"And are you content with your assignment here? I know that many young officials hope to be sent to the coastal cities instead of to the interior."

Jia Huan smiled. "It is true. Officials do not compete for a place in this province. Most wear jade charms in the hope that they will not be sent to the southern borders. They are afraid of the fever and they dislike the villagers. But I am different. The project of educating the ignorant tribes in these wilder areas is fascinating to me. They are subjects, and yet they are not yet civilized, not truly Chinese."

"This is your first assignment away from the capital?"

"It is my second. I went first to Macau. If there are no more books, I will blot these pages and grind more ink so that we may continue our inventory."

While he waited for Jia Huan, Li Du's gaze fell on the tea set. Remembering his observation the night before, he again counted the teacups. There were four small cups, but only three large ones. None appeared to have been used, and there were no cast-off leaves in the slatted tray. He lifted the lid of a small jar. It was stocked with fine tea, just like the one in his own room. He picked up the teapot, still heavy with water. Its rounded sides were ice cold.

Troubled, he set the pot down and went to the corner of the room where Pieter's bags were arranged, neatly, against the wall. He knelt, and carefully opened one of the worn cloth satchels. Inside were the humble and well-used tools of the traveling scholar: a set of writing utensils in a leather envelope, a warm blanket of brown wool, a scratched and dented pot, a set of small knives, and several packages of dried fruit and savory preserved meat. Only one item stood out as bright and new, and Li Du picked it up.

It was a soft brown leather purse, roughly square in shape. A large, circular piece had been cut from one side and replaced with a richly embroidered circle of fabric. The inset cloth depicted three foxes leaping through juniper bushes against a background of shining sky blue. The dye was exquisite, bright color transformed into thick, gleaming threads.

Li Du recognized the style. Purses such as these were worn by Khampa and Tibetan merchants, and used to carry tea leaves. When the caravans stopped, the horsemen could brew their butter tea quickly and conveniently using the small churns that they carried slung to the saddles of their horses. Li Du inhaled, and raised the purse to his nose, surprised by its strong fragrance. It smelled of perfume, heavy and floral, and vaguely familiar. He removed a pinch of what was inside. It was black tea.

Then his fingers caught the sunlight, and he saw, clinging in the crevices of dark leaves, a fine, powdery residue, a color between white and pale green. It was too thin and pale to be dirt or sand. He touched his finger tentatively to his tongue, and recoiled as a tingling, freezing sensation seized his mouth and throat. He coughed and spat.

Jia Huan turned around and rose quickly to his feet with a look of confusion. "What —"

"I am all right," said Li Du, moving to the desk. But he was unsteady on his feet, and by the time he reached it, he was forced to put out a hand to keep from falling. He closed his eyes and took a deep breath. He opened his eyes to see Jia Huan looking at him with concern. "I am feeling better now," he said. "Truly."

"But what is the cause of your distress?" asked Jia Huan.

With his free hand, Li Du tipped the pouch, spilling a small amount of the leaves onto the piece of paper on the desk. They scattered across Jia Huan's neat calligraphy like black ravens flying over a wintry forest.

"What are you doing?" asked Jia Huan.

"These leaves are coated with poison," Li Du said. Jia Huan's brows drew together. He leaned down to look more closely. To Li Du, the leaves now seemed twisted and vile, the pale powder shining in the sunlight.

"This is not dust," said Jia Huan quietly. "But you are sure that it is poison?"

"Yes."

"It cannot be a coincidence," said Jia Huan. "This poison must have been the cause of the priest's sudden death."

Li Du did not respond immediately. When he spoke, his words came slowly. "It must have been," he said, "but it is strange."

"Very strange," Jia Huan echoed. Then he straightened his shoulders and smoothed the emotion from his pale features. "I must inform the magistrate at once," he said, and picked up the purse. "I will bring this to him."

Li Du nodded.

"And I will send for the doctor. You do not look well."

Li Du shook his head. "I am recovering. It was not enough to do me any real harm. I require a few moments, merely, to rest. I thank you for your concern, but as you said, you should inform the magistrate at once."

When Jia Huan was gone, Li Du sank slowly into the chair at the desk. The memory rose before him of Pieter van Dalen leaving the performance the night before. Li Du's last glimpse had been of a tall, cloaked figure disappearing into the dark. Closing his eyes, Li Du tried to follow Pieter beyond the border of his own memory.

He would have made his way along the lantern-lit garden paths to the guesthouse. He would have lit the two candles. If he wanted tea, he could have summoned a maid to bring it. But, Li Du recalled, Pieter had not liked to be served tea. He had preferred to make it himself. So, instead of summoning a maid, he would have gone to the brazier in the courtyard and filled the pot in his room with boiling water from the kettle. Then he must have taken the purse full of tea from his bag. It would have been too dark to notice the pale powder mixed into the leaves. What then? A pinch of tea in a cup, hot water, the swirling leaves, and death.

Li Du held up his hand and examined the sheen that still clung to the tips of his fingers. Now recovered from the shock of the discovery and the physical effects of the toxin, he was able to think more clearly. He had seen this powder somewhere before. Moreover, he was certain that he knew what it was. But where had he seen it? It had been years ago, in a different life, in a locked drawer. The powder of — and then he remembered — of jewelvine root. This was ground jewelvine root, and he knew why it was familiar to him. In a moment, Li Du was up and out the door, on his way to the library.

The sun was fully up now, and the pale stone guardians watched him with impassive countenances, their features indistinct and flecked with the shifting shadows of cypress needles, as he passed between them into the library. He recalled the earnest vitality of Pieter van Dalen as he had met him for the first time — striding through the shelves of bound silk volumes, speaking to Li Du as if they were in the middle of a conversation they had begun long ago. *Unfortunate men,* Pieter had said of the Ming History authors, *commissioned by their conquerors to write the story of the defeated dynasty.* What had he called it? Li Du frowned. *A deadly exercise in tact.*

He turned sharply at the sound of a tap on the floor, and saw an old man with a walking stick approaching him from a patch of sunshine in the far corner of the room.

"Who's that?" The man's voice was a croak. "Won't have them saying I don't look after the place. Who's that, then?" His Chinese was heavily accented, guttural and difficult to understand.

"I apologize for startling you. We have not met, but I am a guest in this house. My name is Li Du. You are Mu Gao, the librarian?"

The man stopped just in front of Li Du. His back was so bent that it was difficult for him to lift his head to inspect Li Du's face. His features proclaimed him a local. Wrinkled, papery skin hung from a long face with high cheekbones and a sharp nose. He chewed thoughtfully on his lower lip as he assessed Li Du with rheumy eyes.

"They don't call me librarian," he said finally. "I'm the caretaker. I do the dusting and sweeping. No need for more — not many visitors to this place, not usually."

"My impression of the library was —"

Mu Gao interrupted him with a little jab of his cane into the air. "So you're the one the magistrate said would give me advice? The royal librarian? Well? Look around you. See any dust? Smell mildew? No? That's right. Nothing wrong with my work."

Li Du hastened to reassure the old man. "You take wonderful care of it," he said. Mu Gao eyed him suspiciously, and Li Du continued. "I was going to say that this is the most beautifully kept library I have seen in a very long time. There is no dampness, and I see that the books are in fine condition. I wondered, though, how you keep the insects from eating the paste and ruining the bindings?"

"Jewelvine root," said Mu Gao, instantly. "After that, only task left is to sweep away the insects with the dust."

"Of course," said Li Du. "That is what I used also. Tell me — do you keep it here in the library?"

"Where else would I keep it? Not needed for anything else, is it? Except some use it for killing fish, but not around these parts."

"Is it kept in a locked place?"

Mu Gao grunted. "No. I keep it in a drawer, same place as the papers and inks. Why are you asking me about jewelvine? Is this something to do with the dead man? I don't know anything about it, but they told me he died in the normal way."

Li Du was cautious. "I have no certain knowledge," he said, "but it appears now that he did not die, as you say, in the normal way. I must speak with the magistrate."

"But it is clear what happened," said Tulishen, after he had shut the door to his
study. "Surely you have seen objects like
this one during your travels through the
province?" He motioned toward the embroidered purse that rested on the desk in front
of him.

"I know that this purse is in the Khampa
style, but —"

Tulishen broke in. "And must have been
given to him by the Khampa with whom he
traveled. You recall what I said to you when
you arrived. His fate was sealed when he
decided to travel with thieves and murderers."

"But why would Brother Pieter have carried it with him, yet only used the tea leaves
for the first time last night, when there was
tea already provided for him in his room?
And what reason would the Khampa traders have to give a foreigner, with whom, to
my knowledge, they had no quarrel, poisoned tea leaves in a purse readily identifi-
able as being of Khampa make?"

Tulishen's eyes narrowed. "The answers
to your questions are unimportant. Of what
significance was his decision to drink the

tea last night, or on any other night? And as for the reasons they had for killing him, I would remind you that these people are barbarians, not yet graced by civilization. We speak of horsemen who cut their dead to pieces and throw them to the vultures. What other rituals must they practice, still more abhorrent than that? Perhaps this tainted gift was retribution for a perceived offense. Their ways are inaccessible to Chinese people. To try to understand them is as useless as trying to understand the thoughts of beasts." Tulishen nodded, approving of his own reason.

Li Du shook his head. "Brother Pieter spoke warmly of them. He told me that they were hospitable, generous people. He liked them."

"Then obviously he was misled. Cousin, I have been very patient. I can see that this sad event has upset you. But you must understand that it is essential for all of us to move beyond it, to attend to matters of greater significance. You are no longer accustomed to the way a city is run. Administrators, especially in a place such as Dayan, so far from the capital, are selected for our intuition, our experience, our ability to read a situation and do what is best."

"But surely you plan to do something.

Surely you will send soldiers to question the Khampa traders, to bring them here to be questioned, and punished if they are guilty."

Tulishen gave Li Du a look of pitying condescension. "There are considerations of strategy, of diplomatic relations with Tibet, of what is prudent when you look at the situation from a more sophisticated perspective. The situation with Kham is very delicate at present. If the Emperor wants to risk a war in order to investigate the death of a foreigner, then he will issue his commands accordingly. But it is not for me to destroy the Spring Festival simply because one foreigner has died."

"Then you are not going to investigate?"

"As I have said already, it is clear what happened." Now Tulishen's tone contained a warning.

"Excuse me, Cousin, but it is not clear. There are inconsistencies that cannot be ignored. The poison in the tea — I recognize it. It is powdered jewelvine root, a poison kept here in your own library."

Tulishen's face tensed. "If this jewelvine is in my library, there is no reason for it not to be on a caravan also."

Li Du persisted. "And there is a teacup missing from Brother Pieter's room. If he brewed the tea himself, drank it, and died, then the cup from which he drank should still be in the room. If it is not, then someone must have taken it. Someone in the mansion —"

"A teacup?" Tulishen struck the desk before him with an open palm and stood, glaring at Li Du. "Do not be so foolish. If someone removed a cup from the room, it was to clean it. Is it your goal to undermine the festival? Are you so envious of my success that you would use the death of this man against me? You bring more shame upon yourself."

The words hung between them. Li Du was aware of the impulse to return Tulishen's insult, to say that he could never envy a man doomed by his own small-mindedness to a never-ending cycle of frustrated ambition. Instead, he said simply, with no change in his expression, "My concern is for the truth."

"And mine is for the will of the Emperor," snapped Tulishen. "The Son of the Dragon has traveled a year for this moment. The festival must be all that he expects it to be. These are not frivolities. Displays of power unite the empire, and inspire loyalty across generations."

"Consider if you are wrong, and the

Khampa are innocent. Then the murderer is here, in the city, or in your home. What threat does that pose to the festival?"

Tulishen's voice shook with anger. "I will hear nothing more from you. Your intention was to depart the city today. I command you to do so. Your papers are here."

"Then," said Li Du, "you choose not to seek an answer."

"You have too simple a view of the world," Tulishen replied. "Your attitude has already brought grief to you and to our family. Now I must ask you again to leave this house. You have a capacity for making yourself unwelcome in your own empire. Let us hope that this is the last time you must be told. It is embarrassing for both of us."

"Yes," Li Du said, quietly. "It is."

Avoiding Li Du's eyes, Tulishen made a show of rolling and re-sealing Li Du's papers. When he looked up, his attention was caught by something over Li Du's shoulder, and he nodded with an expression of relief. "My Lady Chen," he said. Li Du turned and saw her, tall and composed, lower her head gracefully in deference to the magistrate. He wondered how much she had heard.

"Excuse my interruption," she said. "The Emperor's portrait has just been delivered."

"Ah," said Tulishen. "That is very good. But first I must speak to you about the salt commissioner. There is some question over where he is to sit at the first banquet. Li Du, here are your papers. Take them." He held out the sealed roll. Li Du took the papers, bowed to Lady Chen, turned, and left the room.

At the end of the hallway, three servants were carefully removing the layers of cloth from the portrait of the Emperor. As Li Du approached, the final panel of sheer green silk slipped away from the painting and fell at his feet, almost tripping him. He stopped, and as one of the servants gathered the cloth into a bundle, he looked at the image that was now revealed.

The Kangxi sat behind a square desk. He was dressed in the unadorned gray robe and red hat of a scholar, and his feet, in soft black shoes, rested on a low footstool atop a scarlet rug. One foot was braced, as if he were about to rise, but his relaxed shoulders conveyed stillness and solidity. His expression was gentle, but behind him, carved onto a marble screen, were climbing dragons whose scaly coils strained and bunched to fit within the confines of the frame. In his right hand he held a brush poised above a sheet of unmarked paper.

It was an image created to inspire loyalty, and it was masterful. In it, the Emperor was simultaneously rarefied and relatable. The Emperor was an approachable scholar, a compassionate man with an appreciation for beauty and an understanding of sadness. He was also a descendent of dragons, a powerful warrior who had subdued the provinces and whose rule was sanctioned by divine ancestry. Whatever words he chose to write on the blank sheet before him could never be challenged, be they poetry, command, or judgment.

The portrait is a game of perception, Li Du thought, *as are the festival and the empire itself. And* — Li Du was aware of the cold heaviness in his chest that always preceded the memory — *as was the execution outside the Forbidden City five years ago.* The time had been deemed appropriate for the Emperor to make a stern example of condemned traitors, and so it was done. The deaths had been cruel and, Li Du would never cease to believe, unjust. The search for the truth had been as minor a concern to the Emperor then as it was to Tulishen now. For those in power, facts were merely materials that could be used, modified, or ignored for the purpose of maintaining control. Tulishen was not entirely stupid.

The people of Dayan would accept the culpability of the Khampa because they wanted to. The festival would proceed, and any unease would be lost in the clink of coins, the glow of lanterns, and the spectacle of performance. Li Du had no place here. He turned his back on the painting and left the mansion.

By midafternoon, his pack heavy with supplies purchased from the market, Li Du was in need of a hot meal, and found himself outside the inn. He eyed the bright, peeling festival announcements pasted on either side of the door and the symbols of good fortune painted onto the lintel. He sensed more than heard the bustle that would surround him once he went inside. Shifting the pack on his shoulders, he hesitated. Then he caught the fragrance of fresh rice and rich broth, considered the cold nights ahead of him, and stepped through the door.

The small, narrow entrance was deceptive; it opened into an extensive labyrinth of courtyards and guesthouses. One hallway or covered walkway after another dead-ended in secluded gardens, each one indistinguishable from the others. But he came eventually to the central common room and found it full to capacity. Those who could not find a place at the tables crowded together around plates of food held by anxious maids, and raised their arms to demand more tea or wine. Servants scurried through the packed spaces clutching trays piled high with dishes, avoiding elbows and knees and gesturing hands. The multitude of voices clamored with excitement, and the topic of conversation was immediately apparent. They were all talking about the death at the mansion.

The innkeeper was in the kitchen issuing instructions to the cooks while he tossed flat circles of dough into a pan of spattering-hot oil over a flame. His fingers were coated in oil. The rest of him was dusted with flour, and his forehead glistened with sweat from working over the fire. Whenever he looked up, he surveyed the room full of patrons with beaming pleasure. When he noticed Li Du, his eyes sparked with recognition, which he made a quick, unconvincing effort to hide.

"Sit here," the innkeeper said to Li Du immediately, gesturing to a small space at a table beside the fire. "Go ahead and set down your pack. Here, see, there is still some space. Not too close to the fire. You'll be wanting the stew, I think." Li Du obeyed, shifting the heavy pack from his shoulders to the floor, and taking his place on the bench. The innkeeper gestured to a nearby maid, and a bowl was set before Li Du as quickly as if it had been conjured from the air. As Li Du began to eat, he saw the innkeeper's gaze move around the room, restless and observant.

"I'm called Hoh," the innkeeper said. "You're a guest at the mansion, aren't you?"

"I was."

Hoh made a show of concentrating on his work. He scooped a handful of wet, greasy dough from the bowl beside him into the pan, which was supported over the flame by a sturdy ring of bricks, and began to press and stretch the dough into a flat circle using his knuckles and fingers. Li Du could see that the motions were automatic, the busy fingers mere indicators of the calculations and judgments that were taking place inside the man's head.

"It's a bad business," said Hoh. "My guests are very upset over it. They were all just on the same roads themselves, you know, the same roads as those Khampa. The bandits are becoming bolder, more dangerous. Thieves can smell money, you know, and there's too much coin and rare goods changing hands at festival time. And why, you might ask, why does the innkeeper complain when his inn is full? I will tell you — it is because I keep a good house, and I do not like my guests to be anxious. Very upsetting for you, wasn't it? In the room just next to his? You might have shared tea with him." The words were sympathetic, but Hoh's expression was one of eager curiosity.

When Li Du did not reply, the innkeeper continued, his hands working faster and more deftly as he settled into his own chatter. "There is another one of those priests here, you know. The young one, with the hair like old hay. He can't communicate with anyone, unless he's asking about plants. He has a passion for every weed that grows in the ground. I told him to go find Doctor Yang. The doctor knows a thing or two about plants. Strange people, these foreigners, more strange than most foreigners who come through this town. I heard you speak their language. So the old man really said nothing to you? Nothing about why they wanted him dead?"

"Brother Pieter admired the Khampa. If they were indeed responsible for his death, I can offer no explanation for it."

Hoh's eyes widened and his plump cheeks quivered. "If?" he said in a loud whisper, leaning forward even as he handed a wait-

141

ing maid a plate heaped with fried dough. "Then you do not think they did it?"

Li Du looked thoughtfully at the eager innkeeper. "How is it that you know so much about what happened that night?" he asked.

Hoh waved his hand dismissively. "Oh, I have a pretty set of ears in the mansion. Do you think I don't know who you are? The magistrate's cousin. And I know that you used to be a librarian. And that you were exiled from the capital. You see? Nothing escapes me."

"I see that it does not."

"Well," Hoh said, annoyed, perhaps, by Li Du's reticence, "I'm sure I didn't mean any offense. Everyone is anxious. A murder, and now the storyteller has disappeared. He was doing a great service entertaining my guests. I would hire him to stay in Dayan awhile, if my wife would let me have the money."

"Hamza is missing?"

Hoh used the tips of his fingers to flip the flat dough in the oil, spattering a few drops over his apron. "I wouldn't expect an artist to miss an opportunity to perform for an emperor, but who knows? Can't predict what people will do, can you?" Hoh sighed and changed the subject. "No talk of the Emperor changing his plans, I hope?" Li

142

Du heard the first real suggestion of anxiety in Hoh's voice. "Because," said Hoh, "my guests will be very disappointed if there are cancellations. The whole city is in great anticipation."

"I know of no changes." Li Du's bowl was empty, but he used his last piece of bread to soak up the final traces of savory stew, his mind turning to the journey before him.

"Of course it's all set," said Hoh, "once the Emperor makes his prediction. What a fearsome sight that will be — the sun going dark. And the Son of the Dragon himself. My inn will never see such prosperity again. No — never again like this." Hoh wiped flour onto his apron and added, "Not a good time for inauspicious events. You don't take risks when the Emperor's coming. Too many spirits hanging around, and something bad could happen. I have all my jade hanging on my door."

Before Hoh could pry any further, Li Du thanked him and took his leave of the inn.

The sun set and the moon rose, parchment yellow, the marks on its surface like traces of lead someone had tried to rub away. Li Du walked alone on the path to the mountain. A painter could have captured it well: a defeated curve of shoulders at odds with a determined stride against a mountain that filled the sky.

That night, sleeping at the base of a gingko tree in the courtyard of a Buddhist temple, he dreamed of the red glow of lanterns lit at dusk in Beijing. His dream lingered on the color: red tea in a white cup, scarlet lacquer on the sides of drums, blood on the executioner's platform in the capital city, the decree, in imperial scarlet ink, of exile. The Vermilion Bird of the South, blazing in Tulishen's library. What was the character on that shelf? *Emptiness.* That was it. *Emptiness.* No, that was in the north. The southern constellation was *ghost.* He was a ghost in the library, and the books were rearranging themselves, shifting into disorder, mocking his efforts to return them to their proper places.

■ ■ ■ ■

4 Days

■ ■ ■ ■

CHAPTER 7

The path was as steep as a staircase, and after three hours Li Du began to notice the effects of high elevation. Thorny rose vines and berry bushes gave way to azaleas and oaks. The wind grew sharper and colder, sweeping down from alpine meadows. The air thinned; a deep breath no longer satisfied his lungs. When he took too large a step he teetered, and he was aware of his laboring heart.

Dayan was behind him, and he could see the path ahead winding, empty, all the way to the low ridge. It would not be difficult to reach it before dark. He would camp there, and tomorrow he would follow the trail down to the banks of the Golden Sand River.

Sun pooled like bright liquid between the shadows of trees. Old oaks stood, tall and peaceful with crusty bark and bearded branches, like friendly philosophers enjoying a slow and eternal conversation. Limestone crags jutted from the ground to form sharp-edged mazes. Beneath his feet, firm-packed dirt alternated with spills of gray scree that slid and clattered as he walked across it.

At midday, he came to a side trail and followed it to a rocky promontory over a deep ravine. It matched the description he had read in his gazetteer, so, reassured that he was on the correct path, he decided to make himself a bowl of millet. He arranged his utensils on the rocks and left them there while he located a small stream to fill his pot with water. He returned, made a fire in a crevice far from any dry brush, and prepared his meal. When he had finished, he sat on a comfortable patch of moss to eat and to take in the view.

It was very quiet. After a while, a tendril of cloud drifted into the narrow gorge below the precipice where he sat. The cloud thickened into a winding, ponderous snake. It continued to expand, slowly filling the ravine until it rose to the level of the promontory and engulfed Li Du. The world around him became white, and he could no longer discern the shapes of trees or rocks, or the contours of the path on which he would continue. The south summit of the mountain, visible a moment before, was gone.

The quiet deepened into silence. Li Du did not move, but rested his eyes on the soft, white expanse. As he watched, the cloud shifted and broke. He saw, as if through a window, a tree on the opposite side of the gorge. It was a dead, hollowed oak, blackened by fire. Only one branch remained, reaching out perpendicular to the trunk. The vapor thickened, the window closed, and the tree was gone.

Another opening appeared. Through this new window Li Du saw movement, and thought he could make out the rounded back of a little bear trundling across a clearing into a copse of evergreens. Again the mist moved, erasing the scene. The next break in the cloud framed a waterfall, a still, silver column too distant for him to perceive its tumbling energy. That window closed, another opened, and he saw a tree. It was in the same place as the tall oak he had seen minutes earlier. Only this one was not hollow, but alive, its limbs and trunk whole and draped in garlands of lichen.

He imagined then that the shifting clouds contained thousands of years, and that he had seen the same tree in two different times. What if every moment of that tree's existence, the whole of its past and its future, existed at once, here in this blank and infinite cloud?

An eerie suggestion of his own insubstantiality pulled at him. He, too, was inside the void. If someone standing on the other bank of the ravine were to see Li Du through a window in the mist, what would that person see? Perhaps Li Du would appear as a child, an elderly man, a ghost, or a memory of an old poem. In this place, the present was of no consequence, and he was adrift. It was a feeling he had longed for over the years of his exile.

The entire cloud was beginning to dissipate, and Li Du walked to the farthest edge of the overlook. From that vantage point, the city of Dayan was visible in the distance. He could just see the long, walled rectangle of Tulishen's mansion, and the layered roofs of the pagoda on top of Lion Hill. It was impossible now to detect any movement on the streets or in the surrounding fields. It was like a model of a city, a cold replica in ceramic and paint. *And yet,* he thought, *today it must be more crowded than it was yesterday, the inn more raucous, the market bursting from its confines, spreading through the quieter streets.* He turned away.

It took him a little while to clean his pot. He dried it over the fire, then wiped it so that it would not dampen or soil his books. His pack was beginning to wear through in the places where the sharp corners of the volumes pressed, and he rearranged them slightly to preserve the newest set of patches. He hefted the pack onto a stone ledge, looped the straps over his shoulders, and pushed through the azaleas, back to the path.

When the sun began to sink, it tinted the green and gray slopes and cliffs with rich amber. Li Du was high enough now that he could see the spine of the dragon extending its sharp peaks to the north. The summits beyond the first one were all bare rock veined white with snow, impassable. Their western aspects were soaked in deep sunlight, becoming more saturated even as their eastern counterparts receded into cold shadow.

His eye was drawn to movement along a ridge as sharp and thin as a ripped edge of paper. Dotted at equal intervals, like round white beads on a string, was a herd of sheep. They moved all at the same slow speed, so that the spaces between them did not change as they traversed the ridge line. A little way down the slope, Li Du could see the shepherd, a dark spot with a hat and walking stick. They were so far away that Li Du would never have noticed that there was a person there, were it not for the bright white sheep at the junction of rock and sky.

According to the description in his gazetteer, once he reached the far side of the meadow the path would begin to slope down. At that point he would find a series of caves, large enough to provide comfortable shelter. The author urged the traveler to explore the caves in daylight, and in particular to observe the threads of sky through the stone at different angles. Li Du's feet were tired and beginning to ache, but the meadows were blustery and cold. He kept walking.

The trail had just begun to angle downward when he smelled fire smoke and heard the clang of bells and snorts of horses. Remembering the warnings of bandits in the hills north of Dayan, he paused, uncertain what to do. Ahead of him the path dropped, as promised, into a thicket of azalea trees. He remained where he was and tried to discern the exact direction from which the noise came. He scanned the darkening meadows for alternate routes, away from the strangers.

A rock clattered somewhere to his left, and he turned to look even as he took a small step backward away from the sound. It was too late. He had been seen, and the man who approached him now was tall, unsmiling, and pointing a musket directly at Li Du's chest.

There was no doubt that the man was a Tibetan Khampa. He towered over Li Du. His hair hung loose to his shoulders, framing high cheekbones and a sharp, straight nose. Despite his obvious youth, the skin around his eyes was creased with long, deep wrinkles, the result of enduring freezing wind and blinding snow. The hilt of the knife that was sheathed at his belt was wrapped with bright red yarn strung with silver and turquoise beads.

Li Du waited, very still, while the man evaluated him. When he saw the man's face relax slightly, Li Du said, "I am traveling alone. May I continue that way?" And he pointed behind him, away from the sounds of the camp.

The man shook his head and said something in Tibetan.

"Do you speak Chinese?" Li Du asked.

The man shook his head again, repeated what he had said, and gestured with his musket for Li Du to follow him.

They walked down a narrow path through dense, twisting azaleas, and Li Du began to glimpse firelight through the branches. In a few minutes the trail widened into a clearing.

It was a good site — flat, and tucked far enough below the ridge to be out of the wind. The horses and mules, thirty or forty animals, had been relieved of their cargo and their harnesses and were grazing. Four separate fires crackled in shallow pits, each ringed by neat stacks of baskets and wooden saddles. The caravan members were tending to the horses, gathering wood, adjusting leather covers over piles of tea bricks, and preparing food. They looked up curiously as Li Du and the guard passed them.

At the far edge of the clearing was a small hut, a bare structure built from trunks and branches and stone. These buildings were used and maintained by whomever happened to be there, whether a herder tending yaks or sheep, a hunter, a traveler, or a merchant caravan. Li Du had stayed in many over the years.

There was a fire inside this one, and the light shone through the cracks in the wood, warm against the violet and blue twilight. On the roof, fresh cuts of meat were arranged to dry. Pale smoke curled around them through the spaces between the roof beams. The guard had to bend almost double to pass through the leaning door opening, and Li Du followed him inside.

A man and woman were preparing food in one corner, and two men sat opposite each other on either side of the fire. At first Li Du did not recognize the young man who had exchanged his embroidered silks for homespun clothing, and who sat with rounded posture staring into the fire. But when he looked up, Li Du blinked in surprise.

"But you are not a stranger," said Hamza, straightening from the fire. He beamed at Li Du, and Li Du felt himself returning the smile automatically. But he hesitated before speaking, and looked at the others in the cabin.

The man sitting across from Hamza began an exchange, in Tibetan, with the guard. While they were talking, Hamza gestured for Li Du to sit beside him, and spoke in a voice just above a whisper. "Do not be anxious. These are my friends, and they are only bandits on occasion. But they will want to know why you have come in search of them. Or" — he rubbed his unkempt beard thoughtfully — "did the magistrate send you after me?"

Li Du also kept his voice low. "I was not looking for anyone at all. I departed the city yesterday, and I was going to stay the night in one of the caves." He proffered Xu Xiake's published journal.

Hamza took the book and perused it. At one page he stopped, and read: *"The local people speak of Mu Ring because he crossed a river in thick mist to win a battle. Curious, I made a point of visiting that river, and found it to be quite shallow. The histories record the bravery of Mu Ring's action, but it is not difficult to cross a stream. This shows how unreliable books are . . ."* Hamza grimaced. "Your snobbish scholars are very good at ruining stories. I would like to hear more about this soldier who crossed the river. Perhaps the mist was in fact a ruby-eyed demon writhing its vapor coils — but now I must explain to my friend who you are."

The guard had left the hut, no doubt to return to his post, and the other man was waiting patiently for Hamza. Hamza began to talk to him in Tibetan, and when he had finished he said to Li Du, "Your brows are lifted. I have impressed you? I know most of the words uttered in this world. It is a particular skill of mine. Now I have told them who you are, and assured them that

156

you are a traveler, not an official like your cousin. The two here preparing our stew are Norbu and his wife, Yonzheng. The innkeeper Hoh says that his bread is the best, but Yonzheng's is better. And this man is Kalden Dorjee. It is his caravan."

Kalden acknowledged this introduction with a shy nod directed more at the fire than at Li Du. Nothing about his appearance suggested fearsomeness, except perhaps his hands, which were large and scarred and thickly callused. He had eyes that slanted down at the outside corners and a somber mouth, set naturally in a slight frown that suggested worry. For a few moments, as he prodded and rearranged the fire, he looked thoughtful.

"My Chinese is very bad," he said, finally. "Please speak to my friend. I will listen." He gestured across the fire at Hamza.

"Ah," said Hamza, pleased. "Then I shall conduct an interrogation. We will pretend that I am a stern official — a magistrate, perhaps." He affected a posture inspired by formal court portraiture, his back straight, his hands on his knees, his expression suddenly unreadable.

"What," Hamza began, "can you tell us of the situation in Dayan? Is the magistrate sending soldiers in pursuit of these men?"

Li Du shook his head. "He is not. But you know that the magistrate has blamed the Khampa for the murder of Brother Pieter?"

Kalden's jaw tightened almost imperceptibly. Hamza answered, "We do. I left Dayan as soon as the rumor reached the inn. Kalden and I have been friends for many years. I came to tell him what had happened. Tomorrow I will go back to Dayan."

"You have known each other a long time? But I was under the impression that you were from India."

"Were you? That is strange. I am from Egypt, originally, but when I was eight I joined a ship's crew as cabin boy, and that is how I came to Tibet."

"But you cannot sail from Egypt to Kham."

"Rivers do change their courses," said Hamza, slightly patronizing. "But I have more questions for you. Why does the magistrate suspect this caravan?"

Li Du paused, aware of his own part in the assignation of blame. But he was honest. "The magistrate ordered a search of Pieter's belongings, and asked me to itemize the Latin books. I found a leather purse filled with poisoned tea. The purse was just like that one." He pointed at a purse hanging from a split in a wall beam.

Kalden made a comment in Tibetan, and Hamza nodded. "Kalden wants to know why you think that he is guilty of murder simply because you discovered poison in a purse that might have been placed there by anyone."

"Your friend misunderstands," said Li Du, firmly. "I do not think that he is responsible for Brother Pieter's death. There is evidence that someone who was inside the mansion that night was involved."

"If that is so, why were the Khampa accused at all?"

"That was the conclusion the magistrate drew from the presence of the embroidered purse. He believes that someone on this caravan killed Pieter over some offense he caused."

Hamza's expression darkened. "No one here would have done such evil. And no one made a gift to Pieter of any purse or tea. I would have seen it."

"I went to the inn to find you, in order to ask just that question. How did you hear so soon that the Khampa were accused of the crime?"

"The innkeeper's niece. She is a maid at the mansion, and every time there is gossip she appears like an *ifrit*, out of the air, to whisper the rumors to her uncle."

Li Du thought about this, then said, "In this instance, I think that the gossips were put to clever use."

"Explain this."

Li Du chose his words carefully. "The magistrate's attention is fixed on the Emperor's arrival. He cannot consider the death of Brother Pieter beyond its potential to impede the success of the festival. If important guests are upset, or if the Emperor sees the crime as an inauspicious portent, the entire celebration might be canceled."

"But that could still happen."

Li Du shook his head. "The Khampa already have" — he glanced at Kalden, who was listening intently — "have a reputation for banditry. The magistrate was clever. He found an explanation that would satisfy the need to place blame, and reassure the visitors that there was no danger in the city."

"And," said Hamza, understanding, "he made sure that the gossiping maid knew of it as soon as possible. I have always thought that I have nothing in common with a bureaucrat. But I see now that the magistrate is capable of telling a tale. Perhaps we share something after all."

Li Du waited while Hamza and Kalden spoke at some length. Kalden was mostly silent, nodding and affirming in low monosyllables. Then Hamza turned to Li Du. "The Khampa can bear the indignity of a false accusation," he said, "but you are sure that the magistrate is not sending soldiers after them?"

"I am sure. There are no soldiers to spare. But there are other concerns."

"What concerns?"

"When the Emperor hears the magistrate's version of what happened, it may influence him against Kham and Tibet. And the relationship between the empires is already unstable."

Kalden shook his head. Hamza gave a little smile. "That is not Kalden's concern. The quarrels of emperors and kings do not reach the caravans. And their home villages are high in the mountains. They dwell with their families among stones and stars, so high that trees cannot grow. You will see, when you go north."

Kalden spoke again, and Hamza translated. "He says that the murderer will be punished, if not in this life then in another. It is not their concern. It is not yours. These are the troubles of the powerful schemers. It is better to stay away from them. And he says that you may share their food and fire tonight."

Li Du thanked Kalden, but the caravan leader waved away the gratitude.

CHAPTER 8

While Li Du and Hamza were talking, the two cooks had, with quiet competence, prepared a cauldron of stew and a stack of hot, salty, fried bread. With their hands wrapped in cloth, together they lifted the heavy pot, carried it outside, and called the camp to dinner.

Li Du followed Hamza and Kalden out of the crooked hut. Night had fallen, and the gaps in the clouds were crowded with stars. The stew was placed close to the largest fire, and the horsemen began to help themselves. Li Du ladled a portion into his bowl, and accepted one of the potatoes that Norbu had plucked from the white-hot ash. He scraped away the blackened potato skin with his knife. The inside was soft and steaming hot. A sip of stew soothed his tired bones and revived his exhausted spirits. He stretched his sore feet out to the fire and drew in a deep, contented breath, enjoying the voices around him even though he did not understand the language.

The cold on his back and shoulders made him shiver in spite of the flames, and he reached into his pack for his blanket. As he pulled it out, he noticed that someone's tea purse had been left on the ground. He looked for its owner and, seeing no one, he picked it up and examined it. The round, embroidered patch set into the leather frame depicted flowers and birds, not foxes, but the style and quality of the thread were identical to the one he had found in Pieter's room. He inhaled — it smelled of horses and good black tea.

When he looked up, Hamza and Kalden were approaching. Kalden had a small cask with him, and he indicated that Li Du should present his cup for wine. Li Du protested that this was too kind, but Kalden would not accept a refusal. He took Li Du's cup and filled it to the brim with clear wine. Then he filled Hamza's and his own.

"We liked the foreign monk," said Kalden, in his deliberate, simple Chinese. "He should not have gone to Dayan. But his soul has left that city. Do you understand my words?"

"Yes." Li Du held his cup with both hands and raised it deferentially to Kalden. They drank. The wine was strong, and Li Du felt its warmth settle in his chest before it coursed to his fingers and toes. As he reached to set his cup down on a flat stone he stopped, and brought it back to his lips to taste it again.

"But this is Lady Chen's wine," he said.

Kalden looked questioningly at Hamza, and they had a brief exchange. Then Hamza said to Li Du, "When Kalden brings his caravan so far south, they always buy wine from Snow Village. It is the best in the province."

"Snow Village?"

"It is not far. You passed very close to it on the road from Dayan."

"Lady Chen said that it was her family wine. Is she from that village?"

Hamza nodded over his shoulder at the cabin roof, where the meat still smoked. "We bought that sheep from a Snow Village herder. She mentioned the lady's name."

"What did she say?"

"I asked the old woman if she would attend the festival — I told her that I was going to perform. She was very suspicious of me, and with a disapproving squint she told me that she didn't like crowds, didn't like stories, and didn't like city food. But she confessed that she wanted to see if the

Emperor could really command the moon to cover the sun. Then she boasted that the most beautiful woman at the festival would be from Snow Village. Of course I asked who it was, and she was offended that I did not know already. The Lady Chen, she told me, a consort to the highest official in Dayan. Her place there is a matter of village pride."

Li Du nodded. For a peasant woman to attain that status required not only beauty, but skilled manipulation. She had to be clever, and ruthless.

Hamza said, thoughtfully, "I will have to look at her more closely when I return tomorrow. You understand I have seen many beautiful women. Princesses, queens, one of whom lived in the sea and had scales of every color. I have even seen one of your Chinese fox spirits. So I have a very high standard."

Hamza looked up at the sky, in which stars were embedded like diamonds. "It is good that you are staying with us tonight. This mountain clatters and roars in the dark hours. I think it is monsters who are rattling the bamboo stalks that bind them. Better to be with a caravan. Better, at least, than sleeping in a cave with that dry old book. What traveler wrote it?"

"His name was Xu Xiake, a scholar of the Ming Dynasty. His obsession was correcting errors in previous texts. The Golden Sand River in the valley below us was not known to be the source of the Yangtze until he wrote that it was."

Kalden asked a question, and Hamza translated it. "He says that when the Ming ruled China, the Mu family were in command here. Kalden's grandfathers fought them — a good-natured enmity: the Khampa raiding Dayan, the Mu raiding Khampa towns. More an exchange of goods than a feud. But he wonders what a Chinese scholar was doing here during the Mu reign."

Li Du considered what he knew. He had read Yang Sehn's *Genealogy of the Mu*, in addition to Xu Xiake's account of Mu Zheng's hospitality. Mu Zheng had himself been a student of Chinese literature, and had charmed Xu Xiake by asking the scholar to edit his poetry for incorrect characters and repetition.

"The Mu," he began, "had pledged loyalty to the Chinese Emperor even then. Officially, they were vassals of the Ming. But no real effort was made to institute Ming bureaucracy here."

"So it was the Kangxi who truly subdued

167

the Mu."

In any other company this would have been a delicate, if not impermissible, subject. Here, Li Du realized, he could be almost as frank as he was in the privacy of his own mind. Not yet acclimated to this new freedom, Li Du began cautiously, with a question.

"Do you know of the traitor general Wu Sangui?"

Kalden shook his head, and Hamza said with a shrug, "I have heard of him. But my turn to tell a story will come later."

Li Du looked at the fire, calling to mind the young Kangxi, and the empire that, at the tender age of sixteen, he had yet to claim. But the history of Wu Sangui had begun before that, when Kangxi's father was not the first Qing emperor, but only a Manchu warrior determined to lead his army through the Wall and make China his own.

Li Du took another sip of wine. "Wu Sangui was a powerful soldier of the Ming court. But he betrayed the last Ming emperor. It was he who opened the palace gates to the Manchu. And so the Kangxi's father, the Shunzhi Emperor, took Beijing, and Wu Sangui became his most trusted servant, an honorary Manchu. He fought countless battles for the Shunzhi, and it was with his might that the Qing Dynasty began.

"When the Shunzhi died, the Kangxi was not yet old enough to rule. And so the empire was put under the command of his uncles, the old Manchu regents. They had no intention of ever allowing the young prince to assume the title of emperor. But when he was sixteen years old, the Kangxi wrested power from his uncles. This was, you understand, a terrible risk. Those who plotted against him were very powerful, and at any moment he might have been assassinated.

"No sooner had he accomplished this feat than rumor reached him of Ming loyalists gathering here, in the southwestern provinces. The Kangxi was then still a boy, and for him, these were wild lands, choked with jungle and poisonous insects and cannibals. Nothing in his own experience, or that of his ancestors on the frozen plateau, had prepared him to do battle in a place like this.

"So he sent his most trusted general — Wu Sangui — to fight the traitors, and to subdue the local people, whom he suspected of aiding their former masters, the Ming."

Kalden spoke. "I remember now. Here he was called a different name. He was hated."

Li Du nodded. "Wu Sangui fulfilled his task with terrible brutality. Many of the Mu family were slaughtered before Wu Sangui found the last Ming prince hiding in the forests with his supporters. After he defeated the small army he brought the prince to Kunming for execution. He strangled the young man before an audience."

There was silence. Then Hamza said, "I told you that these mountains were haunted by ghosts. The monsters rattling the bamboo. Are the Ming truly defeated? There are none left?"

"None that threaten the Kangxi. Those who survived retreated across the borders of the empire to the jungles."

"And the Mu?"

"The Mu were weakened by Wu Sangui's campaign against them. As I said, he succeeded in his mission. But instead of returning to the capital, triumphant, he remained in this province and declared himself the ruler of a new empire. He claimed this land as his own, and accused the Kangxi of being a descendent of barbarians, illegitimate, ill bred, and undeserving of power.

"In that month the Qing dynasty could have fallen. But it did not. The Kangxi was saved by the Mu."

"After he had ordered their deaths?"

"Yes. He called for their aid, and they gave it. They hated Wu Sangui more than they hated the Manchu. They defeated their enemy, and the Emperor had his corpse scattered across the empire. To repay the Mu, he allowed them to keep their independence. For a time." The strategy, Li Du remembered, was referred to by Beijing strategists as "using barbarians to rule barbarians."

"And that time ended."

"The Mu family weakened, slowly. There was illness, and bad luck. The Qing bureaucracy was installed one piece at a time, and met no resistance. Now Tulishen governs Dayan. And the only member of the Mu family still living in the mansion of his ancestors is the old servant, Mu Gao." Li Du thought for a moment and, moved by the attention of his audience, by the firelight, and by this new sense of companionship high in the mountains, added, "You see why the Emperor's visit to Dayan is so important. This province has not been easy for him to control. It has frightened him. He knows that he has never won its soul — the ghosts, as you say, remain in the mountains where he cannot make them rest. That is why the festival must be a spectacle unlike anything this province has ever seen.

That is why he has chosen to come to Dayan for the moment of the eclipse. He wants this province to be his — he wants it to forget the time when the Mu family lived in the mansion. And I, for one, have no desire to be there when the people are won over by theatrics that distract from —" He stopped, surprised into silence by his own emotion.

When he spoke again, his voice was level, his tone deliberate. "And I will not be there," he said. "The Emperor would not welcome the presence of a man he exiled. And my cousin would do anything to avoid displeasing the Emperor. My intention has always been to journey north, to make use of my exile by following the paths of the scholars and seeing with my own eyes what I have only read. There is nothing I can do in Dayan."

Hamza was regarding him intently as he spoke, and when Li Du had finished, Hamza gave a small smile. "True stories," he said, "are too bitter. Perhaps you should leave the storytelling to a professional." He held up his hands, drawing the eyes of the audience from Li Du to himself. "Now," he announced, "it is my turn to tell a tale.

"But unfortunately, it must be in Chinese, as the great scholar among us does not count among his many learnings the language of Kham." There was a chorus of friendly protest and disagreement, but in good cheer, and those who did not speak Chinese went to one of the other fires, while those who did remained to listen. Li Du gratefully settled into the shadows, ready for the distraction that Hamza was about to provide.

Hamza smiled again, and began:

"There was once in the land of Egypt a Sultan. He was the cruelest sultan who had ever come to power in that land.

"Around his palace there were always heads mounted on stakes, and they never had time to rot, for they were constantly being replaced with new heads: heads of men, heads of women, even the heads of dogs that had barked too near the palace.

"There was in the service of this Sultan a vizier, a man as wise and gentle as the sultan was tyrannical. His name was Jaffar, and only he was capable of tempering the sultan's fury, for they had been friends since childhood, before the sultan grew into a cruel man and the vizier into a kind one. Whenever he could, Jaffar convinced the sultan to show mercy, and the poor souls in the dungeons placed all their hopes on his influence.

"Besides Jaffar, there were many lesser

173

advisers within the walls of the palace. These men spent their days hoping that the Sultan would not ask them anything, for they knew that if their answers were not to the Sultan's liking, their wives would be widows by sunset, and their heads would be displayed for all to see.

"Now, it happened at the time of this story that one of the advisers had a visitor. This guest, a relative of his wife's, was a judge from the faraway land of China. This man had a reputation for cleverness that had reached as far as Egypt, and beyond. His name was Judge Dee.

"Judge Dee was enjoying his time of leisure with his cousin and her family, and was much taken with the sun and sandstone of the city. But on the third morning of his stay, the sultan summoned all of his advisers to his audience chamber. Judge Dee's host bid a tearful farewell to his wife and daughters, and was about to go to the palace when a messenger arrived from the sultan. The adviser read the message and turned to Judge Dee with fresh tears in his eyes: 'My honored guest, I am ashamed that my hospitality has led only to danger for you. The sultan sends word that he has heard of your reputation, and requests your presence also in his audience chamber.'

"Judge Dee, though impressed by his relative's sorrow on his account, was intrigued, and agreed with good cheer to accompany the man.

"They assembled with the other advisers in the royal audience chamber, where the sultan in his gold and ruby robes and his great silver and silk crown paced in distress. The assembled sages knelt with their heads bowed before the great king, and fixed their eyes on the floor, as it was law to do in the Sultan's presence.

"The Sultan spoke in a voice hoarse with grief: 'You who call yourself wise all know the only true wise man in this kingdom, my vizier Jaffar. He has been murdered, and in a manner that appears impossible. I cannot rest until I know what befell him. There is among you a man from distant lands renowned for his wisdom. Step forward.'

"And Judge Dee, who was well aware of his talents and had no false modesty, stepped forward and said, 'O, Sultan, I am a visitor to your land, but in my own city, I am known for solving just this kind of impossible problem. Allow me to turn my mind to your question.'

"The Sultan dismissed the other advisers. Eyes still fixed on the floor, they left the chamber in great relief, pitying the foreigner whose head they felt sure they would see, severed and staring, on the palace walls by

175

the end of the day.

"When they were alone, the sultan said to the judge: 'There is in the palace grounds a tower, an isolated place designated for solitude and contemplation. Jaffar was the only person with a key to that tower. Yesterday he went into it, locked the door, and did not come out. After some time I insisted that a servant accompany me into the tower, to reassure myself that he had simply left without being noticed, for I feared that something had happened.'

"As he spoke, the Sultan led Judge Dee to the base of the tower, in which was set a single small door. The Sultan opened the door and walked with the judge up the long stone staircase rising in a spiral to a single room at the top of the tower. And there, in the center of the humble apartment, was the dead man, dressed in a robe of simple white cotton. He had been strangled, and his face was so swollen and terrible to behold that the servants who accompanied them looked away in horror.

" 'As I said, the only door was locked,' repeated the Sultan.

" 'And the walls are too smooth to scale,' said the judge, thoughtfully. 'Is it possible that he let his assailant in?'

" 'No,' replied the Sultan, 'for the assailant

would have needed the key to lock the door behind him when he left, and look — the key is still here around the vizier's neck, where he always kept it.' The sultan pointed to the key strung on a golden chain around the dead man's neck.

" 'I see,' said the judge, much perplexed. And he retired to the quarters provided him to think.

"He began by dismissing every possible method of breaching the tower. There was no way anyone could have climbed, flown, or burrowed into it. It must have been unlocked, and locked again, with a key. The Sultan had told him that only Jaffar had a key. Well, that was not strictly true, for Judge Dee had seen the Sultan himself unlock the door with a matching key of his own, as surely he had when he discovered the body.

"But why would the Sultan, known throughout the kingdom for the delight he took in execution and public torture, kill a man in quiet, alone in the tower? Murders like this one, Judge Dee knew from experience in his own kingdom and in others, were committed in order to gain wealth or power, by murderers afraid of being caught. The Sultan had no need of such subterfuge, for he could murder at will without punishment.

"A master, thought Judge Dee, has nothing

to gain from the secret murder of a servant. And the more he pondered the question, the more puzzled he became.

"Sunset came to the jeweled palace, and the time came when Judge Dee had promised to provide an answer. He approached the Sultan's audience chamber slowly, afraid for the first time in his life that he had been given a problem he could not solve.

"As he was about to enter the chamber, the servant beside him whispered: 'You showed great disrespect today when you looked at the sultan. You must keep your eyes on the ground in his presence, in accordance with the law of the land. I give you this advice in the hope that it will save your life, for you are a stranger here and do not know our ways.'

"The judge gave a deep sigh and, at peace, entered the audience chamber.

"The Sultan sat on his throne. Judge Dee kneeled and said, 'O, Sultan, I have the true answer to this murder. Are you sure that you want to hear it?'

" 'I do, for that is why you are here.'

" 'Sultan, you told me yourself that no one could have entered that tower but through the door.'

" 'Yes,' said the Sultan.

" 'But Sultan, there is no door in your palace that is locked to you. Therefore, it is you who

178

must have killed the man.'

" 'Your insolence is punishable by death,' replied the Sultan. 'What reason would I have to kill my dearest friend?'

" 'Forgive me, oh Sultan, but your reputation in this land is a fearsome one. You have killed men for no reason at all. But what I could not understand is why you would have killed in stealth. You, who even now have three hundred heads adorning the walls of your palace.'

" 'You are contradicting yourself, judge. The problem seems as impossible as it ever did.' "

Hamza stopped speaking. His audience was rapt. He smiled and broke the spell to ask: "And what did the judge say to this?"

A voice came from the small group: "Was it a great bird who flew through the window and killed the vizier?"

Hamza shook his head gravely.

"Was it an arrow shot from the ground?"

"No!" cried a voice next to the speaker. "He was strangled, remember?"

"Judge Dee took a breath. 'It was, as you say, a contradiction. I found myself believing that it could only be you that had killed the man in the tower, and also that you could have no reason to kill your vizier in this way. It was not until I was about to enter your audience chamber this evening that I learned the truth. A servant reminded me to lower my eyes in

179

your presence, for that is the law of the land.'

" 'Ah,' said the Sultan.

" 'And then I remembered your voice when you spoke to your advisers this morning, hoarse as if you had been grieving.' Judge Dee paused. 'Or as if you were disguising its sound. And I remembered the servants unable to look closely at the face of the dead man, as horribly contorted as it was.

" 'You are swathed in the finery befitting a sultan, and the body in the tower wore the same simple robes that Jaffar wore every day.

" 'You, O Sultan, are not the Sultan, but Jaffar, the friend of the tyrant, and it is the Sultan who lies dead in the tower, clad in a simple white robe.'

"And Judge Dee looked up at the face of the man on the throne, and saw in those sad eyes the truth of his answer.

" 'And now you know the truth, judge, so judge me,' said Jaffar.

" 'I will pronounce my judgement. The grief in your voice is real, for you have killed your friend, a man you loved as a brother, despite his terrible actions. The Sultan was a cruel tyrant, a despoiler of his own land. You killed him because you could not bear to watch him destroy so many lives. My cousin tells me that you have always been a voice of counsel and reason in the face of the tyrant's madness.

180

Rule well, oh Sultan, and do not let the beginning of your rule define its course.'

"And with that Judge Dee left the silent Sultan, and returned to the house of his cousin, where there was much rejoicing at his safe return. But the answer to the problem he refused to reveal, and on the next morning he left the kingdom with many thanks to his cousin for his hospitality, and set out on the seas to his next adventure."

Kalden was frowning slightly. He asked Hamza a question, and received a short reply.

"What did he ask?" Li Du was curious.

"Why the vizier invited the judge to investigate, when he himself had committed the crime. I replied that a good storyteller does not explain everything. And now it is time to rest. Tomorrow I return to the city, and before the week is out I will have told a tale to the Emperor of China himself. I will confess — that is not something I have done before."

During the night the clouds moved away, and the moon shone so silvery bright that it cast shadows on the ground. Li Du awoke and marveled at the illuminated landscape. The moonlight shadows were sharper than daylight ones — every pebble on the dust had its perfect double inked beside it.

A line of poetry came to him, from an old scroll that he knew so well he could still picture its exact placement on the library shelf: *Forever bound to passionless roaming . . .*

"Well, Li Bai," Li Du said, addressing the moon as if its white face were that of the poet himself. "After a thousand years among the stars, do you ever witness an event in this world that makes you wish you could return?" The white face of the moon looked back at him sadly.

Li Du had left a city in which a murderer now rested, complacent. The man, or woman, who had desired the death of Brother Pieter had succeeded. There was not going to be an investigation. The crime would slip away like a leaf down a stream, forgotten amid the manufactured splendor of the festival. Li Du listened to the clacks of bamboo in the wind and the snaps of the watchman's fire. And he made his decision. In the morning he would go back to Dayan, and he would discover the truth of what had happened there.

■ ■ ■ ■

3 Days

■ ■ ■ ■

CHAPTER 9

"A local story tells of a rich man who saw his reflection one day in a stream, and realized that, though he had many gold and silver coins, he had left very little time."

Hamza had been practicing his art since they left the caravan at dawn. Content to address the rustling leaves and placid mules, he made no demands on Li Du's attention. They were a strange pair: the small scholar in patched blue and gray, lost in his own thoughts, riding beside the straight-backed storyteller, clad once again in embroidered silk, his obsidian beard sculpted to a point, one hand on the reins and the other raised in elegant gesticulations as he spoke. The two mules were almost identical, white-flecked gray with large, twitching ears and tranquil dark eyes.

Thanks to the mules, they arrived at the outskirts of Dayan not long after midday. As they approached the center of the city, they dismounted so that they could guide the worried animals more easily through the crowds. Hamza raised his voice over the thickening clamor.

"The rich man went to his village market to buy himself some years. But he was told that there were none for sale. So he traveled to Dayan. But there were no years for sale here, either. He traveled from one city to the next, but was told again and again that there were no years for sale. Finally, he came to Beijing, and hunted through each stall in their great bazaar. But he found no years. So he stopped, and looked behind him, and he saw that all the lakes were dried and all the rocks were crushed to dust. And this, the story says, is the origin of sorrow."

Hamza's words were almost lost in the bustle of the Dayan market. In the single day Li Du had been away, the city had transformed. Performers had begun to arrive, and a carnival atmosphere pervaded the streets. Lilting operatic recitations blended with the repetitive cries of vendors. Jugglers and acrobats commandeered empty spaces, and the spectators standing in concentric rings around the shows rendered many of the smaller alleys impassible.

Their progress through the crowd was slowed further by the two mules, who walked shoulder to shoulder beside them, ears twisting anxiously in response to the cacophony. Hamza, with the exception of a few competitive glares leveled at the other performers, was untroubled by the chaos. "If I saw years in the market," he said, "I would not buy them. Wine is another matter."

Hamza had paused and was looking through the row of temporary stalls into a busy store whose walls were lined with shelf upon shelf of gleaming bottles. Li Du, who had last received money six months ago from a wealthy relative in Guizhou, was aware that his purse was beginning to feel light. *But,* he said to himself, *in the days that are to follow, a cup of wine in the evenings may almost be a medical necessity.* So he pulled out a piece of silver and offered to watch the mules while Hamza purchased two bottles.

Minutes later Hamza returned, a bottle in each hand. "This one is for me," he said, holding up a sealed jar, glazed a deep green and incised with wild geese. "It reminds me," he said, "of the young princess who wove capes of stinging nettles to save her brothers from a sorceress who had cursed them to appear as birds. And this one is for you." He thrust his hand forward proudly

187

to display the bottle, white and blue porcelain in the Ming style.

Li Du accepted the bottle and examined it. The pattern was a simple, painted, blue design, pleasingly bright and transparent, the white porcelain shining through it. On it were two lines of a poem, the words slipping down the neck of the bottle in simple calligraphy: *The path of stars slants low toward you.*

"Did the merchant tell you that the wine was good?"

Hamza made a dismissive gesture. "I had not the time to get the truth from him. I chose these because I liked the bottles."

They put the wine away carefully, and continued on. "So," said Li Du, "you would not buy years? You would not extend your life if you could?"

Hamza shook his head. "Bargains like that usually conceal traps. And endings are not always sorrowful. You Chinese just think they are, because all of your stories end with lovers committing suicide — beware the peppers."

Li Du's foot caught on the edge of a woven basket, sending a few of the peppers heaped in it sliding down to the ground, where they glowed like setting suns. Li Du hastened to put them back in the basket

188

before they were trampled, glad that the vendor's attention was elsewhere. Beside the baskets of peppers were buckets full of honeycombs, studded with liquid jewels, half sunk in deep wells of honey.

He straightened up while his mule waited patiently, and they continued on. Ahead of them, an elderly woman was bent almost double under the weight of the basket on her back, in which were fitted two large pig heads with cloudy half-closed eyes. Bobbing away, they stared back at him until they were lost from sight amid bolts of cloth. It was silk, spooled out from rollers for buyers to examine, bright ribbons of color blocking the path and casting tinted shadows on the people who ducked underneath.

Hoping to find a less densely packed street, they turned right into an alley that was familiar to Li Du from his first day in Dayan. He recognized the hanging, tangled bridles adorned with gleaming bells, and the stacks of coarse saddle blankets. The fishmongers would be somewhere ahead, beyond the incense. He caught the scent of smoky rose and night jasmine, and came to an abrupt halt.

Hamza, mimicking Li Du, sniffed the air, then raised a questioning eyebrow. "You want to buy perfume?" he asked.

189

Li Du was peering through the crowd at the cluttered market stalls that lined both sides of the alley. He saw the telltale haze of smoke blurring an area just ahead of them on the right, and guided his mule toward it, Hamza close behind.

The incense came from a leaning, ramshackle set of tables covered in cloth drapes streaked with gray ash. Lit coils, cones, and sticks all sent sinewy lines of smoke up into the air, where they mingled and spread. It was a sensual, heavy combination of flowers: rose, jasmine, osmanthus.

But it was not the incense seller that held Li Du's attention. It was the low table tucked beside it. The table was so humble and small, so crowded amid the jumble of vendors, that it would have been easy to miss. Sitting on a stool behind it, a peasant woman, her head swathed in a pink wool scarf, was bent over a piece of embroidery. She was drawing a length of thick blue thread up through the cloth. On her back a swaddled baby slept, its head on her shoulder, peeping from under an embroidered blanket. Another child stood beside her, bundled in warm clothes, with ruddy pink cheeks and a solemn stare. The smoke from the incense clouded the area in the almost suffocating fragrance.

"What is it?" asked Hamza, trying to see through the bustle.

Li Du pointed. On the table in front of the woman, arranged in two neat rows, were ten leather purses inset with embroidered pictures of foxes and junipers.

When Li Du bent to pick up one of the purses, the child next to the woman pushed at her shoulder, and she looked up quickly.

"Do you want to buy something?" She had a strong accent and a loud voice.

"I wanted to ask you about these purses," Li Du said.

"Are you an official?"

Li Du began to say that he wasn't, but Hamza interrupted. "He is the magistrate's cousin."

She looked surprised. "The magistrate's own cousin? I didn't think anything was going to be done. I told one of the guards, but he said that in a crowd like this there will always be pickpockets, and that I should pay more attention. He said there wasn't a chance of finding the thief, so I had better not bother him about it again."

"You mean," said Li Du, finally understanding, "that one of these purses was stolen from you?"

"Isn't that what I just said?" The baby woke up and began to play with the woman's hair.

Li Du looked again at the purses. "When did this happen?"

"Three days ago. In the afternoon."

"And what occurred exactly?"

"It was crowded, like it is now. Mountains and oceans of people. I was busy — I sew while I wait for customers. I didn't see the thief's hand reach out and take one. Noticed it missing later when I counted. That's why my daughter is here now — to watch while I sew."

"And what pattern was embroidered on the stolen purse?"

"They are all the same — like these ones."

"And you make them all in the Khampa style?"

Her face softened a little bit. "My mother taught me," she said. "She was from Kham. She sold purses like this."

"And do you know if anyone else in Dayan sells them?"

"No one does. See how fine the embroidery is? And the thread is dyed with my mother's own recipes. The colors are very bright. I don't usually make them to sell, but I came for the festival. The other people in my village told me that there will be good business."

"And the incense burning next to your

table — it is always the same?"

She nodded. "Yes. I put my table here because I like the scent. Does that matter?"

"It is essential," said Hamza. "He is a very clever investigator."

The woman gave Hamza a suspicious look, unsure whether he was in earnest.

"I am sorry that it was stolen from you," said Li Du, "and I will do what I can to address the theft. Allow me to buy one for myself."

The woman smiled for the first time. "Well — that is good of you. They cost a quarter tael — you see how fine the quality is."

Li Du did not dispute the high price, and paid the woman under Hamza's silent scrutiny.

When they were finally out of the market crowds, on the quieter street leading to the mansion, Hamza said, "How did you know that the woman would be there?"

Li Du roused himself from his thoughts. "When I found the purse in Brother Pieter's room, I noticed that it did not smell as I would expect an object carried by caravan to smell. It was perfumed. I did not think it was important, but when I caught the scent of the incense in the market I recognized it. The threads absorbed the fragrance."

"Then the thief who stole the purse from the market is the murderer."

"I think it is likely. It was taken on the afternoon of the day Brother Pieter died."

Li Du hesitated. They were almost at the inn, and Hoh was already standing outside, no doubt having been informed of their approach. The innkeeper waved and gestured for them to hurry, pointing toward his kitchen, his cheeks red and smiling, his hands dusted in flour.

"Not too loudly," said Hamza under his breath. "The innkeeper can't be trusted with secrets."

Li Du nodded. "There is still a long while before sunset. If you would be willing to take the animals, and to ask the innkeeper whether I might have a room at the inn, I will go and speak to the magistrate."

"What will you tell him? He is not going to be happy to hear what you have found out."

Li Du looked back at the mountain, once more a distant, silent shape, as if it might provide the answer to a question. Then he sighed, and said with a small smile, "Somehow I must convince him that the truth is important, but I worry that the evidence of the purse will not be enough."

"Because," said Hamza in a low voice,

"your cousin will choose safety and convenience over truth. Your Chinese bureaucrats do not like to take responsibility. And your cousin is a real bureaucrat — he is a cog."

Li Du agreed with the frank assessment. In the bureaucracy, the punishments for failures were often heavier than the rewards for successes. Tulishen would do everything he could to avoid looking again at the murder.

Li Du adjusted his hat, raised his chin a little higher, and said, "He is a man of the law. I have to trust that he will not turn away from justice."

"And I will hope so also," said Hamza, grandly. "And while you are gone, I will convince our good innkeeper to give you a room. You and I shall dine together this evening." And, taking the bridles, he went to meet Hoh. Li Du crossed the cobbled square to the gates of the mansion.

Tulishen met him in a covered pavilion built in the middle of a deep pond. It was accessible only by a high, arching stone bridge, the railings of which were studded with white marble lions. The pavilion itself was round, with slim columns holding up its high roof. Cold radiated from the stone and icy water, chilling the shaded interior.

Across the water, through the plum and willow trees on the bank, Li Du could see the book-sunning room at the back of the library.

The magistrate wore a robe of dark blue silk and a black furlined jacket. His draped figure distorted the banded shadows of the columns. He looked irritated and impatient.

"I was composing a response to the governor of Dali," said Tulishen, "who will arrive in the city this evening. His courier is waiting in my office. I almost did not believe the guard when he told me that my cousin had returned and wished to speak to me on an urgent matter. Why have you come back to Dayan? Now you want to plead for the Emperor's forgiveness after all? His words are gold and jade. You cannot undo them."

"That is not why I have come back. I am here because I want to discover who killed Brother Pieter."

Li Du waited, but Tulishen was facing away from him, his hand on the railing of the pavilion, his gaze directed down at the water that lapped against the marble. A slow, white fish swam in a ponderous circle, looking for food in the plants that gripped the stone beneath the half-frozen surface.

Tulishen began to speak, still without looking at Li Du. "When you were a boy, the family thought that you would be the one who would advance us. You were so clever. Our mothers imagined you as a magistrate, even a governor, in one of the port cities. Up to a point, you met every expectation. You attained the highest academic degree. You won honors. And then what did you do? You had yourself appointed librarian, and you expressed no ambition ever to be anything else. And in that — that humble career — you became friends with scholars who in your ignorance you did not recognize as traitors. Your exile humiliated us more than your obscurity ever could. And I myself did not escape punishment for your actions."

"You are a magistrate."

Tulishen laughed — it was a thin, bitter sound. "Yes. I am a magistrate. Posted to a miasmic village a year's journey from the capital. Surrounded by diseased insects and ignorant peasants. I, who have dined with governors, princes, even at the Emperor's own table."

Li Du's reply was quiet. "I never wished these troubles on you," he said.

Tulishen absorbed this, then turned to face Li Du. "And yet," he said, "you are here now to bring more trouble to me — to my city, my guests, my prospects."

"It is the murderer of Brother Pieter who threatens you."

Tulishen made a gesture as if to sweep Li Du's words away like hovering flies. "I have heard this already," he snapped. "Your opinion did not interest me two days ago, and it does not interest me now. Nothing has changed. The situation has been resolved. You cannot dispute that you yourself found, in the dead man's room, a purse of Kham make, filled with poison. The man had traveled with the Khampa. This is the explanation, and if you have come back to try to convince me otherwise, then you have wasted your time."

Li Du produced the small embroidered purse from his pocket. He held it out to the magistrate. "Do you recognize this?"

Tulishen snatched the purse from Li Du. He turned it over in his hands, and Li Du saw him swallow. Tulishen looked up at Li Du. "How did you get this? It was locked in my own office. I know that it was there. How did you take it?"

Li Du was calm. "That purse you are holding is not the one that was found in Pieter's room."

"But this is some trick. What have you done? It is the same purse."

"It was made by the same artisan. She is a

198

woman of Kham, but is, at this moment, selling these purses in your own market here in Dayan. She is here for the festival. And on the day Brother Pieter died, she was in the market, selling these purses. I spoke to her not an hour ago, and she told me that on that day, one of them was stolen."

The skin of Tulishen's knuckles stretched over the bones of his hands as he clutched the railing. He was silent.

"The Khampa did not give Brother Pieter the poisoned tea," said Li Du. "Someone here in Dayan stole the purse from the market, and used it to implicate the Khampa."

"No," Tulishen said. "This is nonsense. I will not hear it."

"It is the truth."

"You are a fool. The festival — the Emperor's arrival — that is all that exists. You have no idea of what must be accomplished in these final days — of the delicate situations, the decisions, the responsibilities, the cost. Accommodation, food, entertainment, security. The traders arriving in the city must be monitored, the caravans searched, strangers interviewed. Hundreds, thousands of people. Weapons, captive beasts, diplomats who must all be welcomed with appropriate ceremony. The festival field still

199

being prepared. And all the time the Emperor coming ever closer. Three days, Cousin. *Three days.* There cannot be a murderer in the city. Not now. When this is over — when the festival is behind us — then, perhaps, I will look into this further. Before that time, it is out of the question."

"But you must see that Pieter's death is related to the arrival of the Emperor. It is too much of a coincidence —"

"A single cutthroat is no danger to the Emperor of China. The matter can wait."

There was a small cough from the edge of the pavilion. Li Du and Tulishen turned to see that, unnoticed by them, Jia Huan had crossed the bridge and was waiting to address the magistrate. His presence seemed to calm Tulishen, who looked at the composed young official with a kind of desperate reliance.

"Is the courier still waiting?" asked Tulishen.

"He is, but that is not why I have come."

"Then what?"

"I am sorry, Magistrate, but I had to inform you at once. There is some very strange talk in the city."

"What talk?"

"Everyone is saying that the Khampa did not murder the Jesuit. They are saying that there is to be an investigation to find out who the murderer was. And —" He glanced at Li Du.

"And what?" Tulishen demanded.

"They are saying that the magistrate's exiled cousin is going to solve the case, so that he may present the truth to the Emperor and be forgiven for his own crimes."

Both Li Du and Tulishen stared. Then Tulishen turned on his cousin. "Was this your doing?"

At that moment Li Du realized exactly whose doing it had been. He had a sudden urge to laugh, but checked the impulse and said, gravely, "I know nothing of this. But as you said to me before, Cousin — rumors can appear without warning, and they can be powerful. Clearly someone had a romantic notion of an exile redeeming himself. And, equally clear, people enjoy the idea."

"But this is not to be tolerated. Jia Huan — you must be exaggerating. Who told you that this gossip is in the city?"

Jia Huan was apologetic. "It was Hoh's niece, Bao. She came to me immediately when she heard. I did not believe her, so I went to the inn myself. What she says is true. The entire place is afire with the news. The merchants and nobles — all of the guests are speaking of it."

Li Du almost pitied his cousin. Tulishen's face was drained of color. "What should be done? My career — my legacy — everything depends on the success of the festival." He faltered.

Li Du silently thanked Hamza for his help, and understood that the time had come for him to do what he had returned to Dayan to do. "Cousin," he said firmly, "you cannot ignore this. I am sorry, but the situation has gone beyond your power to control. The Emperor will hear, one way or another, of what has happened. I take this responsibility willingly. I will help you —"

Tulishen held up his hand in a signal for Li Du to stop. Li Du looked at his older, successful cousin, striped with shadows, the rings on his fingers clicking softly against the cold marble rail as he leaned on it.

"I am not a stupid man," said Tulishen, wearily. "I see that this farce cannot now be avoided."

Li Du began to answer, but Tulishen interrupted. "You will report your findings to me. You will provide an answer on the evening before the Emperor's arrival. If you do not, I do whatever I deem necessary to reduce the harm you have caused."

"Whatever you deem —"

"By coming here, by bringing me this" —

Tulishen held up the purse that he had crushed in his hand — "you say to me that you want to have this burden. I am giving it to you. Perhaps you have been outside of the bureaucracy too long to remember the risks that come with a choice like yours. But now it is too late."

"I understand."

"Then I will inform Lady Chen that you are to have what help you require. You may come and go freely from the mansion. How will you begin?"

"I wish to look again at Pieter's belongings. But before I do that, I have several questions for you."

"What questions?"

"I wish to know what Brother Pieter said during your formal introduction. You said that he came from Agra. What else did he tell you of himself?"

"Nothing of importance that I recall."

"You complained that he spoke too much. Surely you remember something of what he said?"

Tulishen made a show of thinking. "I did not think at the time that it was necessary to pay close attention. I do not remember all the details."

"But something . . ."

"Yes, yes," said Tulishen, impatiently. "He

went on at length about his fascination with China."

"He told me that he was in Beijing forty years ago," said Li Du.

"Yes. He wanted to come to China, but was still a student, a novice. Apparently it is not usual to send the inexperienced brothers far from their homes, unless they are going to their holy sites. That is why he spoke Chinese so passably, for a foreigner."

"So that they would allow him to come to China?"

"Yes. As you said, forty years ago. He boasted to me of his work on the Observatory. He told me he built one of its instruments. Jia Huan — you remember. He spoke to you as much as to me. Of course he was not aware of the rudeness of addressing a secretary when a magistrate is present. But tell my cousin what the old man said."

Jia Huan was clear and succinct. "Because I came last month from Beijing, and had some knowledge of the Bureau of Astronomy, he wished for me to tell him which of his brothers are still in that city, and what new instruments have been added since his time."

"But none of this is relevant," said Tulishen. "His speech had no substance."

Ignoring Tulishen's obvious desire to end the conversation, Li Du said, "When Pieter spoke of his decision to travel to Dayan for the festival, he said that he had not seen *these* mountains in many years. Do you know what he meant by that?"

Tulishen raised his eyebrows. "Ah," he said, "I did not realize that you did not know. The old Jesuit had been to Dayan before."

Li Du had asked the question without any certainty of the answer. He concealed his surprise. "Why have you not mentioned this before?"

"What reason was there to mention it? It was a long time ago. Thirty years. The Mu were still in power here."

"But what was he doing in this far part of the empire?"

"He told me that he traveled here to explore a part of the empire that he had not seen. He stayed for two years in a village near Dayan. Then his superiors ordered him to travel to Tibet. That is all I know."

"But isn't it possible that he made an enemy here? Someone who has held a grudge all this time?"

Tulishen sniffed. "I do not think it is likely. This place is very different than it was thirty years ago. The Qing have a presence here now. The old families are gone."

"Not all of them."

Tulishen's patience was exhausted. "If you want to know about that time, then I suggest you ask Mu Gao or his cousin, Old Mu, at the clerk's office. But I doubt they will be able to help you. The local people, as you know, do not possess any great wit. I have no more time to spend here. Jia Huan will take you to where the dead man's possessions were stored."

He began to walk away, then stopped and turned back to Li Du. "In my opinion, Cousin, if you have any chance of finding your supposed murderer, which I still think is unlikely, you had better look among the foreigners."

"Why do you think that?"

Tulishen frowned. "The dead man was arrogant and indiscrete. His dithering and his insinuations were often troubling, and on occasion, deeply offensive. But that is not motive for murder. Whatever secrets he brought with him to my home came from foreign cities. The foreigners all have their agendas. Probably it was the young Jesuit — he didn't want the old man stealing the Emperor's attention."

"And the merchant, Sir Gray?"

The frown deepened on Tulishen's face.

"I want you to be cautious with Sir Gray. Do not ask him impertinent questions. These treaties and matters of trade are beyond my jurisdiction. If the Emperor plans to make an agreement with the Company, we must not be accused of hindering it. Question him with tact. Tomorrow you will find him on the festival field. Certain objects in his tribute have given him some authority there."

And with that, Tulishen turned his back on his cousin.

CHAPTER 10

Li Du stared down at the worn books he had arranged on the desk like a mosaic. He and Jia Huan were in an unused study reserved for the magistrate's son when he visited. In one corner of the room was a bed with green curtains embroidered with flowers and insects. The bookshelf was bare except for several thin volumes of essays and a pile of albums by famous calligraphers. Jia Huan had pushed to the edges of the marble-topped desk a white jade musical stone and a forest of clean brushes arranged in five separate jars.

The books were as Li Du had seen them on the morning after the banquet. He picked up the *Flora Sinensis,* remembering Pieter's intention to offer it to Brother Martin. It was, Li Du had learned years ago, a book with a strange history. Its author, the Jesuit missionary Father Boym, had been a guest of the Ming court for many years when the Manchu invasion began. He had watched the fall of the Ming, and, devastated by what he feared would be an end to the intellectual and spiritual development of China, he had rushed to Europe to plead for help on behalf of the failing dynasty. He had published the *Flora Sinensis* to persuade his king to defend the fragile delights of the dying empire, but his efforts had failed to convince.

Li Du admired an illustration of a mango, depicted with care both whole and in cross section. A brown-inked tree trunk climbed up the left side of the page, its high branches bending with the weight of the fruit.

"What is it you hope to find?" asked Jia Huan.

"When I looked at these books before, I did not know that Brother Pieter had been murdered. I think it is necessary to look at everything again, from our new perspective."

Jia Huan looked down at the illustration on the page. "It is poorly rendered," he said. "The balance is incorrect."

Li Du reexamined the drawing. It had certainly not been done in the Chinese style. In addition, the weight of the ink in the words Boym had copied in Chinese suggested improper stroke order. But the depiction of the plant itself was marvelously realistic.

"There is a Jesuit painter in the capital," said Jia Huan, "who paints portraits. Our court painters have begun to imitate his style. They say that the lines of perspective are essential to create a convincing copy of the subject."

"You disagree?"

"The Jesuit painter would do better to learn from us. Our artists are more subtle. A painting should be more than a crude replica of reality."

"You speak as an artist. Painting and calligraphy are near relations."

"Yes."

"Do you really dislike the foreigners so much?" asked Li Du, mildly.

If Jia Huan was aware of the significance of the question, it did not deter him. "You served in the Emperor's own library," he said. "So you must see the situation as I do. Their ugly languages corrupt our poetry. Their brushes will never do honor to our mountains. They try to replicate our porcelain by studying the heat of our kilns and our methods of grinding minerals. But they have no understanding of our art." Jia Huan's expression became more intense. His quiet voice was sharp with conviction.

"One of the Jesuits said that we Chinese see the Western priests as geniuses fallen from heaven, that we have put off our *peacock tails* and recognized their superiority. Does that not anger you?"

Li Du tried to put himself in the place of the proud young official who stood beside him, so devoted to the idea of the empire. Had Li Du ever shared that resolute faith? Or had it always rung false, as it did for him now? He said, "The author of those words had a tendency to exaggerate. Not all the Jesuits share Father Kircher's sense of superiority. But do you truly have no interest in learning what they have to teach?"

Jia Huan had recovered his composure. "The scholar Zheng Dai," he said calmly, "reminds us that an entire year of study is not enough to learn a single word."

Li Du nodded, remembering. "But after a decade has passed, the student who studied the word for a year will see it suddenly in the arc of a sword or the fall of a blossom, and will know its meaning."

"The foreigners are a burden on the progress of the empire. They distract our scholars with cheap entertainment."

Li Du looked down at the books on the table. "I must ask you," he said quietly, "about your movements on the night of the

211

murder."

Jia Huan seemed taken aback. "I do not care for the foreigners, but I assure you, it was not I who killed the Jesuit."

"I am not accusing you. But on the night of the murder, you did not remain in the courtyard during the performance. I saw you come and go. Did you see anyone close to Brother Pieter's room, or notice anything out of the ordinary in the mansion?"

"My errands did not take me past the Jesuit's room. And as for unusual activity in the mansion, it is all unusual at this time. The construction, the crowds, the foreigners — nothing is as it normally is."

"And what were your errands?"

Jia Huan's brows drew together. "There have been so many small tasks," he said. Then his face cleared. "There was more graffiti," he said. "I removed it in the afternoon, and began to copy it. Then the banquet began and I had other obligations — accepting deliveries and seeing to the comfort of the guests. I returned to the library to finish my work while the story-teller was performing."

"This graffiti — is it all the work of the same person?"

"I do not think so. There are at least two styles of writing."

"And what is the content?"

Jia Huan looked slightly uncomfortable. "The usual rumors," he said, "that do not bear repeating."

"It is possible that they have some relevance to the case."

"I do not think so. The messages are not creative. The same ugly stories that the Emperor has already proved to be entirely untrue."

"I do not know them."

Jia Huan spoke quickly. "The posters say that the Emperor is illegitimate. They say the fourteenth prince schemes against his father, that the last Ming emperor was murdered . . . and all the expected imagery of the clear wind that cannot blow away the bright moon. As I said, trash that does not bear repeating."

The bright moon still shines. The clear wind cannot blow it away. Li Du remembered the line of poetry well. In any other language, it contained no offense. But *clear*, pronounced *qing*, and *bright*, pronounced *ming*, revealed the true meaning of the poem. The poet had been loyal to the Ming Dynasty. He had died for his words, but they had remained powerful among the dwindling ranks of those who still did not accept Qing rule.

"And you have no knowledge of who is

responsible?"

Jia Huan shook his head. "No one in Dayan has yet caught sight of any culprit. But it is only a matter of time before someone does. And the magistrate will not be lenient. Not at this time."

Li Du was quiet. Then he said, "The murderer was someone who was in the mansion that night, who knew where Brother Pieter was staying and also that he had traveled with the Khampa. Everyone who fits that description is a suspect."

"I understand." Jia Huan looked as if he were about to say more, but at that moment they were interrupted by a voice behind them. They turned to see a small maid standing in the late afternoon sunlight.

She bowed her head respectfully. Then she beckoned to Jia Huan. "The magistrate requires your assistance."

Jia Huan bowed apologetically to Li Du. "I regret that I cannot be of more help to you. Please inform me if there is anything more you require."

"I will. Thank you."

As Jia Huan left, Li Du saw that his face had once more become that of the efficient secretary, his opinions smoothed away into the mask of intelligent servitude.

The titles of the books told Li Du little more than he already knew. Brother Pieter had been fluent in Chinese and Latin. He was an astronomer, and he had been working on a manuscript about the construction of observatories. Like Li Du, he carried with him the books of scholars who had preceded him, and like the scholar Xu Xiake, he had enjoyed correcting the errors in previous texts.

Li Du was retying the twine around the unfinished manuscript when he noticed that several of the pages were different from the others. Their content matched that of the rest of the manuscript, but the paper itself was different. While most of the pages were clean, separate sheets, these were rough along the left side. These were blank pages torn from a book, probably a journal. But there had been no journal among Pieter's possessions.

As he began again to retie the twine, he fumbled, and several pieces of paper fell to the floor. He knelt to pick them up, and saw that one page was not written in Pieter's handwriting. It was a letter addressed to Pieter. He read:

It was my great pleasure to partake of the hospitality of the Jesuit house in Agra. I am safely returned to Calcutta, and have had the opportunity to consult the books here on the matter that we discussed over that very fine dinner. Your cellars have brewed beer far better even than that of all the merchants in Calcutta, who consider themselves so superior in all things culinary and commercial.

The copy that we have here in Calcutta is, as you guessed, the translation made by Fr. Michael Boym, and contains the details you requested on the Chaldean priests that are not recorded in the text as it was translated by Fr. Athanasius Kircher in his *Prodromus Copticus*. I include a copy of the Boym with this letter, and hope it will aid you in your research.

The roses are in bloom here, and when the city is not overwhelmed by the stench of sewage, their fragrance is beautiful indeed. I hope this reaches you before your journey to China, and that said journey is a great success. As you know I have been only to the capital, and not a day goes by that I do not recall some small detail of what I saw there. I fear I speak of it too often, and am a great bore to my friends. I wish that I had the strength to attempt such a voyage myself, and to see with my own eyes the plants and strange flying creatures in Fr. Kircher's illustrations. I wonder, do they actually exist? I look forward to your report, and wish that my old bones were not as rickety, my mind not as wandering. If I could have my youth back I would travel to every corner, every village and mountain in the world.

And finally, as to our conversation before I left, I must admit that in my heart I agree with you. Our purpose, this conversion of the heathen, troubles me also. But we must not allow ourselves to stray too far from our orders. The Dominicans grow ever more determined to sabotage our brothers in China, and I urge you to be cautious. They speak ill of us to anyone who will listen, and while they are still forbidden to enter any part of China other than Portuguese Macau, they do what they can to do us harm from a distance. Did you know they had a Jesuit ship searched there? They spread the rumor that it was full of gold bars, coated in chocolate. What imagination! They say we are debauched, decadent, corrupt, when it is they who plot constantly against us. I am not easy in my mind when I think of our future in China.

I am eager to read your draft on the construction of small observatories for the study of astronomical phenomena. Your ideas and knowledge on that matter are unmatched. It is perhaps better that you have conducted your study outside of Rome, where there is still so much empty talk required before one can present new theories.

Your humblest servant
Fr. Martin Walpole.
Calcutta, Dec 8, 1707

Li Du stared at the name. The two men had claimed never to have met each other before. Yet this letter from one to the other was dated only several months ago, and implied that they had met in person. Had he misunderstood? He tried to recall their conversation at the banquet. They had conducted themselves in the manner of strangers. He was certain of it. Li Du read the letter again. Then he put it in his pocket.

He checked the other books, but found nothing further. Finally he picked up Pieter's Bible. After a brief hesitation, he tucked it under one arm, and left the room. Outside it was still light, but the sun was beginning to burn heavy and molten as it sank lower in the sky. The mansion was bustling with activity in preparation for dinner, and it took him a moment to get his bearings. Once he did, he set out deliberately in the direction of the library.

Mu Gao was there, sitting alone at his small table in the corner sipping a bowl of soup. He set the bowl down with an appreciative smile, which turned immediately to a scowl when he noticed that someone had come in.

"So you've come back?" he said, when he saw that it was Li Du.

"I have. I am investigating the murder."

Mu Gao grunted. "Not surprised," he said.

"You knew the Khampa were innocent?"

"Innocent? Not them. Horse-lovers and wife-thieves."

"But you don't think they poisoned Brother Pieter."

"Not the way they do things. Fought them myself, when I was young. Never knew them to poison their guests. I'm not saying they aren't yaks' asses." In Mu Gao's thick accent, the words came out in a string of

219

burring and growling punctuated by flat, emphatic syllables of affirmation or denial.

"I wondered if I could ask you some questions."

Mu Gao looked doubtful, and Li Du prepared to be scolded for interrupting his dinner. But the old man did not scold him. Instead, he looked down at his steaming bowl of soup. "But I have no food for you," he said, in a mournful tone. "We cannot sit and talk if you are hungry."

Li Du protested that he was the one at fault, and encouraged Mu Gao to continue eating. It was only after many reassurances that Li Du was expected at the inn for dinner very soon that Mu Gao agreed to continue his meal in Li Du's presence.

"I wanted to ask you," said Li Du, "about the man who died. Did you recognize him?"

"Recognize a strange-lander like that? I would if I'd seen him before — people don't look like that here. What do you mean?"

"He visited Dayan thirty years ago."

Mu Gao's mouth dropped open in surprise, displaying his four remaining teeth.

"You do not remember?"

"Thirty years?" Mu Gao's expression was vague, bewildered. Then a hint of recognition sparked in his eyes and he began to wag his finger at the level of his ear, thinking. "Maybe I heard of him. The young foreigner in Dayan, or hereabouts. Just thought of him that way. That was about thirty years ago."

"But you didn't meet him?"

"No. I was taking caravans to the tea forests then — fell in love with a southern girl and stayed there for a while. Pretty women in the south. And tea families are almost as good as yak families for money. But my wife had yaks — you can't do better than a pretty wife who owns yaks." His gaze became distant and unfocused.

Li Du, realizing that he was tiring the man, said, "I will leave you to finish your dinner. Perhaps I may return tomorrow to speak to you a little more?"

Mu Gao nodded vaguely. But as Li Du rose to go, he raised his chopsticks in the air and clicked them together to get Li Du's attention. "Wait," he said, "don't you want to know about the fight?"

"The fight?"

Mu Gao nodded vigorously. "The dead man. He fought with the other one. The bald one."

"When?"

"On the day he died, of course. That's the important day, isn't it? Why would we talk about it if it wasn't that day?"

"Can you tell me what happened?"

Mu Gao looked down into his bowl of soup, and for a moment Li Du thought his attention had wandered. But after he had plucked a dumpling from the broth and eaten it, Mu Gao spoke again. "Yes, I'll tell you. It was after you yourself spoke to him. In the sun room. You left the library. I saw you as I was coming back."

"Where had you been?"

"I went to drink tea with my friend. I didn't want to be in the library when the bald merchant was having his boxes brought in. He was scolding all of us. I wanted none of it. But I came back, and saw you leave. The other one, though, the dead man, he went into the room of treasures. Stayed there a long time, rustling about with the boxes, I heard him."

"And when did the argument occur?"

"Almost time for the banquet. The gongs were ringing. And the dead man, he came out of the treasure room. But the bald man had just come in, and saw him. That's when it started."

"Why were they arguing?"

"How would I know? They weren't talking in any language I've ever heard. Didn't understand a word. Jia Huan — he was here copying that new graffiti. Very uncomfortable, we were. He and I looked at each other, but what were we going to do? None of our business."

Li Du wondered if Jia Huan had been about to mention the argument when he had been called away by the maid.

"So you had no idea why they were angry at each other?"

Mu Gao grumbled. "Not really at each other. It was the bald one angry at the dead man. Seemed like he didn't want him in the treasure room. Maybe thought he was stealing. The other one — the dead man — he didn't raise his voice. He was polite. But the bald man's face, and his head, too, went red as a pepper. Thought he might fall over in a fit."

"And how did it end?"

"The dead man left first. The other one went into the treasure room, then came out and went out toward the banquet." Mu Gao ran his tongue across dry lips. "That's all I know," he said. "But why have you made me talk so much? Look at my soup. It is almost cold."

"I will not take any more of your time," said Li Du.

Mu Gao sniffed. "At least you are more polite than most people. Doesn't mean you can take that book away from the library."

223

He pointed at the Bible Li Du still had tucked under his arm. It took him several minutes to convince Mu Gao that it had not come from the magistrate's library. Once he had, he wished the old man a pleasant evening and took his leave.

He made his way along the paths to the very back of the mansion until he came to the base of the wooded hill. He started up it, toward the tombs of the old Mu kings. The path was cobbled, and led steeply through the tall cypress trees from one brightly painted pagoda to the next. Each building was perched on an artificial outcrop, and surrounded by little waterfalls and rock gardens. Down the columns ran lines of ancient poetry painted in a romantic style. Inside, clean cushions gleamed in soft silk, viper greens and golds.

About halfway up the hill he glimpsed the white marble of the tombs through the trees, and followed a path that led to them through dense shrubs and rose vines. He came to the graves, which were set into the hill, their white marble covers like carved doors leading into the sloping ground. Scattered among them were low tables and stone benches, there for visitors to sit and consult their ancestors.

Pieter's grave was obvious. The dirt

around it was new, and the marble was not yet streaked or cracked. There were no words carved into it. On either side of the flat white cover two standard, blocky dragons stood guard. A few slips of imitation money fluttered in the breeze like translucent leaves.

Li Du slid the book under the claw of one of the stone guardians. It gave the indifferent dragon some personality, and Li Du imagined the creature reading the parables and poems in the thick foreign tome when there were no humans present.

The sun was setting now, and the light was fading to violet blue. Sounds drifted faintly from the mansion below: voices, dinner gongs, and the thuds and jangles of doors being pulled closed. He put one hand on his knee to straighten up, and as he was brushing the cold dirt from his robe, he saw something sparkle on the ground.

Nestled among the fallen oak leaves was a tiny silver ornament. It was leaf shaped. No, a feather, with delicate striations etched into its face. At one end a ring joined a length of silver chain, strung with three pearls.

It was the feather of a phoenix tail, and the last time Li Du had seen it, it had dangled from the comb in Lady Chen's hair.

He found her in one of the small banquet halls. She was speaking to an attentive maid, and continued to speak as Li Du approached.

". . . more powder for the consort house. Be sure that it is not the white lead variety, but the other one, the morning glory seed. The ladies prefer it — the white lead is too sticky. And you must also buy rouge, the safflower with added attar. Choose one with a strong pigment. We will need extra for the concubines who are to attend the banquets. They may not have their own cosmetics, and they must look sophisticated, or it will reflect poorly on our house. Can you remember all of that? I will not have time to tell you again in the morning."

The maid departed in a flurry of curtsies and nods, and Lady Chen turned to Li Du. "The magistrate has explained the situation to me," she said. "The household is, of course, at your disposal."

Her face, moon white, was composed, suspended above a gown of maroon satin. She reminded Li Du of the tower rhubarbs that he had seen growing on shale slopes in the high alpine meadows. It was a plant known as the aristocrat of the mountain, and in the woman who now regarded him, he saw something of the isolation and strength that opposed the studied perfection of her costume. Her hair was dressed with turquoise and pearls.

Li Du said, "I am sorry for the anxiety that these events must have caused you."

"I appreciate your courtesy," Lady Chen answered, with a hint of impatience, "but it is not necessary for you to be so tactful. The success of the festival is as important to me as it is to the magistrate. I want to know what is happening in my home, and I want to know what it is necessary for me to do. I do not have the leisure to indulge in distress. You have questions for me?"

Her posture was rigid, and in her fixed expression Li Du saw her determination to maintain control of the conversation. He wondered if he could relax her guard before showing her the silver feather.

"I do have questions," he said. "Could you describe to me the tea sets in the guest-rooms? Are they identical?"

"In form, yes. The patterns differ, but they were all commissioned together from the same kiln. Why?"

"And the sets are all complete, as far as

you know? None of the pieces have been lost?"

"It is very fine quality. I would not dishonor the magistrate by providing his guests with cheap porcelain, or with imperfect sets. I conduct strict inventories of all our valuable goods regularly — paper, rugs, statues, cushions, and of course the porcelain. The last time I examined the guestroom tea sets, they were whole."

"And when was that?"

Lady Chen took the time to search her memory. The silence did not fluster her, and when she spoke it was with assurance. "It was ten days ago. I inventoried the tea sets, the cushions, and the paper and brushes."

"But on the night Brother Pieter died, I counted only three teacups in his room."

She arched an eyebrow. "Do you mind if I fold these table covers while we speak?"

Li Du gestured for her to continue. She picked up a green satin cloth and folded it deftly as she said, "If there is a cup missing from the room, it must have disappeared very recently. The maid who cleaned the room should have noticed. But this has been a difficult week for the servants. The death of a foreigner frightened them. The cook was terrified that she had prepared the food badly."

"I understand. You will tell me if the cup is found?"

"Yes. And I will ask the maids what they know of the matter. Does this mean that the poison was in a cup of tea?" She asked the question a little too quickly, with affected disinterest. Her expression was unreadable.

"I cannot answer you," replied Li Du, "because I do not yet know. But I have another question — of a slightly delicate nature."

"Yes?" Lady Chen set the folded cloth down and picked up another.

"Do you know the name of the concubine with whom the merchant Sir Gray had an assignation on the night of the murder?"

Lady Chen looked faintly amused. "He had no tryst with a woman hired by this house."

"You sound very sure. These meetings do call for — for some privacy. Are you certain that it did not occur?"

The hint of humor brightened into a smile at once charming and superior. "There are many good reasons to know which men accept the overtures of pleasure women and maids on banquet nights. I question the women very thoroughly, and they know that the consequences of lying to me are severe.

I trust you will not repeat this information. As you say, there is a certain assumption of privacy. But I can assure you that he was not with a woman."

Lady Chen was regarding him still with a trace of mockery, and he decided that the time was right to try to catch her off balance. He drew the ornament from his pocket.

"I found this," he said. "I believe it is yours."

He was relieved to see her composure waver. A tiny furrow appeared between her brows, and she stretched out her hand to take the silver-and-pearl feather from him. He set it gently into her open palm.

"Yes," she said. "It is from a piece of my jewelry. It must have fallen from my hair. Thank you for returning it to me." She avoided meeting his eyes.

"I found it beside Brother Pieter's tomb. Can you tell me how it came to be there? I understand that the burial was performed without ceremony. Not even the magistrate was present."

Lady Chen's hand closed in a fist around the ornament. She said, coldly, "Of course I was not at the burial. And I did not visit the man's grave."

"Then how did a jewel from your hair

come to be there?"

"I was visiting a different grave. I go there to honor my own ancestors — my mother was a distant cousin of the family that used to rule this province. I do not speak of this often — the Chinese nobility does not admire the local bloodlines. I would prefer not to speak of it now."

She gave the explanation smoothly, but Li Du noticed that her eyes remained on the cloth that she was folding, and that the silence after she finished speaking discomfited her as it had not before.

Li Du said, "On the night of the murder, you served wine to Brother Pieter."

Lady Chen drew in a sharp breath. "If you are suggesting that the poison was in the wine, it is impossible. I served all the guests from the same bottle. You yourself drank from it."

Li Du pressed. "But can you tell me what made him spill the wine? Had he perhaps seen something at the edge of the garden, or heard something that upset him?"

"You are misremembering. He was tired, and he spilled some wine. That is all that happened."

"Then why did you go after him soon after he retired?"

Lady Chen's gaze snapped up to meet his.

She said, very firmly, "I did not go after him. I was going to fetch more wine."

"But you did not have a servant with you to carry it."

"They were occupied. I can carry a bottle of wine without help when necessary."

"And when you returned, you did not have any wine with you."

"No — I was going to get the wine. I did pass close by to the guestrooms, and I thought I heard voices. I continued on, and then there was a sound of someone falling. That is why I went to the guesthouse."

"And what did you find there?"

"Only the dead man. I called for help, and when Bao — the maid — arrived, I sent her at once for the doctor. I knew that there was nothing that could be done. He was not breathing."

"And after that?"

"You know what happened after that. I came straight to the stage courtyard to tell the magistrate what had happened."

"And you saw no one at all either on your way to or from the guesthouse?"

"No. But I was walking on the main path. There is another, a more hidden way, under the willow trees. But there are no torches there at night. If someone were leaving the guesthouse and did not want to be seen, that is the path the person would have taken."

"Thank you, Lady Chen. You have been very patient. It is late, and I know that you have many demands on your time."

And with a respectful bow, Li Du turned and left her there, watching him go.

It was dark. Li Du had obtained a lantern from an open storage room and now held it before him, walking slowly in the small pool of light, peering at the dark shapes that loomed beyond its border. As he traversed the zigzagging flat bridges over the ponds, a cold wind blew through the withered lotus stalks. They rotated slowly in the water, as if they were turning to look at him. He shivered and quickened his pace, careful not to miss a turn. Demons traveled in straight lines, and the sharp angles of the bridges were built to evade them.

When he passed the guesthouse where he had stayed, he saw the small path leading into the willows in the direction of the library. It was as Lady Chen had described it, unlit and obscured by hanging branches. He began to make his way down the path, walking carefully on the flat stepping stones.

He passed through a moon gate draped with thick vines, and found himself in a rock garden behind the library. In the center of it grew a plum tree, its branches black veins against the sky. The rocks varied in shape and size, each chosen for their resemblance to miniature mountains, castles, and cities.

Li Du had never cared for rock gardens, and this one was particularly eerie under the bony fingers of the plum tree. Removed from the mountain, the looming stones were strangely unsettling.

He could see the path continue through the garden and the lights of the guesthouse where Pieter had died not far beyond. Lady Chen had been right. If someone had wanted to approach or leave the guesthouse at night without being seen, he, or she, would have taken this path.

Li Du turned around and looked at the rocks. Almost all of them were taller than a person, but at least three were small enough to lift. He knelt beside one, set the lantern down, and eased his fingers into the cold earth. He tilted the rock up, but saw only wet dirt and the indistinct movement of insects. He lifted another rock and found the same. Feeling slightly foolish, he lifted the third. Crushed beneath it, amid a scuttling family of beetles, were the bright fragments of a blue porcelain cup decorated with red flowers.

CHAPTER 11

Hamza reached with his chopsticks into the copper pot that sat between them, and plucked a jade green pepper from the depths of the chicken stew. He regarded it as if he had found a treasure, but before he could begin the story of the magical pepper or the tale of the butter coins — Li Du was learning to identify the signs of Hamza departing one world for another — Li Du spoke.

"Have you noticed," he said, "that every person in this room has looked at us at least once since we began our dinner?"

Hamza put the pepper in his mouth and chewed thoughtfully. He swallowed. "It is my striking appearance. But I am accustomed to being admired. I am not discomfited."

"You do not think they are looking because you told everyone here that I am going to solve a murder in three days' time?"

"I did not tell everyone." Hamza was indignant. "I selected my listeners with care. Tell me — before the rumor reached the mansion, were you succeeding in convincing the magistrate to pursue the killer?"

"No." Li Du leaned forward a little bit over the stew and added: "And you should know that your efforts produced an immediate effect."

Hamza grumbled. "I would have enjoyed seeing the reaction myself."

"I think that you would have."

Imagining it, Hamza gave a satisfied smile. Then he pinched the tip of his beard to neaten its point. "If you fail," he said, "it will be very bad for you." He might have been speaking on the subject of a light rain about to begin on a summer evening. "Yes — it will be very bad. Your cousin will not hesitate to sacrifice you in order to save himself. You are an exile. He is a magistrate. He can say what he wants about you, and the other officials will believe him."

This had already occurred to Li Du. "Are you implying that he could accuse me of the murder? I doubt he would go so far. But if you foresaw this risk, why did you go to such effort to put me in the position I am in now?"

For a moment, the flame in the lantern

closest to them went still, and cast a uniform glow through the thin silk shade. Lit this way, Hamza looked like an illustration, his beard a single brushstroke, gleaming ink, his burnished face and black eyes unmoving. Then he spoke, and the spell was broken.

"Remember that I traveled with the man who now lies dead in the ground. We traversed mountain passes so treacherous that even the caravan horsemen dared not speak or move in their saddles. I saw how his bones shook and pained him. I saw his lips move in silent prayer. But whenever he spoke, it was to express gratitude or to offer help. He completed with grace a journey that frightens even the people who live in those mountains. And then he came here, to this city in a valley, redolent with gold and musks and posturing tourists, and here he is killed, *here in this place.*"

Li Du said nothing. Hamza's shoulders relaxed and he said, "You seek the truth. And so I am helping you."

"Thank you."

Hamza searched the stew delicately with his chopsticks and drew out a soft piece of turnip soaked in oil and broth, steaming hot. He eyed it watchfully, waiting for it to cool, and said, "But I hope you have not forgotten to include me in your list of suspects. The storyteller who spins dark tales, who associates with bandit caravans —"

"— who will not reveal where he is from," Li Du finished.

Hamza's eyes widened in innocent surprise. "But I have told you. My family is from Turkey, originally."

"Ah, not from Mughal lands, or from Egypt, as you said before?"

"You must have misheard. It is necessary for you to listen more carefully, if you are to recognize when people are lying to you."

Li Du kept his gaze lowered as he used his chopsticks to coax the remaining grains of rice into a clump at the bottom of his bowl. "If you insist that you are a suspect," he said, "then tell me what reason you would have had to kill Brother Pieter?"

The question seemed to please Hamza. He smiled. "Perhaps I am such an ambitious conjurer that I could not resist the tale — it winked at me from its thin world. It wanted a body and blood. It wanted to live longer than one night, not to dissolve into the smoke of extinguished lanterns. The characters were already here: the merchant, the wise man, the courtesan, the magistrate, the emperor . . ."

"The exile?"

"All that was needed was a corpse to lie among them."

Li Du, who never wasted food, was still pushing his last bite of rice from one side of his bowl to the other. He said quietly: "I do not believe your confession, and I will not play your game. A moment ago you told me why you want Pieter's killer brought to justice. Were you sincere?"

He looked very seriously at Hamza, who, after a moment, bowed his head. "You see why you are the one who must conduct this investigation," he said. "Truth and I make uneasy companions. We bicker — she tells me that I do not understand her. I respond that she does not understand herself. And so we continue from one city to the next. She does not always like my stories. And I sometimes stray from her side, and she —" He stopped in the middle of his sentence, and Li Du glimpsed the tired young traveler whom he had met on the mountain, by the fire with his friends. It was enough to reassure him.

There was a short silence between them. Then Hamza said, "What will you do first?"

Li Du had just asked himself the same question. "I do not yet know how the poison was administered," he said. "The purse may have been put in Pieter's room, or given to him, at almost any time. He may have consumed tea from it, or he may have ingested the poison in another way. The fact that the teacup was taken suggests that the poison was in that cup, and therefore cannot have been removed until after Pieter had drunk from it. Lady Chen says she arrived at Pieter's room minutes after he died. She told us that she came directly to the courtyard to tell the magistrate. The magistrate was at Pieter's room minutes later, and I followed him there."

"So . . ." Hamza spoke slowly. "The cup was either taken before Lady Chen arrived, or in the time it took her to bring the doctor and the magistrate to the scene."

"Or," Li Du said, "it was taken by Lady Chen. You were still on the stage when I left the courtyard, which means that it cannot have been you who took the cup."

"That is so." Hamza gesticulated silently to himself as he played out the scene in his mind. Then he frowned. "The murderer removed the teacup because the cup contained the poison."

Li Du leaned forward. "That is the obvious explanation. But consider — why would the murderer take the cup, but leave the purse in the room? If the murderer wanted

240

the death to appear natural, he would not have planted a purse full of poisoned tea among Pieter's possessions. Or, the reverse: If the murderer intended to frame the Khampa, then the murderer would not have taken the teacup. By removing the cup, the murderer left a clue to his presence in the mansion that night."

"Or her presence."

Li Du nodded. "Or her presence. The two actions contradict each other."

Hamza tapped his chopsticks idly on the soot-blackened side of the copper pot while he thought. "You said that you found the teacup under a rock?"

Li Du nodded again. "Lady Chen described to me an unlit path leading away from the guesthouse toward the library and the courtyard where you were performing. I followed it, picturing the murderer on that night, clutching the teacup and searching for a way to dispose of it quickly without drawing attention."

"I would have thrown it into one of those deep ponds. It would have sunk into the mud and lotus stalks and never been found."

"The murderer may have wished to do so, but could not. It was a very cold day — there were icicles on the trees. The surface of the water was frozen, so the porcelain would likely have rested on top of it. After that, the rock garden is the obvious alternative."

Hamza looked impressed, but then his expression changed to perplexity. "I do not understand the contradiction of the purse and the cup," he said.

"Nor do I — it does not yet make sense. For now, I think we should ask ourselves who might have benefited from Brother Pieter's death. There were many people in the mansion that night, but only several of us had any connection to him, or knew who he was."

"I cannot think of anyone who benefited from his death."

"There are many reasons to commit murder: to exact revenge, to silence a secret, or, if the killer is insane, then there would not be any rational reason."

"But who hated Brother Pieter? What dangerous knowledge did he have?"

Li Du raised his eyebrows and said mildly, "I do not know yet. We cannot simply state answers to those questions — we must search for them. When you were performing that night, did you see anything strange in the audience? You were the only one with a view of their faces."

"Alas — I see my audience, but not in that

way. I am guided by their expressions. I know when they are aroused and desire more description of breasts, and women tied to trees. I know when their mood is for romance, and I give them stars and gowns made of moonbeams. I know when the children are becoming tired, and need more of sea monsters and flying carpets —" He recalled himself to the moment. "But I remember nothing else."

Li Du nodded his understanding. "Then let us consider the possibilities. The merchant — Nicholas Gray. He and Brother Pieter argued. We know that from Mu Gao. We do not know the content of the argument, but I would guess, from what Pieter mentioned to me about his distrust of the Company, that it was about Gray's employer. I will question Gray — and make use of the fact that he does not know that the two people who heard his confrontation with Pieter could not comprehend his specific words. Also, Gray left the courtyard during the performance and, if we can trust Lady Chen's information, he lied about where he went."

Hamza made a noncommittal sound and Li Du went on: "Then there is the Lady Chen. She is a powerful woman who does not permit herself to act without thought.

But when I showed her the jewel that I had found at Pieter's tomb, she held back a strong reaction. I glimpsed it before she shut it away."

"What emotion?"

Li Du tapped his fingers on the table, frustrated. "I could not identify it. But I am sure she has not told me everything she knows."

"Perhaps she is keeping a secret for the magistrate. She is first consort — he must confide in her."

"Yes — I have not forgotten my cousin." Li Du lowered his voice to a whisper. "Pieter's death appears to have caused him only anxiety and inconvenience. But his adamant refusal to investigate may have had a darker motive."

Li Du set down his chopsticks and thought for a moment. Then he said, "We know also that Pieter came to this province thirty years ago. You did not mention that to me. Did he say anything to you about his time here during your travels?"

"I apologize for my forgetfulness," said Hamza, earnestly. "He did speak of it a little. He had a powerful memory. The horsemen were aghast when he pointed to landslides that had not been there when he first traversed those paths. It seemed to me that he thought of it often — but usually walked alone in the hallways of memory."

Li Du considered. "The city has also changed," he said. "Magistrate Tulishen and his household all came long after Pieter had settled in India. Many local people have died, or moved away from Dayan. But we must not ignore the possibility that someone held a grudge against Pieter all that time. Perhaps Mu Gao knows something more than what he said. I will return tomorrow to try to determine whether the jewelvine did indeed come from the library. If it did, he certainly had access to it."

Hamza hummed thoughtfully, then said, "And what of the efficient secretary, Jia Huan? He is very sure of himself."

"He had the opportunity to go to Pieter's room that night, and he has no love for foreigners in China. But he is an intelligent, ambitious official in the employ of the magistrate. His dislike of the foreigners is intellectual — it is difficult to imagine him murdering one."

"I agree with you."

"There is the younger Jesuit — Brother Martin."

Hamza waved his hand in the direction of the labyrinthine interior of the inn. "The nervous scholar hardly ever leaves his room.

He would be mysterious if he were not such a — what is your saying? A frog in a well. He obviously has no idea at all of what he is doing."

"I will speak to him tomorrow." Li Du told Hamza about the letter he had found among the manuscript pages.

"It is suspicious, but he is one who does not seem capable of murder," said Hamza. "He handles weeds and bugs as a midwife handles babes. I would keep my attention on Sir Gray. He reminds me of a jewel-encrusted crab."

Li Du looked around them. The common room was still crowded with guests in colorful silks hunched like beetles around their tables, talking and gesturing and drinking and occasionally craning their necks for a view of the table where Hamza and Li Du spoke quietly together.

Hoh slipped toward them through the crowd carrying a tray with two cups of wine. His confidence in his own importance shone from his red cheeks and bright eyes. When he reached them, he leaned down close to the table and spoke in a low voice as he served the wine. Li Du saw guests watching out of the corners of their eyes.

Hoh's hands shook slightly with excitement. "So," he said, "what progress have you made?"

Li Du assured him patiently that they had no answers to make public yet, complimented the stew, and thanked the innkeeper for providing him a room. Hoh nodded enthusiastically, as if Li Du were asking him for his opinion and he was giving it. Then he piled their empty dishes onto his tray. He took his time, arranging and rearranging the bowls and plates. With a knowing smile, he turned and maneuvered deftly back in the direction of the kitchen.

Li Du raised his bowl to drink, but as he did so he felt a crisp, thin corner of paper stuck to the bottom of it. He put his cup down and slipped the paper under his sleeve. While Hamza watched curiously, he read it, holding it low and out of sight. Written in a neat, feminine hand were words: *I have information. Meet me in the chess garden.*

The chess garden at the inn was a secluded courtyard some distance from the dining hall. In it were five low stone tables surrounded by stone benches. Overhead, lanterns dangled from rope strung from one side of the courtyard to the other. There was a lit brazier beside the central table. The garden appeared to be empty, so they sat by the fire to wait.

They had only just sat down when a woman appeared from one corner of the garden and walked quickly over to them. She looked around her with the light movements of a bird. When she reached them she said, breathlessly, "My name is Bao. The innkeeper is my uncle."

Li Du remembered the name. "Please sit by the fire," he said. "You are a maid at the mansion?"

Bao nodded and smiled, a thin, conspiratorial little smile as she sat down. She had obviously taken pains with her appearance. Her face was coated with bluish-white powder. Her lips and cheeks were rouged, her eyebrows painted, and her hair thickly oiled. Applied to her small, sharp features, the heavy makeup gave her face a hard, kiln-fired delicacy.

"And there is something you wish to tell us?" asked Li Du.

Her voice trembled, but he saw in her eyes that the attention delighted her. "I have been so frightened waiting here in the dark. I thought the murderer might appear at any moment."

"You do not need to be afraid here," Li Du said. "We are the only ones listening."

Bao's small face was suddenly stern. "My

mistress taught me never to assume that you know who is listening." Bao glanced around her again, swallowed, and licked her lips. "I know a secret about the magistrate and my mistress, Lady Chen. My friend Yue was sent to the capital with the magistrate's son after he visited last year, and she is back now. She told me that the magistrate's son told her that one of the magistrates in the capital has died. His name was Liu, and he was mentor to Magistrate Tulishen when the magistrate — when my master — was a student. Yue says that the Emperor is considering Magistrate Tulishen for the open position. It would be a great promotion, and he wants it very badly."

"And Lady Chen?"

Bao leaned forward with a fierce expression. She looked around the courtyard again, before her words tumbled out. "Lady Chen," she whispered, "is needles in cotton. Once a maid tried to seduce the magistrate, and Lady Chen tormented her so that she swallowed her own jewelry to kill herself. And another maid — she disappeared — Lady Chen made her run into a stone wall so that she bashed out her brains."

Hamza whistled under his breath.

"You knew these women personally?" Li Du asked.

Bao blinked. "No — they were gone by the time I became a maid there. But Yue and Ming and Hua all say that they heard from Na, who married and went to her husband's village, that it happened that way."

"And Lady Chen supports the magistrate in his pursuit of this opportunity in the capital?"

Bao shifted excitedly in her seat. "Lady Chen knows that if the magistrate is promoted to Beijing, he may decide not to take her with him. She is getting old, and has no sons, and he has two new wives, as well as his old ones — I hear they are very refined."

"So Lady Chen does not want him to receive the advancement?"

Bao gave a noncommittal lift of her shoulders. "She does not want to be disgraced, or sent to live in a village. She has no family — she acts very high, but if he leaves her here she will have nothing. That is helpful information, isn't it?"

"It may be," Li Du said. "I do not know."

This seemed to make Bao anxious, and she said quickly, "But I know more. I saw something on the night of the murder. The magistrate said something to the doctor that the doctor did not like. It was just after the doctor looked at the body. The magistrate

250

spoke to him very sternly. I did not hear what he said, but it looked as if he was commanding the doctor to do something that the doctor did not wish to do. What do you think that means?"

Li Du poked at the coals with a stick, recalling his impression, on the night of the murder, of a woman leaving the guesthouse just before he arrived there. "That is very interesting."

Bao fidgeted. "I told these things to my uncle, and he told me to tell you. He said that his guests all want you to find the murderer, and that I should help you. Can I do anything else to be helpful? I can listen for you — at the mansion — and report what I hear? What do you know already?"

Her lips were set into a slight pout, and Hamza said gallantly, "You are as brave and helpful as you are lovely. You make me think of the sirens on the emerald islands of the invisible sea."

Li Du directed a reproving look at Hamza, then said to Bao, "I am very grateful for the information you brought to us."

"So you will talk about the case with me?"

Hamza opened his mouth to say something, but Li Du spoke first. "It is late," he said. "My friend and I will drink some wine here by the fire. You should go back to the mansion before you are missed. And you are right to be cautious — there could be danger."

Looking slightly crestfallen, Bao rose and departed, leaving them alone. They waited for several moments, listening to the swish of her skirts receding.

When she was gone, Hamza said, "We might have kept her here a little longer. She may have had more to say."

"And," said Li Du, "she would have done everything she could to encourage us to talk, so that she could report to her uncle."

"Ah — so she was actually here to spy on us. What of the information she gave us about Lady Chen? Why did you not ask her to say more? A woman who could manipulate a servant into choking on jewels could easily poison a stranger."

Li Du responded with a little smile. "She was lying — or one of the other maids lied to her."

"Well," muttered Hamza, "you are suddenly very sure of your ability to discern truth."

Li Du smiled a little. "I apologize — I am not being clear. She did speak very convincingly. But I know that Lady Chen did not actually torment those maids because I have read the novel from which those stories were

252

drawn. It is the *Dream of the Red Chamber.*"

Hamza, bested at his own art, grunted. "I see," he said. "So did the little gossip help us at all? Or was she only here to creep into our conversation so that her uncle can exchange information for coin, and impress his eager guests?"

Li Du was debating that same question. "What she told us about the promotion gives me one idea. Tulishen wants the position of magistrate in Beijing. The death of a guest in his home threatens his attainment of that position. It is possible, then, that the murderer's goal was to prevent Tulishen from advancing."

"Lady Chen?"

"I do not know."

"And the doctor?"

"I will ask him what Tulishen said to him."

Hamza withdrew into moody contemplation. Eventually he straightened and called into the darkness for a servant. When one arrived, he asked for more wine. It was brought to them, and they sipped it slowly in the warmth of the fire, each lost in his own thoughts as the inn quieted around them.

"One night," said Hamza after a while, "Pieter woke up most of the caravan to give a lesson in astronomy."

The image of Brother Pieter rustling through the camp, shaking the shoulders of sleeping horsemen, instructing them to rise and learn a lesson, took Li Du so by surprise that he laughed softly. Hamza, pleased by the response, went on: "Pieter lamented that he did not have his star charts and instruments with him, but insisted that he could explain to all our edification even without the charts. Instead of turning over and covering their heads to make him go away, the horsemen rose and hunched over the symbols that he made on a flat stone with the charcoal end of a stick in the fire. And he pointed up at the sky, where he said that the bright red star shining there was closer to the earth than it would be for another thousand years.

"Then, because we were all awake already, he said that he would tell us the story of the great competition of astronomers in the capital. Do you know what took place?"

Li Du did. The trouble had begun in 1659, before Li Du was born, but the final confrontation had occurred ten years later, when he was a child. Curious to know how Pieter had told it, he said that he did not remember it well. So Hamza began: "I tell you this tale as it was told to me by the black-robed holy man of Agra.

"Long ago, when China existed only in the pale space between night and sunrise, the first Emperor said that a golden light would appear in the east. His people looked to the horizon, and at the Emperor's command, a dragon with scales of liquid fire appeared there. And so the sun rose on the empire.

"From that time on, the emperors of China have foretold the nights on which the moon would shine full, the nights when it would slice the sky like the cut of a curved blade, and the nights that it would be absent from the firmament. They have announced the arrival of the stars of winter, and those of summer. And they have presided over eclipses.

"But many thousands of years have passed since the first Emperor invited the dragon to his sky. Yes, the dragon's flame still burns. And yes, the mountains have not moved. But there have been changes. Knowledge was gained, and knowledge was lost. The emperors forgot the language of the dragons, and could no longer speak with them. The astronomers discovered ancient patterns in the sky. And they described these patterns in new languages that only they could understand.

"And so it came to be that the emperors of China made their predictions according to calendars delivered annually by the astronomers. This was kept secret, so that the grandeur of the emperor was not diminished in the eyes of his people. The years continued to pass, and the work of the astronomers was disrupted by war and famine and rebellion.

"When the Kangxi's father became Emperor of China, neither the Chinese astronomers nor the Manchu shamans were certain of their knowledge. The calendars had become inaccurate. Months of study yielded incorrect predictions. The Emperor could not rely on them.

"To this court came a great astronomer, the Jesuit Father Schall von Bell. His predictions were so accurate that the Emperor was amazed. The Emperor began to rely on the foreign priest, and to honor him. Where others could not approach the Emperor, Father Schall sat in his company as an old friend. He presided over a new board of mathematics. He translated his books into Chinese. He taught young scholars.

"But the jealous astronomers and shamans hated the man who had supplanted them. When the Emperor died, and the regents assumed power, the old shamans saw their chance. They denounced the Jesuits as despisers of the gods, rebels against China, and teachers of evil. Father Schall was imprisoned and sentenced to death.

"When the moment came for his execution,

a trembling rose from deep within the earth. It cracked the walls of the Forbidden City, and as the palace shook, a darkness came across the sky. A flaming dragon appeared in the heavens, and struck the room of the palace where the sentence had been delivered, exploding it to white and gray ash that whirled through the gardens and mixed with the falling plum blossom petals.

"Terrified, the regents delayed the execution. Then Father Verbiest arrived in Beijing. He was thrown into prison with his brothers, uncertain of his fate. But from his cell, weighted down by nine chains, Father Verbiest called out a challenge. 'Let it be a competition,' he cried, 'for there is coming upon the land an eclipse of the sun. Let your shamans and your astronomers predict the minute the earth will be dark. If I am more accurate than they, then pardon my brothers and accept me as your servant.'

"The challenge was set. There were three predictions: The Manchu shamans said that the eclipse would come at noon, the Muslim astrologer of the Chinese court said that the eclipse would come a quarter of an hour later, and Father Verbiest said the eclipse would not come until three quarters past midday.

"The day came, and the whole court came out to wait together in their finery. The noon hour approached, the water clock dripped its seconds into a lacquered bucket, and the sun blazed. Noon came and went. The quarter hour came and went. Still the sun blazed. Then, as the third quarter of the hour drew near, the crowd burst into noise as a curving, black emptiness bit the sun. At the exact minute that Father Verbiest had predicted, the two disks aligned, and a ring of white light flared around the black emptiness.

"Ever since then, the Jesuits have been responsible for the astronomical calendar. Their role is not publicly acknowledged. Once a year the calendar is delivered, quietly, to the Emperor's chambers. So it was that Brother Pieter came to serve Father Verbiest, and to aid him in the construction of the observatory whose astrolabes and steel measures rise against the northern sky beside the grinning pagodas and mosaic dragons."

Hamza finished and they sat in silence, Hamza looking at the web of white and black and molten coals in the brazier, Li Du looking up through the lanterns at the stars.

"So that is how Pieter related the story to you?" asked Li Du.

Hamza nodded very sincerely. "I removed a few of the less interesting details."

"And added the flaming dragons, per-haps?"

"Not at all — I was assured of the story's veracity on that point."

Li Du smiled. "And how did the Khampa like the story?"

"Kalden Dorjee said that the shamans in his village are not like the Manchu shamans in the capital city. In Kalden's village the shamans are elders, grandfathers to all the children. They share butter tea around the fire, listening to the creaks and murmurs of the yaks in the barns below. They give the children their names — they give comfort. It is only in palaces where the shamans become like bureaucrats."

"It is strange," said Li Du. "In a few days the Emperor will preside over an eclipse here in this place. In order for that predic-tion to occur there were, as you say, bureau-crats, strategies, competitions and argu-ments and decisions and bribes. An entire year of these calculating little moments. But when it happens, no one will think of those things — of a calendar written by foreigners a year ago, or of the Kangxi's calculations about which province was most in need of renewed subjugation. The audience will see only magic, flowers of fire in the sky, dragon canals and acrobats. And when the Emperor appears to exert his power over the sun, they will revere him for it."

"In two days he will be here," said Hamza. "What will you do tomorrow?"

Li Du drank the last of his wine, stood up, and dusted the flecks of ash from his robes. "In the morning I will go to the mansion. I would like to know what Pieter was looking at on the day he died."

■ ■ ■ ■

2 Days

■ ■ ■ ■

CHAPTER 12

Mu Gao was in the library, sweeping the marble floor with a broom woven of dried reeds. Using the broom in place of his cane, he shuffled and swept and shuffled and swept, and with each step the fine dust rose in a cloud. Behind him, most of it settled gently back to the floor.

Li Du cleared his throat quietly, not wanting to startle the old man. There was no reaction. Mu Gao continued to sweep, his eyes on the floor. Li Du moved to stand in front of him, until finally Mu Gao realized that someone was there.

He stopped sweeping and peered at Li Du. "Why didn't you say you were here?" he asked. "It's frightening, a person appearing from nowhere." He squinted. "I've met you. You're the librarian from the big city."

"We spoke yesterday evening." They were standing in one of the seven rows of the philosophy section, surrounded by silk book boxes gleaming sapphire blue. Mu Gao squinted again.

"You told me about the argument between the man who died and the foreign merchant," said Li Du.

"I remember," said Mu Gao gruffly. "You think I don't remember. So you're still looking for the murderer. Well what do you want now? I'm sweeping."

"I came to ask you about the jewelvine that you keep in the library."

Mu Gao's watery eyes sharpened. "That's what killed him then? Jewelvine? You want to see where I keep it?"

Li Du followed Mu Gao to a cabinet against the wall near the main door of the library. It was almost as tall as Li Du, with drawers in a column down the center and two closed cabinets on either side. The dark, lacquered wood was inlaid with faint golden illustrations, the largest of which depicted a drunken poet holding up his bowl of wine and composing poetry for a seated prince.

Mu Gao slid one of the drawers open. Inside, neatly arranged, were several whole roots, wiped clean and dried, a small stone mortar and pestle, and a shallow bowl filled with fine powder. Li Du touched a fingertip gently to the powder and raised his hand to examine it closely.

"Careful with that!" exclaimed Mu Gao. "I wrap my hands when I use it."

"That is wise. Do you keep this drawer locked?"

"No."

"And have you seen anyone taking powder from it?"

Mu Gao shook his head. "Haven't seen anyone touch it. But they come for the things in the other drawers. There's the paste — there — and paperweights, thread, brushes, and ink here. Lady Chen accounts for all of it in her inventories. She's stingy with the paper and ink."

"Then someone may have taken the powder without you noticing?"

Mu Gao sucked at his lips and shrugged. "Sometimes I fall asleep. You think the poisoner is in the mansion?"

"I don't think that anyone outside the mansion would have known to find jewelvine here in this drawer. Can it be purchased in the market?"

"No. I told you, it's my recipe. Never seen it in the market. But I didn't kill him."

"On the evening he died, after the argument you recounted to me, there was a banquet. I did not see you there."

Mu Gao's answer was gruff. "I don't go to the banquets. I was in town drinking with my friend."

"You were there in the afternoon, and again in the evening?"

Mu Gao's lips spread into a gaping smile. "In the afternoon we drink tea. And in the evening we drink alcohol."

"I see. And what is your friend's name?"

"Old Mu."

"A relative?"

"Cousin. Used to be a lot of us in Dayan. We drink together and talk about old times."

"And when did you return to the mansion that night?"

"It was late. The guard at the gate told me the old foreigner was dead. I went to my room and lit incense. I'd talked to him that same day — thought of his spirit wandering the mansion made me nervous. But why are you questioning me? I didn't kill him."

A step on the marble floor made them look up. Silhouetted in the door of the library was the tall figure of Brother Martin, his hair golden in the sun. He came forward, and his green eyes flicked nervously from Mu Gao's face to Li Du's. Then with a look of determination he launched into a spate of nonsense Chinese, repeating and attempting to correct himself as his cheeks turned feverish, uneven red.

"His Chinese is very bad," said Mu Gao.

266

Brother Martin stuttered into silence, then said in Latin to Li Du, "I am so sorry. I am trying to learn but I cannot remember the tones."

"It is good that you are practicing," said Li Du, "and you are doing very well. Are you here to speak to me?"

"To speak to you?"

"You may not have heard that I am investigating the death of Brother Pieter."

"I — What? I thought Brother Pieter — I thought that he was poisoned by the men he traveled with. Sir Gray told me that they were bandits."

"They were suspected at first, but now we know that they were not responsible."

"Ah — Well, if I can be of any use — of course. But I — In fact I came in search of a book. The *Ben Cao Gang Mu*." He pronounced the words slowly and looked anxiously at Li Du for affirmation. Li Du, eyebrows raised, said, "Of course I know that book. And I am sure that the magistrate has a copy of it here. Mu Gao will help us find it in the catalogue."

"Oh, thank you — you are very kind. Doctor Yang recommended it to me for help in my plant identifications. He is taking me with him today to collect herbs, and I thought I would consult the book first."

"But how do you communicate with him?"

Brother Martin gave a self-deprecating smile. "He is very patient. And his knowledge of the plants here puts me in awe. I — I have my own modest understanding of certain species. As long as we restrict our discussion to flowers and berries and trees we can speak together. He taught me to say the title of the compendium."

They located the book on a shelf carved with the constellation called *net,* and carried its ten volumes, bound in faintly yellowed white, to the round center table. Brother Martin opened to a page, and Li Du saw his face transform. His expressions had always fallen along a spectrum of shame, discomfort, anxiety, and confusion. The man Li Du saw now was intelligent, focused. His fingers moved across the page deftly, tapping specific parts of the colored illustrations — a root, a petal, a fruit — and nodding slightly in understanding and affirmation of what he saw.

"This is exquisite," Brother Martin said. "This text — what does it say?"

Li Du read: *"Grows in wet ground; strong and bitter; cures swelling boils and is to be drunk hot."* The words were printed beside a picture of a pink and white flower with dark green leaves and white, clawlike roots.

"And this one?"

"Grows in the south of Tiger Leaping Gorge. Is sweet, cures thirst, and is to be eaten raw."

"This one" — Brother Martin pointed to another illustration — "this is the one I want to see. Kaempfer saw it in Japan — he calls it gingko. It is a tree that the botanists in England say has not grown on earth since before the flood, many thousands of years ago. Explorers have found stone impressions of ancient gingko leaves in Europe, but the doctor says he will show me a living one here. I am — I just can't believe it." His eyes pleaded for his enthusiasm to be understood and shared.

"That silverplum?" asked Li Du. "But it is common here. They grow in the courtyards of the temples. The doctor is going to take you to see one?"

"I am to meet him when the water clocks strikes nine chimes. I have some time still to study."

Li Du considered how to speak to the nervous young man. He decided to wait to mention the letter, and instead to take a more subtle approach. He still had very little sense of who the man was. "I have not had the opportunity," he said, "to speak to you since the night that Brother Pieter died. These must have been difficult days."

Brother Martin kept his gaze on the book that was open before him, but Li Du saw that his eyes were fixed, no longer scanning the illustrations.

"You are very young to have traveled so far on your own," Li Du went on. "Did your superiors not think it wise to send you here in the company of someone more experienced with the ways of this country?"

"I — I am from a small house," said Brother Martin. "I was the only brother among us with the will and ability to make the journey."

"And where did you travel from? You did not come from the north."

"No. I traveled overland from Calcutta. I did hire guides along the way."

"And have you come with some particular purpose? To see the Emperor?"

Brother Martin's reply was quick. "No. I have nothing to say to the Emperor. That is" — he struggled to make himself clear — "nothing to say that is worth his time to hear. I came because I have always wanted to see China. That is, to see its plants. I — I study plants. Their medicinal uses." He indicated the book in front of him. "In England," he went on, "where I am from, originally, there are many scholars and — and other brothers of my order, who have

270

heard of the wondrous plants in the mountains of China. But no one is allowed to come in. I have waited a long time in Calcutta, just hoping . . ." He trailed off.

"And then the invitation from the Emperor arrived."

"Yes. The word spread. I think that it was the East India Company ships that first brought the news. I heard of it, and began to make plans immediately. I thought that such an opportunity could not be missed, even if I had to travel alone. I — I do not care much for Calcutta. The Christian orders — the other ones, you know, the Dominicans and the Capuchins, they are very competitive with each other, and with us. And then there are the crowds, and the disease. It inspires awe. Hindu pagodas across from Mughal minarets and even cathedrals, now. People from every empire, every country I know in the world. But it is not a friendly place."

Brother Martin turned his attention studiously back to the open books, while Li Du considered what he had just been told.

Mu Gao had been observing the interaction with a sleepy expression. Li Du said to him, "I would like to see the item that Brother Pieter examined on the day he died. Will you open the door for me?"

"Won't get me in trouble, will it?"

"The magistrate said that I would be given access to anything I needed."

"All right, then — no bother for me to do it."

They walked slowly between the shelves to the twin doors at the back of the library. As before, the book sunning room was open, the hall of treasures closed. The bright dragons coiled down the wood like hanging vines, white painted pearls clasped firmly in their jaws.

Brother Martin had risen from his seat and followed them. "Are you leaving?" he asked.

Li Du quickly considered the factors and decided that Brother Martin's presence could be helpful. "This is where the tribute from the English East India Company is being kept — you recall that Pieter spoke of it at the banquet."

Brother Martin glanced toward the window. "I only just heard the eighth chime. May I come with you? I am curious to see that device — the tellurion." Li Du nodded. Mu Gao withdrew his key ring from where it hung amid the folds of his coat. He unlocked the door.

The room was cooler and much darker than the rest of the library. It was a cavernous space, the ceiling high enough that the tops of the shelves lining the walls were lost in the dim upper corners. The windows were thin rectangles in one wall, too narrow for anyone to pass through, admitting only narrow beams of light into the room.

On and around a table in one corner was a mass of crates of various sizes, perhaps fifteen or twenty in total, made from rough wooden boards and stamped with the black seal of the Company. A few of the ornate boxes had been removed from the protective crates, and sat on the table, treasures in and of themselves. One was inlaid with mother of pearl. Another was painted with Arabic script surrounded by gold and silver flowers. Another was carved with elephants wearing jewel-studded saddles.

The largest of these was a box of obsidian black lacquered wood. It was a cube with sides a little more than the width of a large man's shoulders. Affixed to each of the four sides was a dragon of hammered gold. The four dragons appeared to claw their way up the sides of the box, and their tails formed hooks that fastened the top of the box to the base. Their arching backs were handles by which the box could be lifted away from its contents, and the mouths of the dragons were open in hisses, the muscles of their bodies tensed to defend the treasure inside.

"This one," said Mu Gao. "After he'd opened this box, he had no more interest in the others. Not that I saw when I glanced in at him."

Carefully, Li Du slipped the dragon tail hooks from their clasps. He gripped the dragon handles on two sides of the box and lifted it straight up and away. He was just tall enough to raise the cover higher than the contents. He set the lid down carefully, then stood back to look at what he had uncovered. Mu Gao looked from Li Du's to Brother Martin's faces with the smug, possessive expression of one who has seen a wondrous sight already and feels ownership over it.

The bottom of the box was the foundation for a cylindrical golden base. From the golden disk rose the empire of China. Li Du's gaze traversed mosaic fields of jade and lapis lazuli, crossed dark quartz mountains, and descended along sapphire rivers to the sea, on which sailed a tiny golden ship with red silk sails the size of a fly's wing.

These glittering imitations of the natural world circumscribed the miniature walls and gates and towers of the great capital itself. He saw the tiered roofs of the drum towers, the obsidian gates of the Forbidden

City. He saw gardens of diamond and sapphire flowers, moonstone and tiger's-eye ponds, cherry trees laden with opal snow, silver and blue and red roof tiles, and there, nestled close to the west wall, a tiny replica of the royal library, his library.

But all of this was, incredibly, only decoration. The tellurion itself rose from the center of the Forbidden City in a chaotic skeleton of jointed rods and spoked disks. Five of these rods were fixed at the end with polished metal spheres of varied size and hue. From deep within the gears and spokes Li Du could hear the soft clicks of mechanical movement. In the center a sixth orb, the largest, rose above the other spheres. It was made of red glass encased in a net of yellow gold as thin as thread, and it was gently, inexplicably glowing.

This tellurion was a treasure to mesmerize kings and poets, an object of art, of science, of magic. Looking at it, Li Du became aware of a prickling at his nape. He imagined the metal spokes unfolding into the legs of a clockwork monster that would crack and crush the mountains and towers of the jeweled empire.

He thought of the nights he had passed alone with the stars, when he had found comfort in the incomprehensible eternity of the heavens. He had felt in those moments, as when he had stood in the cloud on the mountain, that he was removed from the cycle of endings and beginnings. The tellurion had the opposite effect. To him it seemed a faceted prison, forcing all the energy, all of the infinite power of the world into the clicking movements of a cold thing.

"That must be phosphorus," said Brother Martin, intrigued.

"I have not heard that word before," said Li Du.

Brother Martin explained. "They call it the 'fiery noctiluca' as well — the chemical that glows. It is very new — I have seen it at demonstrations."

Li Du leaned closer to the orb. "And it just emits light indefinitely?"

"They say its inner fire is fed with air — a stoppered bottle will dim after some time, but — look here, their little sun has tiny holes — the clockwork must somehow allow a steady stream of air inside. They must have planned it carefully, though — too little air and its fires will dim, too much . . . Well, at one of the demonstrations the alchemist wiped his knife on his apron, and minutes later we saw the cloth burst into flame."

"I understand better why Sir Gray was so

adamant that it not be dropped," said Li Du, remembering Sir Gray's furious commands to the servants as they had unloaded his cart.

"It really is marvelous," Brother Martin said. "Look how the sun sparkles as it burns. The planets are moving around it, but the calibration is so fine that the eye cannot see the movement. It is too slow. A clock for the heavens."

Li Du remembered the night of the banquet and said, "That is how Pieter described it, as a clock."

Brother Martin reached out to touch, very gently, the glowing sphere. "In this model the sun is at the center, as Newton declares it to be. But our church holds the earth to be the center. It is a great debate between men of science and men of religion. The Pope allows for the use of equations that have sound practical purpose, but forbids their assumptions from being called truth. That is the word that causes the trouble. It is a delicate situation, dangerous, for some people." Brother Martin paused, staring at the glowing sun. "Whoever made this knew that without the sun in the center, the object would be of no practical use. It could not have served its intended purpose — to make accurate forecasts of how the heavens will move."

"But," said Li Du, "as a holy man, you must follow the teachings of your church?"

"Yes, of course. But it is a complicated situation. Brother Pieter was an astronomer. For his calculations to be correct, he must have assumed the sun to be at the center. It is all about how one speaks of these things in public circumstances."

"Now that is something our empires and churches have in common." Li Du leaned closer, trying to see some resemblance to the sky in the orientation of the spheres, but could not. He said, wonderingly, "And can you read it now?"

Brother Martin blushed. "Oh — no — I did not mean to imply that I could. I do not speak the numerical language necessary to understand these symbols. I doubt anyone other than a very skilled astronomer could actually use this to make a prediction — the device is almost as difficult to read as the night sky itself."

"Of course," said Li Du, "but its beauty is accessible to any observer. Even a king with no interest in astronomy would be eager to possess such a marvel, I think."

Mu Gao, who had been listening to the Latin without comprehension, said, "After he — the dead man — took off the lid, he looked at the thing inside from every angle. I saw him through the door. Like a poet studying a tree. He was talking to himself and smiling and writing in his book. Seemed very happy."

Li Du remembered the torn pages he had found among Pieter's papers. "A book?" he said. "You mean a journal?"

"Yes. Like the travelers carry, but with the strange foreign binding. Leather."

"And he took this book with him when he left?"

Mu Gao shrugged. "Didn't see. Must have."

Li Du looked at the base of the tellurion. There were hundreds of numbers and symbols etched into its base, ticks and reference points and arrows, none of which meant anything to him. He tried to remember what Pieter had said specifically when he had spoken of it at the banquet, but he had only an impression of excitement and enthusiasm. Whatever had upset Pieter later in the evening, it did not seem to be related to the tellurion.

The ninth chime sounded, drifting through the thin windows. Together Li Du and Brother Martin lowered the box back over the tellurion, and Li Du clasped it shut.

The three of them left the room, and Mu Gao made his way immediately to the pillows by the window.

Li Du and Brother Martin departed the library together, and at the gate of the mansion Brother Martin said, "I am late to meet the doctor. I — I am sure that I cannot be of help to you, but of course — if you have any need of me — well, I will do what I can."

"I'll help you find the way to the doctor's house," said Li Du.

"Oh — no, that is all right," Brother Martin protested awkwardly.

But Li Du insisted, and they walked together at a quick pace toward the western outskirts of the city.

"I find myself a little unclear in my memories of the banquet," said Li Du. "Perhaps I drank too much wine. Would you refresh my memory of where you and Brother Pieter met?"

"Where we met? But — but we met only briefly the day I arrived. I was very ill. I only really spoke to him for the first time on the night of the banquet."

"Ah — I meant to ask where you met before you saw each other here in Dayan."

Brother Martin shook his head. "There is some mistake," he said. "I had never met him before that night."

"Ah — then I am sorry. I was confused. So you did not know each other in India?"

Brother Martin was adamant that they had not. He said, a little breathlessly, "He — he did not — Did he tell you that he knew me?"

"No — as you said, I was mistaken."

They were almost at the doctor's house. Brother Martin started to speak several times, but each time he stopped and reconsidered. Finally he said, "I know that I am a suspect. But I swear to you that I did not kill him. He — he was very kind to me. And I could never kill anyone . . ." He trailed off as they arrived at the door of the doctor's home.

They were welcomed into a modest courtyard home permeated by the sweet fragrance of angelica. Dried herbs and shucked corn hung in bunches from the eaves on all sides of the porch. Doctor Yang led them between woven bamboo trays spread with seeds and roots drying in the sunny courtyard, and into the family's main room.

Brother Martin, unable to remain still, asked timidly whether he might look at the plants and mixtures spread around the room. The doctor nodded and watched benevolently as Brother Martin examined a sealed glass jar full of distilled barley liquor, infused with goji berries that had settled into a deep layer at the bottom of the jar.

Li Du sat with the doctor by the raised platform fireplace in the center of the room. "You are taking him to the temple today?" he asked.

With an indulgent smile, the doctor turned the ears of corn that he had nestled at the fire's edge to roast. "Despite appearances," he said, "the man is clever. He does not know the correct words, but he knows the plants. I am going in the direction of the temple anyway — one of the monks is going to give me dried wormwood. So I will show this man the old gingko."

Li Du accepted the corncob that was handed to him. It was burning hot and he held it with the very tips of his fingers as it cooled. The kernels were cooked to a sweet dark crust, and smelled of sugar and smoke. He inhaled gratefully, almost unwilling to change the subject. But he had come to the doctor for a reason.

"I have a question about the man who died in the mansion."

The doctor's expressive face flattened immediately, and when he spoke it was in a stiff, offended tone. "I made a mistake. The man was very old, and I have never seen a deceased foreigner. It is impossible to make the same conclusions. Their skin, their temperature — everything about them is different."

"But in the moment you did believe that he had died of natural causes?"

"Of course I did. What was it that killed him then? What poison?"

"Jewelvine root. Was his death consistent with that toxin?"

The doctor clicked his tongue, then said defensively, "I've never seen a person dead of jewelvine. But it could have been, in a person that age. If it can't be purged, it would stop the breathing and cause death very quickly, especially in an elderly individual."

"I was told that after you examined the body, the magistrate spoke certain words to you. According to the witness, those words appeared to cause you some distress. May I ask what the magistrate said?"

Doctor Yang slowly poured more water into Li Du's teacup and then into his own, concentrating harder than necessary on the task. Brother Martin's cup was still full, and the doctor returned the kettle to the blackened hook dangling over the flame. Finally he said, "I don't recall. Of course we were all very upset."

"He was not instructing you to say that the death was natural, no matter what you found?"

Doctor Yang was silent, his mouth a straight line over his wispy beard.

"I do not want to bring you trouble," said Li Du. "But I have very little time in which to discover the truth. Even the smallest actions are important to me. Did the magistrate tell you to say that the death was natural?"

After a pause, Doctor Yang gave a short nod. He looked up and saw that Li Du still held the cooling ear of corn in his fingers. "Eat," he said, sternly. "You look too thin."

Obediently Li Du took a bite of corn. It was fresh and sweet. Doctor Yang nodded in approval. "Good. And now I will answer your question, because you have already guessed. The magistrate did as you said. He told me that an old man had died, and that I must not cause a panic. He said that the man had been frail. He said that I was not to mention anything unusual about the death to anyone."

"And did you?"

"I have studied illnesses and remedies my whole life. I told the magistrate the man could have been poisoned. He replied that he would take what action he thought necessary, and ordered me not to bring up the matter again, to him or to anyone."

Li Du nodded. "Thank you for telling me the truth," he said.

Again gesturing for Li Du to continue eating, the doctor said, "I hope it helps you. I am told that you must discover what happened before the Emperor arrives. That is a very great obligation. Will you do it?"

Li Du did not answer the question directly. Instead, he glanced at Brother Martin. "I have more to discuss with that young man," he said finally. "You will bring him back this evening?"

The doctor was taken aback. "I suppose he may have known the use of the jewelvine, but he seems a very unlikely assassin," he said.

Li Du nodded. "I agree. But we all have secrets, and I am afraid he is no exception. Also, he is a brother of the same church as that of the man who died. Even if he is not involved, he may be in danger."

They looked at Brother Martin, who had busied himself with inspecting a pile of walnuts left for hulling, his fingers turning inky black from the juices. As if sensing that he was being discussed, he looked up at them and smiled nervously. Li Du rose, thanked the doctor and his wife for the tea, and took his leave.

It had occurred to him that there was one thing of which he could be certain for the next few hours. Brother Martin's room was empty, and had not been touched by its occupant since he had learned of the new investigation. It was possible that he had left something there that he would not want found.

CHAPTER 13

Hoh was delighted to accompany Li Du and Hamza through a well-tended glade of green bamboo to the door of Brother Martin's room, and left unwillingly when he was called away almost immediately to welcome new guests. Li Du, relieved, watched the innkeeper bustle away before he pulled open the carved doors.

His first impression of the room was that of a long-abandoned home into which nature has begun to reassert itself. The desk was piled with drifts of leaves, early spring greens curling into dry brown shells. On the floor were scattered haloes of brown twigs, wilting petals, dustings of powdery yellow pollen, and crushed seed husks.

It took him a moment before he recognized the methodical human presence within the mess. On the floor by the desk stood three tall stacks of stained and brittle paper. Plants were pressed between the sheets, making some layers thicker and more uneven than others. In an attempt to weigh them down, the piles had been crowned with improvised weights gathered from around the room: jade figurines, a wrought-iron serpent, several books, and, bridging two of the piles, the marble head-rest from the bed.

"Is the man a magician?" asked Hamza, picking up a slim pine branch from a chair and examining it. "I see no runes carved here."

Li Du examined a small leather folder fastened shut with a loop of string. He opened it and drew out a sheaf of papers. They were letters of introduction and permissions to travel, meticulously translated so that each document existed in both Latin and Chinese. He set the letters on the table and examined them one at a time.

He said, half to himself, "These all have Brother Martin's name on them. Martin Walpole — his full name."

"Why wouldn't they?"

"This letter here," said Li Du, holding it so that the light fell on the writing, "is from another Jesuit. This is their sign." He indicated the sunburst surrounding the initials *I-H-S*.

"The letter charges the bearer to collect

plants for the compendium of the world's botanical wonders . . ." Li Du skimmed the rest. "And here it is stamped by the inspection official at the Chinese border, confirming that the bearer of the letter has permission to travel and to collect specimens in this province."

Hamza looked over Li Du's shoulder. "It looks like all the other letters. Every traveler carries documents like these."

Li Du picked up a different sheet of paper and held it beside the first. "This is the letter of permission for Brother Martin merely to enter China. Both of these letters bear the same inspection official's seal. But see the difference in the paper. One of these letters is old, the other new."

"But you do not need to analyze the quality of the paper. Just look at the dates written on them."

"I did," said Li Du. "The permission to collect plants is dated a month ago. But on the letter that grants entry, the one that appears older, the date is smudged. Someone has spilled a drop of oil onto it. See how the paper is transparent?"

"Ah. Then what is the explanation?"

Li Du thought for a moment. He took the letters to the open door and studied them, one at a time, in the sunlight. Then he nodded, confident in his analysis. "The newer letter is a forgery. The older letter is authentic."

"How do you know that?"

Li Du handed the older letter to Hamza. "See how the ink of the official's seal is pressed onto the paper?" He mimed the stamping of the seal. Then he handed Hamza the other page. "This one appears to have been stamped in the same way with the same seal. But if you look very closely you can see brush strokes. This seal was painted, not stamped."

He peered at it again. "It was not poorly done. The forger probably patted it with crumpled paper to mimic the look of a stamp. But I have some experience in this area."

"What experience?" asked Hamza, taking the papers from Li Du and looking from one to the other with a dubious expression.

A forgotten memory was returning to Li Du. "A man once came to the library in Beijing with a manuscript he claimed was written in Li Bai's own hand. The paper was the correct age. The commentary in the margins was appropriate to the period. But Li Bai had a quick hand, and I could see by the weight of the ink that the forger had made the strokes slowly, no doubt concentrating hard to produce them." He gestured at the papers Hamza held and finished, "This is an amateur effort in comparison."

Hamza looked at the papers again. "They still look the same to me," he said, "but then again, I do not spend very much time with paper and ink. Does this explain what Brother Martin is hiding?"

"I am not sure, but I would say that this letter, the authentic one that grants Brother Martin permission to enter China, is at least ten years old."

Hamza's face brightened with understanding. "Ah!" he said. "He cannot have been a traveling Jesuit ten years ago. Not unless he was an exceptional child."

"My thought exactly."

"So how did he come by the letter?"

"Either he stole it, or someone gave it to him." Li Du was thoughtful, remembering Pieter's comment about Brother Martin's name. "Pieter noticed something strange about Martin Walpole when they were first introduced, but he chose not to say anything. I will likewise give the young man the benefit of the doubt until we have spoken to him."

"But what if Brother Pieter's silence was his fatal mistake? What if he knew something about this forger and was killed before he could speak?"

"I intend to be careful."

Hamza ran his finger over the dusty, pollen-coated tabletop and said, "There are more ways to kill a man than by poisoning his tea or stabbing him in the dark. Did you know that in the desert of Samara the sun is so hot that you can burn a man to ash simply by using a mirror to direct a sunbeam onto him?"

"I did not know that," said Li Du, "but I did read once in a book that there is a stone taken from the stomach of a cow that can heal a dying man of any wound."

"The *haranzi*," said Hamza, delighted. "I myself held such a stone to the tail of an injured mermaid, and as thanks she rewarded me with one of her scales, harder than a diamond and possessed of more colors than exist between black and white. I gave this scale as a gift to one of the twelve princesses of Samarqand."

"And do you still have the stone that healed the mermaid?"

"Alas, I do not. I wagered it on a game of *shatranj*, and was defeated. Should you meet a woman who calls herself Diloram and has an elephant tattooed on her left wrist, do not bet your possessions in a competition with her. It is a great shame —

a healing stone would be a comfort in this city."

Li Du acknowledged this with a nod. "I think that we have found all that we can in this room, and we cannot waste the time going after Brother Martin — we must assume that the doctor will bring him back this evening as promised. I will go to the festival field — the magistrate told me that Nicholas Gray will be there today."

Hamza made a dismissive gesture with one hand. "I cannot help you with him. Ambassadors. Trade. Diplomacy. These subjects make me feel that I have fallen into a swamp and am breathing mud. I will go to the mansion and eavesdrop on the servants."

They agreed to meet again at the dinner hour, and Li Du set off again through the streets of Dayan. As he walked, he passed several of the ornate posted schedules of the festival events. He winced slightly at the reminder of the inevitability of the Kangxi's arrival. The date and hour were there, proudly emblazoned, marking the end of his investigation. Two days.

On a low wall in the eastern section of the city, he saw faint traces of gray against the newly painted white. He recognized the tacky streaks as paper glue, and wondered whether this was the site of one of the pieces of anti-Qing graffiti, or whether some eager tourist had stolen an official schedule as a memento.

As he neared the edge of the city, he began to hear the strikes and echoes of hammer blows, the whine of pulleys, and the staccato commands of guards and officials. At the apex of a steep cobbled road the city came to an abrupt end, and Li Du was confronted with the festival field in its last, frantic stages of construction.

Before he could take another step he was hailed by two bannermen wearing identical blue robes with high collars fastened at the neck with copper buttons. Their hats were black, decorated with single peacock feathers and held under their chins by thin silk cords. Each man had, slung across his back, a bow of mottled wood and a quiver of arrows with black and red feathers. Fixed to their slim, blue-and-gold belts were swords in green sheaths from which blue tassels dangled. Their sturdy black boots were slightly turned up at the toes, the white soles muddied from the field. They stood before him, blocking his further progress.

The bannerman on the left, a young man with high cheekbones and two thin tufts of a mustache drooping all the way down to frame his tiny, sharp chin, said, "Visitors are not permitted here until the first day of the festival. Return to the city center — there are entertainers in the market and in the teahouses." His tone was impatient, as if he was tired of giving the same order.

"I am on an errand for the magistrate. Please tell me where I can find the foreign ambassador."

The guard looked doubtfully at Li Du's patched robe, worn shoes, and faded coat. "You are the magistrate's investigator?"

"I am."

The guards hesitated, but a moment later their attention was distracted by raised voices nearby. One construction worker was accusing another of laying down a crooked line of mosaic tiles, thus destroying the fountain pavilion. The other worker was defending himself, and their argument was on the brink of coming to blows. The guards started in the direction of the quarreling men, waving Li Du on toward the far end of the field.

"Go on," one of them said, speaking over his shoulder. "The foreigner is there by the Emperor's podium. Watch where you step — the peasants toss bricks around like they're scattering seeds for planting. Almost had my head taken off yesterday."

Li Du raised his hand to shield his eyes from the glare, and looked at the structure at the farthest end of the field from him. The ground sloped upward from the edge of the city, and the three-tiered edifice silhouetted against the sky appeared to sit on the horizon. Half of it was scaffolded in a clinging skeleton of ladders and ropes, and figures teemed over and around it like sparrows filling the branches of a tree.

Between him and the pavilion was an expanse of furrowed, upturned earth and nearly finished stages painted with bright clouds and dragons and birds. His progress was impeded by the curves of a narrow canal that wound down from the top of the field toward him. It was half decorated and would soon be a serpentine dragon, with gold and iron lantern hooks set on its banks in imitation of claws. Gardeners kneeled on both sides of the water, planting blooming camellias in the cold dirt to disguise the plowed earth and to outline the shape of the creature. Arching stone bridges paved with gleaming vermilion tiles crossed the canal at regular intervals.

It took him almost ten minutes to reach the base of the grand pavilion, and by the time he arrived there he was breathing hard from air thick with dust, smoke, and the smell of paint. He craned his head back to look at the building now rising straight above him, filling his vision, even taller than it had appeared from his vantage point at the edge of the city.

The emperor's pavilion was three levels high, with three broad gabled roofs turned up at the corners to reveal painted carvings in layer upon layer like the gills of a mushroom. On each corner ridge of the roofs paraded sculpted clay guardians: dragons, cats, dogs, lions, and phoenixes, each figure unique in color and pose. Li Du, standing at the base of the structure, was too close to see the top of it, where the Emperor would stand, but he saw the stairs leading up to that level, subtly built into the back of the structure so that the audience in the field would not see the Emperor climb them.

Nicholas Gray was standing with an official beside a stack of ornate wooden beams in an unusual spectrum of shades and textures, whorls and polishes. Next to the piled wood was the dirty, discarded cloth that had been used to protect the pieces from damage on the journey from Calcutta.

Gray had exchanged his gilded diplomat's robes for simple clothes and worn boots. His sunburned forehead was furrowed in concentration, and he was alternating his gaze between the beams beside him and the top tier of the pavilion. He was speaking in clipped Chinese, and the official was nodding obsequiously in response.

When Li Du spoke, Gray's expression was momentarily blank. Then recognition dawned. "Ah," he said, "the magistrate's cousin. You speak Latin. What a relief. I have been struggling with your Chinese words all morning, and the exertion is draining my capacity for clear thinking. Will you help me explain to this man that the beams are to be placed on the top pavilion under my direction? I want the Emperor to be able to see them — they are for him, not for the crowd. I will show this man how they are to be fitted together once they are lifted to the top." He spoke loudly, as if that made his words more likely to be understood, and performed an exaggerated series of movements, miming the process of fastening the wood to the end of a rope and wheeling it up with a pulley.

Li Du translated Gray's words for the official, who insisted that he understood and began issuing orders for the pieces to be tied up and wheeled to the top platform via the pulley, as Gray had indicated. Gray, preparing to help lift the wood, pushed the sleeves of his coat up above his forearms and kneeled to raise one end of a beam. But the official waved him away. The wood, he said, was very light, and they could lift it without assistance.

In the cold brightness of daylight, Li Du noticed for the first time that one of Gray's arms was hairless and traced with the puckered striations of burn scars. The wounds had healed long ago, but the injury when it happened must have been grave. The pull of ravaged skin looked painful even now, and Li Du averted his gaze.

Once Gray was assured that the beams were all being raised to the top level of the pavilion, he dusted off his hands and turned to Li Du. "This wood is very rare — our English elm is as fine as your famous pear tree. That is rosewood, and that one is mahogany. And this here is the finest — it is made from bog oak. Do you see the shine of purple deep in its whorls? Its color is unmatched in the natural world."

"It is an odd shape," said Li Du, scrutinizing the piece. It was a column as one would usually see made of marble in foreign architecture. The flat top of the capital had a large, round indentation in it, lined with velvet.

"Ah," said Gray, with pride. "That was specially designed to display the tellurion.

See how its base will fit there?" He pointed to the round indentation. "It keeps the tellurion at the proper height so that it may easily be admired. We want the Emperor to experience all of the treasures to their best advantage. I am grateful to you for serving as translator just now. It is my hope, before I leave your country, to master not only your language, but your strange version of the game of chess. Perhaps you might instruct me in both."

"You wish to learn the rules of chess?"

Gray smiled. "I have always believed that it helps, when doing business with an empire, to understand the games played by its men. In my country, the pieces on the board are governed by different rules than they are in yours. They have different capabilities, and they have different limitations. You do play?"

"Of course." Li Du hid his surprise. This was a different Gray than the one he had spoken to at the mansion on the night of the murder. Where that man had exuded a ruthless fixation on the Company's interests, this one, sunburned and energetic, gave the impression of efficiency and genuine enthusiasm. Li Du did not know what had cheered the man, but the change was disarming. He understood better why Gray had been chosen as an ambassador.

"Then perhaps," said Gray, "you would honor me with a lesson before I leave the city."

Li Du gave a slight nod. "Perhaps. Has the magistrate told you that I am making inquiries into the death of Brother Pieter?"

Gray nodded. "Of course I hope that you find the culprit soon. I have been assured that the Emperor's schedule will not be affected by your investigation. I trust that is still true?"

"The festival plans are unchanged," said Li Du, and looked at the field. "But will this place be finished in time?"

Gray followed Li Du's gaze and smiled. "Your peasants are exceptional laborers. Their endurance is astonishing. Yes — it will be ready. The architects have timed it so that everything will be new and clean — nothing soiled by mud or trampling. The flowers have just arrived from the greenhouses today — the gardeners did not want to plant them too soon and risk an early spring frost." Gray's smile broadened and he added, only half speaking to Li Du, "If I were not here to see it for myself, I would think this empire beyond the power of imagination to create."

Unsure how to reply, Li Du continued to

watch the scene on the field. To him it seemed a clanging, creaking union of devastation and creation. The people and the horses were working with exhausted intensity. The air sparkled with dry dust. The lunchtime millet bubbled from campfire pots. And at the edge of the field, where the space had been expanded to accommodate the expected crowds, he could see the raw stumps of hundreds of felled trees.

Gray turned to him. "Have you come to ask me about the dead man? I am afraid I have nothing I can offer you. I have no idea who might have killed him. I can only hope that no one else is in danger."

Remembering Tulishen's injunction that he not offend Gray, Li Du spoke carefully. "I do not want to keep you from your work here, but I do have questions for you."

Gray's expression did not change. He shrugged, agreeable. "Of course I want this matter resolved as quickly as possible. If I can be of any help . . ."

"What did you and Brother Pieter argue about in the library?"

Gray frowned. "We did not argue."

"You were overheard."

"Ah," said Gray, his expression clearing. "But that was not an argument. It may have appeared so, but in our culture, men may express themselves with vehemence without the loss of face you take so seriously in your country."

"And what was the subject of this debate?"

Gray directed his gaze upward in thought. "I came upon him after he had taken the liberty of examining the Company's property. You can imagine my distress. He was a stranger to me, and I am charged with the safety of that cargo. He reassured me that he was merely interested in the one piece — the tellurion. You know he was an astronomer?"

"Yes."

"He overheard a description of it during the inventory, he said, and could not resist. Once I realized that the old man meant no harm, I was patient with him."

"And that was the extent of your conversation?"

Gray shifted his weight from one foot to the other, and glanced at the progress of the construction. It seemed to satisfy him. "What do you mean, the extent of it? Who talked to you?"

"If you will pardon me, I am asking you."

Gray looked hard at Li Du, trying to infer what he already knew. "Well," he said finally, "he made some offensive remarks that did upset me. I had relied on him, as a fellow

European, you understand, to support me in my errand to the Emperor. But he revealed to me certain gross misunderstandings of my employer, and indicated that I could not rely on him as I had thought to."

"He felt that the Company was dangerous."

"As I said, he was in error. But he was an elderly Jesuit, and I am a gentleman. He had no actual power to harm my mission, and so I was as patient with him as possible. That is all that happened. I assure you. Are you satisfied?"

"On that point, yes, for now. But I would like you to tell me your movements on the night he died."

Did he imagine the evasiveness of Gray's small eyes as he composed his reply? When Gray spoke, his tone was casual, almost disinterested. "You cannot mean that I am a suspect?"

"If I may be frank — you did leave the courtyard just after Pieter left it."

"Yes, but I thought you had asked me this already. I had an assignation with one of the hired women. We met in the garden with the fountains — by the main gate. I was nowhere near the guesthouse."

"That is what you said." Li Du's posture was apologetic, his shoulders rounded in deference to the other man. But his words were clear and confident. "If you will pardon me, I know that is not the truth."

Gray's ruddy face flushed slightly, and the flakes of peeling skin stood out white on his reddened forehead and nose. "I am trying to be patient with you. But remember that I am an ambassador. I have certain immunities that must be respected."

"I understand that, and the magistrate wishes especially that you not be inconvenienced. But I would point out to you that, if you are innocent of the crime, it is in your interest to speed the investigation. You do not wish your audience with the Emperor to be affected by his concern over an unresolved crime."

Gray considered Li Du's words, but did not reply immediately. Li Du quickly weighed his options, and decided to continue with the direct approach. The tellurion was still in his mind, as were the painted event schedules, and the shadow of the looming emperor's pavilion that fell on him and Gray as they spoke. He had to take a risk and move forward.

"That cut on your hand," said Li Du. "It is almost healed now, but on the night of the murder it was fresh. Did it come from a shard of the broken teacup?"

305

"I did not break my cup."

Their eyes met. "No," said Li Du. "It was Brother Pieter's teacup that broke. The one that you hid in the rock garden."

"How dare you —"

Li Du interjected quickly: "I am not accusing you of murder. But I believe that you were in the room when he died, and that it was you who took the cup."

"I don't know what you are talking about. I was with a woman, and when I left her I returned to the performance. I learned of the death at the same time you did."

Li Du shook his head. "I noticed that you have a habit of playing with a silver coin. You were doing it throughout the performance."

Gray scoffed. "How is that relevant?"

"When you came back from the dark gardens, you did not take the coin from your pocket again. Instead, you concealed your hand from view. I think that you did so because it was bleeding from the wound you had just received."

Gray did not reply immediately. Instead, he focused his attention on filling and lighting a slim wooden pipe that he had drawn out of his pocket. The ritual seemed to have a calming effect on him, and finally he said, in an even tone, "I did not kill him."

"Then you admit that you took the cup from his room?"

Gray drew a long pull from his pipe and puffed the smoke slowly into the air. He looked very intently at Li Du. "I do not admit anything," he said. "How do I know that you are not trying to trap me into confessing to a crime I did not commit?"

"That is not my intention."

Gray made an impatient gesture with the hand holding the pipe. "I am a representative of the most powerful Company in the world. I am alone in an empire the workings of which are unfamiliar to me. I would be very naive if I expected everyone here to be truthful. In these political games, lies are part of the language. Honest people are fodder for the clever ones. Do not ask me to believe your promises, and do not expect me to put myself at unnecessary risk."

Li Du thought about what Gray had said. Then he lifted his head and addressed Gray in a formal tone. "Then this is what I propose. I will tell you what I think happened. If my conclusions convince you that I am not attempting to put the blame where it is not deserved, then I ask you to help me, and to tell me what you know."

Gray directed a calculating look at Li Du, then gave a short nod. "I believe that is fair," he said. "But shall we walk as we speak? The wind is cold here at the crest of the hill, and there is a pleasant path there, out of the noise and dust." He pointed down the wild slope in back of the emperor's pavilion.

Li Du squared his shoulders and straightened his hat. They began to walk. Li Du took a deep breath and began: "I know that you did not meet a prostitute that night in the mansion."

"How do you know?"

"That is not relevant. But once I knew that you had lied about where you were, I assumed that your actions must have placed you somewhere close to the scene of the crime. You were seen arguing with Brother Pieter. Whatever he said to you made you follow him that night. Perhaps you only wished to speak with him. Perhaps to threaten him. But you did follow him when he left the performance."

Gray continued to smoke his pipe. Li Du went on.

"You left so soon after Pieter that I suspect he was not yet dead when you reached him. I suspect that you were with him when he drank the tea, and that, before you knew what was happening, you found yourself standing over a dead body. You panicked. It was obvious to you that the tea had been poisoned. You realized how culpable you would appear to anyone who came upon the scene. Fearing discovery at any moment, you realized that without the cup of tea, Pieter's death did not look like murder. You thought that if you took the cup, with some luck the matter would be viewed as an unfortunate, but unavoidable, tragedy. You did not care in that moment why he had died, or who had killed him. You acted decisively in your own interest."

Gray's expression was shuttered. The construction was behind them now, and already the path had become overgrown and mossy. A raven squawked from a nearby tree, and there was a flutter of grouse wings in the bramble.

"Perhaps," said Li Du, "you meant to wash the poisoned tea from the cup and return it to the room, but it was too late. As soon as you were out of the guesthouse you saw Lady Chen approaching. She had heard something and was coming to see what had happened. You hurried to the dark path under the willows and cast about for a place to hide the cup. The ponds were frozen, and you did not want anyone to see or hear you. That is when you came to the rock garden. You lifted one of the rocks and put the cup beneath it. I imagine that when you returned the rock to its place, one of the shards was still visible. You tried to push it out of sight, and you cut your hand on one of the broken edges."

Li Du stopped and turned to face Gray. "Is that what happened?"

Gray gave Li Du a long, speculative look. Then, resigned, he appeared to relax. He transferred the pipe to his left hand, and raised his right to look at the cut, now a thin, pink line. Then he took the silver coin from his pocket and began to move it across his knuckles as he spoke. "It's good luck, the coin," he said. "And it did happen as you say. You understand why I did not confess it. I might have been accused and executed without ceremony. As I said before, we foreigners know very little of how your empire operates."

Gray prodded a quartz pebble with the toe of his boot. "I did not go to threaten the Jesuit. I merely wanted to convince him to help my cause. I wanted him to use his influence to support the Company. The Jesuits may not have as much power as they used to, but I thought that having one on my side would be useful. At the very least I wanted to ask him not to disparage us in the presence of the Emperor."

"He spoke to me of the Company. He was adamant in his disapproval."

Gray shrugged. "I can be very persuasive," he said, then added quickly, "but I meant him no harm. I wasn't going to kill a man just for being unenthusiastic about trade."

He went on. "And what does a holy brother know of this part of the world to make him so authoritative? The Jesuits are interested in their languages, their astrolabes, and their converts. It was not fair for a person with no grasp of the greater situation to criticize my work."

"And what happened when you reached his room?"

Gray looked up briefly at the bare tree branches, his breath in the cold air indistinguishable from the pipe smoke. "I caught up with him just as he was going through the door."

"Did you see whether his door was locked?"

"It was not locked, but that did not seem to surprise him. He greeted me cordially enough, and we went into his room together. He lit the tapers. And that is when he saw the tea. The cup was out on his desk, with dry tea leaves in it already and the steaming kettle beside it."

"What did Pieter say when he saw it?"

"He was pleased. I don't remember what he said exactly. Something akin to 'How considerate . . . the maid has come before me and prepared tea . . . marvels of good hospitality.' Comments of that nature. Whoever put the tea there must have left just before we arrived."

Li Du remembered that the pot had still been quite warm when he himself had touched it some time later. Gray continued. "He poured the water into his cup and asked me why I had come."

"And how was he at that moment?"

"He was distracted. I started to speak, but I could see that he was preoccupied, and not listening to me. I was just beginning to think that I had wasted my time coming to talk to him, when it happened. He gasped for breath and fell to the floor. It was over very quickly. He was dead before I could do anything."

"But you did not cry for help?"

"There was no time! I tell you he stopped breathing, and then it was over. If I could have done anything to help him, I would have, but he was beyond aid. And I was shocked — I was not in possession of my full faculties."

"And what did you do then?"

Gray took a deep draw from his pipe and

looked at the smoke curling in the air before him. "It was just as you said. I panicked. I've seen men die before, but this was . . ." His forehead creased and he said, "It is difficult to explain. Something like this happens — a nightmarish moment — and you look for what is familiar to you. But when it happens in a strange country, the world loses its sense. You want to call out, but you do not know what language is in your head. The shapes, the air, they take on the warped proportions of dreams. I tell you — I can almost believe the talk of curses. In that moment, all I could grasp hold of was my mission in coming to China. I knew that I had a duty to protect myself."

"He was an old man, and you thought that if no one had reason to think of poison, no one would."

Gray did not flinch. "I know that it was not a clever idea. I didn't think of the danger. I didn't think of the murderer who might have been watching. All I could think of was that at any moment someone might walk in and find me standing there. So I took the cup from where he had set it on the desk, and I ran out of the building. I had only just turned the corner around the wall when I saw Lady Chen approaching. And I was standing there with the damn

313

cup in my hand, my blood roaring in my ears."

"And why did you not confess all of this once the blame was placed on the Khampa?"

"Would you have confessed? I had no information that would help to find the actual culprit. I convinced myself that some well-meaning maid had filled the cup with tea from that purse you found in his room, and that the bandits really were responsible. Then you returned, with your questions. How would it have looked, my speaking of it so late? And what impression would such an action make on the Emperor?"

"You did not know of the Khampa purse that the murderer had planted in the room in order to implicate them. So you could not have known that taking the cup would interfere with the murderer's plans, and draw attention away from the murderer's intended scapegoats and back to the mansion."

"Damn bad luck," said Gray, with feeling. "But you see, don't you, that I did nothing against any law? My actions may have been foolish, but in the moment it was all I could think of to do."

"Did Pieter say anything before he died, or make any gesture?"

Gray shook his head immediately. "There was no time."

"And you saw no one in the gardens on your way to or from his room?"

"Oh — vague figures, certainly. Couples in the shadows, bannermen and soldiers patrolling. No one I recognized, except for the Lady Chen. But now I have helped you — now you know that the murderer prepared the tea just before Brother Pieter and I arrived at the room. And in return — will you keep my involvement between us alone?"

"Sir Gray, I have no investment in the deals made between your company and this empire. And I have no wish to involve myself. I will not speak of any of this unless it necessary to my investigation that I do so."

Gray looked as if he might say more, but something in Li Du's face stopped him. "Then we have no quarrel. As long as I am allowed to present the Company's gifts in the time and manner previously agreed upon, then I am content. And now, if you have no more questions for me, I would like to return to the pavilion — the carpenters will not understand how the beams are to be fitted together."

Li Du acquiesced, and they retraced their steps in uneasy silence. Gray's confirmation

315

of what Li Du had guessed should have been satisfying, but it was not. Gray had acquitted himself well in their conversation, and yet, somehow, Li Du was not sanguine as to Nicholas Gray's innocence.

CHAPTER 14

The Office of City Records had the atmosphere of a beehive. Like all the government buildings in Dayan, it had been commandeered for use in festival preparations. Harried officials in black caps and red robes dashed in and out of the open doors, carrying, arranging, reading, and occasionally dropping ledgers, seals, and velvet bags that clinked when they were set down.

Just as he had successfully nudged his way through the door, Li Du recognized Mu Gao coming out of the building. The old man did not see Li Du squeezed among all the others. He was carrying a bundle of papers under his arm, and his attention was on keeping his balance. He limped down the street toward the mansion, leaning heavily on his cane.

Li Du attempted to ask one of the officials for assistance, but the young man shook his head with an expression of panic and began to stammer a garbled excuse until he was interrupted by a corpulent merchant in purple silk who yelled that he was still waiting for a receipt for the silver.

"I was promised four places on the fourth platform," he cried. "I just gave you so much silver that you should give me ten places! Six places then! I want written assurances!"

The harassed secretary had just produced a piece of paper and begun to write on it when a small group of caravan merchants pushed their way inside. One of them consulted a parchment and announced to the room, "Delivery of ten thousand candles for the river flower lanterns. Where do we receive payment?" No one answered, and he opened his mouth to speak again when a bearded man in a yellow robe emerged from another room and roared, "The crystal of at least four lanterns is cracked! They must be replaced!"

Li Du was jostled this way and that until he felt hot and panicked himself. He was beginning to think that he had wasted his time when he felt someone take a firm grip on his elbow. He looked down and saw that an old man was holding his sleeve with an ink-stained hand wrinkled and gray with parchment dust. The man gestured to indicate that they could not speak over the commotion, and ushered Li Du through the crowd until they passed through a small door into the deeper interior of the building.

With each door they passed through it became quieter, until finally they were alone in a dim, tranquil room. The windows were shaded by faded silk screens, amber and beige rectangles of light surrounded by drifting dust motes. The walls were lined with cabinets of lacquered wood, each drawer labeled with black or red painted dates. Some of them had been crossed out and replaced with newer dates. Others had been altered by pasting paper sheets over the originals, on which were written titles such as: *Fourth Register of Temples* and *Ninth Tablet of Tea from the Fifth Reigning Year* and *Porcelain Delivered Tenth Year.*

The room had, in spite of its disorder and slightly musty odor, the sanctified feel of a library. Compared to Tulishen's library this room's paper shades and book spines were poorly matched. The lacquer was scratched, and corners of paper peeped from open drawers. But what it lacked in upkeep it made up for in earnest use. The drawers looked rifled, memorized, studied. The desk was slightly discolored from tea stains on the wood. Clean paper was arranged in colored stacks, and the brushes dangling from the brush holder were still damp.

"If you are actually at the office of records in search of records," said the man, "I'm the only one who can help you. I'm too old to run around counting coins and haggling with nobles over how close they may sit to the Emperor." He made a dismissive gesture that turned into a welcoming wave at a low chair.

"Now, you sit there, and I will sit here, and let me pour you some tea," he said. Li Du watched as he prepared the tea, and noticed that despite his age his hands did not shake. The man lifted the heavy kettle full of water and took it outside to a court-yard fire. When he came back he said, "It was already hot. It just needs another moment to be perfect. But what was I saying? Ah, yes — I'm too old for that nonsense. All those young secretaries terrified they'll be blamed for a tarnished spittoon. And all that silk and gauze delivered every day — if you sewed it all together you could shroud the whole mountain with it. But after the festival it will be torn and trampled trash, all of it. Sad waste, I say. Never liked waste. I'm called Old Mu, by the way, city clerk."

"I think that I have met a relation of yours.

You must know Mu Gao, the custodian of the library?"

Old Mu cocked his head in the direction of the kettle outside, as if he could hear the water reaching its appropriate temperature. He shuffled out and returned holding the kettle, his sleeve drawn down to protect his hand from the hot handle. He talked while he prepared the tea. "Mu Gao is my dearest friend, my cousin. We used to walk together in my wife's garden — *wandering through jade bamboo* — and now that we are too bent to walk easily, we sit and talk, *as the stars go down . . .*" He brought Li Du the cup of tea and passed it to him with both hands, bowing his head as he made the polite offering.

It was Pu'erh tea, and Old Mu had rinsed and steeped it to perfection. Li Du drew in the fragrance that clouded from the darkening liquid, the thick dissonance of fermentation and the dry, insistent power emerging from the unfurling leaves. He sipped and felt his vision clear, his chest warm, and his heart beat with increased enthusiasm for its work. Old Mu took his own cup to the desk and sat down.

"Mu Gao does not seem to take very much pleasure in his work at the magistrate's library," said Li Du.

Old Mu's expression became sad. "Well," he said, "you must not mind him. I am very lucky — my wife is still alive, cantankerous and clever as a good old woman should be, and our children are good strong farmers with children of their own, well outside of the city, where life is not so different from what it was before. But Mu Gao is alone, and his mind is not always clear. He knows that his place is in the mansion — but he was not meant to be a servant there. We grow old, and bitter, drinking together and remembering the days when our family had vigor. We were the most powerful family in the province, you know."

Old Mu pulled himself up and refilled the small cups with water. Then he creaked slowly back down into his chair and went on: "But even in our days of greatness there was never such a festival as this. Every craftsman in the south of China has been working for months on festival decorations." He raised his hands and gesticulated as he listed the items he had seen: "Paintings, screens embroidered with dragons, incense, incense holders, lamps, bells, drums, flags, poems on silk, miniature trees, pear wood chairs, even tiny pleasure boats for the canal . . . It is going to be a spectacle. I'm as eager as the next man to see our mighty

Emperor. It's the crowds and waste I don't like."

Li Du nodded in agreement.

"But," went on Old Mu, "I have not asked you why you are here. I think I know who you are — the magistrate's cousin?"

"Yes, I am. I came here to ask if any records exist of foreign visitors to Dayan. I am interested in the events of thirty years ago, before the Qing magistrate arrived."

Old Mu cooed a little under his breath. "Well," he said, "there's many a cup of tea been drunk in all that time. Hm." He took a key from a drawer in the desk, and moved to a small cabinet in one corner of the room. He opened it, rifled through the contents, and emerged with a ledger, crisp and undamaged, its ink still bright. "Here it is," he said. "And what would that be? The ninth reigning year of our good Emperor. Not many Chinese in these parts at the time. We saw some odd types on the caravans, of course, but that foreigner, the one you're interested in, the one who died, well, he was different as they come. Hair pale as a lotus root in oil."

"You remember him?"

Old Mu nodded. "I do. Would have liked to see him again . . ." He left the sentence unfinished.

"And he stayed in Dayan several months?"
"Almost a whole year, yes, but not in Dayan. We were having one of our quarrels with the Khampa, and he stayed in a safer place. Ah, yes, here it is. He wrote down his name — not in a script I know." Li Du looked down at where Old Mu was pointing. He read, in brushed ink:

Pieter van Dalen

Beside the name was a brief description in Chinese:

Strangelander holy man, traveling with Buddhist pilgrim Xuanzhang, servant Feng (see below). Presented to Mu Zeng gifts accepted with gratitude. 1 small clock for telling hours in central style. 1 book of foreign make, leather binding, with painted pages. 50 taels silver. First letter of introduction bearing seal of Jia Zheng of Board of Rites in Forbidden City. Second letter of introduction bearing seal of Magistrate Tao of Pu'erh prefecture. Third letter from Mu Zhong, son to the cousin of Mu Zeng, current student of respected status in Beijing. Fourth letter bearing seal of Fr. Verbiest, giving permission for his student to bring teachings to greater empire region. Taken in by the hospitality of the Zhao family in Snow Village. Departed ninth reigning year, seventh month in good health with gifts.

"And was it you who wrote this entry?" asked Li Du.

"No — that was before I became a record keeper. I was just a secretary and a scoundrel. This record keeper, Loh, died years ago. He had a good hand, though, and mixed his ink very well."

"This village — is it the same Snow Village that lies on the foothills of the mountain?"

"Yes, that is it. Just over the lowest ridge, on the river side. A long day's journey from Dayan. A humble place, except for its wine."

"And, the Zhao family? Did you know them?"

"Yes — they are a large family."

"And do you know if there was anyone at that time who might have had a motive to wish Brother Pieter dead? Someone who might have held a grudge all these years?"

"No — I cannot think of anyone."

"It was a time of divided loyalties," said Li Du. "The Ming had been defeated, but they still had many supporters, especially in this part of the empire. Might Brother Pi-

325

eter have been involved in some plot? There were Jesuits who wished for the Ming to return."

Old Mu raised his hands helplessly. "I really don't remember anything like that," he said. "We were fighting anyone who happened to be trying to kill us or steal from us. The foreigner would not have been part of that. From what I recall, he was a gentle, prettily mannered young man with a fondness for books and poetry. He did not want to be a burden to anyone. A helpful sort of man."

Li Du stood up and thanked Old Mu. As he left, he turned and asked, "Was Mu Gao drinking wine with you on the night of the murder?"

Old Mu took only a moment to deliberate, then nodded with certainty. "Yes — the banquet night. He doesn't go to the magistrate's banquets. We shared a bottle of good strong wine, raised our cups to the moon and drank to the ancestors."

Li Du thanked Old Mu again and departed the records office. He ate a bowl of noodles at a shop, and felt much better once he had finished. The Sichuan pepper danced, metallic, on his tongue, and the thick, salty broth rejuvenated him. He would have need of the energy, he thought, for his next task. He had to go to the mansion and make a report to his cousin.

Tulishen had inadvertently scheduled two appointments for the same time that evening. Li Du found him pacing in the office with the painting of the Kangxi on the wall, talking half to himself and half to Jia Huan, who stood listening patiently, his velvet cap so clean it might have been new, his expression attentive and sympathetic. As usual he held a bouquet of scrolls of varied size and color under one arm.

"It must be Cheng," said Tulishen. He had glanced up through drawn brows when Li Du had entered, but ignored him. He repeated, with decision, "It must be Cheng. He is a Director at the Board of Revenue. Ju-hai is only — what did you say he was?"

"A second secretary at the Board of Censors," said Jia Huan.

Tulishen grunted. "Yes," he said, with satisfaction. "That is not so prestigious. I will be late to my meeting with him, and keep the appointment with Cheng."

"If I may, magistrate," said Jia Huan, "it is true that Cheng's rank is higher. But Ju-hai has an old connection to the Feng family — they are still on terms of great intimacy. And the eldest Feng son has just been made, by

327

imperial appointment, the Chief Master of the Government College."

Tulishen was silent for a moment. He rubbed his face with both hands, pressing his fingers to his eyes, then blinked several times as if to clear his vision. "If I did not have so much on my mind I would have remembered." He turned to Li Du. "You see how important navigating the web of connections is?" He returned his attention to Jia Huan. "I would not want to snub a friend of the Chief Master of my son's school. Already there are too many wolves and too little meat in that place. Obviously Ju-hai must not be offended. I will keep the meeting with him, and put off Cheng. Make the proper arrangements."

"I will offer your sincere apologies to Cheng. Perhaps we may find one extra seat on your viewing platform for him?"

The deep wrinkles along Tulishen's brow smoothed a little. "Yes," he said. "Yes, that will keep him happy. After all — Cheng is also an important ally."

Jia Huan straightened and adjusted the documents under his arm. "Then I will see to it directly," he said.

He waited for the expected dismissal, but Tulishen, with another look at Li Du, said, "Stay until we have heard what report my cousin has to make. You may be required for some task that has proven beyond his capacity to accomplish."

Tulishen and Jia Huan both looked at Li Du expectantly, and he prepared to speak. But Tulishen interrupted him before he could begin. "I can see that you have no answer for me. I did not think that you would. I told you from the beginning that you were fishing for the moon with this stubborn notion — this determination to find an assassin whom I am sure will never be found. You wish now that you had let it alone, do you?"

"No. I —"

"Well, it is too late. You have thrown off all the balance, and now you have the Emperor's attention. Jia Huan — show him."

With a glimmer of apology directed at Li Du, too subtle to be perceived by Tulishen, Jia Huan drew out one of the scrolls and handed it to Tulishen, who unrolled it. Li Du moved closer to see. Even after many years he recognized its dimensions — one *chi* high and two *chi* broad. It was the stationery reserved for correspondence with the Emperor. Written on it was a letter in neat black ink, but the margins around it were filled with comments in red like flame sparks bursting on the page. Li Du silently skimmed the letter and the margin notes.

"That is the Emperor's own hand," said Tulishen, darkly. "It is the letter we wrote" — he gestured at Jia Huan — "and it has been returned to us with the Emperor's reactions." Tulishen skimmed through the red, pointing.

"He is interested in the case . . . eager for its resolution . . . he hopes to be diverted by the solution . . . he suggests another foreigner was responsible . . . foreigners prone to competition and quarreling amongst themselves . . . but here — see here." Tulishen's finger shook slightly as he indicated the powerful crimson slashes of the final comment at the end of the letter.

"Above all," it said, *"there must not be too many incidents. An excess of incidents in the border provinces places too great a strain upon the empire."*

Tulishen looked accusingly at Li Du. "As you can see," he said, "I wrote that your investigation is going well. So tell me — have you learned anything from your questions? Your forays to the dead man's grave? The clerk's offices?"

"No."

Tulishen stopped pacing. He looked hard at Li Du through narrowed, swollen eyelids.

"No?" He was incredulous. "That is all the answer I am to expect? Just — no?"

Li Du was deferential, but his voice did not waver. "You appointed me this task because you would not take it upon yourself. You told me that you could not possibly give it your attention. So I will not burden you now with the tangled threads and ill-cut pieces that occupy my thoughts. I have heard many things, but I have not fitted them into their proper places. I do not know what is relevant, and what is not. Surely you do not wish me to waste our time by listing all of it to you?"

"This — this impudence," said Tulishen, "from you."

Li Du said nothing.

"So," continued Tulishen, "you have information but you refuse to share it with me. Are you somehow unaware of the gravity of the situation?"

"I am aware, Cousin. And I have a question that I wish to ask you."

"What question?"

"Do you hope to fill the position in Beijing recently vacated by Magistrate Liu?"

Tulishen exhaled sharply. "That is my concern. It is not auspicious to discuss such matters, and it is no business of yours."

Li Du considered. Tulishen was incensed.

His skin was sallow, and his fingers fidgeted with the cuffs of his long sleeves. He looked, Li Du thought with just a flicker of sympathy, exhausted and genuinely overwhelmed. "I have a reason for asking," he said. "Do you have enemies here?"

"Enemies?" Tulishen was startled. "N-no," he stuttered, "but — but of course there is competition for a position as high as the one I hold. I have rivals. Everyone has their ambitions. But what are you implying?" He peered at Li Du, suspicious, uncertain.

Wearing an expression of humble concern, Li Du said, "Have you considered that the murderer could have wanted to sabotage your promotion by destroying the festival?"

Tulishen stared; then awareness dawned. "I had never thought of that. Do you believe that I am in danger?"

Gently, Li Du shook his head. "It is an idea only," he said.

But the shift of attention to himself as a victim had comforted Tulishen and improved his mood. He said, with a suggestion of warmth, "Your concern for my safety is touching, Cousin."

"I apologize for prying into your personal affairs. You and the Lady Chen must be very proud that this opportunity has arisen."

"Of course Lady Chen is pleased," said

Tulishen, a little too quickly. "Lady Chen is very loyal to this family, and has my best interests always in the forefront of her mind. Ask Jia Huan — she has been invaluable in the preparations for the festival. Tell him."

Jia Huan's praise was effusive. "The Lady Chen has spent the last months devoted to the study of fashions of the capital. She has read all of the manuals. She questioned travelers. She practiced every delicacy with the cooks in the kitchen to ensure that the Emperor's favorite dishes are made to his satisfaction. She has trained the servants to be ready for all of the customs that are unfamiliar to them. They have memorized the correct tunes to play when the Emperor drinks tea, and those to play when he drinks wine."

"And," Li Du asked, casually, "will she enjoy Beijing?"

Tulishen blustered slightly. "Lady Chen in the capital? I am not sure that such a relocation is appropriate for one of her background. She is of a good local family, but among more polished ladies she does not appear to good advantage."

"She is a beautiful woman, and as you say, very devoted to the family."

"Yes, she is beautiful. But you know the peasant blood must assert itself eventually in a woman. Village beauty is a wildflower that blooms only briefly. My younger wives will retain their delicacy for many years — they have stayed in Beijing these past several years in part to preserve it. Lady Chen begins to show her age, and she has given me no sons. I do not wish to be embarrassed by her among the families of rank."

When Li Du said nothing, Tulishen added, with a hint of defensiveness, "I am not denying that she has been a success here. She has made all of the preparations for the Emperor's comfort at the mansion, and we would be ready to receive him were it not for this — this matter." He gesticulated and looked at Li Du as if Li Du himself was the source of the problem.

Li Du said, "The mansion is impeccable. But what is your opinion of Sir Gray and the Company tribute? Do you expect that Gray's audience will please the Emperor or aggravate him?"

"I am impressed with the man," said Tulishen, "though I had not expected to be. I thought that the treasure would be a meager pile of foreign trinkets, and that the entire spectacle would be an embarrassment, an offense to the beauty of the mansion and the festival field. But this Company, whatever it is, does possess real wealth. I think

334

that the gifts cannot but please the Emperor. The muskets in particular are of a new design that I must admit is better than any we have tried to produce. And the Persian perfume glows from glass bottles that resemble hollowed gemstones. There is white coral from the depths of the sea —"

"And the tellurion," added Li Du.

"Yes — that too is very fine. And an intelligent gift, more intelligent than I anticipated from foreigners. It will augment the festival, not detract from it. And the Emperor will like it."

"Because of its connection to astronomy? To the eclipse?"

Tulishen grunted affirmation. "And the chimes."

"What chimes?"

Li Du read greed in his cousin eyes, and envy. Tulishen went on. "The miniature city built at its base is not just a statue. It has certain mechanisms inside it, similar to those foreign clocks with figures that dance when the hour is struck. The ship moves up and down on the waves, the trees blossom with pink jewel flowers, the bells swing in the tiny towers. Only the striking of the hour is, in this unique device, the eclipse. When it begins, so will the display, all for the Emperor's personal enjoyment. Picture it

— the festival field dark, filled with lanterns like the stars in the heavenly path, and the Emperor high above the crowds holding the world in his hands . . ." Tulishen's gaze was far away, imagining it.

Li Du thought about it also. The tellurion had been a marvel even as he had seen it, glittering, in the cavernous, dim room, its movement imperceptible to the human eye. To see it perform during the eerie moments of darkness as the sun became a black disk, a door into nothing, sucking light from the world — such a sight would enchant even an emperor. It was, Li Du admitted, a gift that would not be surpassed anytime soon within the realm of material objects.

And, Li Du acknowledged, Tulishen was correct. The tellurion was a clever gift, meant to entice, to intrigue. The Emperor was a man of notorious curiosity. The Company had sent its lone messenger, Nicholas Gray, like bait dipped into a pond at the end of a fishing line. The Kangxi would want to meet the clockmakers, the jewelers, the sculptors and astronomers who had crafted the tellurion. He would want to demand explanations from them, to commission new work. But in order to have what he wanted, he would be forced to invite them to his empire. It was a strategy that the Jesuits had employed to great effect in the early years of their arrival, but Li Du wondered whether the Kangxi, despite his reputed fascination with new technology, would be so easily manipulated. He shuddered slightly. The thought of the mechanical click of time within that jeweled skeleton oppressed him. It was as if time itself had been trapped inside, a creature of boundless knowledge forced into a cage too small for it.

"Brother Pieter," Li Du said, "took a special interest in the piece, and I had the impression that he wrote notes in a book — a journal, perhaps — as he examined it. But I have not seen such a book. Do you know where it might be?"

Tulishen looked inquiringly at Jia Huan, who shook his head with a perplexed air. "No — I have not seen anything of that nature. It would be with his other books."

"But it is not," said Li Du. "You and I have examined Pieter's possessions twice now. You are sure that it was not put in a separate place? Or perhaps" — Li Du was struck by the sudden idea — "perhaps it was buried with him?"

Tulishen frowned. "It was not buried with him. Your impression must have been wrong. Who says that he had one?"

"Mu Gao saw him writing in it."

Tulishen exhaled sharply. "In that case you are wasting our time. Mu Gao's memory is rotten. Whatever he says is of no use to you. You should listen to Jia Huan. He can be relied upon."

Jia Huan bowed low in gratitude. Tulishen gave a curt nod and said to him, "I want the arrangements made with Cheng within the hour. Do it yourself, in person. Then you can tell me if he takes offense." He turned to Li Du. "Cousin, I have no more time for this. I must attend to other matters."

When Tulishen was gone, a faint hint of distress crept across Jia Huan's expression. It was as if the magistrate's departure allowed the young man a moment's respite from the unwavering competence that Tulishen took for granted in his new secretary. Jia Huan's brow creased in concentration, but after a moment he shook his head, frustrated. "I don't know what could have happened to it," he said. "I am sorry."

"But it is not your fault," said Li Du. "I asked the question on the chance that you knew where it was, but I think it likely that the journal was taken on purpose. By now it may have been destroyed."

"Do you think it contained a clue to the

identity of the killer?"

"Perhaps. Or the killer thought it might."

Jia Huan waited for Li Du to continue. When he did not, the secretary straightened his shoulders and looked over Li Du's shoulder in the direction of the gate. "You have no further need of me now?" he asked.

"You are very patient," said Li Du. "I know that there is a great deal of pressure being put on you in these final days. No doubt you have borne much of my cousin's anxiety over this investigation."

Jia Huan inclined his head very slightly, but his tone was crisp. "It is an honor to be in Dayan at this time, for a festival that will be unlike any other I have seen. But the murder — it has unsettled the situation. The magistrate is" — he searched for a word, as if afraid of being disrespectful — "he is stretched too thinly between all of the duties that have been placed upon him."

"And this position in Beijing? I may be mistaken, but it is possible that Lady Chen is not as eager for it to happen as the magistrate thinks? After all, it may mean her dismissal from the family."

Jia Huan's face was solemn. He said, "What Lady Chen wants is to remain first consort to the magistrate. She will do what she must in order to keep her place. If the magistrate does invite her to Beijing, his wives and other consorts will present new challenges for her. But she does not confide in me, of course — you must speak to her yourself, if you think this matter has any relevance to your investigation." He looked at Li Du curiously.

Li Du sighed and rubbed the back of his neck thoughtfully. He was tired and stiff, and there was something about Jia Huan's presence that calmed him. The quiet, earnest intelligence that the young man emanated was reassuring, like the first sip of good tea, and Li Du understood why Tulishen relied on Jia Huan in so many areas of governance.

Li Du said, "I confess I do not know what is relevant. I am searching for an enemy in a world that is opaque to me."

"What do you mean? Do you refer to your time in exile?"

Li Du smiled slightly. "Before I was an exile," he said, "I was a librarian, and that gave me little more insight into current politics than I have now."

"So you believe the motive was political?"

"Not necessarily, but I ask myself who could have hated Pieter, who could have wanted him dead. And my mind returns again and again to the Dominicans. Pieter was a Jesuit, and the Dominicans are the rivals of the Jesuits."

Jia Huan considered. "The Jesuit did refuse to support the Company's suit, but it would be foolish indeed for Sir Gray to have reacted so violently, and at such risk to his mission. And yet —" He stopped.

Li Du, who had been glancing idly again at the titles of the books, looked up and raised his square little eyebrows in question. "You have an idea?"

Jia Huan spoke slowly. "The young man, the Jesuit who is here — something about him has always seemed false to me."

Li Du kept his face expressionless, waiting for Jia Huan to continue. But Jia Huan shrugged. "I am not saying that I think he is a Dominican assassin. And I have expressed to you my feelings about the foreigners who try to woo our empire. In my opinion the Dominicans do not have the creativity or the resources to send an assassin, though I allow that they have motive."

"Do you know very much about them?"

"Some. My assignment in Macau was to observe their behavior. The Jesuits irritate me, but the Dominicans are far worse. They understand nothing of China. They know only their own rules, and care only for their own comfort. I am glad that the Emperor holds them all to be fools and idiots."

"I seem to recall that the Emperor granted one of them an audience some years ago — a Dominican was allowed to travel to Beijing."

Jia Huan nodded. "That is true. I met the man — Father De Tournon. I was part of the escort who traveled with him from Macau to the capital. I even tried to instruct him in our language."

With a rueful, frustrated movement of his hands, Jia Huan went on: "It was a waste of time. The Emperor's scorn was ignited from the moment he met De Tournon. The man was sick, and unable to kowtow, so the Emperor ordered his eunuchs to bring a couch so that he could recline during the interview." Jia Huan shuddered slightly at the memory. "The man *accepted.* And he was not aware of the loss of face."

Li Du understood Jia Huan's revulsion, though he did not share it. If De Tournon had attempted the kowtow and had fainted halfway through it, he would have had a better chance of earning the Kangxi's respect. But to accept a chair in the Emperor's presence would be unthinkable to a Chinese person.

"And what was the result of the interview?" Li Du asked.

"The Emperor asked him why he had come. De Tournon made a speech that was as obsequious as it was absurd. He said that the Pope wished to thank the Emperor for his hospitality toward his brothers the Jesuits. But of course the Emperor knew that there was no love between the Jesuits and the Dominicans. He told De Tournon that this was a very flimsy reason for making such a perilous journey. And De Tournon did not even understand that he was being mocked. He began to ramble. He said that the Jesuits were no longer to be trusted, and that their Pope wished to install Dominicans in Beijing instead. I will never forget the Emperor's reply. He said, 'But how can this be true? Your religion forbids you from lying. If the Jesuits cannot lie, then how it is possible that the Pope does not trust them? Are you telling me that your religion is false?' De Tournon stammered and blustered and could make no reply. He was banished in disgrace."

As Li Du was absorbing this story, they were interrupted by one of the maids from Hoh's inn. She curtsied to Li Du. "Sir," he said, "your friend the storyteller says that you must return now to the inn, because the man you wished to speak to has come back."

Li Du thanked the maid, and turned to Jia Huan. "I kept you too long from your assignments. I hope that you will not be chastised."

"It is nothing. The hour is not yet over, and I will see to the magistrate's schedule immediately."

They were about to part, the maid having left to do another errand elsewhere in the mansion, when Jia Huan said to Li Du in a low, intense voice, "I hope that you will not be offended, but I must offer you some advice. I feel that you and I are not so different as we may appear to others. We share concern for the empire. I do not wish to see a fellow scholar destroyed by a situation that, perhaps, you do not entirely understand."

Li Du, wondering at Jia Huan's uncharacteristically urgent tone, said, "Your concern is very kind. But what would you have me do?"

Jia Huan regained his composure. He said, very quietly, almost in Li Du's ear, "For your sake, you must give the magistrate an answer. I have great respect for you because you have tried to find the truth, but if you cannot find it, you must not admit failure. He wants an answer that will satisfy — he will not demand more of you. An answer.

Any answer. Do you understand?"

And without waiting for Li Du to respond, he bowed respectfully, and hurried away.

CHAPTER 15

"If this man is a killer of holy brothers," said Hamza, "then he will not hesitate to kill a librarian. I will go with you."

"If he is guilty," replied Li Du, "then he is too clever to kill me in his room in the middle of the day when anyone might have seen me go in."

"Then I will come with you in order to intimidate him, so that he will not waste your time with more lies."

Hamza was determined to play the bodyguard, so they went together to Brother Martin's door. The carvings in the wood panels were too dense to admit a clear view of who was inside, but Li Du had the impression of a figure pacing through the shadows. He knocked, and the movement stopped abruptly.

"Who is it?" came Brother Martin's voice. Li Du replied in Latin, and the door opened. Brother Martin's face was pale, except for where it had been burned by the sun. The skin was reddened on his cheeks and under his eyes, which were green as emeralds in contrast. The scruff that had glowed on his jaw when he had arrived in Dayan had grown into a short, full beard, and darkened to copper. He wore his usual black robes, but they were rumpled, torn at the seam of a sleeve, and adorned with holly-oak where the spiked leaves had caught in the fabric.

"Yes?" he asked, looking first at Li Du and then, nervously, at Hamza.

"I am glad that you have returned safely from your excursion with the doctor," Li Du said, pleasantly. "May we come in?"

Brother Martin's expression wavered between welcome and trepidation. A glance at Hamza's stern countenance pushed him decidedly toward the latter state of mind, and he spoke in a rush of words. "I — I am afraid that I am very busy this evening. The landlord has even offered to have my dinner brought to me here, because I cannot take the time away from my work. The plants need to be pressed, you see, and if I do not do it quickly they will lose their color as they dry. And — and I must write down my observations before I forget them. Perhaps we could speak at another time?"

Li Du pushed his worn cap back slightly on his head, and looked up at Brother Martin, standing tall and thin in the doorway before him.

"The matter," Li Du said, "is quite urgent. And I believe it would be safer for us to speak outside of public hearing."

"S-safer?"

"Safer for you."

Brother Martin was looking over Li Du's shoulder, as if expecting a line of archers to be standing there, arrows pointed directly at him. He finally stepped back away from the door. "I suppose I have no choice, really," he said. "Come in."

Closing the door behind them, Brother Martin turned and seemed to see the room for the first time as it must appear to other people. The place was even more of a shambles than it had been that morning. The floor was as leaf-strewn as a mountain path. The stacks of paper by the desk had grown taller, and were beginning to list precariously to one side. The desk itself was a jumble of leaves and branches and flowers. Ink had dried and cracked in the inkwell, on which was propped a single chopstick and a broken pencil. Footprints were tracked through a layer of dirt on the floor. Brother Martin hurried to brush debris from the chairs so that they could sit.

"I — I have been lost in my work. Here — this is the gingko leaf. And this orchid — I could barely bring myself to pluck it from its place, it was so beautiful there by the stream. Tea — I am sorry. I should offer tea. I am always offered tea. Would you like tea?"

After he had babbled out the offer of tea, he bit his lip as he glanced around the room. Li Du guessed that Brother Martin had not the first idea of what he would do if they accepted. It was strange to think of this, one of the simplest gestures of hospitality, as an intimidating obstacle. *How different our country must be from his,* thought Li Du. He declined the offer, and sat down in one of the chairs least covered with leafy detritus.

Hamza, meanwhile, walked slowly about the room. He opened a small side door and peered outside at a little private garden. With a grunt of appreciation he descended the short set of marble stairs into it, leaving the door open. He cast a meaningful glance over his shoulder at Brother Martin, then proceeded to circle a pear tree with slow, deliberate steps. This accomplished, he sat on the bench beneath the tree and set his gaze straight in front of him, his arms crossed against his chest, his chin jutting forward slightly. Li Du assumed this to be Hamza's best impression of a bodyguard.

"What is he doing?" asked Brother Martin, with a bewildered look at Hamza, who was now adjusting the point of his beard.

"He is assisting me in my investigation. There are several questions I must ask you."

"Questions?" The pitch of Brother Martin's voice rose a little. He steadied it and went on: "But I told you everything I know when we spoke this morning. I have nothing to add. I have no idea who killed Brother Pieter. I hope the culprit is caught very soon, but — but what more can I do? I don't even speak Chinese."

"That plant, there," Li Du said, pointing at a humble twist of pale root on the corner of the desk. "Do you know what it is?"

Brother Martin glanced at the place Li Du indicated and shook his head, perplexed. "No — I have not identified that one yet. I collected it from the garden at the mansion. Is — is it valuable? The gardener told me I could take a little of anything. I — I didn't mean . . ." He trailed off.

"That plant you claim not to recognize is called jewelvine. And it was jewelvine that killed Brother Pieter."

"It — it was? But you cannot think that I . . . But I had nothing to do with his death. I told you already. You must — you must believe me. I would never kill anyone." His voice cracked, and his face flushed mottled pink.

"And what if Pieter had threatened to reveal your true identity?"

The change was immediate and startling. The bright color drained from Brother Martin's face, leaving it pasty white. His voice was thin and quiet, almost a whimper: "Wh-what do you mean?"

Li Du leaned forward slightly and said, "I would like you to tell me who you really are, and why you are here."

Tears welled in Brother Martin's eyes, and his throat worked as he tried to speak. Finally he managed a ragged whisper. "M-m-my name is Martin Walpole."

Li Du shook his head. "I am quite sure that it is not, as I am sure that you are not a Jesuit."

In response to this statement, Brother Martin made a final, valiant effort to collect himself. He wiped the tears from his eyes and cleared his throat. He drew himself up a little straighter. "I do not know why you are subjecting me to this — this injustice," he said. "I have all the proper documents.

351

Please look at them. I am here to study the plants of the province for — for the glory of God and the church." He rose, took the leather folder from the desk, brushed the dirt from it, and presented it to Li Du with a shaking hand.

Brother Martin sat down again and watched Li Du intently, his whole posture canted forward with anxiety, his hands clasped. Li Du drew the papers from the folder and pretended to look at them. He knew their contents already, and another glance reassured him that his conclusions that morning had been correct. He held up the document granting permission to enter China. "This paper is old," he said, simply. "It was written and sealed at least ten years ago for the real Martin Walpole. You smudged the date with oil, here."

The muscles of the other man's jaw clenched. He opened his mouth to speak, then closed it again. Li Du went on in a matter-of-fact tone. "This other letter, the one that gives you permission to collect plant specimens, is new, but it was not written or sealed by any Chinese official, unless perhaps by one who is corrupt."

Brother Martin stared. Li Du said, almost apologetically, "I can tell a forged seal from an authentic one. And there have been other indications."

"Wh-what do you mean? What indications?"

"I have made the acquaintance of many Jesuits during my life — you see they spend a great deal of time in libraries. But despite their fondness for any volume that is unfamiliar to them, I have never known one to part from his own prayer book. You seem to be using yours as a paperweight. I was also surprised by your ignorance of simple funeral rites. Probably you did not expect such knowledge would be required in order to maintain your disguise. Just as you never expected to meet a real Jesuit in the rural mountain villages of China."

Brother Martin's reply was faint. "No — no, I — I am not — You are mistaken . . ."

Li Du drew another, folded piece of paper from his pocket. "I found this letter among Pieter's possessions. It is addressed to Brother Pieter, and its author is one Brother Martin Walpole of the Jesuit house in Calcutta. It was written three months ago, and it shows that Brother Pieter and Brother Martin were good friends. When he first met you, Pieter was introduced to a person whose name he knew, but whose face he had never seen before in his life."

The other man's eyes widened. "He — he

knew? But I didn't — I am not . . ." He stopped, too upset to continue.

Li Du said firmly, but without rancor: "You are, or would be in the eyes of any Chinese magistrate, a spy."

At this Brother Martin began to shake his head vehemently. "No," he said hoarsely. "No — I am not a spy. I care nothing for politics. I swear to you — I am not a spy."

"Then I will ask you again. What is your real name? And why have you been impersonating the Jesuit Martin Walpole?"

He dropped his head into his hands, and his broad shoulders collapsed. He moaned softly, and said, addressing Li Du only vaguely, "But he didn't say anything. I — I thought that I'd carried it off perfectly. I thought that he believed me."

"You exaggerated your illness in order to avoid meeting a real Jesuit, didn't you?"

The man nodded miserably. "But why didn't he say anything?"

Li Du's response was cautious. "I think," he said, "that Brother Pieter saw before him a young man, a fellow traveler, alone in a dangerous country. He did not confront you because he did not want to harm you before giving you a chance to explain yourself. But he never had the opportunity. He was silenced —"

"No! I know what you are about to say, but it is not true. I would never have killed him. Never. Even if I had known that he suspected me. But I swear — I didn't think that he knew. And I didn't kill him. I didn't. I — I will tell you the truth now."

He took a deep, steadying breath. "My name is Hugh Ashton." He gave a short sigh. "Oh — I had not realized how good it would feel to say it. And you are right. I — I am not a Jesuit. I am not a man of the church at all, may God forgive my blasphemy. How stupid I have been."

"The officials here and at the border must have been too busy to look closely at your papers."

The man who had called himself Brother Martin winced. "The forger in Calcutta assured me that the seal was done well," he said.

"It is passable," said Li Du.

Realizing that Li Du was waiting for him to go on, Ashton took another deep breath. "The whole truth of it is that I am a botanist, and that I have been a terrible fool."

Li Du raised his eyebrows. "Your passion for the trees and flowers of the province is obviously genuine, but why did you conceal your identity? If you are not part of the church, then who is your employer? The

English East India Company?"

Ashton's cheeks reddened again. "I have been so foolish — I do not know how to make you believe me. I have no employer. It — it was all supposed to be a grand adventure. I wanted to be like the famous botanical explorers. I wanted to return to Europe with information and seeds and specimens never before seen in the West." He looked up, his eyes pleading for Li Du to understand.

"I know that it is hard to believe," he went on at Li Du's silence, "but I wanted to be a kind of hero."

"To whom?" Li Du was genuinely curious.

Ashton spread his hands in a helpless, all-encompassing gesture. "To the scientific world. The Temple House Botany Club is the most respected group of botanists in England. Sloane — he sailed to the New World — he returned with chocolate and is now the leader of the botanical society. He is at the forefront of every discovery, every convention. Six months ago, I was traveling through Calcutta. I received a letter, a personal letter to me from Sloane. He wrote that he had heard of me, a young student of botany from his college, and knew that I was in this part of the world. He said that there is a growing fascination with the tea forests in southwest China, and with other rumors of botanical wonders in these mountains — of plants, they say, in the shape of lanterns as tall as a man that emit green light. And of many, many others. He said that the society would be most grateful for any report I could give. So — so I began to dream about coming here myself, becoming one of the greatest collectors in history."

"But why did you not simply apply for permission to do that?"

Ashton's eyebrows drew together and his expression became perplexed. He looked at Li Du as if he was searching for some trick in the question. "But you know why," he said.

"I do not. My own journeys over the past five years have kept me outside the company of others. I do not understand why you could not apply to cross the border, especially when the Emperor had invited foreigners to the festival here."

"Oh. Oh — well — yes." Ashton removed the somber black cap from his head and raked his fingers through his mass of curly hair, leaving it in wild disarray. "Then I suppose you do not know the mood in Calcutta. The foreigners there are all convinced that the Emperor of China is going to close the borders permanently, and that it will happen very soon. Everyone feels that the Jesuits are the last vestige of the Emperor's interest in the West, and even they are being treated coldly now. And as for us — the academics, the explorers, the scientists — we are all turned away as spies. I thought that if I wanted to collect plants, my only chance would be to — to . . . Well, to borrow the legitimacy of a Jesuit robe. I have no great tribute to offer, as Sir Gray does."

"And how did you get the letter of permission from the real Brother Martin?"

"We were friends already. I would visit him in the monastery in Calcutta, and he would tell me stories of his journeys in China. When the invitation came from the Emperor, I took it as a kind of sign. I thought that with Brother Martin's old letter, a Jesuit robe, and a new letter giving me permission to collect, I might get away with it. I planned not to attract much notice, to sort of blend in with the other travelers. But I — I did not picture the situation correctly. I — I only borrowed the letter. I didn't steal it."

With an attempt at bravado he added, "I have tried to keep my wits about me, to continue my work and not panic. But — but I have been so afraid. It has been on my mind that the murderer might have killed Brother Pieter out of hatred for the Jesuits. I — I am willing to die as an explorer, reaching for a blue poppy high in the ice and snow of the Himalayan cliffs, if that is my fate. But to be killed for being a member of a religious order to which I do not truly belong . . ." He stopped, frustrated, searching for words to express his feelings. "I did not want to die," he said finally, "as someone other than myself."

He looked up, intensity in his green eyes. He was terribly vulnerable, and Li Du could see that he knew it. And yet there was a new strength in his bearing. A dogged confidence had begun to assert itself from the moment he had uttered his own name, and he did not fidget as he waited for Li Du to pronounce judgment on him.

Looking at him, Li Du understood why Pieter had not immediately condemned Ashton for lying about his name. Li Du recognized a scholar when he saw one. Now that he no longer had to sustain his false identity, his determined, untiring enthusiasm for his quest radiated from him with almost tangible energy. Hugh Ashton had risked his life, had entered a place of isolation and danger to him, in order to study its plants. He was not really a man of the church, but he knew what it was to revere the work of whatever power had breathed life into the snowy mountains, and painted flowers onto them with colors no painter or poet could ever replicate. Li Du sighed.

"I am inclined to believe you," he said, and added, with a little smile, "and I am not going to turn you in to the authorities for the crime of spying on flowers and trees. If you are eavesdropping on orchids in the hope of learning political secrets, you have bigger problems than the threat of imprisonment."

"And — and you believe that I did not kill Brother Pieter?"

Li Du's expression became grave. He glanced outside at Hamza, who sat, eyes closed, with no appearance of paying them any attention. Li Du turned back to Ashton. "You did not leave the courtyard during Hamza's performance that night. At the moment I cannot see a way that you could have been the one to prepare the poisoned tea for Pieter. It appears, for the present, that you have an alibi."

"Then I am to continue the pretense? Please advise me. I have had no one to advise me in such a long time, and I am —" He stopped, overcome by the relief of unguarded speech.

"I think," said Li Du, "that for now it is the safest course. Your plans were not as foolish after all — after today the crowds will multiply, and the Emperor will be too preoccupied with the festival to pay attention to you, especially if the real killer is found by that time."

"And — and whom do you suspect?"

Li Du did not answer the question directly. He was thinking hard about what Ashton had said. He rubbed his forehead, pressing his fingers to his brow as if the pressure might hold his thoughts in place. "I am hoping that now that you are not afraid of me, you will speak candidly on several subjects. It would help me to know more of what you mentioned a moment ago — the impression outside of China that the empire is going to close to foreigners. And while we talk, I will show you how to serve tea."

Hugh nodded, and smiled. Li Du went out to the garden where Hamza sat, where a kettle hung over a lit brazier. He pulled his sleeve over his hand to lift it, noticing too late that the blackened handle left a line of soot on the cloth. Hamza, with a raised eyebrow, said, "Are we drinking tea now? Is it safe to drink tea with him?" Li Du reassured him, and together they went back inside.

Li Du described to Hugh the method by which one can tell that the water has reached the correct temperature, explaining that it was the sound of the boil, the low rush in perfect balance with the higher-pitched dance of bubbles at the side of the pot, but not the center. He showed Hugh how to use the little pot to rinse the leaves and pour the dusty water into the slatted tray. He provided the appropriate ratios of tea to water, and repeated several times the proper way to hold the pot, to pour the tea into each cup, and to present the cup, gently with both hands, to the guest. Hugh Ashton listened with grateful attention, and Li Du saw how his eyes sharpened with keen interest at the mention of the color, variety, and preparation of leaves.

"So," said Li Du, once they were sipping from their cups, "tell me of these rumors in Calcutta."

Ashton had been watching the tea, long, silver strands of dragonwell, opening and darkening in the golden green water and steam. After a moment's thought he looked up. "The news is coming from the Jesuits who are leaving China. They say that the Emperor is beginning to despise all foreigners. The Jesuits blame the Dominicans, of course, for turning the Emperor against all

362

of us with their mishandling of the audience he has granted them. And the Dominicans blame the Jesuits. They say that if the Jesuits had converted China the way they were supposed to, China would have a Christian emperor by now and would be more sympathetic to Western interests."

"By Western interests do you mean trade?"

"The East India Company is the real Western power now in this part of the world — everyone knows it. Everyone outside of China, that is. And the Company is desperate to use Chinese ports."

"Do think Gray's tribute will succeed?"

"The Company is almost as powerful as an empire in its own right, but it is not powerful enough to take China by force. There was a great deal of effort put into this tribute. The material luxuries and inventions and knowledge of all the Company's lands are packed into those crates. Its value is unspeakable — but you know. You have seen it."

They spoke for a while longer, but Ashton had little more information to impart. Li Du had the impression that the space in Ashton's mind not occupied by his work was lonely, homesick, and exhausted. As for Li Du himself, he was aware of the light beginning to fade from the sky. Another day was coming to an end, and he did not know who had killed Brother Pieter. When the sun rose again, he would have only a single day remaining until the Emperor arrived in the city.

But, he told himself, he was beginning to see the face of the killer, as yet a shadowy form that crept through the alleys of memory and imagination, narrow and lantern lit like Dayan's labyrinthine streets. It stared at him, this visage whose features he could almost trace.

It was as maddening as holding a book to a twilit window, seeing the black ink of words across the page but finding them unreadable, as if he was again a child and the characters were only dancing insects with no meaning. Li Du shuddered a little as the figure in his mind backed slowly out of sight again, to wander freely and unobserved in the back corners of his thoughts.

"Are you all right?" Ashton's pale face wore an expression of surprise and concern, and Li Du recalled himself to the moment. After assuring Ashton that he was well, he rose and took his leave. Hamza bowed formally to Ashton, and left with Li Du.

"You are beginning to feel the sand empty from the top of the glass, my friend," said Hamza, with frank sympathy. "And you are sure that you may exclude that strange warlock from our list of suspects?"

"No," Li Du replied, "I am not sure. But he could not have prepared the hot water and placed it in Pieter's room. That was done minutes before Pieter arrived, and the young *Jesuit*" — he emphasized the word with a meaningful look at Hamza — "never left the courtyard."

"Then," said Hamza, "we will trust in the old saying that the morning is wiser than the evening. I am too tired to speak of these intricacies tonight."

They parted, and Li Du made his way through the darkened inn, listening to the nighttime chatter through windows and doors like water over pebbles. His room was cold and dark, and he lit a candle. The square cot with its marble headrest did not appeal. He sat down at the desk, and his eye caught the wine bottle that he and Hamza had purchased in the market. As he pulled the wax-and-paper seal from the top, he read again the words painted in blue glaze on the side, and cast his mind back to the full poem from which they had come:

A candle shadow on a screen of polished marble
The path of stars slants low toward you

Do you regret stealing the potion that has
   set you adrift
Over sea and sky and snow to ponder
   alone through the long nights.

The wine was strong and burned his
throat, but it provided some comfort, if only
in the warmth it sent to his fingers and feet.
He replaced the seal, prepared for bed, and
blew out the flickering candle. Lying in the
dark, he thought again of the face that
watched him from the shadows of his
thoughts. But as hard as he tried to peer
through the deep twilight curtains in his
mind, he could not identify it. He fell,
finally, into an uneasy sleep.

A sound woke him in the middle of the
night. Still half asleep, he blinked uncom-
prehendingly at the dim room. The foot of
his bed was silvery white. *Frost,* he thought.
*Autumn is turning to winter, and soon I will
hear the morning drums.* Then he remembered that he was far from home, and
looked again at the glowing square at his
feet. It was moonlight, not frost, and the air
was soft with the approach of spring.

It was hushed voices that had woken him.
Two people were speaking outside, but from
the bed he could not make out any of the
words. When he was sure that he was awake

and not dreaming, he crept very quietly out of bed and peered out of the latticed window. Across the courtyard from his room were two figures, merely shadows in the night, but he recognized the round form and excitable voice of the innkeeper Hoh. The man he was talking to was thin, and spoke too quietly for Li Du to hear what he said. There was something familiar about him, but without voice or features Li Du could not identify who it was.

"He is old and he may give it away," he heard Hoh say. The other man made some reply.

"You put us all in danger. What if you were to be found out? It would be terrible, terrible for the whole city. We have protected . . ." Hoh lowered his voice and the end of the sentence was inaudible.

The other man spoke for some time, until Hoh cut him off. "We should not talk here. Someone may be listening, and that is *his* room there."

Li Du saw the gesture at his own door and remained very still, trusting the inky shadows to conceal him. He watched the two men leave the courtyard. Then he returned to bed, and reviewed what he had heard. He was wide awake, and had no hope of returning to sleep. But he must have drifted off, because when he opened his eyes it was dawn.

■ ■ ■ ■

1 DAY

■ ■ ■ ■

CHAPTER 16

That morning, Li Du received a summons from Lady Chen. He drank his tea quickly, accepted a hot piece of fried bread from Hoh's kitchen, and ate it outside, away from the crowd. The weather was getting warmer. This morning there was no frost, and the sun rising over the eastern hill heated the dust and stone and clay as soon as it touched them. Contented cats slept in the troughs between rows of roof tiles, and the animal statues on the ridge poles crouched in defense of each home, stone fangs bared.

Inside the mansion, the gold leaf of the pagoda roofs was being reapplied, and in the sunlight the effect was like curls and clouds of fire dripping from the lintels. Li Du's opinion was that fiery decoration had no place on buildings made of wood, and as he passed the library he was glad to see that the columns at its entrance were still a clean, cool blue.

Informed that Lady Chen was in the banquet hall, Li Du went to that central building. Its heavy doors were open just wide enough for him to pass through. Once inside, he shivered in the chill of the dim, cavernous space and waited for his eyes to adjust. The windows, set with round geometric lattices, allowed in very little light.

Hanging from the ceiling were thousands of silk slips with poems written on them. Ironed and gleaming, they fluttered faintly as air currents rippled through them in whispers. At the far end of the hall, two women were speaking to each other. Realizing that he was concealed by the columns and shadows around the door, he stood still, unsure what to do.

Lady Chen was instantly recognizable by her height, and he identified the other woman by her voice. It was Bao, the innkeeper's niece. They stood just beyond the banquet tables and seats, arranged artfully to echo the labyrinth design of the windows. The two of them were appointing the musicians' corner, a space defined by a thick chrysanthemum carpet in front of lacquered screens and framed by a swag of peacock blue silk that puddled at either end. Pillows and musical instruments required careful placement to await the courtesans who would entertain the guests as they ate.

". . . as if I were one of the junior maids," Bao was saying, her syllables lengthened into whines. "I am your eyes and ears outside the mansion, and you never show me any favor." She kicked a pillow like a petulant child.

"Stop complaining, Bao." Lady Chen cradled a pear-shaped lute and lowered it into place beside a zither on a red lacquer stand.

Bao ignored the warning in her mistress's tone. "And why should you have so much authority over me? We are the same. You are just lucky, and if you do not have sons then you will not keep your luck very much longer."

The words were cut short by a slap that echoed through the hall. The hanging poetry fluttered, as if in distress. Bao put her hand to her cheek.

"We are not the same," said Lady Chen. "Not when you behave so stupidly. Have I taught you nothing? These details they tell us are so important — our birth, our fertility, our beauty. Everything is negotiable, and everyone can be manipulated. Men more easily than women."

"But aren't you scared?" asked Bao. "If the magistrate is promoted, maybe he will leave you here —"

"Hush. Those worries are a waste of time. You must be clever, and you must never make mistakes just because you are tired. You complain that I do not give you special treatment, but I am trying to help you."

Bao hung her head. "I am sorry," she said.

"Good," replied Lady Chen. "Then go find yourself a cup of tea, and when you come back I expect you to behave better. Keep your shoulders back as I showed you — you never know what dignitaries may have just arrived, and first impressions are the most important. And of course — tell me if you hear anything of interest."

Bao smoothed her skirts, then turned and walked toward Li Du. Her cheeks were bright with shame, and when she saw him she started, then looked quickly behind her at Lady Chen, who was watching.

"It is all right," said Lady Chen. "I asked him to come and speak with me. You may go."

With a look of almost aching curiosity, Bao curtsied to Li Du and left the room. He walked across the hall to where Lady Chen stood amid the heaps of silk and glass and pillows. She smiled at him, her lips stained the winter red of holly berries.

"You should have announced your presence," she chided him. "I would never have wasted your time with our quarreling when you must have a great deal on your mind. How does your investigation progress?"

Li Du considered what to tell her. He hoped that she had asked for him in order to impart information, rather than request it. "I am afraid," he said, "that I do not know who killed Brother Pieter."

Lady Chen picked up the pillow that Bao had kicked and set it down with deft precision at an angle to the screen. "But Mu Gao tells me that it was jewelvine that killed him."

"Yes."

"Strange that the weapon of death would come from a library."

"Libraries can hold great danger."

"Ah," said Lady Chen, smiling. "You mean words. Yes, I suppose they can. It is a beautiful library, is it not?"

Li Du was perplexed. "Very beautiful."

"There is none like it in this province. The magistrate is very proud of his collection." Lady Chen kept her attention on her work, but Li Du had the impression that she was trying to guide him to answer as she wished. Uncertain of what she wanted, he said, "I had not known my cousin to take such an interest in books."

"The magistrate is a very sophisticated man," replied Lady Chen with another smile. "But his most impressive accomplishments have all been in the political arena. He has never considered himself a scholar. It is the rarity of books that attracts him, and the prestige of owning them."

"Perhaps he intended the library for the education of his children."

Li Du regretted his words as soon as he spoke them. "I did not mean to —"

"To remind me that my position is tenuous?" Lady Chen reached for one of the vases to set it on the display table, then checked herself, as if the temptation to crush it might prove too much. She looked at the dainty object. "As I told Bao," she said, "only simple people accept their lots. I prefer to compensate for what I can't control with what I can."

"Why did you ask to see me?"

It was quiet, the only sound coming from the whisper of silk overhead and the stifled clamor of activity outside the thick walls of the banquet hall. Lady Chen looked away from Li Du and glanced at the dark corners of the room. Then she picked up the vase again, and after she had set it down on the table she touched her finger to her lips to indicate silence. It was so subtly done that, if he had not been watching her so curiously, he would have missed the gesture.

When she spoke again her tone was light and self-deprecating. "I have a frivolous request," she said. "I am embarrassed to distract you with it at such a time as this. You were a librarian in the capital."

"I was."

"I have been studying poetry in anticipation of a change to my situation. If I am to spend more time in the highest societies, I wish to be conversant in the classics. I understand that improvised compositions are expected in conversation, and I fear I am not educated enough to impress the ladies and gentlemen at court."

Bewildered, Li Du began to say that he was sure she would be much admired, but Lady Chen brushed away his compliment before he uttered it. "In particular," she continued, "I am drawn to the poems of Du Fu. I find them" — she bit her lower lip as if the action of recalling the words of a poem was like the taste of wine on the tongue — "haunting. His work evokes a pathos I have never encountered in words."

"The verses of Du Fu are among the most beautiful I know. But what service do you require from me?"

"There is a book," she said, "in our

library. It contains my favorite of his poems. But the introduction is written by a Master Min, and I confess I cannot make sense of his analysis. I do not understand his interpretation of Du Fu's work. I wondered if, when the business of your investigation is over, we might discuss it?"

"You — you wish me to find the book?"

She waved her hand airily. "Yes," she said. "Just look up the title in the catalogue. *The Laments.*" She said the name very quietly, and her gaze moved once more around the room.

"I will do my best."

"Thank you. You are very patient. But I have been very selfish and careless with your time. My request is so trifling, when your task is so grave. Please excuse me. I remember that I must interview the chefs who have arrived from the Emperor's retinue. They are to be integrated into our own kitchens, and you can imagine the feelings that could be hurt in that encounter. Please, excuse me."

After she had gone, the hall fell into uneasy silence, as if the glistening ornaments were holding their breath. Li Du remained alone for a few moments, thinking. Then, with renewed purpose, he left the empty banquet hall and set out for the library.

He found Mu Gao standing at the top of the stairs between the blue columns, holding his broom. The old man beckoned him inside and said, "So you were asking my friend Old Mu questions? Checking my story? Was I really drinking with him? What do you think — I'm some liar?"

Li Du shook his head and said gently to the old man, "He told me that you two drink together and remember old times. He said that you fought bravely against the enemies of this province."

Mu Gao grunted. "That we did. And for our troubles, what were we given? Well, I can't speak of that. Old times — and now our family dwindles and dwindles. These Chinese people think I am an illiterate, a bumpkin, because I speak bad Chinese. Never asked to be held up to your standards, though. Never did." Mu Gao's voice was angry, but Li Du saw in his eyes a frustrated, bewildered sadness. He remembered what the old clerk had told him about Mu Gao having no immediate family.

Li Du said, "Chinese scholars and bureaucrats can be fearful of what they do not themselves know. But in my opinion, an empire is like a carpet, most beautiful when woven into a pattern. Languages are the colored threads, and without them the empire would be very dull."

Mu Gao was still clutching his broom, but he set it aside, picked up his cane, and gestured for Li Du to follow. "Come. There is no one around and I have decided to show you something."

Mu Gao limped through the shelves of the philosophy section, his cane tapping rhythmically on the floor. Li Du padded behind him. It was like following a crab along the floor of a silver pond, thought Li Du as he moved through the pale sheen of book boxes that rippled across a spectrum of azure and kingfisher blue. At the far end of the bookcase, a dragon was carved deeply into the wood, its outline filled with thick blue paint. Beneath it was etched the sign of the constellation *heart.*

At about the center of the aisle, Mu Gao stopped. Then, with a creaking of joints and muttered obscenities, he knelt on the floor beside the lowest shelf and beckoned for Li Du join him. Mu Gao surreptitiously squinted to his right and left, and through the gap between the shelves, assuring himself that no one was nearby. Then he pointed to a few books bound in the same blue silk as the others.

"I want to show you my collection. I know you're an exile. You're not like the other Chinese. And my friend likes you." He looked directly into Li Du's eyes as he spoke. "And you're a librarian," Mu Gao added, "so you care about the books." He swept his calloused fingertips over the spines of seven books on the bottom shelf.

"I bound these myself," he said proudly, "with extra silk from repairs. The blue dragon" — his voice wavered and he cleared his throat — "the old mountain dragon has slept beside this city from the beginning of time. When I was a child I used to think that maybe one day it would lift right up from the ground, shake off the trees and snow, up into the air . . ." He trailed off, lost.

"What are these volumes, Mu Gao? What have you taken such pains to preserve?" asked Li Du in a gentle voice.

"What's left of our books, of course. My family's books. My grandfather was the last Mu king. He was a man of our culture. He wrote poems and histories. Then the Qing came and almost all of them are gone now. Burned. Why? I don't understand. The Ming were not that way. Doesn't matter now. But these are the only books left, and I won't let them be thrown away like trash, like all the food they throw away every night." His voice became a thin, raspy whisper. "I don't trust the magistrate."

Mu Gao's rheumy eyes shone with tears, and his stare held a plea. He wiped his tears on his sleeve.

"You have done well to keep these safe," said Li Du.

"You won't tell on an old man?" Mu Gao was tired, and the effort of showing his books to Li Du had drained him. He was beginning to look confused, and Li Du said firmly, "I will not tell anyone."

Mu Gao smiled confidingly. Then his mood shifted, as quick as changing weather. "Well," he said, irritated, "why are we crawling around on the floor? Aren't you supposed to be finding out who is the poisoner? I'm almost out of my own secret store of tea, and I'm not drinking the mansion leaves until the madman's been sent to join his ancestors." With Li Du's help, Mu Gao rose to his feet. He muttered about a quick rest in the sunshine, and ambled in that direction.

Li Du paced slowly to the round table at the center of the library, then walked around it, reading the names of the constellations at the ends of each shelf: *willow, net, wall, wings, root, danger, three-stars* . . . His eyes

took in the rows and rows of books surrounding him. Within them, hidden and
bound in silken uniformity, entire worlds
rose and fell. Attackers climbed walls on
ladders of arrows and nets. Traitors died by
a thousand cuts. Dragons hunted pearls.
Friends smoked pipes by willow gates.
Emperors conversed with explorers. Cities
were built and burned. Mountains slept or
crumbled in rivers of dirt and rock. All this
chaos, these contradictions, arguments, lies,
and riddles, was quiet, confined by serene
stitches and tranquil silk panels.

His thoughts turned to Beijing. The imperial library was a small building in the
northeastern corner of the Forbidden City.
Its walls were of black tile like a deep lake,
watery to ward off thoughts of fire, and
thereby, it was thought, fire itself. Inside,
the rooms were separated by massive
painted screens in muted golds and greens.
And the books — they were as familiar to
him as the memorized lines of a poem. He
even remembered their scents. Some were
musky from voyages in saddlebags. Others
had become perfumed by the incense
burned in the consorts' rooms where they
had most recently been read. Others were
peppery from the treatment used to deter
bookworms, similar to Mu Gao's jewelvine.

He pulled himself from the memory as he arrived at the shelf he was looking for, one filled with books bound in black, under the sign of the tortoise. This was where, if he understood the filing system correctly, the book of Du Fu's poetry should be.

He had to kneel again, but he found the *Laments* easily and pulled the heavy box from its place. Behind it lay a second dark, square object, hidden in shadow and camouflaged by the surrounding black silk boxes. Li Du slid it out, and returned the *Laments* to its place.

It was bound in the Western style, with a cover that was worn, scuffed, and stained by water and the round imprints of hot cups of tea that had rested on it. He opened to a page at random. There, drawn by hand in dark lead, were six circles of equal size, each one marked with tiny black stars and pictograph symbols. There were titles in neat, slanting Latin: *Systema Ptolemaicum,* followed by *Systema Platonicum, Systema Egyptiacum, Systema Tychonicum, Systema Semi-Tychonicum,* and *Systema Copericanum.* He carefully turned the pages. They were filled with words and illustrations, all in the same confident hand. This was unmistakably Brother Pieter's journal.

Li Du carried it with a light step to the

sun room. He heard a purring snore behind him, and saw that Mu Gao was already asleep on his cushioned bench at the far side of the library. Through the large windows of the sun room he could see the mansion paths crowded with activity. Guards and bannermen and secretaries hurried in every direction, while servants scrubbed the marble statues and beat the dust from pillows.

Open on the table in front of him, Pieter's journal looked like a tired, white moth resting its wings. The contents were devoted entirely to astronomical observations and calculations. Pieter had charted the trajectory of the moon with dotted lines surrounded by pinprick constellations. He had described the sky from various vantage points in the mountains. He had summarized the Tibetan understanding of the constellations. And he had mused on the construction of portable measuring devices. Li Du's eyes rested with pleasure on the accompanying drawings, which depicted several astrolabes in the Persian style, the sketches complete with the curling, dense flowers and vines incised into the layered faces of the instruments.

In the imperial library Li Du had seen original journals of famous travelers, and remembered their pages to be a patchwork of different inks and lead, scratched-out phrases and rejected words, reflecting the excitements and frustrations of the adventures. Pieter's journal was different. Nothing had been erased, crossed out, or altered. It was as if Pieter had simply written down what was already clear and perfected in his mind. Were it not for the chronological organization, lead pencil writing, and empty pages at the end, it might have been a published book.

On the second-to-last filled page there was a sketch of the tellurion, lightly, almost lovingly rendered. The kingdom of gems was indicated only by a few abstract lines for the purpose of showing its scale relative to the rest of the device. It was the planets and clockwork that had captivated Pieter.

Below the sketch and onto the page opposite ran a long trail of calculations, the result of each one serving as the starting point for the one that followed. In this section Pieter's work was not flawlessly executed. The handwriting was rushed and uneven, and Pieter had written numbers only to strike through them and replace them with others. A seven had been turned into a rough six, then crossed out and changed back to a seven. One equation had been repeated twice with different results, both scratched over with lead.

Li Du sighed and allowed his head to fall forward into his hands. The journal contained an astronomer's observations of the world. There was no mention of any name or circumstance that suggested a motive for murder. But how had it come to be in the library? And how had Lady Chen known that it was there? He tried to ignore the suggestion of a slant in the shadows on the floor. It was past noon.

The sound of footsteps jolted him from his thoughts. He closed the book, tucked it in a pocket of his robe, and followed the sound to the back of the library. He found Nicholas Gray struggling to open the hall of treasures. Gray was again in his ambassador's clothing, black velvet and heavy jeweled chains and rings. His sunburned skin was peeling white on his large nose, and he smelled of cloying tobacco and anxious sweat.

He swore as he rattled the key in the lock. "You," he said, when he recognized Li Du.

"Do not push the key so far into the lock," Li Du advised.

"So every damned person in the mansion knows how to get into this room except for me?" Gray hissed the question. "The magistrate assured me that the tribute would be kept behind a locked door, but he did not tell me who else had a key."

Li Du glanced across the library. Mu Gao's bench was now empty and shadowed.

"I asked to be allowed in," said Li Du. "The magistrate gave orders that I was to have access to any room I needed. The treasury included."

Gray's nostrils quivered and he looked at Li Du with piercing eyes. "I should have been consulted."

"I assure you, nothing was disarranged."

"And you found nothing relevant to the death of the Jesuit. I know that you did not. There is nothing to find. Brother Pieter had no connection to the Company, to the tribute, or to me."

"And yet he spent his final hours examining the tellurion."

Gray shrugged. "He was an astronomer. Of course he was interested. There was no need for him to do it in secret. I would have let him admire it."

"You and he quarreled the day you met."

"A disagreement between intelligent men is not a quarrel, as I told you before. Are you telling me that I am still a suspect? I told you the truth in the field. His death has only caused me anxiety. The magistrate assures me that the Emperor has been informed of the situation and is not himself concerned by it. The murderer must have come from somewhere else, and left Dayan when the task was complete. It seems that you are the only one who still insists on pursuing the issue, but you cannot think that you will find the answer before tomorrow, if you do not know it by now." The key turned finally in Gray's muscular hand and he swung the heavy door wide to let light into the dim room. The great, black box that fit in puzzle pieces around the tellurion rested solidly on the table.

"There is still time," Li Du said.

"Of course," Gray replied. He went inside, leaving Li Du standing in the doorway. Li Du watched as Gray leaned over the box and put a hand flat against its side. Gray was frozen, barely breathing, like a doctor taking a patient's pulse. After several seconds Gray relaxed and removed his hand. "Good," he said. He removed a small panel to peer inside the box. "The gears still turn and the sun still glows," he said quietly. "For one more day I must protect it. Then I am discharged of my duty. Now if you will excuse me, I will continue with my inventory. The magistrate has promised to meet me here tonight and review the exact order in which the items are to be presented. I will not have my audience cheapened by poor timing."

Now to the inn, thought Li Du as he left the library. He was almost out of the mansion when he saw Tulishen, Lady Chen, and Jia Huan walking in his direction. They were deep in conversation, but when Tulishen looked up and saw Li Du, he flushed slightly and stopped in the middle of his speech. He recovered quickly, and raised a hand in curt acknowledgement.

"What progress?" he asked.

Li Du was careful not to glance at Lady Chen. "I have found Brother Pieter's journal," he said.

"Ah," said Tulishen. "And does it tell you anything?"

"He does not name his killer, unless the name is encoded in astronomical calculations." Li Du retrieved the journal from where he had tucked it in a pocket of his robe and held it up, open, so that they could see. "It is a record of planetary movements, not human ones," he explained.

"Do you truly suspect a code? Or is it your fatigue that causes you to speak in this way?"

"Fatigue?" Li Du was looking at the pages.

"Yes," Tulishen repeated, with a meaningful look at his companions. "You are being unclear," he said to Li Du, in a louder, more deliberate voice.

Li Du closed the book and looked at his cousin. "The language of astronomy," he said, half to himself. "Yes, yes, perhaps I am fatigued. You caught me lost in thought. I am afraid I am not very clear."

"Well, Cousin, I will leave you to these wanderings." Then, to Li Du's surprise, his cousin moved forward and, with one hand on Li Du's shoulder, ushered him away from Jia Huan and Lady Chen so that they could speak in private.

"Cousin," said Tulishen, and his voice was almost kind. "You set yourself too ambitious a task. You should have been guided by me. Perhaps I should have been more protective of you. You are overburdened here in society after your years of solitude. The Emperor will understand. He has far more important matters on his mind than our domestic disturbance. You will be allowed to go on your way."

Li Du took a step back from Tulishen. "I am not overburdened," he said. "And there is much for me still to consider. There is time."

"You should rest," said Tulishen, in a harder voice. Then he turned to Jia Huan. "It has come to my attention that tourists are stealing mosaic tiles from the field. I want more guards posted there, now that all is in readiness. Go see to that now. And you know that this evening the ambassador wishes to rehearse his presentation with the tribute."

"Your pardon," said Jia Huan, "but I have already sent extra guards to the field. I assumed you would wish it."

Tulishen was pleased. "That is very well done," he said. "You are as always of great use to me. And what of the issue with tomorrow's banquet?" Before Jia Huan could reply, Tulishen turned to Li Du and explained, "We were prepared for a certain number, but did not know until this morning that there will be Muslims who do not eat pork."

"The innkeeper Hoh will contribute beef dishes and bread," said Jia Huan. "I confirmed this with him on my way here."

"And," Tulishen went on, now to Lady Chen, "I want you to bring some of your wine to the magistrate from Pu'erh. He is expecting special treatment. The Emperor's decision not to visit Pu'erh has been a blow to him, and we must not allow his jealousy of our success to upset the evening."

Tulishen continued talking, and barely noticed when Li Du gave a little bow and slipped away. He was just outside the inn when he caught up with Mu Gao, who was heading in the direction of the city offices. He carried a jar of wine and a jumble of papers in the basket on his back.

"You are going to see Old Mu?" asked Li Du.

"Yes I am," said Mu Gao, and glanced up at the sky. "It will be a fine evening. You want to drink wine with us tonight?"

Li Du smiled. "I am grateful for the invitation," he said, "but another time, perhaps."

"Your choice," said Mu Gao, and clattered on his cane down the alley.

CHAPTER 17

"We know," said Hamza, studying a moth that had landed on the little stone table in front of him. "We know . . ." he repeated, trailing off as the moth fluttered up into the branches of a cherry tree. He yawned and shook his head. "I do not know what we know," he said, moodily, "only that I begin to suspect this city is an evil place."

They were sharing a late lunch in the courtyard outside Li Du's room at the inn because they had been unable to find seats or to hear each other speak among the crowds and clamor in the dining hall. The warmth that had arrived early that morning had remained, and in the sunshine it was almost hot. A crow squawked from an unseen perch among the mossy patchwork roof tiles, and the sky was blue. Li Du had opened the doors and windows of his room.

"If we believe Sir Gray," he said, "we know that the poisoned tea leaves were in a cup on Pieter's desk, beside a pot of freshly boiled water, when the two of them arrived at Pieter's room."

Hamza reached for his cup of wine, and frowned when he saw that it was empty. He set the cup down. "And do we believe this Nicholas Gray? During my travels I have seen the results of their methods of *diplomacy*. The Company is like a seducer who first charms his victim, then leads her deep under the sea to drown her in the mountains of the underworld. Brother Pieter knew this also. First there is negotiation. Then there is death."

The word hung in the air for a moment before Li Du responded. "For Gray, the murder is an inconvenience that has hindered his mission. What he wants — what he has been told to do — is to charm the Emperor with visions of the wealth that foreign trade will bring to China. A dead body, that of a man whose holy brothers are looked upon with some favor by the Emperor — it casts a pall over the festival and, possibly, over the negotiations. Gray would not take that risk lightly. He would have needed a very strong reason to kill Pieter — something more than rivalry or dislike."

"And how do we know he did not have such a reason? I don't like him."

"The story he gave does account for the missing cup. So let us assume — just for the present — that he spoke the truth. What then do we know of that night?"

Hamza ran his finger around the lip of his empty bowl. "You go on," he said. "This straightforward thinking is not natural to me."

Li Du ignored Hamza's apparent disinterest and said, "How did the murderer want Pieter's death to appear?" Hamza waited, and Li Du went on. "We were meant to think that Pieter returned to his room alone, prepared tea himself — he mentioned several times that he drank red tea in the evenings and also he did not like to be waited upon — and died the natural death of an elderly traveler who had undertaken a journey that was too difficult for him."

"But then what about the purse?"

"The murderer assumed that if the death was declared to have been natural, the purse would never have been noticed. It would have been buried or discarded with the rest of Pieter's modest possessions. The purse was put there in case the doctor recognized the signs of poison and reported those signs to the magistrate. If that happened, the purse would have been found and the poison identified. The blame would then be placed outside the mansion, far away from the actual killer. The Khampa gave Pieter the poisoned gift and he, unsuspecting, prepared their tea for himself that night. And that is exactly what the magistrate did believe. The plan was a clever one. But —"

"But I am confused again. How did the murderer give Pieter the tea? Pieter would not have simply served himself tea from an ornate pouch he did not recognize."

"The poisoned tea that Pieter actually drank was not in the pouch. We have Gray's evidence on this. When he entered the room with Pieter, the tea leaves were already in the cup on the desk. And there was a pot of water, freshly boiled, beside the cup. The murderer must have been there only moments earlier to fill the pot with water from the kettle in the courtyard. Pieter assumed, as the murderer meant him to, that the tea had been prepared for him by a servant."

Hamza squinted in the manner of a person trying to read text that is too small. "So the murderer did not account for someone else being in the room with Pieter."

Li Du nodded. "Exactly. The murderer did not expect there to be a witness. As it happened, Gray was happy to keep the crime a secret in order to protect himself from suspicion. The problem for both of them occurred when Gray, in an effort to hide the poison, took the teacup from the room. He was acting in his own interest, but his interests would have been better served if he had left the scene as the murderer wished it to appear. The missing teacup achieved exactly what the murderer wished to avoid — it drew attention to the people in the mansion. But even with this knowledge, I fear we are no closer to knowing who arranged the poisoned tea."

"The rash young scientist, the striding fool," said Hamza, dreamily.

"You refer to Brother Martin?" *The so-called,* Li Du added silently.

"Magicians with obsessions are dangerous."

"He is a botanist, not a magician, but I take your meaning. He has proved himself a liar, certainly. But he does have an alibi — he never left the courtyard, and could not have prepared the tea and hot water."

"Then what of your cousin, the magistrate? He did not leave the courtyard either, but if he wanted Pieter dead there are many who might have done it for him. People of rank can hire assassins."

"That is so, and he is the one who told the doctor to lie about the circumstances of Pieter's death. But what could be his motive? Tulishen, like Gray, is devoted to the success of the festival. He only asked me to remain in Dayan in order to enlist my help in avoiding trouble from the foreigners. What threat could Pieter have posed to Tulishen that would be worse than the consequences of a murder occurring in his house?"

"Then we come," said Hamza, with another look at his empty bowl, "to Lady Chen. I find her nose very attractive."

"She has," said Li Du, "an unusual beauty. Her hair and her clothes have all the sophistication and style of the high courtesans in Beijing, but on her they seem almost a" — he searched for a way to express himself without incurring Hamza's mockery — "a lacquer. There is a deeper strength in her that is hidden by all those —" He gestured at his head in a vague illustration of pins and jewels.

Hamza's face took on a catlike expression. "So you like the Lady Chen, do you? Perhaps she likes you also. Why do you think she directed you to the journal? And how did she know where it was?"

"I think she is the one who took it from his room."

"Why?"

"I do not know."

Hamza huffed impatiently. "Your answers do not satisfy. What of Mu Gao? He is a bitter man."

"That is true, but his anger is not at the Jesuits. He might have wanted to sabotage the festival, but he could have done that without killing a stranger. Of course, Pieter was in Dayan as a young man. We must not forget that."

As he spoke, Li Du opened Pieter's journal and began idly to scan its pages. Hamza looked over his shoulder and sighed. "I remember him making those diagrams in the mountains," he said. "But they are nonsense to me. How does anyone understand this language?"

"With some patience," said Li Du.

Hamza's attention moved from the book to Li Du's open window. His face brightened when he saw the desk, on which sat the bottle of wine that they had purchased at the market. It gleamed cheerful blue and white. "Is it possible," he said, "that you have wine left? I finished mine on the evening we bought it." He picked up the bottle and shook it. "But this is at least half full," he said, delighted.

Li Du raised an eyebrow. "It is hardly the time of day for wine."

"You are mistaken. Wine is as good in

sunlight as in moonlight."

His attention on the journal, Li Du gestured for Hamza to help himself. *Why,* he was thinking, *why did Pieter write these final pages so poorly? Was he upset?* Pieter had been meticulous on every single page of the journal. He had sketched out one complex equation after another without a single mistake. What had made him slip on that final day? Had something distracted —

Li Du was pulled violently from his thoughts by the sound of porcelain shattering on the floor of his room. As he turned, he saw Hamza fall to his knees, then topple to the floor, clutching the carpet as he began to shake with violent convulsions.

Instantly Li Du was on his feet, the journal forgotten. He glanced from the wine bottle on the desk to the broken cup on the floor, and knew with cold certainly that Hamza had been poisoned. He understood this, understood that it might be too late, but even as his sense of dread increased he was running across the courtyard, crying out for help. Above him the tree branches against the blue sky were like a cracked mirror. The bamboo groves were like walls and the crooked paths distorted and endless.

He almost collided with a maid who was lighting an incense lantern, and it swung crazily, stirring the fragrant smoke into a gray cloud. She let out a startled cry. He told her to fetch the doctor to his own rooms without delay. She gathered up handfuls of her draped silk skirt and rushed away toward the main entrance of the inn, and Li Du continued his own headlong run until he came to the shut door of Hugh Ashton's apartments. He called, and pounded so hard the iron handles rattled in their fastenings.

The door opened and Ashton's pale face peered out. When he recognized Li Du he relaxed momentarily, only to tense again as he reacted to Li Du's expression. Li Du cut him off before Ashton could speak. "Hamza has been poisoned and is dying. You must help him." Ashton stared, and in a burst of frustration Li Du pushed past him into the room.

"Here," Li Du said, sweeping his arm to encompass the plants that filled the space. "Somewhere here there is something that will help. What did you learn from the doctor? *Think!*"

The panic in Li Du's voice galvanized the young scholar, and with a low exclamation he rushed to the stacks of paper and pushed the weights from the top of the piles. A small jade ink stone broke into three pieces on the floor. Its lion's head rolled into a corner. The books that had been stacked on top of the piles fell to the floor in bedraggled heaps of fanned pages and covers.

"I know what I am looking for," muttered Ashton as he tore through the sheets of paper separating the plants that he had meticulously pressed and labeled. The yellowed sheets fluttered through the room like feathers, settling one by one onto the floor in a crackling layer. Ashton whispered under his breath: *"Thea chinensis . . . Pimentae jamaicensis . . . Ricinus chinensis sebifera . . . adiantum . . . mandragora . . ."* He stopped, triumphant, and held up a brown root. "This one," he said. "Where is he?"

Together they hurried from the room. Li Du led Ashton through the courtyards. Li Du only barely registered that they were abandoned, and that everyone must be out in the streets enjoying the performances. As they came close to Li Du's room they heard muffled voices. Just outside the door, several maids were huddled, crying and whimpering in distress and indecision. One of them managed, in little gulping gasps, to tell Li Du that the doctor would be there soon.

Inside, another servant stood helplessly over Hamza, whose breath was a weakening rattle from his throat. His skin was waxen. As they knelt beside him he spasmed; his back arched and his fingers curled into stiff claws as his face contorted in a cry of pain.

Ashton's face registered horror and he said with a shaking voice, "I need something to crush the root." Li Du grabbed the heavy marble inkstone from the desk, and was surprised to find it full of ink. The cool liquid ran black down his fingers and over his hand. He ran his sleeve over the stone to wipe the rest of the dripping ink from it as he put it in Ashton's white, outstretched hand. Ashton crushed the root against the floor then forced Hamza's mouth open and the juicy pulp into it. He closed Hamza's jaw so that his teeth bit down on it and he swallowed.

At first it seemed as if they were too late. Hamza's body was racked by new shudders, and his mouth opened in helpless agony. Then his clutching fingers went still, the muscles of his face relaxed, and his head fell to one side. For one terrible moment it appeared that the life had gone out of him. Then his chest rose once, fell, and rose again. The horrible, rattling wheeze was gone, and Hamza was breathing normally. He was alive.

At that moment Doctor Yang arrived, his thin cheeks bright from running and his beard spread across his chest in wispy disarray. His entrance brought a comforting waft of dried angelica into the room. After one glance at Hamza he began to issue orders. He told the frightened maids to stop gawking and to bring him hot water, cold water, clean towels, and clean robes. They scurried away. While he spoke he was simultaneously examining Hamza, preparing poultices, and mixing herbs. Li Du saw that his hands were gentle, his wrinkled fingers pressing softly, ascertaining temperature and pulse.

Hugh Ashton had stood up and retreated to a corner as soon as the doctor had arrived. Li Du remained on his knees, watching Hamza's face for signs of recovery and waiting for Doctor Yang to say something. But the doctor's words were reserved for giving commands, and when he did address Li Du it was only to ask him to pour more hot water into the cup that the doctor had prepared. Li Du reached for the fresh pot that had just been delivered by a maid, and started at the sight of his own blackened hand. Remembering the spilled ink, he frowned as he poured the water. He had not left ink in the ink stone — he was certain of it. As he gazed around the room, without really looking, he noticed a dim corner of white that looked like a piece of paper. It was far enough under the bed so as not to be visible to anyone who was not crouched, as he was, on the floor. But he hardly had time to remark on its presence when the doctor finally leaned back and hummed with a little sound of satisfaction. The maids had cleaned the floor around them, and Hamza had been undressed and clothed again quickly in warm, thick robes.

"He will recover," said Doctor Yang, with assurance. "He can be carried to his own room. I have given him an herb to make him sleep, now that the poison has been countered." He looked up at Hugh Ashton with pride, and said to Li Du, "You may tell the young foreigner that the nightshade root certainly kept this man's heart beating. He paid good attention to what I taught him. I told you he was not an imbecile, however poor his communication skills."

Li Du repeated this to Hugh Ashton, who stammered that he had not done very much, and that he was only relieved that there had not been another death. He bowed awkwardly.

"Where was the poison?" asked the doctor, turning to Li Du.

"In my wine," said Li Du, and brought the bottle to the doctor.

"You did not drink it?"

"I was about to. Hamza drank first."

Doctor Yang reached for the wine and sniffed it. He nodded, and said something in the local tongue that expressed in growling vowels and guttural consonants his opinions on the corruption of wine with poison. "You know that you must be very careful now. *This* was obviously no accident." Li Du heard the emphasis and understood that the doctor was referring to Tulishen's attempt to cover up Pieter's murder.

"The same poison?" asked Li Du.

"No. Blackhood leaves are my guess. And I see by the way your face falls that you know this will not help you catch the villain — this plant grows on all the mountain slopes in the province." Doctor Yang looked at Hamza's drawn face. "Your friend was lucky," he said. "He is young and strong, and had a little time in which to fight for his life. Very lucky. A bigger sip, even, and his soul would be gone from his body even as we speak."

"Will he be well soon?"

"After rest. But here is the innkeeper. I think that if we all work together we can move him easily. He will be more comfortable, I think, in his own room."

Hoh stood at the door, wringing his hands and speaking in breathless phrases. "In my inn," he said, "in my own establishment. I don't know how it could have happened. Poison! It is evil. It is treachery. But I am responsible. I am responsible. Everyone will think so. The guests rely on me. They put faith in their host . . . an ancient trust . . ."

"He lives," said Li Du, reassuringly. "He lives and now you must help us make him comfortable and safe."

The distraught Hoh put his hands to his face and shook his head. "It just cannot be. Someone must have come and poisoned — but where was the poison?" He saw the bottle and the crushed wine cup. "In your own wine?" he cried. "In your wine that you kept in your room? But you might both have died. I keep a good place. I work very hard. I never — I would never . . ."

"Be calm, old friend," chided Doctor Yang. "Wolves howl and ghosts weep, but innkeepers must be calm. Now we must get this poor man to his room."

"Yes — yes, of course," Hoh sniffed and dried his eyes. "But only allow me to ask — is there a way to stop the rumors that will spread now? Is there a way to keep my guests from leaving? He did not die, after all. . . ." Hoh stopped.

"Well, then," he said to the answering silence, "what will happen will happen. I'm the first one to say there's no stopping a rumor. But please" — he turned a pleading face to Li Du — "you must find this madman quickly. I do not know what will befall this city if you don't. I just don't know."

As soon as Hoh had collected himself, he sent for two strong servants to bring an extra door panel from the storage rooms. They lifted Hamza gently onto the panel and carried him through two courtyards to the door of his own room, where maids had been sent ahead to add warm fur blankets to those already on the bed. In addition, stone foot warmers had been placed, hot from the stove, at the end of the mattress.

"He will be better soon. Let him rest for a while now. Leave a maid here to call for you if there is some problem, and if his condition worsens at all, send for me immediately."

Li Du's own pulse and breathing were beginning to return to normal, and a thought occurred to him. He put out a hand to stop Hoh from turning away. "You said that you do not want this rumor to spread," he said to Hoh, addressing also Doctor Yang.

"I would do anything," said Hoh, pathetically. He raised his hand to rub away the sweat gleaming on his forehead, and his thumb left a faint white trail of flour across his brow.

"In that case," said Li Du, "use your authority over your staff to keep this quiet. Doctor, did you tell anyone what had happened on your way here?"

"I told no one."

"Then only a few of us know."

"But the secret cannot be kept for long," said the doctor. "Hoh is right. Rumors can't be controlled in a crowd like this."

"Not for long, no," agreed Li Du. "But it was my wine that was poisoned. The Emperor comes tomorrow. Why, then, would the killer risk murdering me when tomorrow my investigation will be over? I think — I hope — that it means I am close to an answer. If I can just have some time, without the magistrate becoming involved, I feel that I am very close now to the truth."

"You will have as much time as we can give you," said Hoh. "I will speak to my servants."

They were just about to leave when Hamza awoke and requested, groggily, that Li Du remain behind so that they might speak alone. After receiving instructions from the doctor on when to drink each of the herbal medicines arranged on the table beside him, Hamza and Li Du were left alone.

Hamza's voice was raspy, and he directed his words to the ceiling: "There was once," he said, then swallowed uncomfortably and ran his tongue over dry lips. Li Du brought him the ginger infusion, and Hamza sipped it. "A merchant of Bukhara."

"You must rest," said Li Du, alarmed. "This is no time for a story."

Hamza pursed his lips and directed at Li Du a look of regal affront. He was about to continue, but Li Du stopped him with a firm shake of his head. "You may tell me of this merchant of Bukhara when you are well."

After assuring himself that the maids would not cease their watch over Hamza, or waste any time coming to him should there be any cause for worry, Li Du took his leave.

Back at his room, he took the wine bottle and the one unbroken bowl, his own, into the courtyard and poured the remaining liquid into the dirt among the bamboo stalks. He returned to his room, pulled the doors and windows tight shut, and fastened the metal bolts in place. Finally, sure that he was alone, he knelt on the floor and looked under the bed.

As he had thought, there was a sheet of paper there. He flattened his shoulder as best he could against the floor, and reached

411

his ink-stained hand under as far as he could. His fingers just reached the corner of the paper, and he edged it toward him. It was not dusty, as he had expected it to be. And it was not blank.

It was a letter addressed to the magistrate, using the magistrate's old name. He stared at it, unable at first to comprehend what he saw. Finding suddenly that his legs had become weak, he sank to the edge of the bed and sat there, his back curved forward over the crisp sheet of paper. He read:

Honorable Cousin Li Erfeng,

My thoughts dissolve like rotting leaves in a deep pond. I do not remember who I am. Perhaps I am just a ghost. The unbearable moaning in the stone caves grows louder in my mind. I always thought, alone in those cold places, that it was the sound of the mountain winds. But I begin to fear that it is my own silent voice.

Five years I have wandered. I know that I will never be allowed to return home. There remains one simple task. I hope that in death I will find the path of stars to the celestial dragon. Or am I doomed to the crooked way of demons? I accept my fate with the little dignity

412

that is left to me.

Before I go into the darkness, I offer my confession. I killed the Jesuit. In my hatred and envy I wished him dead, and so I poisoned him as he and his kind would poison the empire. I do not regret this act.

I am no more.

Li Du

CHAPTER 18

He read the letter again. Then he stood up, went to the desk, and wrote neatly at the top of the page: *The following letter is a forgery. I, Li Du, am not the author.* He opened a drawer, put the letter inside, and shut it. As soon as it was out of sight, he felt better.

A forgery. As a librarian he had encountered hundreds of forged documents. He had always enjoyed looking for the small indications that separated the authentic pages from the counterfeits. It was gentle work: feeling the weight of the paper, studying the color of the ink, and searching for anachronistic vocabulary.

But the letter he had just found was more than just an imitation of his handwriting. It was a forged reality. He closed his eyes and allowed himself to follow the lie it conjured. Li Du, the dishonored exile, had lost his mind somewhere in the wild darkness of the mountains. He had come to Dayan, where his insanity had been sharpened by bitter resentment of his cousin's success. The prattling Jesuit, a reminder of the capital, had become the object of his malice, and soon, the victim of it.

Once the Jesuit was dead, Li Du's guilt had consumed him, and he had cast himself with pathetic delusion into the role of the detective. Now, on the eve of the Emperor's arrival, his illness had risen to a fever and, unable to escape his demons, he had chosen suicide. A maid would have found him dead in his room, and a search would have revealed the letter where it lay under the bed, fallen from his lifeless hand. In the morning the magistrate, with proper grief and shame, would have told the Emperor the sad ending. The Emperor would have nodded, the festival would have begun, and the tale would have been absorbed and diluted among the crowds.

It was the killer's third suggestion. The first was that an old traveler had died naturally after a long journey. The second was that the same traveler had been brutally and senselessly poisoned by bandits too far away to pursue.

The features that had eluded Li Du were becoming more clear. It was a forger who waited in the shadows, a forger not only of ink and paper, but of worlds. Like painted screens placed in front of a real landscape, these altered realities were moved softly, silently into place.

They were convincing worlds, each tailored to an audience that would not look closely for the hallmarks of illusion. Those who had supported the idea of Li Du as the exiled detective might as easily and with as much titillation see him as the murderer, the scholar driven mad by rejection and solitude. And then the festival, liberated from the anxiety of an unresolved mystery, could proceed with all the beautiful decadence that had lured the thousands of people to Dayan. The killer had arranged his realities with a reverence for the desires of others. Behind this care lurked a certain pride, and the satisfaction of skilled craftsmanship.

Li Du stood up, noticing as he did the ink that still stained his hand. He knew now why the ink stone had been full. It had been turned into a prop. He opened the drawer, removed the letter, and kept it folded in one hand. Then he pushed open his door and ventured out across the courtyards toward Hamza's room.

When he arrived, he found the storyteller

propped up on pillows, looking disconsolate. He brightened when he saw Li Du.

"So you have come back," he said, "because you wish to know what happened to the merchant of Bukhara?" His voice, usually strong and clear, was a croak.

Li Du told the maids that they were dismissed, then sat down on a chair beside Hamza's bed. Hamza looked at him curiously. "Give me some of that brew I am supposed to be drinking," said Hamza, "and I will tell you." Li Du handed him the cup. Hamza sipped the tonic, winced, and handed it back to Li Du. He was still very pale. But he swallowed and drew himself up a little straighter.

"The merchant had a — a servant that he trusted. One day the merchant was sitting on silk cushions in the sunlight waiting for his servant to bring him a pastry . . . oh . . ." Hamza's face grew drawn and tense, and he shook his head in frustration.

"You are still very sick," said Li Du. "You do not need to speak."

"But I do," said Hamza, quietly, and cleared his throat to continue. "The servant came back from the market. And he was very upset. He said to the merchant, *'Master, I saw Death in the market today and he cried out and pointed when he saw me. I fear for my life. Please may I go this evening to Sa-marqand so that I may escape him?'* The merchant gave his permission, and the servant rode off in haste."

There was a pause while Hamza took another sip of medicine, which elicited another grimace. "The merchant — he went to the market and found Death there. He asked Death, *'Why did you frighten my servant by calling to him in that way?'* And Death replied — he replied, *'Sir, I was merely surprised to see your servant here in Bukhara, for I have an appointment with him tonight in Samarqand.'* "

Hamza gave a weak laugh.

"The tale means," said Li Du slowly, "that a man walks to his own fate."

Hamza nodded. "Do you know why I have told you this story?"

Li Du shook his head. Hamza returned his gaze to the ceiling. "You have been many years in the mountains," he said, "because you do not want to think of home. Now you have come here, where the Emperor is also to come, and where Death has come also. You must consider why you have come. Now show me what you have there in your hand."

Li Du handed him the letter, and Hamza read it without comment. Then he frowned

418

and cast it down on the bed as if it were hot to the touch. "That is an evil message," he said, "if ever I saw one. It is unnatural to create such a false copy of a person."

Li Du's eyebrows went up slightly. "That is exactly the way I saw it," he said. "But it was done with skill by a person with a talent for storytelling."

"For — but then you think now that it was me after all?" Hamza's tone was light, but he kept his gaze down and plucked at the blanket at he waited for Li Du's response.

"No." Li Du shook his head and leaned back in the chair. "No," he said again, rubbing the back of his neck thoughtfully. "You did not write this. Your artistry is of a different nature. You create your worlds to transport your audience into realms of wonder. They are not meant to be mistaken for the truth. The murderer's worlds are much closer to ours, illusions constructed around us as we walk through life, replacing our truths with lies. There is a perfection to the way they are built."

"Perfection? You offend me." Hamza's voice was slightly slurred, and he sniffed the cup of the doctor's medicine. "This is making me tired," he said. "How am I to help you when I am sick and slow minded? I have learned not to drink so much wine before sunset." He set the medicine down and looked at the letter again. "Where did you find it?"

"Under the bed, where it might easily have fallen."

"Under the bed," said Hamza. "Like Hassan's letter."

For a moment Li Du thought Hamza was delirious. Then he remembered. "You mean the letter written by Nuraldin in your story," he said.

"Yes," Hamza mumbled. "Six days ago. My first performance in the mansion. Letters under beds. My deepest apologies if I inspired a villain."

Something was bothering Li Du, and his brow furrowed as he struggled to identify what it was. Hamza was continuing, speaking now more to himself than to Li Du. "The letter in the story was the key to a good life. This letter is a mark of death."

Li Du realized what had occurred to him. "But it was seven days ago," he said, "not six."

Hamza blinked. "Seven, then. How would I remember such a detail when I was just poisoned? And anyway I have never found days so important."

And in that moment Li Du understood.

"But they are important," he said. "They have never been so important as they are now. I have not seen it until now. I have not seen any of it. The motive. The motive for the crime. The days."

Hamza gave a low moan. "You are either being clever or making no sense, but they are both the same to me because my head aches too painfully to understand any of it."

"What was it about Brother Pieter that made him a threat?"

Hamza struggled to answer. "To the people here? A foreigner. A holy man. An old scholar —"

"A scholar, yes. But most important to him was the study of the stars. An astronomer. He was an astronomer."

Hamza shook his head slightly as if to clear it. This caused him discomfort, and he stopped and closed his eyes. "But," he said tensely, "but what is the danger of an astronomer?"

"Knowledge."

"Of the heavens. But what have the heavens to do with people?"

"Here in Dayan, at this moment, everything." Li Du removed Pieter's journal from his pocket and opened it to the final pages. He pointed.

Hamza leaned over to see. "The jeweled

421

model of the heavens," he said.

"And the days."

"I cannot understand you. What days?"

"You will be angry, but I must go to the mansion immediately." As Li Du expected, Hamza opened his mouth to protest.

"No," Li Du said. "You are not yet recovered. I will not be long, and when I return I will explain everything."

"But —"

"I know who killed Brother Pieter, and I know why. There is not a second to waste."

CHAPTER 19

The sun was setting. Li Du followed the paths through the gardens, none of which bore any trace of human presence. There were no scuffs on the flat cobblestones, and no footprints in the dirt. There were no smudges on the marble railings of the bridges. The ponds were clear, and even the carp looked as if they had been burnished to a new shine. The curtains that screened the covered gardens were all draped and cinched in spills of silk and velvet, falling coquettishly into soft pools on the polished stone. Citrus and incense mingled in the air.

When he came to the entrance of the library he paused. The four stone guardians — the bird, the dragon, the tortoise, and the tiger — gazed ahead with unmoving solemnity. He felt somehow reassured, and, after directing a brief, respectful nod at the still figures, he squared his shoulders, straightened his hat, and climbed the stairs.

Inside he could hear the sound of voices from across the wheel of shelves. He made his way through a dim chasm, around the filigreed table, to the open door of the hall of treasures. The sun no longer reached its high, thin window, and the room was already lit with candles.

The magistrate and Nicholas Gray stood on either side of the table. Between them was the tellurion, uncovered, on its golden base. Behind Tulishen, Jia Huan was making a notation in a small book. In the dim corner that shared a wall with the main room of the library, Mu Gao sat in a chair, idly poking his cane at unseen bugs on the floor. Lady Chen stood quietly observing, her robes a column of gray velvet embroidered with red birds. Her shoulders were blurred by a cape of squirrel fur. She turned, her face white and attentive, when Li Du stepped into the room. But she did not interrupt the conversation that was taking place.

"The tellurion," Gray was saying, "is the most important piece of the tribute. Its presentation must be worthy of its quality. You are certain that the meeting will not exceed the time allotted? The Emperor must have the tellurion before he proceeds to the festival field for the eclipse. And we need sufficient time to place it on the podium so that he will see it when it chimes."

"Yes, yes," said Tulishen. He was tired and impatient. "It is all arranged as we have discussed before. The Emperor is always precise. I assure you — there will be no unexpected changes to the schedule."

Li Du spoke from the doorway. "And of course," he said, "the moon will not wait on anyone's convenience."

Tulishen and Gray looked up sharply. Tulishen frowned. "As you can see, Cousin," he said, "we are occupied with decisions of great importance to the empire's diplomatic relations. If you have come to speak to me about your situation, you must wait until the ambassador is satisfied that our preparations are complete. I do not require a report from you. The sun is setting on the day before the Emperor's arrival, and your investigation is over."

"As you say, my investigation is over, but —"

"I am glad you understand," Tulishen interrupted. He was turning away when Li Du's next words stopped him short.

"But I am here because I know why Brother Pieter was killed. And I know who killed him."

For a moment there was complete silence. Lady Chen's eyes flicked up to meet Li Du's, and even from across the room he felt the tense energy in her stillness. Then Tulishen said, with an uncomfortable smile, "Li Du, I was afraid of this. As I suspected, your exile had put too great a strain on your mind. Please do not make the situation worse by flinging accusations that you cannot possibly prove. Jia Huan will escort you back to the inn. You are overtired. Jia Huan —"

With a deferential bow, Jia Huan set his work down on the table and moved forward toward Li Du. But he had not taken two steps when Li Du shook his head and said firmly, "I will speak." He turned to Sir Gray. "What I have to say concerns you — can you follow my meaning if I speak in Chinese?"

"I understand you," said Gray. Several beads of perspiration had appeared on his brow, despite the chill in the room. "But I am not sure you understand the gravity of this interruption. Whatever happened to the Jesuit, it is in the past. What happens tomorrow matters not only to your empire, but to the kingdoms of the whole Western world. The eclipse —"

"There is not going to be an eclipse

tomorrow, and Brother Pieter was killed because he knew it."

Mu Gao's cane fell with a loud clatter. Lady Chen opened her mouth to speak, then closed it again as she withdrew into silent calculation. Tulishen stared, stunned, at Li Du.

"But that is impossible," Gray burst out, his face a mask of confusion and horror.

Tulishen found his voice. "How dare you make such a claim," he said, turning furiously on his cousin. "You would challenge the divine knowledge of the Emperor? The eclipse *will* happen tomorrow, and to claim otherwise is to say the Emperor made a mistake. That is beyond madness. It is treason."

"There was no mistake. This was a deliberate act of sabotage."

"The Emperor's conversations with the gods cannot be sabotaged," cried Tulishen. He was about to continue, but Li Du interrupted him in a harsh tone that surprised Tulishen into silence.

"Stop, Cousin. Let us speak for once of reality," Li Du said. "The Emperor makes his prediction based not on a dream, but on a document. A document can be altered. It can be forged. The calendar of astronomical events that the Emperor carries with him now, that he has carried with him through all the months of the southern tour, is a fake."

"But the tribute." Gray's voice was hoarse and there was panic in his eyes. "What — what does this mean? The clockwork is set to the eclipse." He swallowed and pointed at the tellurion where it sat on the table, the light of its red sun gleaming on the gold planets and scattering flashes of crystal and diamond across the surface of the tiny city. "When will it chime?"

"When the eclipse begins," said Li Du. "Not tomorrow, but on the following day. Pieter knew —"

Tulishen broke in. "Why should we believe any of this? You make extraordinary claims but you offer no evidence. You spin a tale that threatens all of us. Are you trying to make us join you in this madness?"

"I will explain everything to you. But in order to make you all understand, we must acknowledge certain truths about the festival."

"What truths? Speak." Tulishen crossed his arms across his chest.

Gray's attention was still fixed on the tellurion, but with an effort he turned and looked expectantly at Li Du. After a moment's pause, Li Du began.

"For many years the Emperor has harbored anxieties regarding this province. It is a border territory, distant not only from the capital, but from his ancestral lands in the north. More than one rebellion has had its beginning here. The jungles carry deadly fevers. And even the most ambitious officials fear the bandits and the power of the local families who remember past wrongs. The Kangxi has always known that this province is part of the empire only in name."

Mu Gao gave an approving little grunt, quelled immediately by a look from Lady Chen.

"This year," Li Du went on, "the astronomers in the capital saw that an eclipse would be visible in its totality here in Dayan. The Emperor saw a chance to demonstrate his divine legitimacy over these people with whom he shares neither blood nor history. He announced his southern tour. And beginning then, almost a year ago, preparations have been underway. You, Magistrate, have planned a festival of unmatched splendor and decadence. And you, Sir Gray, have traveled a great distance carrying tribute of immense value in the hope of impressing the Emperor. All of this effort has had at its center a fixed point: the eclipse of the sun. But who really named the day of eclipse?"

"The Jesuits," said Gray immediately. "The Jesuits have been responsible for Chinese astronomy since the days of the last Ming emperor."

"Yes. The creation of the annual calendar of astronomical events is entrusted to the Jesuits at the Bureau of Astronomy. Since the competition in the capital many years ago, their superiority in this area has not been challenged. Every year they produce a new calendar. It is delivered, discretely, to the Emperor, who uses it to make his divine predictions. This year, someone exchanged the real calendar for a false one. The copy is identical in all but one detail: the date of the eclipse."

"How could you know this?" asked Tulishen.

"Because Pieter knew it." Li Du removed the journal from his pocket and held it up. "Brother Pieter was a skilled astronomer. Imagine his delight when he arrived in Dayan and learned of the device brought here by Sir Gray. A clockwork model of the heavens. To everyone else, the tellurion is a mysterious, beautiful toy. But to Pieter it was an exquisite tool with a very specific purpose.

"On the day of the banquet, Pieter examined the tellurion."

"Without my permission," said Gray. "But I made sure that he did nothing to damage it. Why is this important?"

"He made notes in his journal. At first when I read it I was very discouraged. I could make nothing of the calculations. But I did notice one small detail. The final pages were the only pages in the book that contained errors. The only pages with numbers written, struck through, and written again. The two numbers that he appeared unable to reconcile in his equations were 'six' and 'seven.' This meant little to me until the moment I realized that *on the day he died, the eclipse was predicted to occur in six days' time.* Pieter was using the tellurion to predict the alignment of the celestial spheres, and it was telling him that the eclipse was not six days away, but seven."

"But who killed him?" It was the first time Lady Chen had spoken. Her words were clipped and cold. Her hands were clenched together tightly.

Li Du looked at the faces that were all turned to him. "Each of you," he said, "had the opportunity to poison Brother Pieter that night. Lady Chen —" He turned to face her. There was no fear in her expression, only restrained impatience as she waited for him to continue.

"Lady Chen left the courtyard several times during the storyteller's performance in order to bring more wine. She might have stopped at the guestrooms and prepared the poisoned tea during any one of her absences."

"Are you accusing me?" Her voice was like ice.

Li Du met her gaze for a moment, then shook his head. "No," he said. "There is no connection between you and the forged calendar. You had no motive to kill him."

He glimpsed just a trace of surprise in her expression before she smoothed it away. He turned then to Sir Gray. "You also left the performance that night."

Gray's nostrils flared and he gave Li Du a furious look. "I told you," he said through gritted teeth. "I spoke to Brother Pieter that night. I saw him die. But I had nothing to do with his death."

"And yet you were the only one who was seen quarreling with him. He disapproved of your Company's strategies. Perhaps this concerned you more deeply than you revealed. Perhaps you feared his ability to turn the Emperor against you. And if you were involved in the forgery of the calendar, then you had yet another reason to kill him."

"That is not true," said Gray. "And you

know that it is not true. I am as shocked as any of you to learn that the eclipse will not happen tomorrow."

"But how is it possible that you did not know? You carried the tellurion with you. Your mission was constructed around the eclipse."

Gray was livid. "It never occurred to me that I would be required to help the Emperor *make* his prediction. The tellurion was calibrated by our astronomers and clockmakers in Calcutta. When I arrived there, it was given to me. My only instruction was to keep it safe, and to be sure that it was presented to the Emperor in time for the eclipse. My itinerary was already set according to the Emperor's announcements. So how could I possibly have imagined that this blasted piece of metal was ticking toward one moment while the Emperor marched toward another? Everyone knows the Emperor of China has not made an incorrect prediction since he took the Jesuits into his employ. How was I to — And now it is all in jeopardy!"

Li Du waited until Gray's tirade was over. Then he said, "It is not unreasonable to suppose that you were involved in the calendar plot. The Company, after all, has reason to harm the Emperor."

Gray tensed, but said nothing.

"The Emperor has refused the Company's requests for years. If he were to be publicly humiliated before his people, it might provide you with an opportunity to take advantage of the situation."

"This is preposterous," said Gray.

Li Du acknowledged this with a little bow of his head. "Not preposterous," he said, "but also not what happened. The tellurion proves as much. If the Company had helped to sabotage the Emperor's calendar, why also send what is, essentially, a correction of the error, to the Emperor as tribute? The two actions make no sense together. No — the altered calendar was a threat to the success of your tribute. And so I realized that you were not involved."

"You play a dangerous game," said Gray softly, "accusing an ambassador when you knew already that it was not me. If you are going to accuse foreigners, why not drag in that missionary who skulks in his rooms? He is the secretive one."

Li Du bowed his head, but there was no shame or capitulation in the gesture. "Neither you nor Brother Martin killed Brother Pieter."

"Then who did?" Tulishen broke in.

Li Du turned to face his cousin. "Let us

434

speak for a moment of you, Magistrate. You did not leave the performance that night, but you had the power to command his death. Any of your servants might have prepared the scene at your order."

"I?" Tulishen's face darkened. "The murder has caused me endless inconvenience and anxiety. I would never have upset the preparations for the festival with such an act. And I know nothing of calendars."

"Perhaps. But it was you who insisted that the cause of death be declared natural, though the doctor saw that it was not. And it was you who refused to listen to my reasons for suspecting that the Khampa were not responsible. You insisted on that explanation, in spite of evidence to the contrary. Either you were remiss in your duties as magistrate, or you were framing the Khampa deliberately in order to cover your own crime."

"No!" cried Tulishen. His face was waxen. "Why? Why would I kill him?"

"But you did deliberately try to cover up the murder."

"No, I — I believed that those explanations were the correct ones. You must understand the strain I have endured. I had no time. There is too much required of me. I may have misjudged, but I did not kill the old man."

"I know now that you did not, though for a time I suspected you. But that was before I discovered Pieter's journal, before I understood the true motive."

Li Du paused, and the silence deepened. "Pieter died because he was an astronomer. Because he was curious. And the person who killed him is the same person who sabotaged the Emperor's calendar a year ago in Beijing. A person who knows how the web of the empire is woven, and is capable of breaking and spinning it into new patterns. There is only one person who could have done this."

"Who?" whispered Tulishen, in a strangled voice. Gray's hand clutched the back of the chair so tightly that his knuckles were strained and white as a skeleton.

"It was Jia Huan."

Tulishen started and looked behind him, as if he had forgotten Jia Huan's presence. "But that cannot be," he said.

Jia Huan's face was very calm. There was only a gentle suggestion of hurt in his countenance. "I must speak in my defense," he said to Tulishen. "Your cousin's imagination has led him far astray." His clear voice emanated the gentle authority of efficient servitude.

"Tell me, Magistrate," said Li Du. "Why have you been trying to convince me that I have lost my mind? You imply that I have succumbed to strain, that I am overtired. Ask yourself whether these thoughts were your own. Or were they given to you by Jia Huan? Did he suggest to you that my sanity should be questioned? Did he imply, perhaps, that my exile has driven me into such shame and jealousy that I cannot be trusted?"

Tulishen was startled, but he recovered quickly. "Jia Huan's thoughts are always of my convenience. He would have betrayed —"

"An hour ago I discovered that the wine in my room contained poison. Under the bed I found a letter, written in counterfeit of my own hand, confessing to Pieter's murder. I was to have committed suicide. Had Jia Huan prepared you to accept that lie, too?"

Tulishen did not respond immediately, but looked from Li Du to Jia Huan, doubt and indecision clear on his face. Lady Chen stepped toward him, apparently concerned, but she stopped herself and waited.

Then Tulishen's expression grew cold and hard, and he turned suddenly to face Jia Huan. "Jia Huan?" he demanded.

Jia Huan gave a soft smile, and it reminded Li Du of a painted portrait. "Can you imagine it?" he said. "Picture our Emperor, tomorrow at noon, standing on that tiered pavilion, his arms raised in command over the dark and the light. And before him a crowd of thousands, waiting. And the moments would tick by, one after another, closer and closer. Then the time would come, the moment, his moment. And then it would pass. And still he would stand there. His arms would tire like those of any man, and finally he would lower his hands while the bright sun mocked him from the sky."

As he spoke Jia Huan's own arms had lifted slightly in imitation of the imagined Emperor. He had closed his eyes. Now he opened them and looked around him.

"This is madness," said Tulishen, taking a step backward.

"You do not fully understand," said Li Du calmly. "Jia Huan had a reason, a cruel motive for his work. The sabotage of the calendar was intended to humiliate the Emperor, but the true victims were to be the Jesuits. He wanted them to be blamed for the Emperor's mortification — they were responsible for the production of the calendar. He believes that the Jesuits should be banished from China, and his hatred of them was such that he was happy to sentence them to death."

"So it was you." Lady Chen's voice was icy. "You killed" — Li Du heard the almost imperceptible catch in her voice — "you killed the guest of the magistrate's home. You betrayed and endangered us all."

Jia Huan's response was unconcerned. "I do not believe," he said, "that it is reasonable now for me to deny it. It appears that our exiled scholar has succeeded in his task."

"Then it is all as he says?" asked Tulishen. "The calendar?"

Jia Huan bowed his head in acknowledgment. "Yes. I created the false calendar for the reason he says. And I killed the old Jesuit."

"But I do not understand," said Tulishen. "We are speaking of the Forbidden City. A low secretary cannot forge an official document. Someone would have caught such an egregious violation."

"It is not impossible," said Li Du, "given the unique circumstances. Recall that the Emperor does not desire the role of the Jesuits to be widely known. The calendars are delivered without ceremony, and very few people are involved in the proceedings.

439

Jia Huan was a secretary at the Bureau of Astronomy, and I imagine that they were as impressed by his efficiency as you have been. He watched the calendar as it was made, and created his duplicate slowly. It is a long process. The calendar is ornate, painted and decorated in the Western style. Jia Huan learned these techniques during his time in Macau. I am sure that the Dominicans were happy to give him the help he asked for when he told them his plan was to harm the Jesuits."

"He is working for the Dominicans?" The question came from Gray.

Jia Huan answered in a hiss. "They are more foolish than the Jesuits. They thought they had recruited a spy. They thought that once the Jesuits were banished they would be allowed in."

He stopped, and Li Du began to speak again. "He knew that the Emperor was planning a southern tour, and that during that time he would be separated from the Bureau of Astronomy. Jia Huan had only to wait for the circumstances to cohere, and they did. The details of the tour were announced. The calendar was finalized. The forgery was complete and the exchange was made."

Jia Huan gave a slight frown. "You tell it

in such a flat way," he said. "Are you not impressed by my audacity? I was very clever. I manipulated so many of them. I was just another black-robed secretary eager to carry out my orders. I fooled the Emperor of China himself."

Tulishen's eyes widened. He opened his mouth to speak, but no sound came out and he closed it again.

Gray's gaze was turned inward in intense deliberation, but now he looked up. "How did your entire empire not see it? All your elite scholars and officials? Not one of them noticed the error?"

"No one would dare to question the Emperor," said Li Du. "Perhaps some star-gazers and shamans across the empire came to their own conclusions. But the Emperor's official prediction is not something to challenge."

Jia Huan listened to the exchange with an amused expression. He addressed Li Du. "You found the journal. That was lucky. And you understood the old man's notes. But how did you know it was me?"

Li Du answered, "You made several mistakes."

"What mistakes?"

"You pretended that you could not speak Latin, but on two occasions you revealed to

441

me that you did. The first was when you quoted the *China Illustrata.* You said that you read in a Western book that the Chinese see the Jesuits as geniuses fallen from heaven and have put off their peacock tails. Those are the exact words of the text, but I know that the *China Illustrata* has never been translated into Chinese. The second was when you told me that Pieter and Sir Gray had argued over Pieter's refusal to support the Company's suit. I knew from Sir Gray that this was the content of their disagreement, but Mu Gao told me that they spoke in Latin. The only way you could have known the subject of their argument was if you understood the language. You learned it, I assume, in Macau. And you were employed at the Bureau of Astronomy a year ago when the calendar was made. I imagine you would have preferred that not to have been mentioned, but the magistrate brought it up when you first met Brother Pieter."

Li Du paused for a moment, then said, in a thoughtful voice, half to himself, "But it was more than that. I have been forming a picture in my mind of the person who killed Pieter. The murderer provided answers meant to appeal to one person more than any other, the person with the power to

442

cover up the murder. The magistrate was willing to believe that the death was natural. He was willing to believe that the Khampa were responsible. He would have been willing, I think, to accept my confession and suicide. I asked myself who had the talent and knowledge to manipulate the magistrate in this way."

Tulishen began to protest, and Jia Huan turned a pitiless face to him. "So easy," he said. "A strong man pursues truth. But I knew I could count on your cowardice."

"I do not wish to hear any more of this," snapped Tulishen. "You are caught, and your evil words no longer have power. You will be turned over to the Emperor, and he will sentence you to a painful and dishonorable execution for your crime. He will want to know why, if your hatred was for the Jesuits as you claim it is, you were willing to subject your own Emperor to humiliation."

"Because," said Jia Huan in a tired voice, "he is weak. The Jesuits flattered his vanity, and so he allowed them to insinuate themselves into the empire. He would not have made such a decision if his own ancestors were Chinese. But he is Manchu. He does not share our blood. He deserves a reminder that he must rule with more wisdom and pride."

Jia Huan's gaze became unfocused and distant. "And then the Emperor, punished for his vanity, would show his wrath against the Jesuits. Those *holy men,* as they call themselves. Beneath their condescension lies only sick envy. It oozes like pestilence from their delusions, their hypocrisy. They want what all foreigners want. Our wealth. Our porcelain. To open China to the world. How meaningless — China is the world. No other empire, no other language, no lands, and no earth need exist. These pathetic foreigners scrabble for our silver and our tea like fish driven mad by flesh. And after the Emperor had sent them to their graves the borders would be shut for an age."

"But why was it necessary?" It was Lady Chen who spoke. She had turned her back to Jia Huan, and posed the question to Li Du. "Brother Pieter might not have discovered the plot. Why was it necessary to kill him?"

"Lady Chen's question is wise," said Tulishen. "The murder was a foolish risk."

"It was evil," said Li Du sadly, "but it was not foolish. Jia Huan's skill is his ability to know the desires of those around him. He saw that Brother Pieter would not stop once his curiosity was piqued. This is a characteristic of Jesuits, but anyone could immediately see the curiosity burning in Pieter. As soon as Pieter mentioned his interest in astronomy, I believe Jia Huan began planning for his death. With the tellurion in the mansion, Jia Huan knew that it was only a matter of time before Pieter discovered the truth. And when Jia Huan overheard the argument between Pieter and Sir Gray, and knew that Pieter had already examined the tellurion, he knew that he had to act immediately."

"I would have taken the journal," said Jia Huan, "but it was not in the old man's room. And there were too many people about for me to return and search for it. First Gray, then Lady Chen, then the doctor and the rest."

"You tried to make the death appear natural. But in case that failed, you planted the tea to indicate the Khampa. And finally, you decided to conclude the investigation by framing and murdering me on the eve of the Emperor's arrival."

Jia Huan nodded. "You were meant to be drinking the wine now, as you usually do, as twilight falls on Dayan."

"Hamza drank it instead."

Jia Huan did not seem to hear him. "What did you think of my letter? Did I capture your voice well?"

"It was your madness and isolation in that letter, not mine."

"But it would have been believed. Your cousin was ready to believe it."

Tulishen began to bluster. "I promise you, Li Du. I did not know. You must admit that your actions have been strange. But I would never, I assure you . . ." He trailed off.

Meanwhile Jia Huan had turned to the tellurion. "It is beautiful," he said quietly. "Not the gems and palaces and mountains. They are there to impress the greedy and unintelligent. But this —" He reached a finger gently toward the glowing red sun. "This is very clever. The foreign company offers the world to the Emperor of China. A flattering metaphor. But China will not be taken." He paused thoughtfully, then added, "It, too, would have mocked the Emperor tomorrow, with silence, knowing and hiding the true time of the eclipse from him. . . ."

"Step away from it," said Gray. "It is time for this bizarre confession to end. I want to know what is to be done. The Emperor will be here in the morning, and everything is thrown into confusion. Brother Pieter's death was tragic, and Li Du has shown himself a superior mind to this villain, but now there are greater concerns to address.

446

The future of our empires are at stake, and cannot be left to misunderstanding and grief because of a madman."

"The ambassador is right," said Tulishen. "Mu Gao — summon the guards to take the traitor away." Mu Gao rose and tapped his way out of the room and across the library floor.

Jia Huan did not struggle when the guards arrived. When he was gone, Lady Chen went immediately to the magistrate and began to whisper in his ear. As she spoke, Tulishen's face began to clear. The color returned to his skin and he pulled his shoulders back to stand straighter. When they had finished their whispered conference, Tulishen turned to Gray. "I understand your concern," he said, "but the situation can be faced. You will see how the powerful in our empire can restore order under any circumstance. Cousin," he said, turning to Li Du, "you have been of service to the empire and you need have no worry that your presence in Dayan will bring the law upon you. The matter is now one of politics and strategy, and your help is no longer required. You may go."

Too relieved to care that Tulishen's condescension was already reasserting itself, Li Du bowed and left the room. In the library he found Mu Gao. "You!" said the old man. "You did very well. And tomorrow you will drink tea with me and my friend. You will come?"

"I would like that," said Li Du, and meant it. "Will you be in the Office of Records?"

"Yes — yes. That is a good place. We will meet there. Old Mu will want to hear it all."

Li Du left the library to find that it had grown dark outside, and the stone guardians were lantern lit. As he looked at them for the second time that evening, there rose before Li Du's eyes an image of a distant future. He saw the tortoise's shell patched with moss, the lion's snout chipping to rough stone, the bird's feathers smoothed away and the dragon's features indistinguishable from those of a humble dog. What did time have in store for them? What empires would they see rise and fall? With a tired sigh, Li Du turned and walked away.

"But what I don't understand," said Hamza later as they sat together in his room, cheerfully lit by candles and a brazier by the open door, "is —" He stared at the steam rising from his cup. "No," he said. "No, I don't understand any of it. Tell it to me again." He was already much recovered, and was nibbling at a warm piece of bread while the inn clamored around them in drunken revelry and loud competition over who knew the most about the strange events of the evening.

Li Du sighed. "The festival was created around the eclipse of the sun."

Hamza waved his hand. "Yes — yes, I know. Very important. Display of Emperor's legitimacy in distant provinces."

"Jia Huan killed Pieter in order to protect a plot to eliminate the Jesuits from China."

"And you say the Dominicans were involved?"

"The Dominicans believed that Jia Huan was working for them. They thought the fall of the Jesuits would give them a renewed chance at winning the Emperor's favor themselves."

"But they were as stupid and misguided as the woman who stole her neighbor's magical stewpot."

"I can only assume your analogy is correct. Jia Huan used the Dominicans to acquire the information he needed in order to forge the calendar."

"So," said Hamza, handing Li Du the piece of bread so that he could warm it again in the fire, "the Emperor made a prediction using the calendar that was wrong."

"Yes. And because it was all happening during the southern tour, there was less scrutiny. The Emperor would spend the entire year far away from the Jesuits at the observatory. The calendar proved accurate all year, so what reason was there to doubt its accuracy now?"

Hamza nodded. "So the Emperor was to have been embarrassed. The Jesuits were to have been blamed."

"And Pieter posed a threat to the plot just when it was about to succeed."

"And Jia Huan killed him. Pieter spoke of how he loved red tea in the evenings." Hamza's voice was sad.

"As well as of his journeys with the Khampa. And of course, Jia Huan knew about the jewelvine in the library. Jia Huan saw a way to kill Pieter. He stole the Khampa purse from the market — as Tulishen's chief secretary he was aware of all the traders and merchants, even the humble ones, who had entered the city to sell goods in the market."

"Then the night of the banquet . . ."

"Jia Huan had many duties that evening, which gave him an excuse to move freely through the mansion. It would have been easy for him to plant the Khampa purse during dinner when everyone was occupied.

450

Later he had only to make the final arrangement of the hot water and tea on Pieter's desk. He kept watch on the stage courtyard, and as soon as Pieter rose to leave he went quickly ahead of him to the room. He left just before Pieter and Gray arrived."

"And yes — Gray was there and took the cup. I understand that part."

"From that moment onward Jia Huan did all he could to manipulate the magistrate into covering up the death. He urged Tulishen to blame the Khampa. And when that failed and it seemed as if the murder might affect the festival after all, he prepared a scene in which I was to have committed suicide, having written a note confessing to the crime."

"Well, I wouldn't have believed it of you," said Hamza, staunchly.

"Thank you."

"So what is going to happen tomorrow?"

Li Du looked at the fire. "I don't know," he said.

"You don't know?"

"I wanted to know who killed Pieter. Now Jia Huan is caught. I have little doubt that the Emperor will find a way to save face, but that is not my concern."

"And the ambassador? Was he furious?"

Li Du gave a little smile. "He was greatly

discomfited, yes."

Hamza shook his head. "The political games are very strange," he said. "Do you think the Emperor will bite the Company's lure and catch the empire on that silver hook?"

"Again, I do not know."

"For a man who has just proven himself a clever and brave detective, you do not know very much. What of Jia Huan? What will happen to him?"

"He will be judged and condemned by the Emperor himself. It will all be done very quietly."

"Yes," said Hamza, staring into the brazier coals, "as are so many violent things."

Li Du lay in bed for a long time, unable to sleep. Through the inn's walls he could hear songs of revelry over the deep crackle of bonfires and the clatter of tin cups full of wine. Bridles jangled and horses snorted and stamped. Even in the dead of night more people were arriving. Meat was grilling in great wafts of savory smoke and spice, and game tiles rattled like river pebbles. The festival was almost upon them.

When Li Du finally went to sleep that night, he dreamed of being lost in a library whose books were spinning stars that would not remain on their shelves. They moved around him in bright circles and arcs, so that he did not know where he was or how to find the volume he sought.

1 DAY

CHAPTER 20

Tulishen rode out before dawn in full court attire. His blue satin robe was as stiff and shining as if it were made of hammered metal, and the wide white cuffs of his sleeves covered his wrists and hands as he held the reigns of his horse. His hat, obsidian black, formed a stiff curve across his creased forehead. Around him rode his finest bannermen, armed with bows and arrows, and carrying pennants that fluttered blue and yellow in the wind.

While Tulishen was greeting the Emperor outside the city, Li Du was enjoying a plate of fresh steamed dumplings. The dough was as translucent as flower petals, and the pork and spring green scallions inside were steaming hot and seasoned with salt and red pepper. As he ate, he observed the changes that had worked their way through the city during the few hours he had slept.

A new schedule hung on the wall beside

his table, so new that the ink used for the thickest brush strokes was still wet. Where the original schedule had announced the eclipse, this new version provided a list of renowned performers who would take the stages that afternoon. The eclipse, again in bright crimson, now occupied the middle hours of the following day.

But it was in listening to the conversations around him that Li Du perceived the real effort that had been made the night before.

"It was an azure dragon, not a phoenix," came a reproachful voice from a nearby table.

The others at the table questioned the speaker, a fat merchant in green silk, on how he could be sure.

"Because I heard it directly from one of the magistrate's own attendants, who was present when the communication from the Emperor was received. An azure dragon heard that the Emperor was here and in its excitement flew through the sky to visit him. It appeared to him in the sacred pond by the temple outside the city, and the Emperor *spoke* to it."

There were impressed gasps from the listeners.

"Yes," continued the merchant, "the dragon appeared in the pond as the Emperor's own reflection. Of course the subject of their conversation is beyond our comprehension — they speak in a celestial language — but the Emperor, who is very wise, saw that when the dragon flew through the night sky toward this province, its whiskers stirred the stars — as ripples disturb flowers that have fallen in water — and altered their position."

"But is that a bad portent, or is it auspicious?"

"Oh, it is a very good portent. And the Emperor has changed the time of the eclipse in order to account for the dragon's movement. It will be tomorrow, which means that the acrobats we saw in the market will perform today."

A rouged woman in purple robes sighed loudly and said, "Is it possible for this festival to be more fine than it is now? Personally I do not think so. Have you seen how clear the sky is today? And I think I caught a hint of early osmanthus fragrance in the air. And the mountain is so picturesque!"

They all agreed that the view was very fine, and so the conversations continued. Everyone was speaking of the Emperor's encounter with the dragon and subsequent revision of the schedule. When eventually the subject was exhausted, the talk turned to the delicacies that were to be served at the upcoming banquets, the invitees to the most exclusive events, the operas and the lanterns and the luxurious promise of the festival. Li Du finished his dumplings and walked out into the square.

Children ran through the shifting maze of people and horses and shadows, chasing stray cats and shrieking with holiday abandon. The cats climbed easily to the rooftops, from which vantage points they could ignore their tormentors and search for fish left unwisely in upstairs kitchens. Old women sat in groups outside on stone benches, wrapped in shawls and watching the crowds with suspicion and satisfaction. From their ears hung heavy jade earrings, tiny disks polished so smooth they looked wet. All through the streets the travelers, noble and poor, milled and shopped and ate and spat and tried to catch glimpses of wealthy officials and their consorts.

At the Office of Records he found Mu Gao and Old Mu already in the clerk's little room, which was filled with dusty sunlight and the smell of dark tea.

"He has come!" cried Old Mu with a smile. He stood and came to the door, ushering Li Du inside. "Mu Gao has told

460

me everything that happened last night. What a scandal. I can picture it all. It is delightful, and you have our respect, even if the magistrate will not give you the credit you deserve. What difference does it make when you, like us, are outside of the pecking order?"

Mu Gao was looking at Li Du from under his heavy, wrinkled eyelids. "Kept us all up late, though, with all the scurrying that followed. A dragon spoke to the Emperor. Bah. The usual nonsense."

"Pay no attention to my old friend," said Old Mu. "By now you know that he is a curmudgeon. Tell me — is your friend the storyteller recovered?"

"It is kind of you to ask. He is well, and insists that his conversation with Death was so illuminating that he would not have missed it."

"Foolishness," muttered Mu Gao.

"And," Li Du went on, "he is planning to perform tonight at the banquet. He told me that if he had died he would have performed as a ghost."

"Unnatural," said Mu Gao, but Li Du saw grudging amusement in his eyes.

"And what will you do now?" asked Old Mu. "For a week you have been keeping your balance on the tiger's back. A dangerous situation, but more dangerous once you decide to get down."

Li Du accepted a cup of tea and breathed deeply, enjoying its fragrance. He took a sip and said, "I have not spoken to the magistrate today, but I understand that as long as the Emperor is satisfied with the resolution, I am free to leave Dayan when I please."

"Then why don't you leave now, while you have the chance? The magistrate cannot be happy that you've shown him to be a fool. All this time he thought you were chasing invisible assassins, and then it's his own secretary. He'll want to forget all of it as quickly as he can. Don't expect any commendation from the Emperor. That's not the way the magistrate will direct things."

Li Du smiled. "I agree with all you have said. And I do not plan to remain here long. But I wished to speak to the two of you together before I left."

"You honor us," said Old Mu. "Let me pour more water into your tea. It is good tea — my own private store. I haven't trusted any of the other leaves, what with all these plots and schemes in the air. I tell you, I'll be relieved when the Emperor's gone and the crowds leave. My elbows are bruised just from walking down the street. Too many people."

"I don't like it either," said Mu Gao darkly, with a belligerent look at the multitude of dust motes in a sunbeam.

"I remember," said Old Mu, "when I was a boy, my father told me that when the Emperor — the old Emperor — toured the eastern coast he sailed on a boat from one city to the next. And the performers sang and danced on stages built on the water. Very grand, he said."

"Your father traveled to the east?"

Old Mu nodded. "The Mu was a strong family, and a curious one, before the Qing."

He looked at Li Du, curiosity crinkling the corners of his eyes. "Now," he said, "why did you want to speak to us?"

Li Du took another sip of tea. "I wanted to discuss," he said, "what you two have been secretly doing ever since the arrival of hundreds of strangers to the city gave you the excuse to make mischief."

Mu Gao fumbled his teacup, and several drops splattered across the desk, where they remained like jewels in the sunshine. Old Mu put his hand on his friend's arm. "I do not think he means us harm," he said, but his fluffy white eyebrows were drawn together in concern.

"We're just old ghosts," said Mu Gao.

"Just old rotting books. Haven't done anything."

"The two of you," said Li Du, "have been spending your evenings pasting anti-Qing graffiti from one end of the city to the other."

The old men became silent, their eyes cast down.

"You have taken advantage," Li Du went on, "of the fact that the Chinese officials pay no attention to you, to wander through Dayan with your piles of papers. Even Jia Huan, who was so adept at knowing all that was happening in the dark alleys, did not think that you were the ones behind the vandalism."

Old Mu drew in a deep breath. He raised his eyes to look at Li Du. "Then how did you know?"

"On the day I met you here, I saw Mu Gao leaving this building with a sheaf of blank paper under his arm. I asked myself why, when there was a good store of paper at the mansion, he was obtaining it from this office. The reason, I realized later, is that Lady Chen conducts strict inventories of all the valuable items in the mansion, including paper. You needed to get it from this office, where it is not so carefully counted."

Mu Gao grunted and tapped his fingers on the table.

"Also," Li Du went on, "you used tea to age the paper so that its fine quality would not call attention to this building, or to the mansion. I noticed stains on the table in the book sunning room in the magistrate's library. They are the same as the stains here on this desk." Li Du pointed to the irregular dark patches on the wood. "Spilled tea would not make this stain. But damp tea leaves, rubbed against the surface, would."

The two old friends looked at each other. Old Mu refilled Li Du's cup with water, and waited tensely for Li Du to break the silence.

"I did wonder," said Li Du, "how it was possible that no one saw either of you, or heard the tap of Mu Gao's cane in the night. The magistrate had demanded information on who has been pasting the offensive words to the walls of the market. He was sure that someone would come forward with a description of some culprit."

"We were lucky that no one saw us," said Old Mu.

"It was not luck," Li Du said, with a little shake of his head. "Of course you were seen. But the magistrate made an error. He thought it inevitable that anyone who saw the culprits would report what they saw. He did not consider that every local person in Dayan might choose to protect the vandals rather than betray them."

There was no response, and Li Du went on. "The innkeeper Hoh was careful to tell me when I first met him that Mu Gao should not be considered a suspect in any crime. His family is as old as yours. The Qing may have reduced you to servitude, but the old families of this province would never send you into danger. You are the last of the Mu family in Dayan. This is your land."

"We have stopped," said Old Mu after a short silence. "We will not do it anymore."

Li Du nodded. "I overheard your conversation with Hoh that night at the inn. I did not realize at first that it was you, but once I understood the subject of your argument, I knew. The stakes have become too high. The arrival of the Emperor and his soldiers puts you too much at risk, and if you were to be caught, there would be consequences for all the families here."

"Yes," said Old Mu. "The time has come for our little game to end. We wanted only to cause the magistrate some worry. Make it all less easy for him."

"We weren't killing anyone," said Mu

Gao. "But what are you going to do? Turn us over to be locked up?" Suddenly he leaned forward. "They killed us," he said, fiercely. "They sent that blood-thirsty traitor general to subdue us. And when he rose up against the boy Emperor, who was it who came to the aid of China? We did. We fought for the Emperor who cared nothing for us. And now we are called *uncooked,* uncivilized, uneducated. Turned our temples into their summer homes. Painted over our paintings. So we put our messages on their walls. You condemn us?"

"No."

The two old men stared at him.

"I am beginning to understand," said Old Mu, his face brightening, "why you were exiled."

Li Du thought for a moment before he began to speak again. "Mu Gao showed me the seven remaining books of the Mu kings, and told me that the rest were destroyed. Why not write them again?"

Mu Gao made a gesture of dismissal. "We are not intellectuals," he said. "We do not know how to write books."

"Why not try? No one will bother you. That is clear. The bureaucrats and officials sent here from the capital keep their attention on their own careers. They do not notice quiet activities outside of their imaginations. If you write what you remember, it can be read and known by others."

Old Mu hesitated. "I don't know," he said finally.

Li Du sighed. "Consider," he said, "that yesterday we apprehended a murderer at the mansion. Jia Huan had taken cruel action to protect a cruel purpose. He manipulated everyone around him with his lies."

"And a good thing he's put away where he won't kill anyone else," said Mu Gao. "I always thought that there was something wrong with him. Too calm. Too eager to do everything he was told."

"But what has happened since then?" asked Li Du. "I woke up this morning to more lies. Jia Huan's actions have been concealed, as if they never happened. Brother Pieter might never have come to Dayan. Everyone's attention is fixed, as it always was, on the festival, on the schedule —" He stopped, newly aware of his sense of disappointment.

"Everyone worrying about how to protect the Emperor's vanity," said Old Mu, quietly. "Yes, I see the contradiction."

"I do too," chimed in Mu Gao. "The problem is the whole stinking festival. The whole mess."

"And that is why," said Li Du, "I urge you to put your anger to a use that may, in time, be treasured by those not yet born. Write something that will be a counter to the other books — the ones written to preserve the deceptions and protect them through the passage of time. Write the truth. Or, at least, write your truth."

Old Mu turned to his friend. "We could do it, you know. On those nights with the moon and our cups of wine, we could write. My wife is very clever. She could tell us what she remembers, too."

"Well," said Mu Gao. "It could be possible."

"You have given us much to think on," said Old Mu.

"In that case, I should be on my way."

"Before you do, I will give you a list of villages. Your Chinese letters of invitation are nothing compared to the hospitality you will receive if you go to these places and say that we sent you. Knowing two old Mus still gets you something around here." He pulled a sheet of paper from a drawer, dipped a brush in ink, and quickly drew a map. "Here," he said, pointing to a mark he had made, "ask for my uncle's stew in a copper pot. It will make the stiff fancy banquet tonight seem like greasy old market food for tourists. You will see."

A short while later Li Du took his leave, the paper folded in his pocket. The two old men were arguing companionably over the names of the plants that used to grow in the old temple outside Dayan.

CHAPTER 21

At the inn, Bao was enjoying the attention of a rapt audience. Hamza and Hugh Ashton were among the listeners at the edge of the crowd, and Li Du joined them. Hamza explained in a whisper the subject of Bao's account. Sir Gray had presented the Company tribute, and Bao was one of the lucky servants who had been selected to carry and unveil each gift.

"I expect her to expire from self-importance at any moment," Hamza concluded under his breath. "And our friend the scholar is confused, so you should translate for him." Hugh Ashton looked relieved to see Li Du.

"It was in the secondary banquet hall," Bao was saying, "because the first hall is being prepared for tonight's banquet, which I will also be attending. The secondary hall is filled with birds in golden cages, each one hanging from a golden chain so that it is like a high jungle canopy of golden trees. I helped to hang them."

"But what was the Emperor like?" came a voice from the audience. "What did he say to the foreigner?"

Bao lifted her chin to a haughty angle. "The Emperor is more wonderful in appearance than any portrait. His robes were so bright I thought at first a dragon had come from the sky and perched on the carved throne. The seventeenth prince was there too, and he is very handsome. He looks like a gentle youth, but they say he is almost as skilled at hunting as the Emperor himself."

"Did the foreigner look very afraid?"

Bao tapped a slim finger thoughtfully against her cheek, allowing the eagerness of the audience to build before she answered. "The Emperor emanates the wisdom of a god, and the poor ambassador was clearly overwhelmed by the majesty before him. Yes, he was very afraid."

"And did he stutter? Did he forget to kowtow?"

Bao shrugged. "No," she admitted. "He did not do so badly. He spoke through a translator, which was wise because the Emperor's speech is so refined that any foreigner would sound a fool in conversation with him. The ambassador was clever not to try."

She considered. "But his clothes are so strange for a man. The cloth at his neck is so limp and flimsy, like a dancer's veil. And he fastens his coat so tight across his chest that it bursts out like this." She mimed a round belly, and puffed out her cheeks to imitate Gray's round face. The women in the audience giggled.

"We carried the objects one by one before the Emperor, and he asked so many wise questions. He wanted the ambassador to tell him the age of each of the old bronze vessels from Arabia. He wanted know what gods they honored, and what they had contained, and whether they were still made today. And when he saw the portraits of the foreign kings he asked if the likenesses were good, and what powers each of them wielded in their kingdoms. There was a white coral tree. The Emperor asked how it had been cut from the ocean, and what instruments had been used to polish it, and whether there were larger corals. When we brought him the spools of green wool — it was nothing like the rough horse blankets — he wanted to know the ingredients in the dye and the size of the looms and the number of sheep needed for each length of fabric. The Emperor's questions showed

473

him an expert in all matters."

Bao's audience nodded and murmured among themselves. She drew her small shoulders back even straighter. "Then at the very end, that was when we brought out the finest treasure of all. The one with the jeweled city. The Emperor was very intrigued by it, and he summoned five scholars who travel with him in order that they could examine it and explain its nature to him. But they could not!"

There were gasps, and Bao nodded vehemently. "They could not say why its center emitted light, or how it could move the way the ambassador said, like a clock. The ambassador was very pleased then, for the Emperor was truly impressed."

Voices urged her to continue, and she cocked her head coyly, pretending to need time to remember what happened next. "Well," she said, "then the ambassador explained it. He said that inside it had the same contents as a clock, but that instead of chiming on an hour it would chime on the eclipse, when the earth was dark. He said that at that moment all the little rivers and oceans made of gemstones will move as if they were real water. The Emperor asked the ambassador to show us this wonder there in the hall. But the ambassador — and

I admit he seemed brave at the time — said that it was not possible."

"Why?"

"Was the Emperor angry?"

Bao shook her head. "No, the Emperor was patient, and he listened to the ambassador. Just the way a clock's chime cannot be initiated before its appointed time, so this device, he said, cannot be cajoled. Tomorrow, when the moon takes its place before the sun at the Emperor's command, the tellurion will reveal itself to him, and to him alone."

There were nods of approval and interest. "And the Emperor was pleased," said Bao.

"What of the ambassador's suit? Will we trade with these foreign strangers?"

Bao looked slightly bored. "I do not know about all that," she said, "but the Emperor did say that nothing about these Western inventions is truly new to our empire. All the foreign wisdom was already explained in ancient times by our own *Book of Changes.* And our craftsmen could make any of these toys themselves, should the Emperor command them. Of course the ambassador had no choice but to kowtow and take his place in the audience, even though the Emperor did not answer his requests directly. But what did he think?

That our Emperor would simply say yes?"

Laughing, the audience members broke into smaller groups to discuss their own interpretations of Bao's account. Li Du finished translating for Hugh Ashton. "I have no mind for these political games," said Ashton, shaking his head in confusion. "It does not sound to me as if Sir Gray could possibly have been satisfied. However foolish I have been, I am glad that I did not come to China in the hope of securing a promise from the Emperor. The Company cannot have had great hopes of success."

Li Du nodded. He was distracted, thinking about the tellurion. It was fitting, he thought, that it would share the pavilion with the Emperor during the eclipse. The tellurion, after all, was a symbol of control. It suggested a world that was predictable, a world that had tamed the spinning infinite of the unknown. A world that fulfilled an Emperor's fantasy, as long as the Emperor remained the glowing center around which everything else was ordered.

Jia Huan had seen this illusion of control for what it was, and seen the opportunity to replace it with an illusion of his own. To crack the Emperor's complacency, and remind the empire of the chaos that waited, ready to spread as wide and dark and infinite as the stars in the sky. And perhaps, in this and only in this, Jia Huan had been right.

That evening, while the Emperor was resting before the banquet, Tulishen sent for Li Du.

"You will not be required to see the Emperor," said Tulishen, who was enjoying a small meal in his private quarters. He reached his chopsticks eagerly from one dish to another, and kept his attention on the food even as he spoke to Li Du. "It has all been taken care of, and the Emperor has decided that it will be best if the incident is kept secret."

"But so many people know. There must be rumors spreading through Dayan."

"The attention of the crowds is easily diverted. Of course we will monitor carefully what is being said, but the death of the foreigner is already fading from public memory."

"And what is to happen to Jia Huan?"

"The Emperor has ordered his death."

Li Du was silent.

"But this is what you wanted, is it not?" asked Tulishen. "I hope that you are not disappointed when I have gone to so much effort on your behalf. You never wished an audience with the Emperor — that is what you told me when you first arrived in Dayan. Today I argued that your role in the matter was very small, that you behaved with respect and loyalty, and that you are anxious to do what is asked of you. I have acted in your interest, and I plan to make a gift to you of silver taels and letters that will ensure your access to good Chinese families in the north. I will be disheartened if you do not appreciate all I have done for you."

"What was the Emperor's reaction? Does he understand that the Jesuits were not to blame for the mistake in the calendar?"

"Ah," said Tulishen, with a little gesture that caused dark sauce to drip from his chopsticks onto the table. "You are concerned for the safety of the foreigners. Well, perhaps you have reason to be. The Emperor is not pleased. Jia Huan is obviously insane, and if I had not been so occupied with preparations for the banquet I would easily have seen as much myself. But if the — what do they call themselves, the Jesuit's rivals —"

"The Dominicans."

"Yes. If indeed they were involved, then this is exactly what the Emperor has been predicting. The foreigners bring their ugly, petty squabbles to China, and cause trouble in his court. They are not of great use anymore in the capital, now that our own scholars have learned what they can from them."

"Is the calendar no longer to be trusted to the Jesuits?"

Tulishen shrugged. "I do not know. That the sabotage was possible speaks to gross ineptitude in the capital. The Emperor will need reliable officials in positions of power there. These young ones like Jia Huan may appear very clever, but they are easily manipulated by thoughtless ideologies. Yes — the Emperor will be making new appointments."

"And you hope that you will be one of them."

"What a sour tone you are taking. As usual you fail to differentiate between what is important and what is not. The matter is no longer your concern. You have no sense of the broader implications. You did well. You were a help to me. As I said, I will provide you certain gifts for the next stage of your journey. But remember — *there is no banquet, however sumptuous, from which the guests do not disperse.* Your part is ended, just as you wanted it to. You are lucky that the Emperor has chosen to overlook your involvement, as an exile, in affairs of such gravity."

"Then I am now free to leave Dayan?"

"Ah," said Tulishen, gesturing again with his chopsticks, "there is one more task for you here. It is, in fact, more of an honor than a task. Sir Gray has requested that you be on the viewing platform with us tomorrow to translate for him if necessary. He is uncomfortable with the variety of accents and dialects among the official translators. And he wishes to thank you for your efforts, which saved him considerable embarrassment. What else did he say?" Tulishen paused to remember. "Ah, yes, he said to remind you that you promised to play a game of chess with him before you part ways. He feels that he has become more accomplished at the game."

"He could have told me these things himself tonight at the banquet."

"Perhaps, but you will not be seated close to each other. As you and the storyteller have become friends, I have placed you with the performers. I am sorry that you will not have a view of the Emperor from your seat, but you have seen how much anxiety and effort has gone into the table arrangements in these final days of preparation."

Tulishen wiped his mouth with a delicate white napkin and stood up. "Now please

480

excuse me. The musicians are to begin soon, and the guests will make their kowtows and presentations of wine. Perhaps you and I will speak again later in the evening."

They parted with the unspoken understanding that neither of them had any intention of speaking to the other at the banquet, where hundreds of guests would be vying for the Emperor's notice.

Li Du, knowing that it would be some time before the lower-ranking tables would be seated, walked the paths of the mansion that snaked upward toward the pavilion on the hill. From the higher vantage point he could see the mountain rising beyond the sloping roofs. He thought of the Khampa and wondered whether they had returned by now to their home villages, or whether they were camped on one of those jagged snowy passes.

The sun had set, but the air was still bright with the cooling fire of the day. The mountain was the color of slate against the sky that glowed pale yellow and green. The great dragon was quiet, more like a shape cut from the sky than an object with dimension and weight. Li Du felt that he was looking at a distant painting that required only a few lines to convey an entire world.

CHAPTER 22

The first banquet of the festival began just after sunset. Li Du sat with Hamza at one of the tables farthest from the Emperor. Around the seated guests, servants moved to and from the tables like swallows, taking plates away and replacing them with new ones, pouring wine and tea, trimming wicks, refilling the rice bowls and providing fresh chopsticks to replace those that had fallen to the floor.

Around the perimeter of the hall were the guards, bannermen of the Emperor and of the magistrate, stern and perfect in round black hats tied with slim bands of silk under their chins, single peacock feathers falling down their backs, wearing swords in green sheaths with gold details and blue tassels hanging from the hilts. Their cloaks were somber, crisp gray, which, rather than making them unobtrusive, made them stand out against the busy embroidered finery of the banquet and its guests.

Boys with rouged cheeks poured wine, and the table was heavy with food, delicacies and tributes from all over the province and from neighboring provinces also. The bronze wine vessels glowed, and acrobats cartwheeled and jumped and somersaulted down the center aisle. The table was heavy with food, glistening with oil and with the gentle beads of condensed steam.

Within Li Du's reach, there were deer tails, bear paws, boar tongues, pheasants, organs, bones of tigers, geese, pigs, fish, salmon, duck, shrimp, carp, wild onions, leeks, mushrooms, and bamboo slices. There were many more dishes that he could not reach, reserved for the guests of higher rank, as was the finest porcelain.

Hamza looked over his shoulder at a maid who removed a bowl of picked-over bones, and said to Li Du, "There is a story of a princess who had to impress a sultan at a banquet. She put the bones left from the feast in her sleeves, and when she danced for the court she flung her arms up gracefully, and swans flew from the silk around her slender wrists. Of course, when her jealous stepsisters tried to copy her, they only scattered bones in the face of the sultan."

"Is that one of the stories you will tell

tonight?"

"Perhaps."

"You mean you do not decide in advance what stories you will tell?"

"Sometimes I do. In this case I am sure of at least one. The rest will depend on the faces I see before me, and what I find inspiring about the atmosphere." Hamza looked around him appreciatively. "It is a fine banquet," he said, "but I must say that it is nothing compared to those of the Mughal king."

"The Emperor does not like ostentation beyond what is appropriate, especially when he is traveling."

Hamza lifted his eyebrows in an incredulous expression. "Have you not noticed that there is a dragon the length of an entire village carved into the eastern field?"

Li Du smiled. "For an emperor and an eclipse, such decorations are expected. Anything less would be considered cheap, I understand."

"Well," said Hamza, "I must go prepare my other self."

The guests invited to the performance drew in their breaths in amazement when they came to the garden stage set at the base of Lion Hill, on the west end of the mansion.

The lanterns were lit from the hill's crown all the way down to the stage, around the stone pavilion where the audience was to sit, and onto the raised dais where the emperor's throne had been placed. It was as if a river of stars was flowing down through the darkness, each twinkling, some with red, others with white flame, and still others inexplicably blue or green. The sky was starry, but there was no moon.

The flagstones were covered with blankets and soft shining cushions of silk perfumed with musk and ambergris. The incense burners breathed flowery smoke into the air, and the guests looked like dark butterflies in their finery.

Hamza began:

"There was once a man named Sayih who decided, after many travels, to return to the kingdom of his birth.

"So he sailed over three oceans until at last he saw the mountains of his own land. He climbed to the high passes where blue ice glowed with inner light. He trod the paths through the dark forest where ancient trees debated philosophy in the old language. Finally, he crossed the desert whose sands were the crushed mirrors of a previous age. And at last he came to the gates of the city that had been his home.

"Now it happened that the Sultan of this kingdom — whose palace stood in this very city — had been for some time in a black mood, for it had occurred to him that his kingdom and all its wonders would someday crumble to dust. The thought had thrown him into such a state of melancholy that he had secluded himself like one in mourning, and little had been seen of him.

"His advisors had come to him with a solution. 'O, great Sultan,' they said, 'the answer to your melancholy is simple. You must record the beauty of this kingdom. Summon the greatest artists to your palace, so that you may judge which among them can produce the most exact copy of all the delights of this land. The winner will become your court painter, and will make paintings so that the wonders of your realm will never be lost.'

"The Sultan was well pleased, and word spread throughout the kingdom of the competition that was to take place. When the day scheduled for the judgment finally arrived, the entire city was in a state of excitement. The advisors had arranged for the Sultan to view the paintings in the golden pavilion in his favorite garden, high on a hill at the center of the city. The citizens gathered to watch.

"There were three contestants. The first was a stern, proud man who had studied the artists of the past. The second was a woman from the east of the kingdom renowned for her command over every color in existence. The third, as you may have guessed, was none other than Sayih.

"At the Sultan's command, the first artist pulled the cloth from his painting. It showed a feast so splendid that everyone who saw it swallowed with sudden hunger. As they stared, a nightingale flew from its perch and tried to pluck a grape from the painted banquet table. The bird fluttered away quickly, for it was a vain creature and embarrassed to have appeared foolish.

" 'This must be the greatest painting,' said the Sultan, 'for it has fooled the natural world into believing that it is real.'

"Nevertheless, he commanded the second artist to remove the cloth from her work. But she bowed low and said, 'O, Sultan, there is no cloth over my work.' And the Sultan was amazed to find that the artist spoke the truth. The drape of cloth was not real, but was itself the painting.

" 'Then this must be the winning painting,' said the Sultan, 'for it has fooled the Sultan of the kingdom.'

"Only Sayih's painting remained, and the advisers and crowd muttered among themselves that it was impossible for this stranger with old clothes and an untrimmed beard to improve on the work of the first two artists.

" 'Remove the cloth,' said the Sultan, 'and show me your painting.'

" 'Great Sultan,' said Sayih, 'You wish to capture your kingdom in a painting that copies it exactly, and this is what I have brought you.'

"And he lifted the cloth away.

"The Sultan raised his eyebrows and approached the painting. In the frame he saw the crowds before him, so real that they appeared to move and breathe. Beyond them he saw the sparkling deserts, beyond that, the shifting trees of the towering forest, and beyond that, the icy glow of the mountains.

"Then the Sultan stepped forward and reached out to touch the painting. But of course his hand passed through it, for it was an empty frame.

" 'Great Sultan,' said Sayih, 'I have journeyed through all the lands that you see, and beyond the far oceans. Only today have I returned to this city, where the markets overflow with sweet fruits from the dry desert trees, dark berries from the forests, and musky herbs from the mountains. And as I passed through the streets I inhaled the scent of this place, and ate its food, and greeted old friends, and sat in the warm sunshine by a marble fountain. There is no painted illusion that can capture your kingdom.'

" 'So,' said the Sultan, 'I was right to mourn, for there is nothing to stop it all turning to dust.'

"The Sultan began to sink once more into despondency, and the crowd grew silent.

" 'O, Sultan,' said Sayih, 'do not despair. For I have seen many wonders in my travels and can describe them to you for your enjoyment. I can tell you of the reflections of the old gods in the desert ponds. I can tell you what the trees in the distant forests are saying. I can tell you the source of the glow in the mountain ice. And I can tell you what lies beyond the oceans.'

" 'Well,' said the Sultan, 'if you can tell me a tale that is of interest to me, perhaps I will not throw you into prison for your impudence.'

"And so the traveler told the following tale. . . ."

And Hamza went on. He told of kingdoms under the ocean, of one-eyed giants and sailor rogues. He told of a jester who was murdered three times, and of twin sisters who saved a prince from a curse.

The hour was late when he was allowed to stop, and he bowed deeply, as drunk in his own way as the audience in theirs. One by one the lanterns on the hill winked out, snuffed by servants who trudged up the paths in the dark and made sure to dampen the grass so that no spark could start a fire.

■ ■ ■ ■

The Eclipse

■ ■ ■ ■

CHAPTER 23

Half an hour before the eclipse was to begin, the only cloud in sight was draped luxuriously over the eastern shoulder of the mountain. Below the festival field the roof-tops of Dayan sloped in layers and levels of mossy gray. For the first time in weeks its streets were quiet and empty. That was because every resident, its guests, its merchants, and its officials were gathered in the festival field. There were, according to the secretary whose task it was to tally the register, more than six thousand people in attendance.

Li Du had been given a seat on one of the eight viewing platforms built on either side of the emperor's pavilion. From this vantage point he could see the entire length of the field and the city beyond it. The performances had all been halted in anticipation of the eclipse, and the crowds surged up over the stages so that the only thing visible other than people was the flashing water of the canal that snaked from one end to the other. Even the small tiled bridges were obscured by the people standing or sitting on them.

Shading his eyes from the sun, Li Du looked at the pavilion that rose three levels higher than the other structures. It looked nothing like the skeletal, scaffolded stage that he had seen before. Now its entire base was gold plated and covered in etched dragons with jade and emerald scales and ruby eyes. From that glinting foundation rose the tiers of the pavilion, the top of which was held up by more dragons, carved in wood. These were unusual dragons, different from the traditional Chinese style. Their bodies were broader and decorated with carvings of geometric tangles and knots and braids. These dragons were the beams contributed by Nicholas Gray, and appeared to hold the uppermost platform aloft on their claws and tails.

Li Du returned his attention to the people around him. Magistrate Tulishen sat in the center on a wooden chair padded with silk cushions. Lady Chen was engaged in discussion with the first consort of the magistrate from Dali, shaded by a parasol made of a net strung with pearls and hung around the edges with a fringe of tiny golden fruits. It was the maid Bao who held the parasol, and Li Du could see by her pinched mouth and white fingers that it was very heavy. Lady Chen smiled and nodded sympathetically while the other woman spoke, but occasionally her glance wandered to peruse the faces of the other high officials and ladies. She wore a dark blue robe embroidered with silver, and her hair was dressed with silver butterflies.

Hugh Ashton had acquitted himself well in his interactions that day, with the help of Li Du as his translator, and Li Du was relieved that the young scholar had not been regarded with any particular suspicion. Now Ashton sat on his own chair, quiet and tired, lost in thought amid the excited babble of words that he did not understand. Li Du had not seen Hamza, Mu Gao, or Old Mu for some hours, and imagined, with a little bit of envy, that they were somewhere lost in the comfortable solidarity of the milling crowds. He guessed they were close to one of the clouds of steam issuing from the food stalls scattered throughout the field.

Li Du looked at the sky, in which the sun shone so bright it seemed to him that it was determined to ward off the approaching moon, or to melt its attacker in its obstinate fire.

The only unoccupied seat was Nicholas Gray's. Tulishen was watching the Emperor, who had begun to ascend the stairs to the top of his pavilion. Tulishen turned his head sharply when Li Du rose and leaned down to ask him quietly, "Where is Sir Gray?"

Tulishen looked at the empty chair and frowned. "If he made other arrangements to view the eclipse, he should have told me. There were many important individuals who offered expensive favors in return for space among us. I could have pleased two more of them, since your translation would not have been necessary either."

"Does it not seem strange to you that he would give up such a vantage point, so close to the Emperor and to his Company's own work?"

"Perhaps it is a little bit strange. But likely he has become distracted, or could not make his way quickly enough through the crowds. You see the chaos down there. Without soldiers to create a path through them, it would be difficult to move from one place to another now."

The Emperor now stood on the top of the pavilion, towering above them and above the crowds that began to cheer at the sight of him. Li Du could barely make out the planes of his face, stern as a carving. His costume was a mixture of Manchu and Chinese style, saffron silk emblazoned with red dragons accented with blue and green swirls of embroidered cloud. In the glaring sunlight he shone as if he were an extension of the golden pavilion itself, a giant standing above his empire, glinting and invulnerable. Behind him on the pavilion stood a line of archers in gray, still as statues. On the ground at the base of the pavilion were more soldiers standing in ranks between the Emperor and the people.

Li Du felt the back of his neck prickle. He glanced at the ground in case Nicholas Gray was only now approaching, but there was no sign of him. The consort who was speaking to Lady Chen laughed, a false, affected warble that increased Li Du's anxiety. Something was wrong. Why wasn't Gray here? Gray had been obsessed with this moment, even more obsessed than everyone else, from the time Li Du had first spoken to him. Gray's concern, through everything that had happened, had always been with the moment of the eclipse. It was the chance to please the Emperor, to charm him and entice him with the skill of foreign clockmakers and jewelers. Gray would never have given up this place, the closest to the Emperor of any in the field.

The faces of the crowd were too numerous, and Li Du knew that there was no hope of identifying Gray among them. He noticed individuals only to lose them again: two old women kneeling and bobbing their heads in prayer, a mother trying to hush an upset baby, three men arguing and gesticulating at the sun, each of them wanting to be the first to see the eclipse begin. Anxiety, like the crackling pressure in the air before a storm, fed upon itself and urged the crowd to murmur more loudly and to look around them in anticipation and fear.

He returned his gaze to the emperor's pavilion. Now the soldiers at the base of it were preparing the fireworks that would burst from the mouths of stone dragons, surrounding the pavilion in sprays of colored fire. The display had been meticulously planned.

From the top of the Emperor's pavilion there drifted a chime so faint Li Du could not tell whether it was real or imagined. The Emperor raised his arms, and a sudden hush fell like a shadow across the field. There was something impossible about that silence in a space filled with so many breathing souls. Li Du glanced at Lady Chen and saw that her eyes were full of tears. He felt an answering sting in his own eyes.

Then the cries began, and all over the field arms were raised, pointing at the sun. The nobles on the carved platforms fumbled for their disks of smoked glass and raised them to their eyes. They all looked at the white, burning sun and saw, very slowly, the perfect curve of darkness dipping into it.

Li Du heard a second ghostly chime. What was the Emperor seeing? Li Du pictured the tiny sapphire oceans shifting underneath the jeweled ships, the tiny drums tapping in the bell towers, the cherry trees clicking into pink gemstone blossoms. And the glowing glass sun. What was it called? Phosphorus. A chemical of fire. *Everything,* he thought, *everything has been about this moment. It has all come to this moment. This moment.*

The light began to change. The entire world was dimming, imperceptibly, into night. Li Du looked at the carved wooden dragons clutching the emperor's pavilion. He heard the strike of flints from the ground behind him as the fireworks were placed in their positions. And suddenly he knew with absolute certainty what was about to happen.

He stood up. No one looked at him. He put his hand on Tulishen's shoulder and whispered in his ear. "You must get the Emperor down from the podium."

"What?" Tulishen was uncomprehending.

"If the Emperor does not come down now he will die."

"But —"

"There is no time."

"You — you are serious? But what can I say to him? It cannot be done."

"Think of something."

The sky was growing darker and darker, and Li Du could no longer make out the features of the people in the field. They were thousands of faceless human shadows, standing in wonder at the sky. Any moment now the fireworks would hiss and scream and explode into the darkening air above them.

Tulishen still hesitated. Li Du reached out and grasped his cousin's arm. "When darkness comes it will be too late. You are the only one the guards will allow to pass. You have to trust me."

Tulishen looked down at the hand that clutched his sleeve. The sun was now half gone. The moon continued its inexorable carving away of the white light. "Do it now," Li Du said, and took his hand away. Their eyes met, and what Tulishen saw in his cousin's expression brought an end to his hesitation. Tulishen's eyes widened, with dawning horror he lifted his gaze to the top of the podium. He stood up, and without a word or look at anyone, descended the stairs.

No one paid any attention. The Emperor and the sun held them transfixed, breathless and still as statues. Only the decorations moved, the tassels and jewels and feathers stirring slowly as they were caught by the careless breeze.

At the base of the emperor's podium, a guard moved to block Tulishen's progress. But at the magistrate's harsh command, the guard bowed deferentially and moved to let him pass. Li Du watched as Tulishen climbed to the first level, then to the second. The sun was now three-quarters covered. Tulishen was at the third level. He had reached the top. The Emperor and the soldiers turned abruptly as Tulishen in his midnight robes stepped onto the platform. Li Du heard another chime and thought he could see the small red glow of the tellurion's sun. How stupid they had all been. What had Ashton called it? Phosphorus — light and fire.

Hurry, Li Du urged silently. The Emperor shone in his yellow and scarlet robe like an echo of the sun that was almost completely covered. Tulishen said something. The Emperor responded. There was hesitation, then decision.

From the high pavilion there was the sound of a drum and then a cry in unison delivered by the soldiers of the Emperor's guard who stood there almost invisible.

"The Emperor will walk among the people," they announced. "The Son of the Dragon will be one with his subjects as the sun is now with the moon!"

Only one white sliver of light remained in the sky, and now its brightness intensified, shining with the last of its strength through the final space allotted to it by the implacable moon. The Emperor descended, moving at a stately pace, down the stairs, slowly, slowly away from the podium and toward the crowds that fell to their knees around him as the announcement reverberated again and again through the multitudes.

"The Son of the Dragon walks among his people!"

Then darkness came. A great ring cut the sky. The blackness at the center of the ring deepened, so dark now that it was not just devoid of light, but an insistent absence. The universal clockwork had moved into its appointed place, and the crowd was united in a cry of wonder and amazement.

Many things occurred then. The noise of the crowd rose into a new cry of awe and reverence. The Emperor was for a moment lost to sight even to his closest guards in the darkness. The flints sparked. Fireworks whistled into the sky and burst in bright chrysanthemums, sprays of color spreading and winking away to be replaced by new explosions. And in that beautiful chaos that had been planned with such precision, the center of the emperor's pavilion was engulfed in searing flame. It blended with the fireworks around it, and as the fire spread to the huge wooden dragons they too burst into flame. The nobles around Li Du jumped as they felt the rush of heat reach them. They stared as the pavilion became a pyre. Li Du imagined that he saw the shattering and the twisting spokes of the tellurion, gears and jewels hurtling through the flame and catching its light before they fell to the shadowed ground.

Through his daze he felt someone looking at him. He turned and saw that it was Lady Chen. Their eyes met and she held his gaze. Then, with no sign that she understood anything of what had happened, she turned back to look at the Emperor and the magistrate proceeding through the crowds. She joined the rest of the nobles in applause.

The crowd continued to prostrate itself in waves around the Emperor. The eclipse began to reverse itself, and the light was returning to the field and to the sky. The sun seemed stronger for having been restrained, and Li Du blinked as the glare struck his eyes.

The fireworks stopped when the light had fully returned. The performers returned to the stages and struck up their music once more. As the people recovered from what they had seen, they began to drink and eat and converse, sharing their impressions of the eclipse that had begun to alter in each of their memories the moment it ended. The orchestras struck up familiar tunes, the acrobats began their cartwheels, and the opera singers again took up their tales of love.

The Emperor was again surrounded by his retinue and escorted to the performances that appealed to him. The noble people who had been given the honor of seats close to the Emperor were already rushing down the field in the hope of continuing to ingratiate themselves.

Li Du walked to the base of the burning podium, where several officials stood in frightened confusion, unsure whether the fire had been planned or not. He looked down at the grass, and saw at his feet the scattered glitter of precious stones. He knelt and picked up a pale silver sphere — the moon, he guessed. He knew there was no chance of finding the sun. It had been the center of the explosion, and the ruby glass that had held the pent-up fire had melted away to nothing.

CHAPTER 24

Magistrate Tulishen came in person that evening to tell Li Du that the Emperor wished to see them both. The private sitting room into which they were admitted was filled with the items that the Emperor always brought with him when he traveled: reference books of foreign and Chinese origin, volumes of classical poetry, history, and philosophy, calligraphy brushes and paper, and a small, simple chiming clock.

Mingled with the delicate tools of academic contemplation were heavy allusions to the hunt. An enormous chair rested on a tiger-skin rug. On the wall, hung between two stringed instruments, was a painting of the Emperor on horseback circling a speared and bleeding boar. In a corner of the room, a large piece of natural rock sculpture sat on a pedestal in evocation of the mountain wilds.

Li Du almost didn't notice the guards who

stood unmoving at the doors and windows, but when the Emperor came into the room they prostrated themselves in practiced unison. Li Du and Tulishen also lowered themselves into the kowtow, and remained with their faces to the ground until the Emperor commanded them to rise.

At such close proximity and in such a humble setting, Li Du had expected the Emperor to appear diminished. He found, when he raised his eyes, that the opposite was true. The Kangxi, wearing an unadorned blue robe and a red hat, was more impressive than any of the pomp and splendor that usually surrounded him. The signs of age on his face — a loosening and hollowing of skin and a weary droop of his mustache — only intensified the brightness and intelligence of his eyes. Li Du read humor in that face, and pride, and, strongest of all, curiosity.

He lowered his eyes immediately, aware that it was the law. He was aware of the Emperor assessing him, and of Tulishen, who was holding himself rigid, barely breathing in his effort to maintain the correct posture. The Emperor addressed Tulishen first.

"The assassin has escaped Dayan, but he will be caught. There may be traitors hidden in this province, but the web I have cast is more tightly woven than theirs. I had hoped that you would have addressed this situation with more discipline during your time here as magistrate."

Tulishen, not permitted to speak unless commanded to, opened his mouth and, with trembling lips, prepared to beg forgiveness for his failures. But the Kangxi gave an impatient wave. "I dislike it when my magistrates quail before me as if they were weak men. A superior man is quiet and calm, and expresses himself without obsequious fear. I understand the situation. This province is untamed. You will serve me better in the capital, where I may rely on you to strengthen connections with certain old families. You accept this change?"

With obvious effort, Tulishen kept his voice from shaking. "This servant accepts with humility and gratitude the honor that is bestowed upon his unworthy family."

"We will discuss the assignment of a new magistrate to Dayan. And when you arrange your household in the capital, you will include the consort Lady Chen. She possesses an exotic charm that will make her popular. Does she have sons?"

"She has no children."

"That is unfortunate, but perhaps the

change of location will be auspicious." The Emperor paused, then with his thumb and forefinger began to move the beads that hung across his chest, clicking them one at a time along the strand. "Though," he mused, "I do not agree with my advisors on the importance of auspicious and inauspicious signs. Everything is not predetermined. Years ago I was on a hunt in the north, and in the deep forests I became separated from the others. Suddenly I heard crashes of thunder very close to me, and I fled the clearing where I stood. When I looked back, I saw that lightning had struck just where I had been standing a moment before. I realized that if I had not run, and had been struck by that bolt, everyone would have said that such was my fate. So you see that human action cannot be discounted. You see the relevance?"

It was not an invitation to speak, and the Emperor allowed the silence to become a setting to better display his next statement. "Today," he said, "the foreigners tried to assassinate me with a clockwork device. It could be said that my fate was predetermined when the weapon was built and set to chime the hour of my death. And yet I am not dead. The Li family has done me great service today."

He turned to address Li Du. "I have always declared my deep respect for scholars. Almost always, when a scholar is accused of a crime against me, I am merciful. Only once in my reign have I executed a scholar for written words. You were a friend to his family, and you were exiled for your failure to recognize his traitorous behavior."

Li Du kept his gaze lowered.

"Today your action has altered your fate," continued the Emperor. "How did you discover that the tellurion was a weapon?"

Tulishen looked sharply at Li Du, who ignored him and spoke to the Emperor. "I interviewed Sir Gray in the course of my investigation of the death of Brother Pieter —"

The Emperor held up a hand to stop Li Du. "A matter," he said, "that there is no further need to discuss. In some circumstances, secrecy is essential. An Emperor is responsible for the history of reign, and there are certain events that do not merit placement in history. But tell me about this Sir Gray."

"The tellurion was coordinated with the eclipse. Sir Gray was adamant that there be no change to the schedule that might diminish the effect of the tellurion."

"But that is not in itself suspicious."

"No, but I saw Sir Gray's face when I revealed that the eclipse would not occur as expected. His eyes turned immediately to the tellurion. He is an impatient, forceful man, quick to be angry. But what I saw in his face was not anger. It was fear. Fear of the object itself."

"He thought it might burst into flame at any moment, until you reassured him that it was not so."

"Yes. I did not understand the significance of his reaction at the time. It was not until today, when he failed to take his place of honor on the magistrate's pavilion, that I saw what was going to happen. The carved dragons that were a gift from the company —"

"The ugly wooden sculptures." The Emperor pursed his lips in distaste, and gave a low, scornful grunt, as if the aesthetic offense was more disturbing to him than the plot against his life.

Li Du went on. "They were made to be part of the stage on which you would stand. When I visited the field, I heard one of the officials remark that they were not as heavy as he expected. He attributed his confusion to the unfamiliar wood. In fact they were hollow, and packed with sawdust and perhaps a trace of gunpowder that would ignite when the tellurion exploded. When the final chime struck at the point of total darkness, the clockwork cracked the glass sun. The chemical inside it bursts into flame when it is touched by air. It is an invention of their alchemists."

The Emperor absorbed these explanations without expression or comment. Then he nodded and said, "I understand the strategy of this Company. It is a common one, and I have read about it in detail in the *Seven Military Classics,* though in general I consider such texts a waste of time. A general who seeks to win a battle by studying a book will always lose. So the Company wanted to destabilize my empire, to introduce chaos in order to make China vulnerable."

"They recognized a unique situation that they could turn to their advantage."

"Ah," said the Kangxi, with a sudden and unexpected smile. "You are very clever. I can see by your face that you and I are sharing thoughts. This is rare — usually I must decide whether to go to the effort of explaining myself very slowly until my officials understand. Magistrate, do you know what your cousin and I are considering together?"

"With deepest apologies," replied Tulishen, "this servant does not know."

"We are thinking," said the Emperor, "of

how this foreign Company had the audacity to plan the assassination of an Emperor. They do not have the strength to attack China, and so they tried to alter the current of my own strength so that it would drown me. I see by your face that you are too nervous to understand me."

The Emperor squared his broad shoulders and raised a finger. "I declared my intention to preside over an eclipse of the sun here in Dayan. The people were to witness my divinity. I invited foreigners to cross the border and attend. We provided the Company with a stage on which to enact their own charade. Against the backdrop of the festival and the eclipse, my death would have seemed as divine as the power I intended to display. My sons would have known. They would have planned to avenge me. But the empire would have been in chaos, and none of the princes are wise enough yet to lead. That is what this Company hoped."

Li Du heard something in the Emperor's voice and, aware of the powers of perception directed at him, he kept his expression carefully under control, allowing no sign or suggestion of what he was thinking to alter his appearance. He was thinking about the second prince, about rumors that had begun years ago, that he was eager to rebel against his father. How had the Company known so much? And how had Gray escaped? The Emperor may have cast a tight net across the province, but the crown princes had their own resources.

The Emperor spoke again. "My instinct about these foreigners has been correct. I predict conflict with these Western empires in the future. I will not allow this attempt on my life to enter my history, but I will not forget it. Now I wish to speak to my close advisors on the apprehension of the assassin. You are both dismissed. And for your services, Li Du, I grant you an end to your banishment. You will not be reinstated to your former position, but to a new one, as head librarian of the Forbidden City."

Lady Chen was outside the kitchen issuing instructions to a cook. "Remember," she was saying, "that the Chief Commander of the Cavalry does not care for bird's nest, and finds the sight of it unappetizing. So you must not place it near him when you serve the table. If he is not there when you serve, you will know his place by the purple and green porcelain. Do you understand?"

The cook nodded that he did, and hurried back through the smoke-blackened doors into the kitchen, repeating Lady Chen's words to himself in a whisper.

When she saw Li Du, Lady Chen nodded in greeting and walked over to him. "We have not spoken," she said, "since the night you named that snake who had disguised himself in our home. And since that time, a great deal more has occurred."

"As you say."

"When I saw you speak to the magistrate I knew that there was grave danger. I will confess to you that in that moment I turned all my thoughts to the wish that he would listen to you this once. He does not like that you are more clever than he is."

Li Du shook his head modestly. She smiled at this, aware that her comment had pleased him in spite of his effort to brush it aside.

"You have heard," she said, "that I am to accompany the family to Beijing?"

"My congratulations. And do you look forward to the change?"

"To see the capital city? A woman would be out of her wits not to be filled with excitement at the prospect. The official who is to be the new magistrate in Dayan is also here without his wives, and will need someone to maintain the mansion. I have recommended my maid Bao for his consideration as first consort."

Li Du blinked. "Bao? But you quar-reled . . ."

"For someone who has been out of society for years, you have navigated the complexi-ties of our situation very deftly. You have shown yourself adept in understanding politics, science, even the bizarre religion of the foreigners. But I assure you — the work-ings of a household remain beyond your comprehension. Bao has been useful to me, and I admire a woman who is not docile. I would never have left my own dirty village if I had not had some spite in me. It is a good quality, when kept under control."

"I have been meaning to thank you for leading me to Brother Pieter's journal."

Lady Chen waved a pale hand dismis-sively. "I noticed it during my inventories in the library and thought it might of impor-tance to you."

"You will pardon me, but I do not think that is what happened."

Lady Chen's countenance changed, and her voice adopted the formal, authoritative edge that she used with servants. "But that *is* what happened. And now I must ask your pardon. Tonight's guests are beginning to arrive, and the musicians have not yet taken their places. The chimes last night were out of key, and one the guests complained."

Their steps had brought them to a secluded place on one of the garden paths. Seeing no one, Li Du said, "You have concealed the truth about your past in order to keep your position in the magistrate's family. I know as well as you my cousin's concern about reputation. I know that your status as daughter of a village leader was important to him in his decision to accept you into his home. He considers family lineage an essential aspect of a person's worth."

Lady Chen stopped abruptly, and the pearls and silver in her hair trembled above her still face. Li Du had stopped also, and she spoke to him very quietly, without turning to face him. "You have misunderstood," she said. "I am not as fearful as you think. I know how to shift a situation to my advantage. But I prefer to control exactly what is said about me, and when it is said. A consort who does not have the security of marriage must have power over the opinions of others. The time may come when my parentage is valuable to me, when I might wield it as an attractive mystery." She spoke, not with bitterness, but with flat resolve. "It would have been inconvenient for . . . for complications about my past to have come up during the past weeks. The magistrate needed me as his confidant, not as another problem to consider."

Now she met Li Du's eyes. Finding sympathy in them, she gestured impatiently and began to turn away. She stopped when Li Du said, so quietly that she would not have been able to hear his words had she not guessed what they would be, "Did you know that Pieter was your father from the moment you met him?"

There was a long silence. Then Lady Chen's posture and expression relaxed almost imperceptibly. "No," she said. "Not at first. When I learned that he had come to Dayan before — that was when I began to wonder. My mother was a widow when the foreign man came to stay with her family. It was not a very secret romance, and it invited no particular condemnation. My aunt and uncle were very happy to call me their own when my mother died. As for my father — he never knew that she was with child when he was called away by his superiors."

"And Pieter? He recognized the wine, didn't he."

"Yes." The catch in her voice was so slight he almost missed it. "I was foolish that night," she said. "But even I sometimes am too romantic. The storyteller was there, and

518

the lantern and the fine guests from the capital. I was emotional, and I thought to test him. I poured his wine, and I said very quietly that it was my mother's recipe, and that she told me once that my father had given the wine a name, a strange word that I remember laughing at as a child. *Cassiopeia,* after a queen whose throne is fixed in the stars."

"And he remembered."

"I do not know what I meant to do. It was an impulse, and when he left so suddenly I was truly concerned for him. And I wanted to talk to him, to know something of him. But when I arrived at his room he was dead."

"And you took the journal."

"It was horrible." She closed her eyes tightly, remembering. She opened them and looked again at Li Du. "I could not understand what I saw. But he was, after all, a stranger to me, and I collected my thoughts quickly. I had the idea that the journal I saw him carrying might tell me something of him, and I took it. Of course I realized later that it was in a language I cannot read. I — I could not destroy it, so I hid it in the library."

"And what made you decide to lead me to it?"

"As I have told you before, there are no secrets from me here. I followed your investigation. I heard of your conversations with the storyteller. When I realized that your goal was in fact to bring the killer to justice, not to gain some advantage for yourself, I decided to help you."

"It was the journal that set me on the path to the truth."

She shook her head. "It was your own determination," she said, "and I admired it. I did not know the foreigner, but neither did I want his killer to go free. My mother loved him. Are you going to speak of this to the magistrate?"

"I see no reason whatsoever to do that."

"I did not think you would. And now there are tasks to which I must attend. I would prefer not to discuss this again. Now that the household is to move to the capital, I must consider all that is to be done, and all that will be different. Perhaps you and I will meet again in the north."

She bowed her head in formal dismissal, as if they had been discussing a matter of household business, and Li Du, with an answering bow, took his leave of her.

Some hours later, Hamza and Li Du were sitting in one of the inn's courtyards, as it

520

had become their habit to do. The inn for once was almost empty, its guests of rank well into their wine at that night's banquet, everyone else well into their wine on the festival field. There were to be candles in the dragon canal that evening, and all day people had been buying folded lotus leaf boats in which to float the tiny flames down the stream. From where they sat, Li Du and Hamza could barely hear the booming and crackling of fireworks and the cheers that followed, carried on the wind from the high field.

"It has been an evil month in Dayan," said Hamza, without rancor. "An excess of bad intentions whose final alchemy was the dissolution of both schemes. Two villains, each one unaware of the other."

"And I," said Li Du, "I almost helped one of them succeed."

Hamza furrowed his brow. "But you foiled them both. What is your meaning?"

Li Du rubbed the back of his neck and looked up as a new star appeared among the crooked branches of the plum tree. "When I corrected the calendar, I doomed the Emperor to death. I set the festival back in line with the clockwork so that the Emperor and the weapon were once more scheduled to meet." He shivered. "If I had not discovered Jia Huan's sabotage, the tellurion would have remained dormant during the false eclipse. It would have burst into its strange flame on the following day, probably nowhere near the Emperor."

Hamza sighed. "What will you do, now that you have your pardon?"

"I have not yet accepted the position in Beijing."

"Can you refuse it?"

Li Du remembered the Emperor's face as he had seen it earlier that day and nodded. "I believe the Emperor would respect the whim of a scholar recluse."

Hamza chuckled. "I thought you were determined to avoid that title. And what of your library? The grand library of the empire. You don't want to return to it?"

"I do. But perhaps not quite yet."

"Brother Pieter told me," said Hamza, "that on the island of his birth, the sea rises so high that it brings shells to the doorsteps and paves the streets with seaweed. You know there is a way to Europe if you travel first north to Tibet. Kalden Dorjee and his caravan are camped outside of Gyalthang for the month, and we should return his mules to him. Perhaps he would guide us as far west as Lhasa."

"We could," said Li Du, "see the young

Jesuit safely to India, if we are traveling that way."

"You are right. And I have an assignation in Agra with that eager Frenchman who wants to bind my tales in one of his books. I still condemn it as a foolish project."

"You do not approve of putting stories into writing."

"Books are for government records and alchemical recipes and all the insipid wisdom of Confucius, not for stories. You do not agree?"

"I would not imprison words unread in the dark, but I am not sure that I trust them to a place as fragile and prone to distraction as memory."

"Books can burn or be eaten by worms."

"Storytellers do not live forever."

"It is a point of fact that some of them do."

"Let us say, then, that we serve a common cause."

Together they watched the stars flare and twinkle and cloud together across the moonless sky. The coals burned red in the brazier, and their lacquered wine cups gleamed as green as spring bamboo in the fading light.

ABOUT THE AUTHOR

Elsa Hart was born in Rome, Italy, but her earliest memories are of Moscow, where her family lived until 1991. Since then she has lived in the Czech Republic, the U.S.A., and China. She earned a B.A. from Swarthmore College and a J.D. from Washington University in St. Louis School of Law. She wrote *Jade Dragon Mountain* in Lijiang, the city that has grown up around the old town of Dayan. It is her first novel.

The employees of Thorndike Press hope you have enjoyed this Large Print book. All our Thorndike, Wheeler, and Kennebec Large Print titles are designed for easy reading, and all our books are made to last. Other Thorndike Press Large Print books are available at your library, through selected bookstores, or directly from us.

For information about titles, please call:
 (800) 223-1244

or visit our Web site at:
 http://gale.cengage.com/thorndike

To share your comments, please write:
 Publisher
 Thorndike Press
 10 Water St., Suite 310
 Waterville, ME 04901